WHS McIntyre is a partner in Scotland's oldest law firm Russel + Aitken, specialising in criminal defence. William has been instructed in many interesting and high-profile cases over the years and now turns fact into fiction with his string of legal thrillers, The Best Defence Series, featuring defence lawyer, Robbie Munro. He is married with four sons.

Forthcoming from the same author in 2017

Good News, Bad News
Last Will

PRESENT TENSE

A Best Defence Mystery

WHS McIntyre

SANDSTONEPRESS

HIGHLAND | SCOTLAND

Published in Great Britain by
Sandstone Press Ltd
Dochcarty Road
Dingwall
Ross-shire
IV15 9UG
Scotland.

www.sandstonepress.com

The publisher acknowledges support from Creative Scotland towards publication of this volume.

ISBN: 978-1-910985-25-0
ISBNe: 978-1-910985-26-7

Cover design by Jason Anscombe at Raw Shock
Typeset by Iolaire Typesetting, Newtonmore.
Printed and bound by CPI Group (UK) Ltd, Croydon, CR0 4YY.

With love to my mum for all her advice over the years; especially that I should forget about being an author and be a lawyer instead.

If I hadn't listened, I'd have nothing to write about. And no money.

Acknowledgements

Many thanks to my unbelievably patient wife, Gillian. If not for her roles as both proof-reader and censor, this book would be a great deal longer and probably the subject of several bitter on-going libel actions. Thanks too to my colleague Gail Paton and my sons for their evaluations of the first draft.

I'd also like to acknowledge my fellow members of the Criminal Bar at Falkirk & District Faculty of Solicitors for talking so much rubbish and providing me with so many lines of dialogue, especially for the less sophisticated of my characters. Thanks to Gordon Addison, a lawyer with an in-depth, if slightly worrying, knowledge of helicopter sabotage. Regards also to the Scottish Legal Aid Board without whom I'd suffer from acute low blood-pressure. Finally, thanks to Mrs Bain, my former English teacher, who thought I shouldn't be a lawyer, but be an author instead. Better late than never.

Introduction

It's not easy being a father. Being Robbie Munro's father is practically impossible. Sometimes I look at the boy, how old is he now, thirty-six, thirty-seven, thirty-eight, something like that, and wonder, where did it all go wrong?

I suppose his mother, God bless her, dying when he was just a baby was a setback. That and him wanting to stick in at the school.

His big brother, Malcolm, had the right idea. Captain of Glasgow Rangers and Scotland by the time he was twenty-two. Scored the winning goal in the Cup Final. The Hall of Fame had a space on the wall reserved for Malky's photo until some dirty Kraut ended his career with a tackle that was more of an assassination attempt. He's got his own radio phone-in now and there's not a pub in the land that Malky can't go into without someone offering him a drink. Or a square-go. I told Robbie to follow in his brother's bootsteps and make some real money. Sure, his lack of talent would have been a hindrance, but there's more to football than skill and ability, and even I have to hand it to the laddie, he is a trier. Every team needs someone like that. Someone prepared to put a foot in and leave it there, let folk know they're in a game, create some bruises. And on that subject, what was wrong with joining the Police, like his old man?

One of Lothian & Borders' finest I was, for more than thirty years. Steady work, steady pay and look at me now. Nice pension, nice cottage in the country. What's Robbie got? No money, no house and a legal aid bucket shop on Linlithgow High Street.

That's what happens if you insist on getting yourself an education. Not that I stood in his way. Edinburgh Uni. Fair enough. But a law degree? *'We need more lawyers,'* said nobody ever, and if that wasn't bad enough, when he comes out he specialises in criminal defence. All I hear is presumption of innocence, this, better ten guilty men go free, that. If his clients aren't guilty why are they on trial? It was out of spite, of course. I spent my working life putting them away, and now he's in court, up to all sorts to keep the bampots out, just so they can commit more crime and he can get more legal aid money. I'm just glad we've a government that's putting a stop to all that sort of thing. Innocent until proved guilty? Seriously, the way Robbie talks, he's never met a guilty man.

And don't think my youngest has only failed in his choice of vocation. No, he can be a flop at anything he turns his hand to. Take his love life for instance. The man's not a disaster at relationships, he's a horseman short of an apocalypse. Remember Jill Green, daughter of my best mate Wee Vince? Now don't get me wrong, I always knew she was too good for him, but having inveigled his way into her affections, and after catching her in what can only have been a moment of weakness, or, more likely, madness, and getting her to agree to marry him – what does he go and do? Only lets the lassie jilt him for some good-for-nothing multi-millionaire.

Mind you, you have to feel for the lad. Before Jill,

there was Zoë Reynolds. He really thought that romance was going somewhere. Turned out the only person going anywhere was Zoë. Australia. I mean, the lengths to which some women will go.

Despite all his many failings, Robbie keeps on bouncing back, bobbing about in the toilet bowl of life like one of the great unflushable. Lucky? Sometimes I think he doesn't do the Lottery because it wouldn't be fair on all the other folk. Even his complete failure to family-plan with Zoë, turned out to be the biggest success of his life: Tina, my darling, beautiful and intelligent granddaughter. Living proof that genes skip a generation. The wee pet lost her mum early, just like her dad did. Thankfully that's where any similarity ends.

But that's enough. Let's not cast up all Robbie's failures, there isn't the space here, and, anyway, it's December, Christmas looms, and there'll be plenty more to come in the New Year.

So, at this time, when some people reflect on the past and others look forward, I say forget history and let the future do its worst. Never mind auld lang syne, better to live in the moment, concentrate on the here and now - if only to find out what that son of mine is up to in the *Present Tense*.

Police Sergeant Alex Munro (retired)

1

Clients. They tend to fall into one of three categories: sad, mad or bad. Some people said Billy Paris's time in the military had left him clinically depressed, others that he had a personality disorder bordering on the psychotic. Personally, I'd always thought him the kind of client who'd stick a blade in you for the price of a pint. Friday afternoon he was in my office, chewing gum and carrying a cardboard box all at the same time. The box said Famous Grouse on the outside. I didn't hear the clink of whisky bottles as he thudded it onto my desk.

'Look after this for me, will you, Robbie?' he said. No 'how's it going?' No small talk. Nothing. Just a request that sounded more like a demand.

A number of questions sprang immediately to mind. First up, 'What's in the box?'

With an index finger the size of a premium pork sausage, Billy tapped the side of a nose that was deviated considerably to the left.

'You either tell me what's in it or you and the box can leave now,' I said.

Chomping on an enormous wad of gum, Billy walked to the window and stared out at a dreich December afternoon.

'Billy…?'

The big man clumped his way back over to my desk, wedged himself into the seat opposite and sighed. 'Just for a few days, maybe a week, two tops. Definitely no longer than a month.'

The box was well secured with brown tape. I shoved it across the desk at him. He shoved it back.

'What's the problem?' He tried to blow a bubble with his gum, failed and started chewing again.

'For a start I don't know what's in it.'

'It's just stuff.'

'What kind of stuff?'

'You know. Stuff. It's not drugs or nothing.' Billy seemed to think I wanted to know what wasn't in the box rather than what was.

'Stuff? What, like guns?'

'When did I ever use a gun...?'

'All those Iraqis shoot themselves did they?'

'I was in Afghanistan, and I'm a sparky. I was in the REME. I didn't shoot anybody. I fixed the guns so that other folk could do the shooting.'

The Royal Electrical and Mechanical Engineers was a fine body of men whose recruiting officer must have been having a duvet-day when William Paris took the Queen's shilling. It had taken seventeen years and a commissioned officer's fractured nose for Her Majesty to come to her senses and discharge Billy dishonourably from further service.

'Knives, then?'

Billy rolled his eyes. 'That was ages ago *and* I never got done for it. You should know, you were there. Not proven. Same thing as not guilty.'

It was the end of another hard week, and I'd promised my dad I'd be home to make Tina's tea. 'Listen, Billy.

Stop wasting my time and tell me what's in it.'

Billy held up a hand, as though swearing an oath. 'No guns, no blades, no drugs. And nothing stolen,' he added, reading my mind. 'It's just some personal things I can't keep at my place.'

'You've got a *place*?' It turned out he had: a homeless hostel in Dunfermline.

'It's temporary. I like to keep on the move and I can't leave anything lying about up there. The place is full of junkies. They'd steal the steam off your pish.'

I wasn't buying any of it. Even a light-fingered Fifer rattling for his next fix wasn't going to take the chance of being caught nicking from Big Billy. Not unless they fancied making the headlines next morning.

He sighed again. Hugely. 'A hundred. I'll give you it when I come back for the box.'

I gave one of the cardboard sides a prod with my finger. One hundred pounds to warehouse a box of personal belongings? If he'd offered me twenty I might have believed him. But a hundred? No, there was more to it than that. This was Billy Paris. I'd have to be as mad as he was not to think there was something extremely dodgy going on.

There was a knock on the door and Grace-Mary, my secretary, came in wearing her coat. She stared disapprovingly over the top of her specs at Billy and his box and asked me if she could have a quick word.

'That's me away home,' she said after I'd followed her through to reception. 'I'm minding my granddaughter tonight and need to leave sharp,' she added, as though she wasn't off and running at the stroke of five every night.

'Then let me be the first to wish you bon voyage and God speed.'

3

'You might not want to look quite so happy about everything,' Grace-Mary said.

Why not? I was one client away from the weekend.

'I've just had SLAB on the phone about last week's inspection.' Suddenly that Friday feeling evaporated. 'They want to go over a few files with you.'

'Files? Which ones?'

The Scottish Legal Aid Board's compliance and audit inspectors carried out regular inspections of those lawyers registered to provide Criminal Legal Aid. Fraud was practically non-existent, but the inspectors had to justify their existence someway or other and were famed for their strict adherence to a set of regulations which, unlike the legal aid hourly rate, changed frequently and with little warning.

'You know how they sent us an advance list of files they wanted to examine?'

I did. I'd spent much of the previous weekend going through those files, turning each one into a SLAB auditor's dream, stuffed full of attendance notes fully time-recorded and in duplicate.

Grace-Mary winced. 'When the lady from SLAB turned up on Monday you were out at court, or otherwise making yourself scarce.'

'And?'

'She gave me another list.'

Another list? I didn't understand.

'A different list,' Grace-Mary clarified.

I didn't like the way this was going. 'But you wouldn't have given her the files on that different list. Not before I'd had a chance to look them over.' Which was to say pad them out with all the bits of paper the SLAB boys and girls wanted to see.

4

She sniffed and fumbled in her raincoat pocket for a scarf.

'No, Grace-Mary, you would have told the witch-woman from SLAB that those other files she wanted were out of the office, in storage, destroyed by flood or fire, orbiting the moon or something. You wouldn't have—'

'I couldn't stop her.' Grace-Mary stiffened, buttoned up her coat. 'I went out of the room for a moment and when I came back she was raking around in the filing cabinets, hauling out files.'

'You left her alone in my office?'

'I was making her a cup of tea—'

Tea? For SLAB compliance? That was like Anne Frank's mum handing round the schnapps before showing the Gestapo up to the attic.

'Yes, I made her tea. Why not? I make tea for all your thieves, murderers, robbers and goodness knows who else.' Grace-Mary, my dad and Sheriff Albert Brechin shared similar views when it came to the presumption of innocence.

'Firstly, Grace-Mary, those thieves, murderers and robbers you refer to are *alleged* thieves, murderers and robbers. There's nothing alleged about SLAB compliance. Everyone knows they're a shower of bastards. And, secondly, those thieves, murderers and robbers are keeping me *in* not trying to put me *out* of business.'

Grace-Mary said nothing, just looked down at her desk and the small green tin box sitting on it. By the time her eyes were fixed on mine again I already had a one pound coin in my hand.

'Why didn't you tell me this before now?' I asked, dropping the money into the swear box. It didn't have far to fall.

'I was hoping the files would be okay.'

'Okay? Why would they be okay? You know I don't have time to do a double-entry attendance note every time I meet a client for five minutes or make a trip to the bog!'

'Well, if you're going to start raising your voice...' Grace-Mary yanked a woolly scarf from her coat pocket and whipped it around her neck, almost taking my eye out with the corner. 'I've put the appointment in your diary. See you Monday.' She strode off down the corridor performing an about-turn after only a couple of steps. 'And I've put a bring-back in as well so you'll remember that Vikki Stark comes back from the States a week on Monday.'

A seven day bring-back to remind me of my own girl-friend's return from a trip abroad? As if I needed it. Vikki, legal adviser for a private adoption agency, was off on a two-week lecture tour of America. She and I were now officially an item. Our relationship hadn't exactly been torrid thus far, our times together infrequent, interrupted by work commitments or with Tina there or thereabouts, cramping what little style I had. The last few months had been hectic for me. First discovering that I was a father and then having to try and act like one. Keeping a romance going on top of that wasn't easy. So we'd been taking it slow.

Once Grace-Mary had bustled off, I returned to my room to find Billy Paris standing on my desk fiddling with the fluorescent light strip. It had been flickering for ages so I'd been making do with an arthritic, angle-poise lamp.

'Problems?' Billy asked, when I returned to my office.

'Nothing I can't handle,' I said, wishing I believed that. 'By the way, what do you think you're doing?'

He jumped down and went over to the light switch on the wall. After a couple of practice blinks the fluorescent light came on and stayed on. 'Your starter's knackered,' he said. 'I've sorted it with a piece of chewing gum wrapper, but there's nothing for it - you're going to have to splash out fifty-pence on a new one.'

'Thanks,' I said, 'and talking of money, I think you were saying something about *two* hundred pounds.'

The big man winked at me and his features carved out a grin, revealing teeth, most of them molars. At least he'd disposed of his wad of gum. 'You're a good man, Robbie,' he said. 'You'll not regret it.'

That's when I knew to say no thanks. If Big Billy Paris was ready to shell out two hundred quid for me to babysit a cardboard box, whatever was inside had to be extremely valuable. Extremely valuable and/or extremely illegal.

I showed him the flat of my hand. 'But I'll need the cash up front.'

2

'Well?'

One of the many drawbacks of living at my dad's house was that he lived there too.

I'd sold my one-bedroom flat, been unable to find anything suitable within my restricted means, and had, in a moment of madness, agreed to move into his cottage with Tina. It meant that, with his junk-room redecorated and fitted-out, there was a bedroom for each of us. It also meant that if my dad tried to throw me out he knew I'd be taking his granddaughter with me.

The old man was sitting at the kitchen table when I walked in the back door. Handkerchief in one hand, cup of tea in the other, he was looking decidedly sorry for himself. My daughter sat next to him, a heap of multi-coloured Lego bricks in front of her, my brother on the other side holding the base of a tall structure that had been designed without regard for earth's gravitational pull.

I threw my briefcase into a corner and loosened my tie. '*Well,* what?'

'The wean. You're just letting her go?' He sneezed massively into the nearly white handkerchief.

'She's going to Disneyland. I'm not selling her into slavery. It can't be less fun than sitting around here trying not to catch your cold.'

Tina stood on her chair, stretching to place another brick atop the tower. She dropped the piece. Malky tried to catch it, releasing his grip on the base. The whole thing toppled, crashing down on the tabletop, bits scattering in all directions.

My dad fished a brick out of his cup, shook the tea off and chucked it onto the demolition site.

'Look, Dad. She'll have the time of her life and be back before Christmas. What's the problem?'

Silly question. The problem, as I well knew, was the battle of the grandparents. It had been raging since Tina had come to live with me. If my dad bought Tina a T-shirt, her grandmother would show up with a full designer ensemble. If he bought her a tricycle, next time we visited Tina's gran there would be a motorised scooter waiting. Only the weekend before, my dad had taken Tina to Princes Street for the Christmas market and a go on some of the fairground rides. Now Mrs Reynolds had scheduled a trip to Disneyland. What was I supposed to do about that? Tina loved her mammy's mammy and the feeling was obviously mutual. If Mrs Reynolds wanted to take Tina on an all-expenses-paid trip to Disneyland Paris, with her cousins, I could hardly refuse. *'No, sorry, Tina, you can't go to see Donald Duck, but don't be upset, Gramps will take you and a half-loaf down to Linlithgow Loch and you can feed some of Donald's real-life relatives.'*

Maybe it's because we were brothers that Malky and I were sometimes tuned to the same wavelength. 'How come Mickey Mouse wears trousers and Donald Duck doesn't?'

Okay, some of his wavelengths were a lot shorter

than mine, probably due to the number of footballs he'd headed in his time.

'Creepy, if you ask me,' he said. 'A duck wearing a shirt and no breeks.'

'Gramps says I have to go in a hairy-plane.' At four and a half years of age, Tina had already learned to ignore her uncle's ramblings. She climbed down from the chair to begin the rebuilding work. 'I don't like hairy-planes.'

'Me neither, pet.' My dad reached over and patted her on the head. 'You'd be better off staying at home with me.'

'What have you been saying, Dad?' I asked, as Tina spilled some more bricks and scrambled under the table after them.

'Me? Nothing.' The old man poured tea into a face replete with the shocked innocence of the wrongly-accused.

'You must have said something or Tina wouldn't be talking about not liking hairy-planes.'

'How can I help it if you can't switch on the telly news without seeing a story about some plane or other crashing? It's the anniversary of Lockerbie next week. It's been all over the news.'

'So you've been scaring Tina? Is that where all this stuff about *hairy*-planes is coming from? Have you forgotten that earlier this year she flew all the way from Australia and never batted an eyelid?'

Tina emerged from beneath the table, clutching a handful of Lego bricks. I lifted her up, held her in my arms and ruffled her hair. 'Well, the good news is, honey, no one is going anywhere in a *hairy*-plane. You and Granny, Aunt Chloe and your cousins are all going in a nice big *aero*plane, and the flight to Paris only takes an hour.

By the time you've buckled your seat belt and sucked a sweetie, it'll be time to land again.'

Tina squirmed in my arms. 'But Gramps said—'

Whatever Gramps had said was drowned out by a loud clearing of his throat.

'Never mind Gramps,' I said. 'He was only kidding you on. You know how hilarious he can be. Now put all the bricks away and I'll make your tea.'

On Friday evenings Tina was allowed to eat her meal on her knee while she listened to her Uncle Malky on the radio. Tonight's live football phone-in was to be replaced by a pre-recorded Christmas special.

Tea was mostly eggs. Cheesy omelettes for me and my dad. Boiled egg chopped up in a cup with soldiers for Tina and scrambled eggs for Malky.

'I wanted fried eggs,' Malky said, as I took his plate through to the living room.

'They broke and I knew you'd moan if they weren't runny so I scrambled them instead.'

'How can you break two eggs? One, fair enough, but two?'

I had to accept that while one burst egg could be considered collateral damage, nought for two wasn't a great egg-cracking average. Then again, it had long been a puzzle why when you fried eggs there were always casualties no matter how carefully you cracked them into the pan. On the other hand, with scrambled eggs you could practically lob them into the pot from a great height and the yolks would remain intact, sunny side smiling up at you, demanding to be whisked.

'Then you should have pretended you were going to make scrambled eggs, cracked them into the pan, changed your mind and fried them,' was Malky's solution to a problem that had defied domestic science for centuries.

'Pretend? To what? The eggs?'

'Aye.' He reached for the salt and sprinkled some across his food. 'Just walk up to the cooker, all casual like, and say... "I think I fancy some scrambled eggs tonight," crack the eggs into the pan and then fry them instead.'

'You want me to lie to a couple of unfertilised hen's ova?'

'You seem to manage okay with a jury,' my dad said. 'Now would you two wheesht? Malky's programme is about to start.'

'What's a hen's ova?' Tina asked.

My dad froze so quickly I could have snapped the end off his moustache. Suddenly, Malky was finding my scrambled eggs to be food of the gods, digging in, cramming buttered toast into his mouth without taking time to chew. I was on my own with this one.

'It's just a fancy name for an egg,' I said. 'Ovum means one egg. Ova is if it's more than one.'

'But what does it mean? Unfertil...thingy.'

My dad had thawed out sufficiently to lower his brow. Slitty-eyes sent invisible death-rays in my direction as he leaned forward in his chair to turn up the volume on the radio.

Tina was unrelenting. 'Where do eggs come from, Dad? They come out of a hen's bottom, don't they?' My daughter had clearly been giving the subject way too much thought. 'Is an egg a hen-poop?' She made a face and stared in horror at the contents of her cup.

'No,' I said, 'an egg is not a hen-poop, it's more like... hen-fruit.'

12

Tina looked up at me. 'Baby hens come out of eggs, don't they?'

It wasn't good to ignore your child's questions. I'd read that somewhere. Fob your kid off with some banal answer and you'd only stunt an enquiring mind.

'Well...?' Malky was now also taking an unhealthy interest in hen biology. 'Where *do* chicks come from, Robbie?'

Paying him no heed, I held my daughter's stare. 'You see, Tina, it's only the mummy chickens that are called hens and it's the hens that lay the eggs...'

'What do the daddy chickens do?'

Malky sniggered. My dad emitted a low growl. His knuckles tightened on the arms of his chair.

I ignored them both. I could do this. 'They wake you up in the morning. They go cock-a-doodle-doo.'

Tina was unimpressed. 'But why do daddy chickens not lay eggs? And why is there not a chick in my boiled egg?'

'Well, you see, if there is a mummy chicken *and* a daddy chicken then the eggs have chicks in them. If there is just a mummy chicken—'

'You mean a hen,' Tina said.

So far so good. 'That's right. If there is just a hen—'

'How can a daddy chicken put baby chicks in an egg? And if a mummy chicken is a hen, what's a daddy chicken called?'

Malky began to choke on a piece of toast. The combination of this and the theme tune to his phone-in show was enough to distract Tina while I sidled off to make my omelette. I ate at the kitchen table, away from the radio and Malky's Christmas special, listening to the hoots of laughter coming from the next room. Later, when I went

13

through to collect the plates for washing up, all hen talk had ceased, the radio was off and the TV was on, showing the local news: yet another report on the upcoming anniversary of the Lockerbie bombing.

The wreckage of Pan Am flight 103 flashed up on the screen. I manoeuvred myself between my daughter and the TV. 'Come on.' I reached out, took one of her hands and pulled her off the couch and onto her feet. 'Let's brush your teeth and get you ready for bed.'

'It's too early for bed,' Tina said, pulling free and looking at me as though I were insane. 'We've not even played dominoes yet and how can I brush my teeth if I've just had my tea and haven't had my supper?'

Tina's supper usually consisted of a glass of milk and a biscuit or a slice of toast taken a couple of hours after her tea. It was a snack she could spin out longer than a royal banquet and the fact that she'd not long finished her late tea was no reason for a change in routine.

I glanced over my shoulder at the TV screen and a huge gouge carved out between demolished houses. 'Well, if you put your pyjamas and dressing gown on, I'll let you stay up extra late tonight.'

It was an offer my daughter couldn't refuse and one of which she'd take full advantage. She was out of the room in a shot.

'You can't hide it from her,' my dad said. 'This is the sort of world the lassie's growing up in. Terrorists blowing themselves up, flying planes through windows, running about beaches with sub-machine guns. You know what happened in Paris back in two thousand and fifteen, and you still think it's okay for her to go to Disneyland?'

'Yes, I do. I'm her dad and I say she's going.'

'And what do I tell the bairn if she starts asking questions?' He pointed at the screen. No longer Lockerbie, but the twisted remains of a light aircraft strewn across a bleak hillside. A picture of a young couple, happy and smiling on their wedding day, appeared, the bride white and lacy, the groom in full Highland regalia, both smiling straight into the camera lens. They'd set out to chase the Northern Lights and found the side of a hill.

'That wasn't terrorists,' Malky said. 'Just bad flying.'

The newly-weds disappeared to be replaced by still images of another couple, video footage of the North Sea and a story about a missing helicopter.

I switched the TV off just in time for Tina to come bouncing back into the room wrapped in a big fleecy pink dressing gown. She flopped down beside me, smiling broadly, all ready for a long night of hard domino playing.

I put an arm around her. Maybe my dad was right. Maybe terrorism was a fact of life. But, like the reproductive cycle of the chicken, it was something I was going to put off telling my daughter about for as long as absolutely possible.

3

There weren't many places I'd rather not have been on a Monday afternoon than the offices of the Scottish Legal Aid Board. My usual line of communication with the personnel at SLAB was restricted to abusive online messages and the occasional heated telephone call as I tried to counter their best efforts not to pay me.

The young woman on the opposite side of the desk drummed bright red fingernails on top of the pile of files that lay between us. So cunning was the Scottish Legal Aid Board that they were now recruiting attractive people.

'This is not the first time we've had to warn you about your lack of attendance notes,' she said. Her smile, like her eyebrows, stencilled onto her face. 'It was raised at the last two annual inspections. By constantly failing to keep a proper record of work done, it seems to me you've been flirting with disaster for some time now.'

The majority of cases were dealt with on a fixed-fee basis so it was the same rate of pay win or lose. And that was the problem: SLAB didn't care if you won or lost, just so long as you time-recorded everything you did. Personally, I couldn't see the point. If the fee was the same whether you spent three hours or thirty-three hours working on it, surely the result was all that mattered?

'There are thirty files here,' she said. 'All taken from

your office.' She wasn't only pretty; she could count as well. 'Out of those thirty you have failed one hundred per cent of the time to record advice to the client that under section one-nine-six there is a sentencing discount available for an early plea of guilty.'

'That's because I don't advise people to plead guilty if they've told me they're not guilty.'

'You should have advised them nonetheless.'

Who wrote SLAB regulations – Franz Kafka? 'Are you actually saying that I should advise clients to plead guilty to crimes they say they didn't commit in order to get a soft sentence?' That was like going to the doctor, hoping for a cure, and being told that if you just went off and died it would save everyone a whole lot of bother.

'So, some of my files are not perfect. What about it?'

'Not some. Here's thirty for a start.'

'Thirty? I must have done three, four hundred cases this year.'

I tried my winning smile. It came in second to her frown. She donned a pair of spectacles that somehow only served to make her look more alluring, and picked a sheet of paper from the desk. 'You registered two hundred and eight-five cases with us, and these,' she tapped the top of the pile again in case I was having trouble following, 'represent a random sample of approximately ten percent of your legal aid workload. None of which is satisfactorily completed.'

Not satisfactorily completed? I looked at the name on the cover of the top-most file: Hugh Hendry. Charge: indecent exposure. He'd taken a walk from the dock after I'd explained to nice Sheriff Dalrymple, who'd once been the Tory parliamentary candidate for Morningside and somehow managed to come third, that the lack of public lavatories due to the SNP's council tax freeze was causing havoc for those with weak bladders. Fortunately, he'd formed a reasonable doubt without giving much thought to why the bold Hugh had been jumping out of a bush with his tadger in his hand rather than the other way round. Whatever, it was my turn to tap the stack. 'Ask Mr Hendry if he thinks his case was satisfactorily completed.'

She sighed, took the file and opened it. 'No initial attendance note…' She intercepted my attempt to put her right on that score with a raised hand. 'Illegible scribbles on the back of the charge sheet do not constitute an accurate record of legal advice given and instructions received.'

Advice? Instructions? Hugh didn't need advice, unless it was to stop getting his tackle out and waving it at passers-by, and, as for instructions, all he instructed me to do was keep him from going to jail again. How precisely that was to be achieved was something he was happy to leave to his lawyer, and, furthermore, those scribbles were perfectly legible to the one person who needed to read them – me.

She continued through the thin sheaf of papers, coming to rest on the final page, a scrawled note with the date of the trial and a big NG. 'Not even a final letter to advise the client of the outcome of the case,' she said, closing the file and staring at me accusingly.

Personally I'd assumed the absence of bars and stripy pyjamas would have been sufficient clue for Hugh as to the outcome of his court case. 'You do know what NG stands for?' I said. 'Take a look. How many not-guilties are in that pile?'

'That's irrelevant.'

I pulled the stack of files towards me and started opening them one at a time. 'Not guilty, not proven, pled to one out of three charges, case deserted, not guilty, pled to a lesser charge...' I shoved the files away from me. 'That's a random sample of six cases from the thirty seized from my office. Three acquittals, one desertion and two pleas to less serious charges. Those results are not irrelevant. Not to my clients.'

She sighed and sat back in her chair. 'You are being paid from the public purse. We need to satisfy ourselves that you are doing what you're being paid to do. That's not possible if you don't keep adequate records.'

'Sounds like you've been keeping your own records.'

She smiled thinly. 'You've been warned time and time again.'

'Come on,' I said. 'These are fixed-fee cases. What difference does it make when I do the work or how long it takes? It's all about the result.'

'No, it isn't.' She took the half-dozen files, snapped them shut one at a time and dropped them back on top of the pile.

I could imagine a SLAB compliance officer in hospital. *No, it doesn't matter if you cure me doctor, just so long as you keep an accurate record of your time spent treating me.*

'I was thinking,' I said. 'How about we discuss things in more detail over lunch? Or maybe a drink after work?'

Slowly the frosty expression thawed and a warm summer of a smile spread across her face. 'That would be nice.' Coyly, she patted the sides of the files to even the stack out and slid them across the desk at me. 'Can I bring my boyfriend along? Maybe we can all go out together after his mixed martial arts class.'

Suddenly it was winter again. She stood, I stood.

'Okay, okay,' I said. 'What now? Do you want me to promise to do better until you lot raid my office around about this time next year?' That was the usual way of things and it worked for me.

She walked to the door and held it open for me. 'No, not this time, Mr Munro. This time we have something else in mind.'

4

'You've been what?'

I was still in a state of shock when I phoned Grace-Mary from Haymarket station, just around the corner from SLAB HQ.

'Struck off the register,' I confirmed. 'Forbidden to provide criminal legal aid services.'

'Does Joanna know? If the girl had any sense she'd go back to being a PF. What are you going to do?'

The answer to my secretary's first question was, no. I'd yet to break the news to my colleague who was off on High Court business. Go bankrupt seemed the obvious answer to her second.

'How long is the ban for?'

She with the red-polished fingernails hadn't stated the length of my sentence, though I'd formed the distinct impression it was conditional on a cold-snap somewhere hot.

I wandered down to platform 4 in a daze and boarded the westbound train. Seventy percent of my revenue gone just like that. I'd been permitted to finish those cases I'd started. Thereafter I could take on no new legal aid work. Of course, I could still handle private cases; SLAB had no say in those, but private clients weren't exactly thick on the ground, except perhaps for road traffic cases, and who wanted to

21

spend their life in the Justice of the Peace court arguing over calibration certificates for speed guns? The problem criminal lawyers had was that their clients didn't have money. A lack of money was the big reason most of their clientele turned to crime in the first place. Those criminals who did have money tended not to get caught very often, which was why they were rich criminals in the first place.

In case the day hadn't started badly enough, I arrived back at Linlithgow to be reminded that the one reliable thing about life was that, no matter how bad things got, they could always get a lot worse.

'Mr Munro?'

Two men in black suits walked into reception. The one who'd spoken was a young Englishman, tall and slim, smiling through a full beard that was not so much trimmed as sculpted. Behind him an older man, squat, solid and mean-looking, like a bulldog with anger management issues. For a moment I wondered if SLAB had decided to do away with the niceties and send round a couple of hitmen.

'I'm Detective Inspector Christchurch. This is my colleague, D.C. Wood.' Still smiling, the man with the beard produced a wallet, holding it up to reveal a warrant card on one half, a metal star-shaped badge on the other. 'We'd like to ask you a few questions.' He cast a glance at Grace-Mary. 'In private.'

'Mrs Gribbin is my private secretary,' I said. 'You can be assured anything you say will be kept in strict confidence.' Although Grace-Mary said nothing, I could sense her approval. I didn't know what questions these cops had to ask me, more importantly I didn't know what answers they may later say I'd given them. Better to have a witness. And it would save Grace-Mary the hassle of having to listen in on the other side of the door.

Christchurch gave my secretary a polite nod of recognition and then turned to me again. 'You had a visit from a man called William Paris.'

The box. I knew I should have asked for more money.

'Well?' the man in the beard asked, after a moment or two of silence.

I tried to keep my face as straight as the poker I'd liked to have beaten Billy Paris over the head with. 'Well, what? I haven't heard a question yet.'

The Bulldog stepped forward. 'William Paris. Where is he?' He pushed his face at me. 'Question enough for you, smart-arse?'

'Grace-Mary,' I said, 'show these gentlemen out, will you?'

The younger man frowned at his colleague, bringing him to heel. 'There's no need for any unpleasantness. All we want is a little help with Mr Paris's whereabouts.'

'He's my client,' I said. 'I don't have his address, but even if I did I couldn't disclose it to you without his express permission.'

Christchurch grimaced. 'And that's final is it?' he asked.

'How can it be anything else? If I don't know his address, and—'

'Yes, yes.' The young man lowered his head, studied his shiny toecaps for a moment and then gave Grace-Mary a stiff little smile. 'Do you have a list of client addresses? A database?'

I stepped in front of my secretary. 'I can write it down if you're having difficulty with my accent. I don't have an address for Mr Paris and, if I did, I wouldn't give it to you. That clear enough?'

The Bulldog rubbed a worryingly thick vein on the front of his forehead. Without a word, he came around the far edge of the reception desk, pushed Grace-Mary's swivel chair to one side and pulled open a drawer. After reaching in and scattering the contents on the floor he moved onto the next.

'Robbie, do something!' Grace-Mary shouted at me, as a stash of People's Friends and some knitting patterns fluttered to the floor.

Do something? Like what? Why do anything? It was now reasonable to assume that whatever Billy had left in that cardboard box was highly suspect. I'd had it since Friday. There was no urgency about this impromptu search. Without a warrant, anything these cops found would be inadmissible in court. Better to let them carry on with their illegal search than insist they obtain a warrant, do things properly and land me in whatever mess my client was involved in.

I took my mobile phone from my pocket and, after some fumbling around, managed to find the video camera. I pointed it at myself, then at Grace-Mary and then at the two suits in turn before commencing my commentary. 'This is a video of the premises of R.A. Munro & Co. being searched by officers of Police Service Scotland without either a lawful warrant or my consent.'

As the Bulldog continued to throw drawers about, his senior officer took a firm grip of my hand so that the camera pointed straight in his face. 'Correction,' he said. 'This search is being carried out by Ministry of Defence officers on a matter of extreme urgency and on the grounds of national security.' He released my hand and then directed his colleague to the filing cabinet in the corner of the room. Before the Bulldog had pulled the top drawer out halfway, Grace-Mary appeared in front of me holding Billy's cardboard box.

'I think this is what you're looking for,' she said to Christchurch while fixing me with a hard stare.

The older cop slammed the filing cabinet drawer shut. 'What is it?'

'It's the box that Mr Paris brought here on Friday afternoon,' Grace-Mary clarified.

'Mr Paris left a box with you?' Christchurch asked. 'What's in it?'

Grace-Mary set the box down on the reception desk. 'We don't know. It's not been opened.'

Christchurch studied the box, stroking his beard. 'Is that correct? This box belongs to Paris and it's never been opened?'

'Unopened is the way it's going to stay,' I said. 'Until either the rightful owner, *whoever* that may be, comes to collect it or you show me a valid warrant.'

The Inspector looked to his colleague and gestured at the box. The squat detective made a move to lift it from the desk, but I placed my hand firmly on the lid. 'It's going nowhere.'

Christchurch sighed the sigh of a man whose patience wasn't so much thin as anorexic. 'As I've already said—'

'It's a matter of national security. I know. I heard you.' I pulled the box closer to myself. What had Billy Paris done that could possibly be a risk to national security? Had these cops even known about the box? There had been no mention of it before Grace-Mary had practically thrown the object at them. Surely they'd have come in force if they thought I was keeping guns or bomb-making material? And why wasn't I being arrested?

25

'How about this,' I said. 'You tell me what the threat to the nation is and I'll let you open the box right here in front of me and my witness.'

'You'll *let* us!' the Bulldog barked.

'That's right.' I lifted the box from the table and cradled it in my arms.

'We'll see about that!' He squared up to me.

Christchurch stretched an arm across his colleague's wide chest and eased him away. 'I'm afraid I'm not at liberty to divulge what remains classified information.' He pulled his own phone from a suit pocket and photographed me holding the cardboard box. That done, he took a black marker from a penholder Tina had made at nursery from a squeezy bottle, some coloured paper, a lot of glue and several hundred metres of sticky-tape. 'We will be back. In the meantime, should Mr Paris return to claim his belongings, trust me we will know.' He came over and signed his name across the seal on the lid in a big bold scribble.

What was in the box? According to Billy, no guns, knives, drugs or stolen goods. What did that leave that could amount to a threat to national security? Explosives? Toxins? And yet if that was the case the whole of Linlithgow High Street would have been cordoned off and cops swarming all over the place. You didn't send a couple of Ministry of Defence plain-clothed along to collect bomb-making equipment or biological weapons.

The man in the beard threw the marker pen onto the desk and signalled to his colleague that they were leaving. 'And when I do come back,' he said, 'I'll have a warrant with me and I'll expect to find that box and my signature intact.' He took out his wallet and removed a business

26

card. 'Until then…' he handed me the card. 'If you suddenly remember anything you'd like to share, please do give me a call. Any time.' He gave Grace-Mary and myself each a polite little nod and then left, taking his guard dog with him. He was courteous enough. I looked down at his business card. Courteous and wildly optimistic.

5

'Have you got it yet?' My dad was waiting for me as I dragged my weary self through the back door and into the kitchen.

'Have I got what?'

'If you have to ask, it means you haven't,' he said, after a brief bout of coughing.

I followed him through to the living room where he had a suitcase on the floor, half-packed with clothes for Tina's Disneyland trip. She wasn't leaving for another fortnight. He was obviously trying to make some kind of point. The girl herself was lying on her back on the sofa, playing with a doll.

'Stop being so melodramatic and just tell me,' I said. 'What have I forgotten now? After all, I've got nothing better to do all day than remember stuff for you.'

'It's not for me.' He seized me by the arm and pulled me close, all the better to growl in my ear, 'It's for the wean.' He tilted his head at Tina. She was holding her doll above her head, a strip of kitchen roll tied around its neck, flying it about and emitting accompanying zooming noises, her four-year-old imagination on overdrive.

'Oh.'

'Aye. Oh.' He backed me out of the room and into the kitchen. 'Christmas is three weeks yesterday, and I've barely an orange put by for Tina's stocking. You said it would be no bother. You knew a guy who could get anything, you said. Could get you a window table at the Last Supper, you said.'

I did know such a guy. The problem was he was extremely hard to get hold of other than when he was in trouble and at the moment he was on his best behaviour. Either that or not getting caught.

'It's not that easy, Dad. I've already told you, there aren't any. Not in Scotland. Not anywhere. Pyxie Girl has been withdrawn. They've stopped making them. People queued up outside Hamley's in London for days and were sent away. There's been riots in the U.S.'

The aforementioned Pyxie Girl was one third of a crime-fighting superhero trio called The Enchanted Ones, comprising the aforesaid PG, Mr Magical and their black cat, Blizzard. All Spandex and spells, the TV show was on air almost as much as the adverts for its spin-off merchandise. Such was The Enchanted Ones' popularity that their action figures were this year's must-have Christmas toy. And that was the problem. Tina wanted a Pyxie Girl. While Mr Magical and his feline sidekick were widely available, as was their arch-enemy, Professor Voodoo (it was surprising how many super-villains had doctorates and postgraduate qualifications), Pyxie Girl could not be had for love nor money.

The difficulty was a political one. Exception had been taken to her name. Pyxie most certainly wasn't a girl. She was all woman, and the actress who played the part had been denounced for accepting such a demeaning title. There had been a Twitter campaign and an e-petition. Pyxie Girl action figures were recalled by the manufacturer, at first with a view to repackaging them under the less patronising title of Lady Pyxie, only for that to cause copyright problems with a Japanese animation company who had a character with a similar name and for whom the blurring of the edges, when it came to age and the female form, was not seen as an issue. The result was an ongoing court battle causing chaos at Christmas for hundreds of politically incorrect wee girls and their parents.

'Don't give me any excuses. You promised her,' my dad punctuated his words with a few short blows of his nose. 'You promised she'd have that doll for her Christmas,' he managed to get out before collapsing into a fit of sneezing that prevented me from pointing out that I hadn't promised anything of the sort. He had.

My few months of fatherhood had taught me that children, like clients, should never be promised anything. Ever. Make a child a promise and you might as well open a vein and get it all down on velum, because they'd hold you to your word like Flashman holding Tom Brown to a roaring fireplace. I'd had a father-to-daughter chat with Tina about the whole problem in which, leaving the intellectual property aspect to one side, I'd done my best to explain the predicament in which Santa Claus found himself. It had gone fairly well until my dad had spoiled it all by mentioning how he knew Santa personally. Seemingly, they were great pals.

I led the old man to a chair and tried to push him down into it.

'Firstly, I promised her nothing – you did, and, secondly, sit down and I'll make you a toddy.' I hoped mention of the amber nectar might assist in a change of subject. 'A drop of whisky, hot water, lemon and honey, and your coughing and sneezing will be sorted out in no time.'

'Get away.' He shrugged me off. 'I've got a cold. I'm not marinating a chop.' He pulled out his hanky and blew his nose. 'Just tell me what you're going to do about getting Tina that doll that she wants.' With a final sniff and wipe he stuffed the hanky back into his trouser pocket. 'Sauntering about like tomorrow will do. I think you've forgotten how close to Christmas it is.'

'Christmas? Really? You'd have thought there'd be decorations in the shops or adverts on the telly to warn me about that kind of thing.' I took him by the shoulders and this time was successful in pressing him down into a chair. 'Calm yourself or you'll start coughing again. It's going to be all right. Trust me. It said on the news that they're hoping to have everything agreed between the TV company and the manufacturers any time now. There'll be plenty of stock available come the New Year.'

'The New Year!' The old man launched himself to his feet again. 'What good is the New Year? What do I say to the bairn on Christmas morning? It's the only thing she's asked for.'

'Listen, dad. It's Pyxie Girl that's supposed to be magic, not me. If there's none available, there's none available. And anyway, how come it's all down to me? It was you who promised you'd get it for her. You and Santa...' I crossed my index and middle fingers and held them up. 'You're like that, apparently. Why should it be my problem? I've got her my presents already.'

'Presents?' He blew a blast into his hanky. 'Clothes aren't presents to a four-year-old. Weans want toys at Christmas.'

The conversation came to a shuddering halt when our

31

very own four-year-old came through looking for more kitchen roll because her doll's cape had ripped mid-flight.

'Supper, bath and bed for you,' I said, picking Tina up and holding her in my arms. 'You've got a big day ahead of you helping Gramps get you all packed for going to Disneyland. That'll be fun, won't it?'

Tina looked me in the eyes. 'Can you come too, Dad?'

'Me? No, I'm too old for Disneyland.'

'But Grandma's going and so is Aunt Chloe and they're old, so why can't you come?'

I gave her a hug, put her down and hunkered beside her, holding her hands. 'I've got to stay and work, darling. I have to go to court. I'm not allowed to take holidays just now, but I'll be off for a few days at Christmas. When you get back you can tell me all about Disneyland and we can play with your new toys, and—'

'Gramps says that he's asked Santa to bring me Pyxie Girl.' Tina turned and looked up at my dad all wide-eyed. 'Didn't you, Gramps?' Back to me. 'Gramps says that he knows Santa and that they're friends and that Santa always does what Gramps asks him.' Back to my Dad. 'Doesn't he, Gramps?'

'That's right, pet,' my dad stared down at me like he was Father Christmas and I the little helper who'd sold Rudolph to a venison farm. 'He does.'

My phone buzzed.

'Oh, I meant to tell you, Vikki called,' my dad said. 'You've to book a table somewhere nice for Monday night and she'll pick you up at the office around five o'clock.'

I tugged my phone from a trouser pocket where it had got itself wrapped around a hanky and my car keys.

'Mr Munro?' It took a moment or two for me to place

the English accent as belonging to the man with the beard. 'I need a word.'

'I'm busy.'

'Then I'd be grateful if you'd unbusy yourself.'

'Have you got a warrant yet?'

'No.'

'Then I've nothing to say, and I'd be very grateful if you and your pet bulldog would leave me in peace.'

'Mr Munro, I don't think you appreciate how important it is that you assist with our enquiries.'

'Maybe if you told me what it is that's so important that you expect me to breach client confidentiality, I might be able to help.'

There was a pause, then, 'As I've mentioned previously, I'm not at liberty to divulge any information at this stage.' He cleared his throat. 'I'll be at your office tomorrow, first thing. Be there.'

6

Had the man with the nicely-trimmed beard asked me equally as nicely to meet him first thing in the morning, as opposed to ordering me to be there, I might have acceded to his request. But he hadn't and so I didn't and anyway I had a more important matter to attend to.

Joanna, my legal assistant, was in Glasgow sitting in on a rape trial. High Court work always sounded terribly glamorous and interesting compared to the average day at the Sheriff Court. In actual fact, on legal aid, it was a lot of high-pressure work for the same low-pressure pay. And there were other practical differences between the High Court of Justiciary and the local Sheriff Court. Sentencing powers was one: life imprisonment as opposed to a maximum of five years. Another was the pace of proceedings. Speed-wise we were talking the difference between my two favourite authors: Sir Walter Scott and Raymond Chandler. With the former, nothing happened fast. Scott could take several pages to set the scene of a Highland glen at sunset, allowing the reader to soak in the atmosphere, his fine prose seeping into the mind like a vintage brandy, poured over a ripe Christmas pudding. On the same word count, Philip Marlowe had already smoked a pack of cigarettes, slugged a couple of bad guys, and driven off into a Santa Rosa sunset, necking a pint of bourbon as he went.

Proceedings were underway and grinding slowly when I arrived and slipped in through the side door, past the witness box and into a seat in the well of the court next to Joanna. 'I need a word,' I whispered.

'Shush. Not now,' she said.

Defence counsel was cross-examining in slow motion. I didn't recognise him. He looked very young, with lots of hair poking out from beneath a snowy-white horsehair wig that marked him as a junior-junior. It was day two and we were still on the first witness. I could have rattled through several Sheriff Court trials by now. If a one hundred pound fixed-fee did nothing else, it encouraged defence lawyers to get to the point, get onto the next case and one day, hopefully, get paid.

The practice in the High Court was to stop mid-morning at a convenient time in the evidence, usually around the back of eleven. When the half-hour had come and gone, I started to yawn, the combination of an early rise and the heat of the courtroom.

'I hope we're not keeping your instructing solicitor awake, Mr Hazelwood,' Lady Bothkennar said to the white-wig. I turned my yawn into an awkward clearing of my throat, sat up straight and tried not to catch the eye of the jurors. 'Perhaps some caffeine would help. I'm sure the ladies and gentleman are about ready for a cup of coffee.' The judge turned to the witness. 'That's enough for the moment, thank you. You can return to the witness room, but please do not discuss your evidence with anyone.' Lady Bothkennar stood. 'The court will sit again at eleven forty-five.'

'Court!' The macer called out, and climbed the steps to the bench, opening the door just in time to allow her Ladyship to exit in a swish of red silk.

'Thanks for that, Robbie,' Joanna said. 'Brian has the complainer on the ropes and you start yawning like a narcoleptic hippo.'

From what little I'd seen, far from having anyone on the ropes, it looked to me like Brian was only learning the ropes.

'Sorry,' I said. 'Tina's an early riser. I just came to see how things were going.'

The accused had been arrested several months previously. I'd attended his police interview and then passed the papers onto Joanna. It was around the time I'd been battling for the custody of my daughter and I couldn't remember much about the case other than it was another rape. It wasn't that rape trials were ten-a-penny, but there had been a lot more of them since they'd amended the law on what constituted the crime.

'What is it?' I asked. 'That age-old tale of boy meets girl, boy and girl get drunk, boy and girl have sex, boy phones girl a taxi, girl phones boy the police?'

'I wish it was a too-drunk-to-consent case,' Joanna said. 'At least they usually deteriorate into a beauty contest.'

I knew what she meant. A lot of people on juries were of a certain age. The word rape conjured up to them Vikings and burning villages or women walking home alone being dragged into the bushes. What they didn't expect to hear was a teenage girl saying that she would never have had sex with the accused if it hadn't been for happy hour at the Student Union and those eight tequila slammers, so she'd like him sent to jail for six years please.

In those sort of cases where the accused scrubbed up well, there was no violence involved and it came down to two drunk people having sex, you could almost guarantee a not proven verdict. 'Not that a beauty contest would have suited us either...' Joanna winced. 'You've seen the accused.'

I had, but it had been months since my one brief encounter with him and I couldn't have picked him out from a police line-up. Joanna pointed him out to me. He was standing further across the lobby, a worried-looking man beside an even more worried-looking woman who I took to be his wife. Keith Howie was forty-eight and hadn't worn all that well. According to Joanna, Ruby Maguire, the alleged victim, was sixteen coming on seventeen and pretty.

'And to think we've got ourselves ten women on the jury,' Joanna complained. 'What a waste.'

Most men accused of rape complained if the jury of their peers turned out to be predominantly female. Joanna, like a lot of defence lawyers, was of the view that the more women, the better. She believed that women judged other women much harder than men did, that male jurors looked at the woman in the witness box and saw their daughters, while the females looked at the man in the dock and imagined their sons. Either way, I didn't think it would matter how the jury was made up. This was no beauty contest. It was Beauty and the Beast.

Niceties over, it was time to move on to the reason I'd come. 'Did I mention how exceptionally lovely you're looking today?' I said.

Joanna gave me a lemon-twist of a smile. 'Do you need to? Don't I always look lovely?' She gave me a friendly shove. 'Really, why are you here? Are you checking up on me or something?'

I felt the need to clear my throat. 'Brian, I need a quick word with Joanna. Business.'

The advocate raised an eyebrow, but eventually he took the hint.

'Something's cropped up,' I said after counsel had left.

'Robbie, this is you. Something's always cropping up. Just tell me what's so important that it's brought you out here to interrupt my mid-morning latte.'

I attempted a laugh. 'Well... It's sort of like this—'

'You're going to sack me.' Joanna folded her arms. 'That's why you're here, isn't it? I mean I know business is bad, no one's getting prosecuted these days, but—'

'It's not that,' I said.

Joanna looked up at the high ceiling while tapping a toe on the marble floor. I suggested we go for some fresh air, and we walked together out of the main entrance to stand beneath the sandstone portico where wigged and gowned figures leaned against stone pillars, smoking, chatting and drinking from cardboard cups.

'I was wondering if you'd consider coming in with me,' I said, when we'd found our own few square yards of privacy.

'In with you? In where with you?'

'In with me at Munro and Co.'

'You mean like as a partner?'

'You've worked with me long enough and we get along fine. The punters like you and—'

'Hold on. Let me get this straight. You want me to go into partnership with you?'

That more or less summed it up.

38

'On what? An equal profit-sharing basis?'

'Yes. Eventually. Possibly. We'd have to work out the details.'

'What's brought this on?'

I hadn't expected Joanna to fall on my neck and dampen my suit collar with tears of gratitude; nonetheless, she could have sounded a fraction more excited at the prospect. 'Why does something have to have brought it on? Is it not enough that I as your employer have recognized your talents and want to reward you with the chance to join Linlithgow's premier criminal defence firm?'

'I'll overlook the fact that it's Linlithgow's only criminal defence firm, Robbie, and repeat my question. What's brought this on so suddenly that you need to come charging through here to ask me something that could easily have waited until I was back in the office?'

I hoped the hurt expression I'd adopted, as I studied my shoes and realised they hadn't been polished in a while, would be answer enough. It wasn't. I wondered about telling her the truth, but in matters of business as well as love and the law I found it rarely helped. 'Grace-Mary said something and I wondered if you were thinking of a return to the Fiscal Service.'

'I did give it some thought...'

'And... Well... I don't want to lose you.' I was beginning to sound like the script from a cheesy chick-flick, and yet Joanna was seriously lapping it up. If only there had been a string quartet to burst into tune at that moment.

Joanna placed a hand on my arm, lowered it to my hand. 'You were really so worried I might leave that you dropped everything to come out here and ask me to be your partner?' I thought for a moment there might be

39

tears. I felt her hand tighten on mine. Uncomfortably so. 'And here was me thinking it was so you could tell me you'd been struck off the Legal Aid register.'

She knew. I rescued my hand and flapped it at her. 'Who cares? There's plenty of other work out there without all the hassle of grovelling to SLAB for every penny we earn. Who needs legal aid?'

'You do,' Joanna said. 'It's the mainstay of the firm. She jerked a thumb at the building in whose shadow we were standing. 'This case I'm in just now is legally-aided. It pays the bills. Without it we can't survive.'

'Okay… but back to the whole partnership thing…?'

'Let me ask you a question, Robbie. If you hadn't been struck off the register, would you still be asking?' She flicked a glance over my shoulder. I turned to see junior counsel coming through the revolving doors with one less than three cardboard cups of coffee.

'Definitely… well, probably. '

'Then get yourself back on it,' Joanna said, setting off to meet junior counsel and her mid-morning cuppa, 'and I'll definitely, probably consider your offer.'

7

It had been six long years since my resignation from Caldwell & Craig. That I'd resigned was the version of history I adhered to, though booted-out might have more accurately described the termination of my career at the old Glasgow law firm. I hadn't been back since. Not a lot had changed. The offices of C&C were incorporated within the same great sandstone building, the same portraits of former partners hung in the same gilt frames, and still stared down disapprovingly at me as I walked along the corridor to the office at the end.

Interiorly it had always been reminiscent of a Victorian library: oak flooring, high ceilings, and a prevailing smell of wood polish, leather and dusty law books. That hadn't changed either, but something *was* different. Back in my day, it had been a happy place. People milling around chatting, laughing, sharing stories. Now the few folk I saw dodging in and out of offices had serious expressions and no time to stop and talk with a former employee.

When I reached the enormous panelled door at the end of the corridor I knocked and walked in. Maggie Sinclair was standing behind her desk at the far side of the room, arm resting on a high-backed chair, staring out of a window at the world.

Maggie was mid-fifties, and going prematurely blonde. Following a series of retirements, she was now senior partner, though, unlike her predecessors, Maggie saw herself less as a lawyer and more of an organiser of things, most of which were pretty well organised already, and, like all professional delegators, she was a firm believer in hard work — so long as it was being done by other people.

She turned to look at me as I entered the room, a mixture of mild surprise and annoyance on her face as though I had interrupted her contemplations on some important matter of law.

'Robbie. So good to see you,' she said, with that almost smile of hers. 'How are things in Linlithgow? I hear you have a child.'

'Yes I have. Tina, and she's doing fine,' I said. 'She's all set to jet off to Disneyland with her grandmother in a few days.'

Maggie gestured to the seat opposite and we both sat, acres of mahogany and tooled green leather between us. 'Yes, children are great, but it's good to have some time to oneself, isn't it?'

As I recalled Oneself had packed her own child off to boarding school the moment they'd severed the umbilical cord.

'What age is she?'

'Four and a half.'

'Have you thought about schools?'

I had and decided on the nearest one. It was where all the other children went.

Maggie frowned. 'A comprehensive education is the cheap option. But is it the best?'

'Worked for me,' I said. 'The cream rises.'

'True, and there are all sorts of other unpleasant things that float. When I ask if it's best, I'm not talking about academic achievement. I'm talking about contacts for future life.'

Again, I couldn't disagree. A good number of my old school chums had become regular clients of mine and not all of them were in jail.

'Take Sir Philip Thorn for instance. I was at school with his sister.'

'Who?'

'You must know Philip.'

I did a mental run through of all those knights of the realm with whom I was on first name terms. It didn't take long.

Maggie sighed. 'He's why I've asked you to come and speak to me.'

'Not to offer me a job, then?'

'I'm so glad you've kept your sense of humour, Robbie. Can we get to the point?'

'Why not?' I said. 'After all, my meter is running.'

'Meter?'

'When you called me you said you were after a spot of advice. Legal advice is what I sell.'

'And the day I need to buy any legal advice from you is the day…'

I waited.

'The day…'

'Then why am I here?' I asked, when it became painfully apparent that Maggie wasn't going to come up with a witty rejoinder any time soon. No doubt she'd think of a right good one the minute I'd left.

'To discuss something that might be to our mutual benefit,' she said.

'And what would that be?' I knew perfectly well that Maggie Sinclair did things for her own benefit and nobody else's.

'Philip Thorn is looking for a man.'

'A lot of ex-private-schoolboys are.'

'A former employee who's gone AWOL,' she continued. 'Philip's extremely anxious to track him down.'

'And you do remember that I'm a lawyer?'

'I try.'

'As opposed to a private investigator.'

'Yes, we've already hired one of those.'

'And he didn't come up with any leads?'

'Just the one. You.'

I leaned back in my chair and let her carry on.

'One of the first things the P.I. did was to check on the missing person's criminal record. He phoned the clerk of court, asked who had last represented him, and guess what?'

'Just because I've appeared for someone in court doesn't mean that we exchange Christmas cards.'

'Well, I'm afraid you're all we have at the moment, and, as I've already mentioned, Philip is extremely anxious to receive any information available about this person's whereabouts.'

'How keen?' I asked.

'That depends on the reliability of your information.'

'Try me.'

'William Paris. You represented him in the Sheriff Court, June of last year, on assault and breach of the peace charges. Have you seen him recently?'

44

I took a moment to smooth a rough edge on a fingernail. 'I might have.'

Maggie sat up straight. 'Coffee?' She pushed a button on the intercom.

Refreshments duly ordered, I wondered aloud whether the whereabouts of one of my clients wasn't something we could have discussed over the phone. It didn't need me to come all the way through to Glasgow just to tell Maggie that I couldn't disclose personal information on a client.

The coffee arrived super-quick. 'No one is asking you to breach client confidentiality,' she said, pouring us each a cup. 'Honestly, I never knew you were such a stickler for legal ethics.'

How much of a stickler depended on the answer to one very important question. 'What's in it for me?'

'Naturally, there would be a finder's fee.' She tipped cream from a white porcelain jug over the back of a silver teaspoon and into the murky depths of her coffee cup. She waited until it had bloomed across the surface before looking me straight in the eye. 'So, do you know where this Paris person is?'

'No,' I replied, 'but—'

'But you know how to find him?'

I took a drink of coffee. One thing hadn't changed about C&C, the coffee was still as good as ever. 'It won't be easy.'

'Nothing worth doing ever is.'

Words to live by. That is, for other people to live by. Not Maggie.

'How worth doing is this?' I asked.

'Find this man and I can assure you it will be very worthwhile.'

I felt a warm feeling inside me, and it wasn't just the coffee. 'When I do find him, what then?'

She raised the white china cup and held it poised at her lips. 'Simply tell me where he is...' she took a sip from the cup and set it down once more on its saucer, 'and I'll tell Sir Philip to write us both a nice fat cheque.'

8

When it came to fat cheques and the acquiring of same, I'd always been of the view that there was no time to lose. Unfortunately, I hadn't a lot to go on, only that Billy Paris had told me he was temporarily based in a doss house situated somewhere in Dunfermline.

Working with that scrap of information, I had Grace-Mary phone Fife Council's social work department and find me the addresses of the various homeless men's hostels scattered about the town. After a morning spent visiting the places on the list, only one had any record of Billy. It was an establishment reserved for recovering alcoholics. He'd stayed there for a couple of nights, a week or so back, before disappearing without leaving any forwarding address. Perhaps it wasn't unexpected that, with so many people interested in finding him, Billy would be trying his best not to be found.

I was on my way out when I was waylaid by a scruffy wee guy who looked like he'd not so much fallen off the wagon, as leapt off shouting, 'Geronimo!' He was supporting the frame of the door with a shoulder and pushed himself upright as I approached.

'Got a smoke on you, pal?' he asked, stepping into my path.

'Sorry,' I said, pushing past. 'That's the one bad habit I don't have.'

'You a gambling man then?' he asked, trotting after me, shimmying alongside. I thought if I kept walking maybe he'd lose interest after a few yards and go annoy someone else. No such luck. 'Cause I bet I know why you're here. You're looking for the big man. That right?'

I slowed and took a sideways glance at him.

'You're the lawyer, eh?' he said.

I stopped. We faced each other. His leathery features creased into a knowing leer. One eye looked at me, the other tried to find me. 'That's who you've come looking for, isn't it? The soldier? You're not the first.'

His breath was a biological weapon and the rest of him smelt faintly of fish. I really hoped it was fish. 'And you've got a tip on where he is, have you?' I asked, taking a step back.

He shrugged. It was the kind of shrug that came with a price ticket attached.

'Not much use to me if you've given the same tip to those other folk who've been here,' I said.

He shook his head. 'I've never telt a cop nothing, ever.'

'The cops have been here too?'

'Twice.'

'Plain clothes?'

He nodded.

'Like me then?'

He laughed. 'Naw, son. Not like you. Like cops.'

'One have a beard?'

He nodded. 'English fella.'

'What about the other?'

'Wee guy. About my height. Solid. They weren't happy nobody here would speak to them.' If his descriptions were anything to go by, it certainly sounded like Christchurch

48

and his sidekick. 'Naebody kent anything anyhow.'

'Except you?'

'That's right,' he said, keeping his good eye fixed on me while the other did some scouting about.

Could I trust him? Almost certainly not. Was he the only possible clue as to the whereabouts of Billy Paris? Almost certainly so.

'Okay, then. Let's have it,' I said.

'Not here.' He cocked his head further along the street to a pub door where a couple of thirsty-looking types in tracksuits were sharing a cigarette. 'In there.'

'Big Billy said you might show up,' said he of the wandering eye, a few minutes later, knocking back a shot of whisky and chasing it with a slug from a half-pint of lager.

So far all I'd discovered was that my drinking companion's name was Jim, or Jazza to his friends, amongst whose number I could now count myself: a privilege I felt sure Jazza bestowed on anyone daft enough to buy him alcohol. Jazza had been in the Army with Billy. They'd served for a time together, but mostly got drunk together.

'So you're a pal of Billy's?' I asked.

'Who, me?' Jazza said, as though there was someone else in the pub I was plying with free drink for information on my missing client. 'Oh, aye. Me and Billy are great buddies. He's a good man. Best sparky in the Army. Didn't matter if it was a tank or a Tornado, if it was bust and had wires Billy could sort it for you.'

'That why they kicked him out?'

Jazza laughed and ran a finger through the condensation on his half-pint glass. 'That's a long story.'

49

One I had no doubt he could spin out all day, providing I kept setting up the drinks.

'It'll keep,' I said. 'Right now I need to speak to him urgently.' I waited until he'd made the rest of the beer disappear. 'Where is he?'

Jazza wiped froth from his top lip with the back of a grimy hand. 'He said that if his lawyer turned up I was to say you're not to bother looking for him. He'll be in touch.'

But I wasn't to be fobbed off by Billy's don't-call-me-I'll-call-you message. 'No more information,' I said, 'no more drink.'

Jazza sat up straight on his bar stool, palms of his hands facing me, one eye going down the shops, the other coming back with the change. 'Ah, well now. That's where it gets a wee bit tricky.'

'How tricky?'

Even with his dodgy vision the old guy had no problem catching the eye of the barman.

'Same again, is it?' asked the man in the apron rhetorically, setting up another hauf an' a hauf.

I waved away the offer of more ginger beer and took a hold of the wrist that was attached to the hand that was heading for the newly replenished shot glass. 'Billy Paris,' I reminded him. 'Where is he?'

Jazza pulled his arm away. 'Calm down, will you, son?' He moistened his lips with his tongue, lifted the whisky glass and sank the contents in a oner, good eye partially closed, the other rolling around like a marble in a saucer. 'If you'll recall, I didn't say I knew *exactly* where the big man was. Only that I had a tip for you.'

'Well, I've a tip for you,' I said. 'That's your last drink on me.'

'Don't be like that,' he said, once he'd sconed the half-pint.

'Why not? You've told me nothing and you're drinking like there's a drought.'

Jazza leaned forward at me, simultaneously crooking a finger at the barman for a refill. 'How much I drink is my business.' I doubted very much if he had any other business. He leaned closer, top lip curling. 'All right?' he snarled.

I'd pretty much had enough. 'Don't bother,' I said to the barman who had Jazza's shot-glass poised under an optic. The barman looked at Jazza as though he had any kind of say in the matter. I took two twenties from my back pocket and held one of them in front of Jazza's face. 'I'm paying for our drinks with this.' I held it out to the barman and once he'd taken it, I held the other twenty up in its place. 'And I'm going to leave this one behind. But only after you've told me where Billy is.'

Jazza stared at his empty half-pint glass. The flecks of foam on the inside of the tumbler were drying out nearly as fast as he was. I gave him the time it took for the barman to return with my change to think things over. Nothing. I jumped down from the bar stool and stuffed the coins back into my pocket alongside the other twenty. I was almost at the door when I heard Jazza call to me.

'He's got a son.'

I slammed into reverse.

'Plays football. Big Billy said something about a cup game the boy was playing in. He's going to watch him.'

I took the other twenty from my pocket, laid it gently on the counter, smoothed it flat with the side of my hand, and said, 'Tell me more.'

9

Saturday morning I was in Falkirk, not a free-kick from the late-lamented Rosebank distillery. Sunnyside football pitches. Whoever had given the place its name had a sense of humour. When I arrived shortly before kick-off with Malky and Tina in tow, the home team was already there, carrying out some warm-up exercises under the supervision of a coach in a bright red padded anorak. A few minutes later the away team showed up on the far side of the pitch with a considerable travelling support. There had to be around fifty of them, mums and dads, grannies and grandpas all out to watch their boy run about in the mud chasing a ball. What else was Saturday morning for?

While the coach in the red anorak put the home players through a series of stretches, another, similarly attired, was using a child's plastic spade to pick up dog shit from the penalty box.

'Why am I here again?' Malky asked.

'I thought that I might try my hand at being a football agent,' I lied. 'I've been given a tip about a player. Thought you could have a look at him. Tell me if he's got what it takes. Boys' football, this is where it all started for you. Do you remember when we used to play?'

'No,' Malky flapped his arms, trying to generate some heat. The rain was coming sideways on a chill wind that made no effort to go around us. 'I remember when *I* used to play and *you* used to run around bumping into people.'

As a lad my dad had dragged me along to watch my brother perform. I had stood at the side of countless muddy pitches like this one, trying to understand how Malky could stroll through a game while remaining unfazed and in complete control. There was an inevitability about the way the ball always seemed to end up at his feet, as though he were some kind of soccer black hole and the ball a planet on the event horizon. When I played, for all my charging about, scampering after every loose pass, I only ever seemed to get in a few kicks now and again, and whether that was at the ball or an opposing player was a matter left to fate.

'If this is an under-fourteens game, how come no one's spotted him before now?' Malky asked.

'He's the same age you were when The Rose took notice of you,' I said.

Malky had been scouted as a thirteen-year-old playing Boys' Club football, moved swiftly to the Junior Leagues with Linlithgow Rose and from there to the big time with Glasgow Rangers' first team. A meteoric rise brought crashing to earth by one brutal tackle from a German midfielder.

'That was then,' he said. 'This is now.'

I knew what he meant. Times had changed. Nowadays the best players were scouted and signed up while embryos.

The coach in charge of dog faeces removal walked towards us, plastic spade held out in front of him on which lay the solid, brown stool of a dog with a well-balanced diet and an arsehole for an owner.

'The glamour of the cup, eh?' Malky said to him as he approached. The coach did a double-take. 'Malky? Malky

53

Munro?' He gave my brother a broad smile as he hurled the contents of his spade into the dense undergrowth at the side of the park. 'What brings you here?'

What or rather who had brought Malky here was me. I needed an excuse to attend an under-fourteens football match and my brother was the perfect decoy. If Billy Paris was doing his best to avoid me, as well as the police, my intention was to catch him unawares, make it look like our meeting was by chance. Malky was a good cover. He could also be called upon for childminding duties if I had to spend some time with Billy alone.

'Malky's here to have a look at one of your players,' I said. 'The boy Paris.'

The coach took a moment to wipe his spade on the grass. 'Paris? Nobody in our team by that name.'

'You sure?' I asked, starting to think that a certain swivel-eyed ex-soldier might have outflanked me.

'I've been coaching this lot since they were in the Fun Fours. I think I know their names by now.'

'Paris is his dad's name,' I said. 'Maybe he goes under his mum's.'

'Doesn't matter,' Malky said. 'If he's as good as Robbie says he is he'll be a stick-out.'

There was nothing for it but to hang around and see who turfed up.

Tina, who had been putting her wellies through a rigorous puddle test, tugged at my jacket. 'Dad?' She tugged again. 'I need the toilet.'

The coach screwed up his face in sympathy. 'Nearest toilets are at the changing rooms away across the other side of the parks. The boys usually just...' he gestured to the undergrowth with the spade.

'You'll need to hold on,' Malky told Tina. 'It'll not be long. They only play thirty-five each way at this age.'

The referee arrived. He handed a tattered fluorescent flag to a coach from either side, gathered the players in the centre for a few words of wisdom and, with a short blast from his whistle, the game was underway.

At half-time it was nil-nil, the surface had cut up badly and I thought we might have lost a few of the smaller boys in the trenches. There was still no sign of Billy Paris and Tina was desperate, hopping from welly to welly.

'You'll need to take her over to the changing rooms,' I said to Malky.

'Why don't you go?' he said. 'I'm the one here on scouting business, remember?'

Someone had to take her, and if I was quick we could make it and be back before the end of the game. I took Tina by the hand and was about to set off when the home team's coaches came over with a joint request that Malky give the boys a half-time team talk.

'Just a wee word of encouragement, maybe a tip or two,' said dog-shit coach, when Malky showed signs of reluctance.

Even though by now Tina was jumping up and down, I simply had to hear this.

'Right, boys,' Malky began, as the team huddled around him, drinking isotonic drinks and stuffing their faces with Jaffa cakes. 'You're going to get nowhere against this mob if you keep hitting it down the middle. You need to stretch the game, get the ball out wide and put in a few crosses. Even if you don't score, you'll maybe get a corner-kick. And as for corners...' Malky was warming to the task. 'What's wrong with you?

55

Scared to mess up your hair?' He reached out and ruffled the hair of the nearest player. 'Head the ball! Listen, it's blowing a gale and the corners are only reaching the front post, so you need to get there first, in front of the defender. Here's what to do.' He hunkered down, beckoning the boys in closer. As a unit they shuffled forward, like co-conspirators. It was the only time that day I'd noticed them operating as a team. 'Stand behind your marker. Let him think he's got you covered then, just as the corner is being taken, stamp on his foot, nip in front of him and, bang!' Malky put his two fists in front of his chest and mimed a header. 'One-nil.'

'Does that really work?' asked one of the players, a skinny, blonde-haired boy who looked like a header would snap him in two.

'Not every time,' Malky conceded, 'but, even if you don't score, the defender will probably lamp you one. You'll get a penalty and he'll get sent off. It's win-win. Just make sure the ref doesn't catch you.'

The coaches cast sidelong glances at each other.

Malky wasn't finished. 'Another good move to try is—'

Time for me to step in. 'Don't listen to him, boys,' I cobbled together a laugh. 'Malky's just kidding you on. You only need to remember one thing, try hard and definitely no stamping. Just go out and enjoy yourselves. Isn't that right, Malky?'

'That's three things,' I heard one boy pipe up as I pulled my brother away.

'Right, Alex Ferguson,' I said. 'You've done enough damage. You can take Tina to the loo. I've got things to do here.'

'But—'

I gave him a shove. 'Stamp on your opponent's foot? You should be ashamed of yourself.'

Protesting that winning was what it was all about, Malky eventually allowed me to usher him in the direction of the changing rooms with Tina leading the way. The game restarted and there was no sign of any goals, Billy Paris, or his possibly fictitious son by the time I saw my brother and daughter returning via the neighbouring rugby pitches, trudging through the mud and driving rain like the Grande Armée's retreat from Moscow.

During their absence I had been looking around for Billy by strolling up and down the touchline, engaging fellow spectators in conversation, hoping for some kind of lead on my missing client. I was all set to call it a day when I felt a tap on my shoulder and turned to see a small woman in a big green coat, the hood trimmed with fake fur.

'You here to watch my boy?' she asked, looking up at me.

'Depends,' I said. 'I'm here to see Billy Paris's son.'

She stretched out an arm and a gloved hand appeared from a furry cuff to point at a well-built lad, taking up position in the away team's goalmouth, while one of his team mates, the blond-haired boy, tee'd up a free-kick about thirty yards out. 'That's him. He's the team captain,' she added, in case I hadn't spied the yellow arm band with a bold black C on it.

'Good player,' I said. 'Big and strong. Like his dad.'

'Billy's not here,' she replied, quickly and a trifle too defensively.

'Do you know where he is?'

She looked at me narrowly.

'I'm his lawyer,' I explained.

'Me and Billy don't speak much. I only see him at matches sometimes.'

'He's not here today, though?'

'A lot of games have been called off lately 'cause of the weather. Maybe he thought this one would be too.'

'Should have been,' I said.

She pulled the hood of her coat closer to her face, holding the sides tightly to her cheeks. 'It's all these dads. Things were always worse back in the day, when they were playing. Every time the ref blows for a foul all you hear is, it's a man's game. Men. They forget it's a man's game being played by wee laddies.'

The blond boy took the kick. It barely made it into the penalty box, and a defender sclaffed it clear for a corner.

'Well, if you do see Billy, will you let him know I need to speak to him urgently?'

She sniffed, non-committally.

'Do you know who that is?' I asked, tilting my head at my brother, who with Tina by his side was squelching down the touchline towards us. 'That's my brother, Malky Munro. You might have heard of him. Ex-Rangers and Scotland. He's got his own radio show. Knows everyone who's anyone in football. If he puts the word out on your son there'll be scouts flocking to see the boy. Isn't that right, Malky?'

My brother looked confused.

'I said: isn't that right, Malky?'

He nodded, his mind clearly on more pressing matters. 'I need a word, Robbie.' He pulled me aside. 'It's Tina. We got to the toilets no problem and I... you know... let her get on with it, but when she came out she wouldn't put her pants back on. She said they were dirty.'

'Dirty?'

'Aye, you know, dirty but not with dirt.'

'So where are they?'

'I told her to leave them.'

'Why didn't you just put them in a carrier bag and stick them in your pocket or something.'

'I wasn't touching them.'

'She's a child. They're child's pants. You've got to expect a few skid marks.'

'We're not talking skid marks, Robbie, we're talking handbrake turns here, and I don't know how well things have been, you know... tidied up down there. I wasn't wanting involved. We'll need to get her home for a bath.'

Tina took hold of my hand. 'I'm cold, Dad, and I've got a sore tummy.'

A roar from the home support. The wee woman in the furry hood bounced up and down clapping her hands as the boy with the yellow captain's band wheeled away from the penalty box, windmilling an arm, his teammates chasing him in celebratory mode.

'Told you,' Malky said. 'Never fails.'

I hadn't seen the goal being scored and so couldn't say if, immediately before the ball hit the back of the net, a member of the opposition had sustained a foot injury. The losing team didn't seem to be complaining, just a lot of heads being held in hands, nothing unusual. Except for one thing. On the far side, amongst the forest of away-support umbrellas, a solitary arm was raised and a clenched fist pumped the air, once, twice, before being hastily withdrawn.

'If I'm not back in five minutes, take Tina home,' I told

Malky. 'Tell Dad about her little accident. He'll know what to do.'

As the ref blew for the restart, I was already walking briskly down the side of the park. Billy must have noticed. I could see his bulky frame peeling from the away support and walking equally briskly in the opposite direction.

I broke into a jog, slipping and sliding in the mud. Each step threatened to send me sprawling. I didn't know what Billy had on his feet, but he was covering the ground very quickly for such a big man. By the time I'd rounded the corner flag and was running behind the goals, he was a good fifty yards ahead and increasing his lead with every slippery step. Where was he running to? On our left there was a twenty-foot-high wire fence, to the right a steep embankment and the rugby fields below. To make it to the main road on the far side, he would have to run the length of two football pitches. Could he keep up this pace? I was determined to find out. Extending my stride, planting one foot in front of the next, I ploughed on until in one particularly boggy patch I left a shoe behind. When my stocking foot came down in front of me, my heel skidded on the wet grass. I toppled backwards, arms flailing trying in vain to regain my balance. The fall knocked the wind out of me. I managed to climb to my knees, head bowed and staring at the sodden turf, fighting for a breath. By the time I'd staggered to my feet and recovered my shoe, Billy had an unassailable lead. He could afford to slow down and walk the rest of the way. All I could do was about turn and hope that I could catch Malky before he set off for home.

'What was all that?' Malky asked, when I'd re-joined him. Like most of those present, his eyes were off the football match and onto the nutter who'd gone for a cross-country run in a pair of casual shoes. 'Look at you. Don't think you're getting in my car in that state. Get yourself cleaned up.' He marched off as the final whistle blew.

Tina laughed in a worried kind of a way. 'You're all muddy, Dad.'

'I know, Tina,' I said. 'Let's go home.'

As I reached down for her hand, someone came from behind to take hold of my other arm in a firm grip. 'You promise you'll have your brother send one of the big teams to watch my boy?'

I looked down at an earnest face, bright and shiny and protruding from a ring of faux fur.

'Promise?'

I nodded.

'Then, here.' The woman who had once had the sheer temerity and strong bones to conceive a child with Big Billy Paris, pressed a piece of paper into my hand, then went off in search of her lump of a laddie to tell him the good news. I unfolded the paper. Three letters: TAS, and the name of a place I'd never heard of: St Edzell Bay. It wasn't much, but it was a start.

10

Situated on the east coast, south of Aberdeen, north of Dundee, the private airport at St Edzell Bay was a former RAF base. Cinderella to the ugly sisters at Lossiemouth and Leuchars, it had been decommissioned shortly after World War Two and most of the buildings didn't look like they'd been given a lick of paint since. As I drove down the mile-long access road, a two-seater light aircraft dropped from a low winter sun, landed with a skip and a hop and taxied along the runway towards a series of misshapen hangars between which a control tower protruded like a mushroom from a lawn after a shower of rain. Beyond that a wide stretch of deserted beach dissolved into the North Sea, the top of the waves blowing smoke. Not the day I'd have chosen for a flying lesson. Not that there was any day I'd have chosen for a flying lesson.

'He's not here,' the security guard said, leaning an elbow out of the window of a hut that was partly wood, but mostly glass.

'He did used to work here, though?'

The guard thought about that for a moment. 'Who's asking?'

'His lawyer.' I reached up to the window and handed him a business card. He studied it, lips moving silently as he read.

'It's urgent that I speak to Billy,' I said.

He tossed the card aside. 'Step out of the car, please.'

I alighted. The guard came down from the glass box and met me on the opposite side of a red and white striped barrier. He was so overweight I couldn't see how anyone could miss him, but, just in case, he had on a hi-vis fluorescent yellow bib, over a navy boiler suit. A baseball cap with the initials TAS embroidered across the front was pulled down to the rim of his mirrored sunglasses.

'This isn't about that fishing gear, is it?' he asked, way too casually, taking a quick look around. He jerked a thumb at a stack of newish looking fibre-glass rods that were propped up against the far side of the hut. 'Billy told me the stuff was legit. Said he found it in a skip, and—'

'I don't know anything about fishing tackle. I'm just looking for Billy.'

The features under the peak of the baseball cap relaxed. Two podgy fingers pinched a leg of the sunglasses and pulled them from his face. He stuffed the frames into a breast pocket of his all-in-one, folded his arms and rested them on the barrier. 'Then it's about the...' He cocked his head at some indistinguishable locus somewhere off to his rear and right. 'You know...?'

I didn't.

'The crash,' he whispered, followed by another shifty look about. 'Are they trying to pin that on Billy?'

'Should they be?'

The guard considered that question like it hadn't previously occurred to him. 'Well, he left in a bit of a hurry, didn't he?'

I hadn't a clue what he was talking about, but made a

63

show of mulling over the question. 'I suppose so,' seemed a viable enough answer.

'And he's... you know...'

'What?'

'Well he's not exactly a choirboy, is he?' The guard pushed himself off the barrier. 'I'm not holding anything against him. Served his time. Just 'cause he's been inside doesn't make him a bad person. Well, I suppose it does, but—'

'When was the crash again?' I asked. 'I forget the exact date.'

'Thirtieth November.'

'Oh, yeah. That's right, St Andrew's day,' I said, hoping to sound like I knew what I was talking about. 'And who was it that crashed?'

He stiffened, replaced his sunglasses and gave the peak of his cap a tug. 'What is this? Who are you?' he demanded, arms out by his side as though if at that moment he'd had a gun to go with his mirrored shades he'd have drawn it.

'Don't steam up your specs,' I said. 'I'm not here about the crash. I'm just looking for Billy.'

'Aye, so you've said already. You're not the first. I've had them all up here. Cops, Health and Safety, Air Accident Investigation. All wondering where Billy boy has gone.'

'Cops ask you about the fishing gear — yet?' It was a threat. Admittedly not a very good one. Whatever, it was a threat that sailed past the fat man like a military stealth drone over a radar station.

'I'll tell you what I told them,' he said. 'Billy's all right and I'm saying nothing that's going to stick him in.'

'Good for you.' If threats didn't work perhaps the old

Robbie Munro charm would. 'I can see you're a pal of Billy's and you don't want to get him into any trouble. I'll tell him that when I see him. But how about you answer me just one question?' Before he could form an objection I continued. 'Do you know where Billy is?'

He thought that over. 'No,' he said at last with a decisive shake of the head. He may have had the look of someone who could be lured anywhere by a biscuit on string, but he wasn't going to be led into any rash statements.

'Okay. How about you tell me a little about the set-up here? I take it you're head of security.'

He straightened when I said that, gave the hem of the hi-vis vest a little tug, and then slouched. 'No, that's Oleg. I'm just one of the operatives.'

'What was Bill's job here?'

He scratched the back of his head. 'What did Billy do? Billy Paris?' he said, as though I'd just sprung the topic of my missing client upon him. 'Billy was... I don't know what you'd call him. Janitor, handyman. Wasn't supposed to do security because of his record, except sometimes he'd fill in if one of the boys was off or wanted away early. The rest of the time... Hold on. That's two questions. You said you only had one question and now you're asking more.'

I tried a different approach.

'Who's the boss around here? Who owns this place?' I waved my arms around so that he might better understand.

He pointed to his hat and each of the three embroidered letters in turn. '*Thorn* Aero Systems. Who do you think is the boss?'

Thorn? It could only be Sir Philip Thorn. He of the big fat cheque. The cheque that was contingent upon my finding Billy Paris.

'And Sir Philip isn't here, before you ask.'

I was quite glad about that. It wouldn't have looked too good if I'd been shown into the boss's office and started firing questions at him about the whereabouts of the very man he was prepared to pay me handsomely to find. Not the sort of thing to instil client/solicitor confidence.

'What about this Oleg guy?' I asked.

'Oleg works days. Not like the rest of us. Guess who's pulled nightshift on Christmas Eve? And nightshift the day before.' He stabbed himself in the orange tabard with a finger. 'That's my Friday and Saturday night both buggered.'

'Can I speak to him?'

'He's not on duty.'

'I thought you said he worked days?'

'Aye,' but not Mon-*days*. He doesn't like them. So it looks like you've wasted your time.'

Maybe it did to him, but I wasn't prepared to accept that I'd driven one hundred miles for nothing. I was sure there was still some helpful information on Billy that could be gleaned. I just needed an opening.

Pretending to leave, I did a double-take at the fishing rods propped against the glass hut as I walked away. 'Where do you fish about here?'

'In the sea,' the security guard said. 'Where do you think?'

I laughed at my own stupidity. 'Good choice. I hear tell there's plenty of fish in it.'

He cracked a grin. 'So they say. I've been trying for weeks and never caught a thing.'

I didn't know much about the sport of angling. One summer holiday when we were boys, my dad had taken

66

Malky and me on a sea fishing excursion and we'd caught heaps of mackerel. Some years later I'd had a go at fly-fishing on Linlithgow Loch. That was when I realised that hurling hundreds of yards of clothesline with some feathers tied to the end into a gale force wind, while trying to not capsize a rowing boat, was an over-rated past-time, as well the most ineffectual way of catching fish ever invented. Then again, perhaps it was supposed to be difficult. Otherwise it seemed unsporting for grown men to spend so much time, money and effort trying to outsmart a creature with a brain the size of a peanut. Maybe with me in charge the contest would be more evenly matched. In any event, it seemed I'd found my way in. Once I was off the subject of Billy Paris and onto that of impaling silver darlings on silver hooks, I had the security guard's undivided attention. All I need do was keep feeding a line, let him swallow the bait and soon he'd happily swim into my net.

11

'You'll catch nothing with bread,' I said, looking into a plastic tub filled with stale crusts. We were perched on a rocky outcrop jutting out from the beach, with the tide on the turn and a merciless wind coming straight at us. A spray of surf hit me in the face like a handful of hurled carpet tacks. 'You see that?' I yelled, pointing to the North Sea with one hand, wiping my face with the other. 'It's full of things trying to eat each other.' I spat out the taste of salt. 'They're looking for meat. They're not making sandwiches.'

The man in the hi-vis vest had a name, Hugh, or Homer to his friends, a group to which I was now affiliated thanks to my self-professed and hugely exaggerated knowledge of fishing. I suspected my new friend's nickname had more to do with the Simpsons TV show than a love for the poetry of Ancient Greece. I'd agreed to spend his lunch hour presenting a tutorial on the fine art of angling.

It was while I'd been making a show of inspecting the rods and other fishing tackle, recently acquired at a knock-down price from my missing client, that I'd learned Homer had worked security at the airport for five years, having been kept on when it was acquired by Philip Thorn eighteen months previously. More innocent questions revealed that the airport's security team consisted of nine personnel operating on a complicated rota system, with three on duty at any time around the clock. The airport was only in use during daylight hours. It ran helicopter tourist trips, trained would-be aviators and was the headquarters for a local flying club. The security team's hours were long and tedious. One watched a bank of CCTV monitors from within the main building, while the other two alternated between manning the gatehouse and making regular perimeter patrols, something which, of late, Homer had been contriving to do with a fishing rod in his hand. So far he'd caught nothing but seaweed.

'The best equipment is no good unless you use the right bait,' I said, jumping along the rocks and back onto the beach, shouting at him through the wind. Lugworm casts were scattered everywhere across a seemingly endless stretch of sand. 'You see these squiggly things? Get yourself a spade. Dig right down deep under each one and you'll find a big ugly worm. Best bait in the world. Keep them in a bucket of sand and they'll be happy as Larry.' Happy until he skewered them on a steel hook and threw them into the waves. Not a good way to go, even if you were an invertebrate.

With that piece of advice I'd more or less exhausted my knowledge of angling. Homer was keen to start digging right away. I preferred to view today as more of a theory session. Best not to get bogged down with the practical side of things, like actually fishing. Thankfully, the threat of a sudden downpour put an end to the outing. A great lump of weather was heading our way, a mass of dark cloud dragging a curtain of rain across the waves, the horizon no longer visible. If we ran, we might make it back to the shelter of Homer's glass hut before we were completely drenched.

'Let's go!' I picked up some of the fishing gear we'd left lying unused on the beach. 'Come on!'

Homer remained fixed limpet-like to a rock. Staring out to sea, he removed his baseball cap and used it to wipe spray from his face. I could barely make out his words as the stiff on-shore breeze ripped them from his mouth.

'I can't help wondering what happened,' he called to me. 'He was here one day and gone the next.'

Now we were getting somewhere. During our time on the beach I'd not so much as breathed the name of Billy Paris, hoping that in the midst of our friendly fishing banter Homer would let something slip.

'Did he tell you where he was going?' I shouted back. It was worth a soaking if I could find a clue in my search for Billy.

He replaced his cap and looked down at me as though I were crazy. Maybe I was — spending an afternoon holding forth on a subject I knew very little about. I usually reserved that for the comfort of a courtroom, not a rock in the middle of the sea.

'Homer,' I said, 'did Billy ever say anything that might give you an idea where he's gone? And before you say anything, I know you're not a grass. You're his pal. But I'm his lawyer. I'm trying to help. If I don't find him fast, he could end up in a lot of trouble.' And not just Billy. I'd be in a lot of trouble too if Beardy ever came up with his promised warrant and found a kilo of smack or a gun in that cardboard box.

'I've told you already. Billy just upped and left after the helicopter crash. I'm not talking about him. I'm talking about Mr Thorn.' He stretched a finger at the briny. 'Hard to believe he's out there. Him and his girlfriend. They've not found any wreckage yet. The sea's been so rough the last few weeks they'll probably wash up in Norway or... or...'

Homer's knowledge of the Nordic states dried up as the first drops of rain started to fall. The glass hut was a four-hundred-yard dash. To make it I'd have to have set a new land speed record. I might have tried if it wasn't for the fact that my fishing buddy seemed to be suggesting that Philip Thorn was lost at sea, possibly along with a female friend and a helicopter. How could Thorn be giving instructions to Maggie Sinclair if he was at the bottom of the ocean? More importantly, just how soggy was his chequebook?

Homer clambered down from a slime-covered boulder, his booted feet slipping and sliding their way to the beach where I stood hugging a collection of rods. He picked up the bag of reels and other tackle. 'Don't you not know *nothing* about what happened here?'

When he put it like that, I wasn't sure. However, I was happy to learn something, anything.

'There was a helicopter crash. Mr Thorn who used to run this place died. So did his girl.'

'Philip Thorn's dead?

'Not Mr Thorn senior.' He tilted the peak of his base-ball cap at the North Sea. 'It's not him who's out there, more's the pity. It's wee Jerry. Sir Philip's son.'

12

It was a long windscreen-slapping drive back to Linlithgow. Crossing the Forth Road Bridge at the back of four o'clock I phoned my dad to say I'd be swinging by to pick up Tina and we'd be having our tea out. As luck wouldn't have it my dad was also free that evening and so the two of them, little and extremely large, were waiting for me when I pulled up outside the cottage.

When it came to dining out, the Munro shortlist of eateries was not a long one. Topping the bill was Alessandro's Bistro, as the proprietor liked to call it, or Sandy's Café as everyone else did. I parked outside and before we'd unbuckled a seat belt my dad said he had to go see *someone* about *something* very important. It didn't matter. It was still early and his absence gave me the chance to drop into the office, collect some files and inspect the troops.

'Anything new?' I asked Grace-Mary. It was half past four so she was winding down and preparing for departure.

'If you mean, has there been a steady stream of criminals looking to pay privately for your services, then no. If you mean, am I having to cram all new legal aid appointments into Joanna's diary, then yes.'

Right at that moment my assistant arrived back from

the High Court looking windswept and as lovely as ever. Tina ran over and Joanna lifted her up, did a quick spin and carried her through to my room, with only a brief, 'Hi,' in my direction.

'I take it you've told her?' Grace-Mary said.

'I have, though somehow she already knew.'

'Then good luck trying to talk her into staying,' she said, without so much as a flinch to corroborate my suspicion as to who had been responsible for leaking the news.

'What do you mean? Has she said anything about leaving?'

Grace-Mary pulled open a drawer and began tidying up an already tidy desk.

I planted my hands on the desktop and peered over at her. 'Grace-Mary, has Joanna said anything to you about moving on?'

She didn't look up, allowing me only the minutest of shrugs. Another person who wouldn't grass on a workmate.

I slipped out of reception and into my room. Joanna was sitting in my big, looks-like-leather chair with Tina balanced on some files that were stacked on the chair opposite. The two of them were laughing and giggling and playing some kind of tennis game with a ball of crumpled paper, using the avalanche of paperwork on my desk as a make-shift net.

'This looks good fun,' I said, catching the paper ball and setting it down out of my daughter's reach. 'You know what would make it better? If you had a proper net. A great big one. Tina, why don't you go through and ask Grace-Mary if she's got a long stand?'

Once Tina had skipped off, I removed the files, set

73

them on top of a filing cabinet and sat down in the chair vacated by my daughter. 'How's the rape going?' I asked. We were both lawyers and a chat about a serious sexual assault was just the thing to help break the ice.

'Nightmare,' was Joanna's verdict. 'First of all you've got our client, Captain Sensible, never been in trouble before, family man, business man, Rotarian.'

I had to admit that Keith Howie had looked extremely normal when I'd seen him sitting in the dock. Not young, and with a face I'm sure he wouldn't have chosen for himself if given the chance, but he could wear a suit and make it look like it wasn't for the first time. For me it was a case of so far so good. Any alleged sex-offender who lacked a bad comb-over, stained joggies and specs with beer-bottle lenses was a bonus. 'What about the complainer?'

'Sixteen coming on seventeen, pretty, seems quite timid. I don't think she gets out much. She's lived next door to the accused all her life. Calls him Uncle Keith. When her parents were away for a long weekend she stayed in our client's spare bedroom because she didn't like being in her own house alone.'

'Is she sexually active?'

'Not according to her statement and not that we'd be allowed to ask such a question anyway.'

'Got a boyfriend?'

'Yes, he's nineteen and works offshore. He was in the middle of the North Sea when this is supposed to have happened.' Like Jeremy Thorn and his girlfriend, I thought. Except there'd be no helicopter bringing them home. 'They're both Mormons. Pre-marital sex is a definite no-no.'

'And the evidence?'

Joanna leaned back, picked up the crumpled ball of paper and began tossing it around. 'Complainer goes out for the evening, comes back around midnight and goes straight to bed. Six in the morning our client's wife is woken by the girl screaming that she's been raped in the night.'

'So the girl's claiming to have been raped.' That was one source of evidence. 'And then there's evidence of distress.' That was a second source. Enough at least to corroborate an assault, if not actual rape, but not who was responsible. 'If it was rape, what is there to say it was our guy?'

'He sells kids' toys now. A few years ago when he had a hardware store he put mortise-type locks on the front and back doors. The keys are kept hidden after the house is locked up for the night. Nothing fancy, just under a plant pot on a window ledge, but the girl wouldn't have known where they were.'

'Which means no one else could have got in during the night?'

'And the only other occupants of the house were Mrs Howie and the three kids. All girls. The oldest is nine and the twins are three. That leaves our guy in the frame.'

'There has to be more.'

'There is.' Joanna finished playing with the ball of paper by expertly pitching it into the bin on the other side of the room. 'A lot more.'

'Injuries?'

'Thankfully not.'

'That's good. Leaves the possibility it could have been consensual.'

Joanna shook her head. 'We haven't intimated a consent defence.'

'Why not?'

'Because you're overlooking two things. One, the fact that the victim—'

'*Alleged* victim.'

'All right, alleged victim. You're overlooking the fact that she'd been drinking and, secondly, even if she had been sober enough to consent, you'll recall what our client said during police interview. The interview in which he declined his right to silence. The interview that you attended,' Joanna reminded me. 'Mr Howie made it very clear he hadn't laid a finger or anything else on her. Sex with consent was always a non-starter.'

Joanna was right. I'd not just overlooked that part, I'd forgotten all about it until then. The fact was that some clients wouldn't listen to advice. The innocent ones were particularly bad at it. They knew best. Keith Howie sold toys. I'd only spent five years studying law, another two in training and thirteen as a court lawyer. What did I know? He'd actually believed the interviewing police officers when they said they only wanted to find out the truth. Keen to shovel his version of events at the cops, he'd dug a hole for himself. Telling the cops anything during an interview was like playing poker with a card sharp, showing him what a great hand you had so he could deal himself a better one.

'What do the forensics say?' I shifted in my seat, discomfited as much by what seemed to be developing into a slam-dunk of a prosecution as by the chair I reserved for clients and the wooden ribs that jammed into my lower back.

Before Joanna could answer, Tina skipped back into the room. 'Dad, Grace-Mary says to tell you she only has short stands.'

At the mention of her name, my secretary, attired for a polar expedition, appeared in the doorway to say goodnight. 'And don't forget you're going out for your tea tonight,' she said, before scurrying off. The woman thought she was my mum. It was only five o'clock. Plenty of time. My dad would still be off on his important business.

'The forensics?' I asked Joanna again. 'Any DNA?'

Tina jumped up, plonked herself in Joanna's lap and began playing with the pendant that hung on a thin gold chain about my assistant's neck.

'The Howie file is in my briefcase,' Joanna said. 'The forensic report is inside.'

Joanna's briefcase was more of a satchel, chestnut leather, like a much larger version of the one I'd had on my first day at school. The file inside was neatly assembled and tidy, everything in order. By that stage in a High Court case, one of my files would have resembled a burst mattress.

I extracted the Crown's forensic report and a brief history compiled by the police surgeon who first met with the girl. I recognised the name of the doctor. His reports were about as objective as one of my brother's match reports after an Old Firm game. The *attack*, as the doctor described it with no room for doubt, reasonable or otherwise, despite the lack of injury, had taken place sometime after midnight on Saturday morning. The girl hadn't reported it to the cops until Monday evening when her parents came back. A delay in reporting a rape wasn't a problem for the Crown. Reporting early helped the complainer's credibility. Reporting late also helped the complainer's credibility because it was classic victim behaviour. What didn't help was that the girl had washed and showered between times.

Turning to the Forensic report I saw that swabs had been taken from the girl in all the usual intimate areas. The same with the accused. There was reference to pubic hair samples, combed, cut and plucked. The last of those always made me wince no matter how many reports I read. The swabs were examined using differential extraction, separating the DNA into cellular and sperm fractions. Cellular fractions of DNA belonging to the alleged victim and the accused were found on each individual. This wasn't surprising. The cells could have been transferred innocently just by sitting in the same room. It was the next section of the report and the tests on the sperm fraction that was more problematic.

Deep vaginal swabs had been examined and sperm heads identified confirming the presence of semen. Not good. Now any assault was officially sexual and therefore a rape.

'Evidence of penetration and ejaculation,' I mumbled to Joanna as incoherently as possible. By now she was playing pat-a-cake with Tina and, according to my daughter, losing at it. Up until then I hadn't realised there was a competitive edge to the game. Joanna nodded, not looking up. I continued reading. Tapings had been taken from the underwear worn by the girl on the night in question. These too revealed the presence of sperm heads, but probably due to the passage of time, attempts at obtaining a DNA profile from the samples had been unsuccessful.

No doubt about it, this was a real stinker of a case.

'I'm hungry,' Tina announced, with a final double-handed slap.

Joanna lifted her down and stood up. 'So am I. Where will we go for tea?'

My daughter was in no doubt about that. 'Sandy's!'

'Then I'm having a Caesar Salad. Why don't you have the same, Tina?' Joanna rubbed her stomach. 'Lovely crispy lettuce, croutons and Parmesan cheese all smothered in Sandy's special sauce. Mmm.'

While Tina, face screwed up, considered that option, Joanna took the reports from me, reinserted them carefully into the file and returned the folder to her satchel.

'Could be worse,' I said. 'Could all have been caught on CCTV or witnessed by the Archbishop of Canterbury.' I prised myself out of the wooden chair, rubbing the small of my back. Legal aid lawyers on fixed-fees had a saying that you should never speak to a client long enough for their bum to warm the seat. Perhaps my wooden contraption was the reason I never seemed to have much trouble with long interviews. 'Anyway, it's too late to plead now. Time to don the old tin helmet, fix bayonets and battle it out. You win some, you lose some.'

'But I really want to win this one. I know it should be a matter of complete indifference to me whether our client's guilty or innocent, but—'

'It's natural to want to win,' I said. 'It's your job.'

No matter what anyone said about the public interest or defending liberties, with criminal lawyers, be they for the prosecution or defence, it all came down to one thing — winning.

'No, it isn't just that. It's his wife, Liz. She's lovely.

79

Despite everything that's been thrown at her husband, she's stood by him, believing one hundred per cent that he's innocent. I'll be more upset for her than him if he's convicted. After all, if he is a rapist he deserves whatever he gets, but what's she going to do with three kids and a beast for a husband?'

'She'll do what every other wife does,' I said. 'Divorce him and sell the house and business while he's in jail and can't do much about it.'

'I think she'd wait for him.'

'Ach, some women are like that,' I said. 'They could have the whole thing on video with David Attenborough doing a running commentary and they'd deny it ever happened.'

Joanna hooked her satchel by a strap over the back of my chair. 'It's called standing by your man,' she said, taking Tina's upstretched hand in hers.

'More like wilful blindness.'

Joanna shrugged. 'Not necessarily. Her belief could be based on trust. They've been married twenty-six years. Maybe she knows him so well she can tell when he's speaking the truth. Do you think he is? How can he be?'

I didn't answer. The truth was something I tried not to think about when it came to criminal trials. Just like talk of guilt or innocence, it only clouded the issues. In the end it all came down to proven or not proven. The evidence and how it was viewed by the jury was all that mattered.

'If you want an acquittal, you'll just have to hope Howie puts on a good performance in the witness box,' I said, reaching down to take Tina's other sticky little mitt. 'And this year's Oscar for most believable rape-accused goes to...'

80

Joanna's wry expression suggested that such an eventuality was about as likely as my daughter eschewing sausage, beans and chips for a lump of lettuce. We left the office, swinging Tina between us. Discussions on legal aid and Joanna's future career could wait. At least until after tea.

13

My dad was already sitting at our usual corner table, his breath smelling faintly of that *something* very important he'd gone to meet the mysterious *someone* about. He had taken the liberty of ordering sausage, beans and chips all round, not realising Joanna was coming along too. The old man stood and pulled a chair out for her, simultaneously waving Sandy over.

There had been a time, back when the traitorous Jill, daughter of my dad's best pal, and I had been an item, that the mere mention of Joanna's name would have had the old man scowling and threatening filicide. Now my assistant was almost an honorary Munro; picking Tina up from nursery if I was late back from court, dropping her off at the house, even babysitting from time to time.

'She's a lawyer not a nanny,' was Grace-Mary's take on things, and perhaps I did take advantage of Joanna's good nature, but only because she really didn't seem to mind. In fact, so far as I could make out, she enjoyed it. Vikki was pleasant enough towards Tina, just not a lot of fun. That might change with time. My daughter's other chief female contacts being her gran and my secretary, I couldn't have asked for a better role model than Joanna. If she ever left Munro & Co. I didn't know who'd miss her the most, Tina or me.

Another person who would be inconsolable at Joanna's departure came over to the table, black and white checked apron about his middle, sleeves rolled up to reveal impossibly hairy forearms, and juggling a damp cloth. Sandy had a number of propositions for Joanna, some of them culinary. Eventually he persuaded her against a Caesar salad. His ricotta cheese and spinach ravioli drizzled with homemade pesto was a much better option. And he'd run out of lettuce.

'Here we are, then,' I said, having cleared my plate in a new personal best time. My dad had gone off to help Sandy with a blocked sink in the kitchen and I was sitting between Joanna and Tina who were still eating. I pushed my empty plate away and draped an arm over the backs of their chairs. 'Just me and my two girls.'

'There's only one girl here,' Joanna said, through a mouthful of pasta. She snatched a paper napkin from the silver dispenser in the middle of the table and caught a drip of olive oil that was running down her chin.

'Dad says that Pyxie Girl isn't really a girl she's a woman,' Tina told Joanna while slurping beans from her fork. 'He says it's because she's got those,' Tina pressed a sticky finger against one of my assistant's breasts. 'Like yours.'

I handed Joanna another paper napkin and hurriedly explained how, to the best of my recollection, that wasn't precisely the way the father/daughter conversation had gone.

'Your dad is quite right,' Joanna said to Tina, doing her best to remove bean sauce from her blouse. 'But he should remember that there is a difference between real girls and real women, not just the ones on telly.'

'That's not all he should remember.' My dad pulled up a chair alongside and gave me a nudge. He frowned and tilted his head at the door. I'd heard the bell ping and assumed it was just another customer. It wasn't. It was Vikki, back from her trip to the States. She was looking very nice. All done up, like she was going out somewhere. To dinner perhaps. Shit. That's what Grace-Mary was trying to remind me about.

I went to meet her. She pulled her hand away when I tried to take it. I tried again, this time successfully, manoeuvring her to an empty table.

Over the years I'd been involved in many, too many, one-sided conversations with women for whom I'd once held an affection. A good number of those talks started along the lines of *it's not you, it's me*. This one with Vikki was different. Apparently, it wasn't her. It was definitely me.

'I think there's been too many people in our relationship,' she said, glancing over at Joanna and Tina. 'It's always one or the other, work or babysitting. It's either Joanna or Tina, it's never me. *We'll have to cancel our week away because I've got a jury trial that's going to spill over*, you say. *I can't make the theatre tonight because Tina's got a sore tummy*, you say. And now this. You can't even remember a simple thing like meeting me for dinner. I've been away for two weeks. You've phoned me twice. Twice in two weeks!'

Last time I'd checked, telephones worked in two directions and I also felt a little aggrieved at the cancelled holiday comment. If Vikki had been a court lawyer, she'd have understood that it was impossible to say with certainty how long a trial would last. Any number of unforeseen problems could materialise from nowhere. In the particular instance to which she referred they had, and my trial had gone on for nearly two weeks instead of the three days I'd previously estimated. What was I supposed to do? Stop mid-cross-examination, wave good-bye to Sheriff Brechin and fifteen jurors with a, sorry, I've a plane to catch, see you all in a week's time with a suntan and a sombrero?

Admittedly the theatre thing had been a cop-out. In mitigation, when I'd been told we had tickets to Hamlet it wasn't mentioned that the play was to be performed by an avant garde group of actors and set in the world of a travelling circus. I liked Shakespeare, but I also liked the Prince of Denmark in doublet and hose, not big feet and red nose.

Whether my forgetting our dinner date was really the last straw in a field of stubble or just a good excuse, I could only sit there, feeling like a mis-matched contender, knowing I was about to be K.O.'d by the champ and just wanting the whole thing to be over, quickly if not pain-lessly and with as little humiliation as possible.

Like the firing squad commander offering the condemned man a last cigarette, Vikki consoled me, saying she'd enjoyed our time together, what little there had been of it, wished me and Tina a happy future and, with a peck on the cheek, a sour glance at Joanna and another ping of the bell above the door, she was gone. As these things usually went I'd got off pretty lightly, with the welcome absence of any face-slapping or hurled drinks.

'I never really liked her that much,' my dad said when I returned to the table, dignity almost intact. He had acquired a mug of tea in the interim, Joanna a latte and Tina a milkshake with a large dollop of ice cream floating on top and into which she was digging with a long-handled spoon. 'Bit of a cold fish I always thought. What about you, Joanna?'

Joanna spluttered into her coffee. 'Vikki's... very nice,' she said at last. 'It's just that Robbie...' She grabbed my chin and waggled it. 'Well, he's an acquired taste.'

A hairy hand set down an Americano in front of me. 'No, Joanna, Islay single malt, that is an acquired taste. From the way women treat him, Robbie is more of a bad smell.' Sandy pinched his nose and laughed.

It was bad enough the serving staff making fun of your misery, but when your own daughter joined in... Tina's giggling only ceased when she dropped a blob of ice cream down her front. 'I like Vikki,' she said, while Joanna set about her with a napkin. 'She smells like flowers. But I like Joanna better because she looks like Pyxie Girl!'

'Pyxie Woman you mean! Are you forgetting about these?' Joanna stuck her chest out at Tina and then pretended to rub the paper napkin in my daughter's face. In the commotion, the milkshake was bumped. I managed to grab the glass to stop it toppling, but couldn't prevent some of the contents hitting the table and splashing over Tina.

'And Vikki wasn't all that pretty either,' my dad said, not letting up. Having thus opined he tested the temperature of his tea with a careful sip. 'Not compared to Joanna anyway. Don't you think so, Robbie?'

Joanna, who was still busying herself with my daughter and a bunch of paper napkins, looked up at me, blushing like I'd never seen her blush before.

I was saved by the bell above the door. Two black

suits walked in. DI Christchurch, beard as immaculate as ever, leading the way, the Detective Constable with the permanent scowl not far behind.

'Sorry to intrude.' Christchurch brushed a dusting of hailstones from each of his shoulders and gave a curt little nod of the head to all those gathered at my table. The man was well-mannered if nothing else. He reached into the inside pocket of his jacket.

'What is this?' my dad said.

'Nothing that concerns you, so shut it,' replied the Bulldog.

My dad was on his feet. The D.C. stepped forward and put a hand on his chest. Two men with hair triggers. If I didn't do something fast, Sandy's rubber wood furniture would be matchsticks in two minutes.

'It's okay, Dad. These gentlemen just want to speak to me.'

A glance from Christchurch was enough to make his colleague draw his hand away and back off. The Detective Inspector removed a folded piece of paper and held it out to me. 'This is for you,' he said. 'As requested.'

I took it from him. 'What is it?'

He gave me a polite little smile, the beard failing to conceal a certain degree of smugness. 'I believe, Mr Munro, that you know very well what it is.'

14

It was chucking it down when we left Sandy's. Hailstones bounced like bullets off the pavement as the four of us scurried down the street, me fumbling in my pocket for the keys to the office.

'Look valid to you?' I asked Joanna, once we'd found shelter in the close off the High Street. She'd insisted upon accompanying me back to the office with the two Ministry of Defence cops. I was glad. She'd make a good witness. She was already a good lawyer. I had a feeling I'd be needing both before too long.

In the feeble orange glow of the night light, she studied the document I'd given her.

'Signed, dated and with our office as the locus. I think it's the most legally valid search warrant I've ever seen,' she said.

That went double for me. I could recognise Sheriff Brechin's signature a mile off, the final letter of his name done with a certain flourish of the pen that signalled his pleasure at being asked to subscribe.

'If you don't mind...' Christchurch said, when he and the Bulldog had come in out of the rain. Did it matter if I minded? I had little option other than to lead our small party along the close and up the stairs to my office where the man with the beard took the warrant back from me and gestured to the front door. I unlocked it and we all piled into reception.

'Right,' Christchurch rubbed his hands together, 'where is it?'

I wasn't sure where Grace-Mary had put Billy's cardboard box, and it was only after a good deal of rummaging around that I found it in the cash room wedged between the safe and the wall.

'Signature still intact, I see.' Christchurch turned the box this way and that, inspecting it for any signs of entry. 'Could you just confirm that's how it was when Mr Paris left it with you?'

It was worth a try and smoothly done. The young detective inspector's polite and friendly approach to his job made even the enforcement of a search warrant seem a pleasant enough pastime. But I was yet to confirm to him the provenance of the box. Only Grace-Mary had so far attributed it to my client and she hadn't actually seen him hand it over. Until I knew what it contained I was saying nothing that might incriminate either myself or the man I might later be asked to defend. Two hundred pounds might not get you much, but at Munro & Co. it guaranteed you weren't ratted out to the cops.

Christchurch smiled when I didn't answer. It was almost a mark of respect. I could have liked him. He was courteous, almost friendly, and, talk about diplomatic! The man could have made waterboarding at Guantanamo Bay sound like a surfing holiday. But it was so hard to like cops. Even polite Ministry of Defence cops. I didn't know why. Years of accusing them in the witness box must have had something to do with it. That and my history with local cop DI Dougie Fleming, the man whose notebook contained more convoluted soliloquies than Shakespeare's. Why should I not cooperate with these two guys? They were here, so they said, in the interests of national security, and I was part of that nation whether I approved of those running it or not. Was Billy's two hundred quid really worth it? Why not team up with these officers, find my missing client and collect on Philip Thorn's fat cheque?

The DI pulled on a pair of white linen gloves. 'You've touched this box, Mr Munro,' he said, 'and so I understand has your secretary. You'll have to tell me who else has if I'm to eliminate them from any further enquiries.' He looked at Joanna.

'She knows nothing about this,' I said.

Meanwhile, the Bulldog was stomping about, wrenching open filing cabinets, tossing folders and paperwork about and generally doing his best to annoy me.

'Would you tell him to stop doing that?' I asked. 'Your warrant only covers a search for the box and examination of the contents.' Even Sheriff Brechin couldn't be persuaded to give the cops carte blanche to turn over a solicitor's office.

'I can ask him and I'm sure he will stop so long as you provide me with an address for Mr Paris.'

How many times would he ask me that? 'Like I've told you before, my client is of no fixed abode. Your boy can throw as much paper about as he likes, but it's a waste of time. A bit like his schooldays.'

Christchurch weighed me up and must have decided I was telling the truth. He told the Bulldog to cease, which the D.C. did with a final slam of a metal drawer, turning his attention once more to the cardboard box.

'There's a pair of scissors in the stationery drawer,' Joanna said and then stopped herself. She gave me a guilty shrug as though she'd been caught conspiring with the enemy. To tell the truth I was as interested to know what was inside as everyone else.

'No need.' Christchurch retrieved a penknife from his pocket, opened the blade and held it poised over the box like a surgeon waiting for a nurse to pat sweat from his brow.

The Bulldog shoved me aside. 'You better hope we find what we're looking for,' he said, moving in for a closer look.

I squared up to him. 'Or what?'

Joanna sighed and shoved herself between us. 'You two behave yourselves.'

The Bulldog ignored her. 'We're the government,' he told me. 'You wouldn't believe what we can do.'

'Do I look worried?' I said.

The D.C. smiled. 'Maybe you should be. You're the one with a daughter going off to France with only granny to look after her. Lot of bad people over there. Remember the Friday the thirteenth massacre? Who knows what could happen?'

How did he know about Tina's upcoming trip?

'Step back, constable,' Christchurch said, sternly. But his colleague didn't budge an ugly hair. Shoving his face at me, barrel chest puffed out, the man was begging to be hit, and I was sure he was hoping I'd oblige. Arms by his side, held out from his body, and balanced on the balls of his feet, he was ready for me to make his day. So I didn't. Striking a police officer either led to arrest or a beating or most likely both. I backed away slowly, putting myself out of his reach. He watched me withdraw from the confrontation, the smile spreading further across his face like bread mould on a stale slice. For a split-second I thought that a police assault charge and a good hiding might just be worth it for one good dig at his smug face. Still, as they say, when one door closes another opens and my retreat provided an opportunity for someone else. An opportunity that came with the element of surprise. Joanna used it to her full advantage. From nowhere her right hand scudded hard across the Bulldog's grinning face. You could have called it a slap in the same way as you could have called the sleet battering against my office window, precipitation. The D.C. wasn't balancing on the balls of his feet anymore. He was rocking back on his heels.

There are advantages to be being a woman, aside from a longer life span and always being right. If I'd have belted the Bulldog, I'd have been handcuffed and chewing floor tiles before you could say police assault. As it was, the Bulldog just stood there, teeth rattling, not sure what to do next. He turned to his senior officer. 'You saw that, Sir. Assaulting a—'

'No I didn't and you deserved it.' Christchurch pointed the knife at a chair in the corner of reception by the window. 'Sit over there and shut up or you can go wait in the car.'

The Bulldog took his bulk across the room and sat down where he'd been ordered, gently seething, too proud to rub the side of a face that by the glow on it had to be stinging.

Christchurch ran the blade across the top of the cardboard box, neatly slicing through the tape and the thick black scrawl of his signature.

'What exactly are you expecting to find in there?' I asked.

Christchurch carefully opened the box, pulling out the four flaps one by one and folding them flat. 'I've absolutely no idea,' he said.

15

'Well, that was a lot of fuss for an old pair of boots, some paperbacks, a socket set and four pairs of socks.' Joanna, ensconced in my chair, swivelled gently from side to side.

The whole search warrant rigmarole had lasted less than half an hour. DI Christchurch and his pet Bulldog had left, somewhat deflated, with a box containing, just as my client had said, no guns, knives or drugs, just a few personal belongings which I very much doubted posed any threat to the public, unless the socks hadn't been washed in a while.

I phoned Sandy, asking him to pass word to my dad that I'd be back to take Tina home, and so he could feel free to go off and attend to some more important business down at the Red Corner Bar. According to the café owner, there was no hurry. Grandfather was onto his first and granddaughter her second ice cream.

'So who is this William Paris?' Joanna completed a three-sixty. 'More importantly, what's he done?'

'Who he is, is a client of mine. I've done a couple of cases for Billy in the past, before you came to work for... with me. At the moment it's a scoring draw between him and the Crown. As for what he's done... well, that's complicated.'

Joanna leaned back. 'Try me.'

'Love to, but I've got a daughter who should be in her bed and a father who wants to be in the pub. What about you? Do you not have a home to go to? Come on, I'll walk you to your car.'

Joanna leapt gracefully from the chair. Nipping in front, she stopped abruptly and turned to face me. 'Sorry about you and Vikki. Must have been embarrassing, happening in front of everyone like that.'

I'd been dumped less than an hour before. The shock of the search warrant had doused my self-pity. Now that I'd been reminded I was surprised at how little I was bothered. Was that relief I felt? Had I ever held long term plans for me and Vikki? Why not? Was it because she hadn't made all that much of an effort to get to know Tina? Had I let her? I'd kept telling myself that someone who was head of an adoption agency, as well as a member of the Children's Panel, probably had enough of kids in her day-job without wanting to be bogged down with one in her spare time. Especially someone else's. Was that the reason? The real reason? Or was Vikki right? Was there someone else on the edge of our relationship?

'I'll get over it,' I said.

'That's the spirit.' Joanna gave me what she regarded as a playful punch on the arm and I wondered aloud how the Bulldog's jaw was doing.

'You don't think anything will come of that do you?' she said. 'I didn't mean it. Well I meant it, but not that hard.'

I told Joanna not to worry. To my mind the slap hadn't been hard enough. We walked the short stretch of High Street to where our cars were parked closely together on the pavement outside Sandy's, jammed into a space marked out for the café owner. He didn't have a car and the space was used only occasionally for unloading delivery vans. The rest of the time Joanna and I shared it.

'We'll need to talk about where we go from here,' I said.

'I thought you'd know your way to Sandy's by now,' she laughed. 'It's right there.'

'Seriously, Joanna. My problems with the Legal Aid Board. Grace-Mary mentioned something about you may be looking for another job.'

'It's not going to be easy, Robbie. You not being able to take on new legal aid clients. Like tomorrow for instance. What happens if we have custody cases and I'm stuck in the High Court?'

She was right. Who was going to cover the appearances of those arrested overnight and appearing in court the next day?

'There's bound to be an appeal process,' I said. 'They can't just cut me loose without allowing some kind of redress. Can they?'

Joanna was of the opinion that they very much could. 'And, anyway, how long would an appeal take to be heard? It takes SLAB an ice age to grant a legal aid certificate. How long until they grant you the chance of a review hearing? Even then…'

'Even then what?'

'Even then you have to admit… you do cut a lot of corners.'

'I'll admit I take the occasional shortcut.'

'Maybe, Robbie, but—'

'It's all a load of bureaucratic nonsense.'

'There are rules and you've been—'

'Flirting with disaster?' I laughed. It was either that or cry. 'That's what the compliance officer at SLAB called it.'

Joanna unslung her shoulder bag and reached in to retrieve the car key. 'Robbie, you've not been flirting with disaster. You've been sending disaster roses and chocolates for years now. You and disaster are practically engaged!'

'Come on, Jo. Don't be such a pessimist. We'll get through this somehow. I'll think of something.'

'Will you?'

'I always do. Remember how Mrs Howie is standing by her man? How about you stand by yours?'

'My man?'

'You know what I mean. Your boss slash potential business partner who also happens to be a man. Tell you what. I'll head through to Glasgow tomorrow morning. Your rape is on an old legal aid certificate so I'm okay to deal with it. You can zoom off to the Sheriff Court and take care of any new stuff that comes in there.'

Joanna screwed up her face. 'That could work...'

'But?'

'But we might not have any custody clients tomorrow and, anyway, it's *my* case. Mr Howie will be giving his evidence soon and I think I should be there when he does.'

My mobile phone buzzed. 'Private Number' flashed up which usually meant the police with intimation of a recently arrested client who'd be going to court in the morning. I showed Joanna the screen. 'That'll be the cops,' I said, in an I-told-you-so sort of a way. But it wasn't. Not this time.

'Is that you, Robbie?'

97

It took a second or two for the voice to register with me. 'Yes it's me, Billy. Where are you?'

'Never mind. We need to talk.'

'I tried to talk to you on Saturday. You saw how that went.'

'You took me by surprise. I'd had a bit to drink.'

'It was ten in the morning.'

'Aye, well, for me it was still the night before the morning after. Listen, I'm right off the drink and have got my head out my arse. I know what I need to do.'

'I hope so because the cops are out looking for you.'

'Good,' he said, 'I'm looking for them. I want you to set up a meet. Got to go, I'll phone you tomorrow.' And with that the line went dead.

Joanna squeezed her key fob. Orange lights blinked in the darkness. 'Who's been lifted this time? I suppose I'll have to cover the Sheriff Court after all.'

'No, you won't,' I said, holding the car door open for her. Visions of Sir Philip Thorn's corpulent promissory note danced in my head. 'This is one client I can take care of myself.'

16

'What's it say now?' I asked.

The shadow of my dad fell heavily across my daughter's face, and the rest of her body, and her bed, indeed across most of the small room. He shoved the thermometer under my nose for the umpteenth time. 'Still a hundred and two.'

On our return from Sandy's it had been a normal night for Tina: some TV, a game of dominoes, a bath and a bedtime story. All routine stuff, until supper time when she'd declared herself to be not hungry. Not even for milk and a biscuit. Nothing like that had ever happened before. She looked pale. Next thing she wasn't feeling well and wanted to go to bed. I felt like the world was tumbling around me.

I took the thin glass tube from my dad and held it up to the light. Why did they make the things so difficult to read? 'It's a hundred. Not a hundred and two. I think it's coming down.'

There was a series of rapid knocks followed immediately by the sound of someone marching into the cottage. Kaye Mitchell appeared, framed in the bedroom doorway, hands on hips. 'Right, you two. Out!' Without a word we obeyed, Kaye snatching the thermometer from my hand as we filed past.

The bedroom door closed and opened again with an order for a glass of water. Five minutes later Kaye was in the kitchen where my dad and I awaited her diagnosis, both of us standing by the big wooden table, too worried to sit down.

Kaye, editor of the Linlithgowshire Journal & Gazette, wasn't medically trained, but she was a friend, and, as the mother of a child who age-wise had reached double figures, I figured she had to have been doing something right all this time. She'd also agreed to make a home visit, not something you could expect on the NHS.

'She's not well,' Kaye said, looking around for the kettle. 'You both having tea?'

'What do you mean, *not well*?' I asked, 'Is it serious?'

Kaye found the kettle and began filling it at the big Belfast sink that was filled with dirty crockery. 'I think it's that flu bug that's doing the rounds.'

'I go down the pub for five minutes and this is what happens,' my dad muttered.

'Five minutes?' I said. 'More like three hours.'

'Oh, I see. I'm not supposed to go down my local once in a while because you can't look after your wean? The Olympic torch goes out more than me these days, and, when I do, I come back to find this place is like Emergency Ward Ten.'

I wasn't letting him get away with that. 'You better not be trying to blame me for Tina not being well. Who do you think's given her the flu?'

'Me?'

'Yes, you. Hanging about her, sniffing and sneezing, spreading germs. There's probably a flu factory going on in that moustache of yours.'

'Or,' Kaye said, thinking she was charging to the old man's rescue, 'it might not be the flu at all. It could be the side effects of two ice cream floats on top of sausage, beans and chips.

'That second ice cream was down to you,' I hissed, jabbing a finger at my dad.

'Will you two quit blaming each other and listen?' Kaye lit the hob and put the kettle on to boil. 'To be on the safe side we better take the worst case scenario and deal with it. Plenty of rest and sips of water. Keep a basin and a towel by the bed in case she's sick. If things get worse, or if she's not any better in a couple of days, you'd better take her to the doctor.'

'Well that's Disney out the window,' my dad said, a trifle too enthusiastically. 'She's supposed to fly out on Friday. That's not happening now. I'd better away and give her gran a call.'

'She'll be fine,' Kaye assured me, after my dad had gone off to use the phone in the hall. There was a cordless one he kept leaving around the house in ever new and interesting places. Every time it rang we had to hunt for it. Tina thought it was a game. Eventually I'd wrapped a piece of string around the handset and tied it to the leg of the old telephone table. 'Kids. One minute they're looking sick and pathetic, the next they're up bouncing around.'

'What about her temperature and the hot flushes?'

'I think we can rule out the menopause for another fifty years or so, but you will need to keep an eye on her. Give her some kids' paracetamol, that'll help, and, like I say, make sure she drinks plenty. Keep her fluid balance up.'

First there was my own fluid level to top up. Kaye had filled the kettle far too full and the water was only now starting to boil. She sat down at the table. I remained standing, not yet sufficiently at ease to be making myself comfortable. Not when my daughter was lying ill just a few feet away. I made myself useful by fetching the teapot and taking two mugs and my dad's giant china cup and saucer down from a cupboard. 'Thanks for coming round, Kaye. Tina's had the occasional sore tummy before, but nothing like this. I think I panicked when I saw how white she was and then her temperature.'

'No problem. Kids are a worry. She'll be fine. Just be grateful you've got a daughter to look after you in your old age. Me? I had to get a son, didn't I? Never mind Alzheimer's. First time I forget where I've parked the car he'll have me in a home for the bewildered.' Kaye lifted a newspaper from the table and absent-mindedly studied my dad's half-finished crossword. 'Anyway, where's the lovely Vikki? I thought she was the expert when it came to children?'

'Good at the theory,' I said, taking a carton of milk from the fridge. 'Not so good at the practical.'

'Still, I've got to hand it to you, Robbie. After that terrible business with Jill jilting you for what's-his-name.'

'Hercule.'

'Yeah, whatever did she see in that suave, sophisticated multi-millionaire? No, after the shock of that I thought you might take things easy on the romance front, but here you are, back on the horse, riding off into the sunset with—'

'Vikki dumped me.'

Kaye sat up as I put a mug of tea in front of her. 'When did this happen?'

'Tonight at Sandy's. You should have been there. Everyone else was.'

'Then…' Kaye took a quick sip of tea and made a face. 'Sugar?' I brought the bowl to her. She scooped in two teaspoons' full and gave her tea a stir.

'Then I have some very good news for you,' she said.

17

'Robbie? You? Really? A blind date?' Grace-Mary looked at Joanna, Joanna looked at me.

'It's not exactly blind,' I said.

'Short-sighted?' Joanna suggested.

'What I mean is that she knows who I am.' It was hard not to sound conceited so I didn't try not to. 'By reputation.'

'And that's not put her off?' Grace-Mary asked.

If Joanna had an opinion on the matter she kept it to herself for about two seconds. 'Grace-Mary's right, Robbie. Do you really want to meet a girl who knows your reputation and still wants to go out on a date?'

My secretary gave her a fist-bump and then held Joanna's satchel out to her. My glamorous assistant was bound for Glasgow High Court for what was shaping up to be the penultimate day of HMA -v- Keith Howie.

'It's only a date,' I said. 'Kaye seems to think we're well suited.'

'Kaye?' Assistant and secretary groaned in unison.

'Yes, Kaye. She's a good friend. When I told her about Vikki, she said that my blind-date-to-be has just come out of a relationship too. She thinks we should both get back up on the horse without further delay.'

Joanna took the satchel and slung her bag over a

shoulder. 'Robbie, you fell off your horse less than twenty-four hours ago. Don't you think you should look around the stable before you jump on the first old nag that comes along?'

'We're only meeting for a drink,' I said, 'but I will give her teeth a check, first chance I get.'

Joanna hadn't dropped into the office first thing just to make derisory comments on my love life. She could do that anytime. She'd forgotten to take her satchel with her the night before, otherwise she would have gone straight to court. I took the opportunity of catching a lift with her. I had my own business to attend to in Glasgow that morning. We made the forty-minute drive in under thirty thanks to Joanna's Mercedes SLK AMG, spoils of the infamous Lawrence Kirkslap case. What I wouldn't have given for a few more private patients like Larry.

We travelled mostly in silence. Whenever I tried to start up a conversation I only received the briefest of responses from Joanna, which was not like her. What was the matter? She'd been fine last night. Either she was not happy about the legal aid situation or she was deep in thought about her High Court case. It definitely couldn't be concern over Tina's health, because, to avoid accusations along the lines of why wasn't I with her?, I'd not raised the subject. It had been hard enough to justify my absence to myself without involving Joanna. I really didn't want the flu. It wasn't going to help anyone if I was laid up for a week. Surely Tina would be safe enough with my dad? He'd brought me and Malky up himself, hadn't he? We must have been ill sometimes and we were still hanging together.

'You'll be glad when this case is over and done with,' I said, as Joanna pulled into the carpark not far from the Saltmarket. The trial would have been over by now if not for jurors dropping like flies from the flu. Their illness had resulted in a number of lost days. So far they'd only had three days of evidence, and three High Court days was not a long period of time, although sometimes it felt like it. Ten o'clock start, a break for elevenses, lunch from one till two and the judge looking at her watch from around the half past three mark.

At the last calling they'd managed to assemble thirteen able bodies out of a possible fifteen. It had been seen as an improvement so the judge told the lawyers to crack on with what they had or the trial would never finish.

'Make the most of it,' I said in reply to Joanna's latest non-committal grunt. 'After this you'll be back to the Sheriff Court. You're going to be one busy girl dealing with all those legal aid cases.'

But even that most controversial of topics didn't spark a response. It was for the best. Although I needed to talk to her about the future of the business, I had neither the time nor inclination to do so right at that moment.

I clambered out of the sports car and looked in at my assistant who was collecting her baggage for the day ahead while, it seemed, trying to avoid eye contact with me. 'Joanna...?'

'Yes?' she said absently, rummaging around in her bag for goodness knows what. 'Oh, is that you away? Okay, g'bye then. If I don't see you, have a good blind-date.' Joanna alighted. Even laden down by shoulder-bag and satchel, she still extricated herself from the tight confines of the sports car interior with a deal more grace than I'd managed.

'If you're done for police assault I'll be happy to defend you,' I said, trying and failing to inject some humour. 'And remember what I said about partnership. Me and you. My offer stands.'

As Joanna stood up straight, her eyes met mine over the roof of the car. She held my gaze like she was holding me by the throat. 'Yeah, but maybe it's the wrong one.'

18

'I can't really spare the time, Robbie.'

Maggie Sinclair quickened her stride, extending her lead over me down the corridor to her room at the far end. I knew she never darkened the door of her office until around ten and so I'd taken up position just inside the front door of Caldwell & Craig well in advance.

'I just need a quick word.'

'Sorry, I don't want any discussion about it. Just tell me when you've found him.'

'I've found him.'

Maggie skidded to a halt on the polished wood floor and about-faced. 'Where is he?'

'I don't know. Not exactly. Not right now at this precise moment.' Maggie turned on a heel and set off again with me following. I caught her up at the door to her office. 'But I do know where he will be at eleven o'clock this morning.'

'And where is that?'

'That's the thing,' I shimmied past her into the room. 'I'd really like to firm up on the finder's fee, and—'

'There's an "and"?' Maggie stood with her back to me. I wondered why and then realised she was waiting for me to help her off with her coat. I did. She took it from me, put it on a wooden hanger and hung it on a coat stand in the corner. The only other thing on it was an ancient black gown, which was there to impress the clients. Maggie did court about as often as Santa did Easter.

'Okay,' she leaned against the edge of her desk to indicate this wasn't to be a sit-down meeting. 'The finder's fee is five thousand. I'm happy to split it down the middle.'

Not bad. But why would Maggie be happy with an even division? Okay, so she had simply sub-contracted the job to me, still there was no way Maggie Sinclair was doing any kind of job for a knight of the realm and taking twenty-five hundred for the trouble.

'I think maybe I'll tell Sir Philip the news myself,' I said. 'See if I can't get him to up the price a bit.'

Maggie put a finger to her temple and looked at the ornate coving. 'It could have been six thousand.'

It wasn't enough. Not now that I had an inkling as to why Sir Philip would want to speak to Billy. I thought I could do better.

Maggie pushed herself from the desk. 'You're in a hole...' She'd either heard about my Legal Aid Board striking-off or just assumed I was always in one hole or another. 'And when I try to pull you out, this is the thanks I get?'

'You'll need to reach down into this particular hole a little deeper,' I said, making as if to leave, just a drop of the shoulder, the faintest turn of my head, nothing I couldn't recover from if the bluff didn't work. Three grand sounded not too bad right at that moment.

'It could have been ten. Yes, I think it was ten. I was getting myself confused it's five thousand each, not between us.'

Five thousand? Much more like it, except even yet I

didn't believe her. Still, the week before Christmas, it would do me fine if I could get my hands on the money quickly enough.

'I'd like cash. Or a bank draft.'

'That can be arranged. First of all I need to know where the man is and be able to confirm it for myself.'

I hesitated.

'Oh, yes, I forgot,' Maggie rolled her eyes. 'You had an "and".'

'Why is Thorn so keen on finding my client?'

Maggie shrugged.

'Is it to do with the death of his son?'

'Who cares?'

I did. Sort of. Though the thought of five thousand in readies had helped alleviate my concerns. 'What kind of man is Philip Thorn?'

'A very rich one. I thought we'd covered that.'

'I mean what kind of *person* is he?'

'The Internet has reached Linlithgow, hasn't it, Robbie? I realise you may have to go down to the village well and collect it in buckets, but you do have access?'

'What I want to know isn't on Google,' I said, though there was plenty of information on Philip Thorn available online. He was a self-acclaimed entrepreneur and risk-taker. Starting out in business life as a lad with only a second-hand Rolls Royce, modest office premises on Sauchiehall Street and the financial safety net of an immensely rich industrialist father, Philip had tried and failed with any number of ventures; moving in and out of various sectors just as the clever people were moving out and in.

With the new millennium came success at last. Thorn's

entertainment company, Blunt Instrument, famed for a series of crash-landed TV pilots and washed-out soap operas, turned to music. Sir Philip's company found the talent, hired the songwriters, supplied the session musicians and paid the critics for glowing reviews. Over the next decade it pumped out a succession of girl and boy bands like an over-active intestinal tract after a dodgy curry.

For most artists on the Blunt Instrument conveyor belt, their days in the sun lasted about as long as Frosty the Snowman's summer holidays. Except for one: Glazed Over, a male duo even I'd heard of. Twin brothers, Greg and Tony Glass, had gone global thanks to Blunt Instrument's marketing machine — that and the fact that, unlike Philip Thorn's other protégés, the twins were actually talented, well able to write top-selling songs, sing and even play their own musical instruments. Their first two albums, Twintessential and Double-Glazed, had been chart-toppers across the world, and stadium tours sold out practically before they were announced. When suddenly the duo stopped recording, thousands of followers had gone into mourning, and they weren't the only ones. Shares in Blunt Instrument plummeted and, with insufficient capital to cover new ventures, these days it merely ticked over on its share of Glazed Over royalty cheques. No wonder Thorn was exploring new avenues of business, not that I saw the airport at St Edzell Bay being much of a money-spinner.

Thereafter most of the online information about Thorn fast-forwarded to his company's recent bitter contractual dispute with Glazed Over. The boys, now men in their thirties, had written a musical based on their string of hits. Their plan was to take it to the West End and onto Broadway. Their problem was that when the Glass brothers had signed up with Blunt Instrument they'd been young, gifted and naive to a frightening extent. They didn't own the songs they'd written, not even the performing rights. If they wanted to so much as sing in the shower, Blunt Instrument was due a major wedge of the soap. There would be no musical, not unless Philip Thorn called the shots and received the lion's share.

And so the brothers had decided they'd rather pack it all in than give the fruit of their labours to Thorn. The musical was shelved and the brothers took to the celebrity circuit, regulars on TV game shows and charity sporting events.

It was all interesting enough, and yet it simply confirmed that Philip Thorn was hard-nosed. So were a lot of business people. I was standing facing one at that moment. I wanted a greater insight into the man's character than how he dealt with employees.

'Do you think he wants to do my client harm?' I asked.

Maggie frowned. 'That's a very strange question. I'm going to need caffeine before I can even think why you'd want to know that.' She pressed a button on her phone console. 'Coffee for two, Maria—'

I coughed. 'And...?'

'And have cash-room draw up a banker's draft to the account of Mr Robert Munro for three—'

'Five.'

'Five thousand pounds.'

We waited in silence until Maggie's refreshment and my payment arrived on a silver tray.

'Now,' Maggie said, brain cells suitably revived by

112

finest Arabica. 'You were going to tell me where your client is.' I noticed that while one hand held a china cup, the other rested firmly on the banker's draft.

'I'll tell you,' I said, 'but first of all I'd like to know if the reason Philip Thorn wants to learn the whereabouts of Billy Paris is because he wants to do him harm.'

Maggie leaned back in her chair, took two or three sips of coffee and gave the question I'd posed a great deal of thought. 'You know?' she said, leaning forward to place the white china cup back on its saucer, 'I honestly don't care.'

Unfortunately for me, I did care, if not sufficiently to reject a five thousand pounds finder's fee. Billy Paris was my client and it was my job to care. Philip Thorn's son had been killed in a helicopter crash. Billy, a man I felt sure was sufficiently skilled to arrange such an aviation disaster, had been at the scene at the time. Not only that, but he'd left his post shortly afterwards and was making himself even more scarce than usual. Now the police were looking for him. The sort of police officers who dealt with terrorism and matters of national security. If Philip Thorn was so keen to find Billy, I could think of only one reason: revenge for his son's death. Was Philip Thorn the type of person who might arrange that? You didn't spend years in the murky, drug-ridden world of popular music without making contacts with some seriously unpopular people.

I looked down at the fingers still pinning the piece of paper to the hand-tooled, green leather surface of the giant desk and realised how much I also cared about money. 'I'm meeting him at eleven o'clock.' I thought I sensed the pressure start to ease on the banker's draft.

'Go on.'

'Down at Stewart Street.'

'Stewart Street? Why Stewart Street? Not Stewart Street—'

'Police station? That's right.'

'Robbie, think.' Maggie tapped the side of her head repeatedly. 'The man Paris is no good to us in a police station. Philip Thorn offered me a fee to find him—'

'And you have.'

'Not if he's in custody I haven't.'

'Yes you have.' I couldn't see what the big problem was. 'You were asked to find him, you agreed to do so and now you have. There you are, Phil, your man's down the nick, give me the cash. Contract offered, contract accepted, contract implemented.'

Maggie's head-tapping with one finger turned into a hair-tearing gesture with all ten. 'How many days at law school did you miss, Robbie? If I tell Thorn he can find the wanted man in the nearest cop shop he'll simply say it was the police who found him. Why pay me twent... ten thousand pounds for something which by then will be practically public knowledge?'

'Well, if he's not going to play by the rules...'

'Rules?' Maggie interrupted. 'He's Philip Thorn. He makes the rules!'

'All right, all right. What am I supposed to do? Billy Paris is handing himself into Stewart Street in half an hour.'

Maggie picked up the banker's draft, tore it up into, I thought, unnecessarily small pieces and made a neat little pile of them on her desk. 'Then you'd better stop him. Hadn't you?'

19

If there was one thing a criminal defence lawyer could rely on it was the unreliability of his clientele when it came to time-keeping. It was amazing how prone your average accused person was to a diary malfunction. I spent a large portion of my court time apologising to Sheriffs for late arrivals. With reference to missed buses, faulty alarm clocks and mix-ups over dates, I would beg the men and women in the wigs and starched collars to recall failure-to-appear warrants and ask for cases to be heard though calling late.

I hadn't expected Billy Paris to be any more punctual. Just in case he'd booked an alarm call, I jumped in a taxi and charged the fare to Caldwell & Craig. By ten fifty-five I was on the concrete-slabbed terrace outside the police station, pacing up and down under the glass awning with the big 'A Division Police Headquarters' sign.

I'd chosen to meet at Stewart Street Police Station because it was conveniently situated in the city centre, not far from the offices of Caldwell & Craig, and Billy Paris knew where it was, having visited there a few times previously, though on those occasions not under his own steam. Not only that, but, if Billy was a suspect, before he could be interviewed he would have to be formally arrested and go through the various statutory procedures.

By law that had to take place at a police station.

At ten past the hour I was looking up into the heavy stillness of a sky, thick with layers of dark clouds, when I heard the automatic glass doors behind me open and someone call my name. I turned to see Detective Inspector Christchurch in the doorway, his beard as ever a work of topiary.

'Mr Munro? We're ready when you are.'

'Ready? Is he here?'

'Arrived twenty minutes ago. We were beginning to wonder what had happened to you.'

Five grand flashed before my eyes as Christchurch led me through a series of security doors to a small room, the walls of which had remained unsullied by fresh paint for many years. My client and the Bulldog sat waiting for us. There were CCTV cameras in the corners and a DVD recorder to the side of a scarred, plastic-coated table. The small room was hot and stuffy. I took off my jacket and sat down opposite the police officers, joining Billy on a bolted down, metal chair that made the old wooden seat in my office seem like a lounger.

If I were to have any chance of getting my hands on Sir Philip's finder's fee I had to get Billy out of there. The only chance of that happening was if he kept his mouth shut.

'Let me take that,' Christchurch said, relieving me of my suit jacket and carefully draping it over a spare bucket-seat in the corner of the room that was reserved for appropriate adults during the questioning of children. 'All set?' he asked the assembled company. 'Good.' And without further ado, the Bulldog pressed a button on the DVD recorder. 'Although you are here on a voluntary basis, Mr Paris, it is still my duty to caution you that—'

'Whoah,' I said. 'Voluntary? Who said anything about this being voluntary?' The DI looked puzzled. I helped clarify. 'When I arranged for Mr Paris to hand himself in, I assumed he would be arrested.'

'Why would you assume that?' Christchurch asked. 'Mr Paris, as I was saying, I must caution you that you do not have to answer any questions, but if you do, your answers will be recorded and may be used in evidence. Understand?'

'No, you understand,' I said. 'I may have been born in the morning, but it wasn't *this* morning. I know what's going on here. You question my client for ages, then when he gets fed up and wants to go home you inform him that he's now being arrested, giving you a further twelve hours. I'd prefer it if you started the clock running now. Twelve hours of him saying no comment is long enough for me, thanks.'

Christchurch shifted his gaze to my client, while the Bulldog silently fumed. The D.C. had clearly been put on his best behaviour. No more threats about my daughter. How long would that last? I didn't think good-cop was a role he'd played before.

'Is that correct, Mr Paris?' Christchurch asked. 'Is this to be a no comment interview?'

Billy clasped his hands behind his head and reclined. It wasn't possible to make yourself comfortable in metal seats the backs of which, like medieval torture devices, were tilted at the perfect angle to torment a sitter's mid-thoracic vertebrae, but the big man looked like he was going to try. 'Fire away,' he said.

And so, after the formalities of introducing each of us present in the room for the purposes of the recording,

Christchurch did precisely that. 'Did you deliberately cause to crash the helicopter carrying Jeremy Thorn and Madeleine Moreau on thirtieth November?'

Some would have been surprised at the suddenness of such a question. Not me. Standard police interview technique dispensed with preamble, preferring to hit the suspect with a sledgehammer of an opening question. Wham! *Did you murder him? Did you rape her?* The supposed shock was intended to knock the interviewee off balance. I'd been at hundreds of such interviews. I'd seen a few suspects wobble. Billy failed to stifle a yawn.

'No,' Billy said, 'I never.'

'But you could have?'

'I've just told you I never.'

'I'll rephrase the question,' Christchurch said. 'You'd have known how to go about it – if you'd wanted to?'

Billy wasn't going to answer that, was he?

He was. 'Not difficult. You can find everything you need to know on the Internet in about five minutes. Loosen a jack-screw in the tail rotor system. You'd need tools for that. Easiest way would be to interrupt the fuel link. Block the line someway or fill the tank with compressed air to fool the fuel gauge. Once the engine stops it's possible to auto-rotate a distance and look somewhere soft for a hard landing, but basically a chopper glides like a brick.'

'How would *you* do it?'

'Don't answer that,' I said. Whether Billy was guilty or not, giving an answer from which special knowledge could later be inferred would make a defence to any charge that followed extremely difficult.

Christchurch leaned forward. 'Mr Munro, do I need to

remind you that you are here to ensure fair play, not to interrupt?'

'If my client is here voluntarily, I'll interrupt if I think it's in his best interests.'

'Copper fragments,' Billy said, while I locked eyes with Christchurch. 'Put some in the air filter and they'll liquefy enough to take out the Inconel fan blades, cause a chain reaction and destroy the engine. Either that,' he laughed, 'or an armour-piercing incendiary round from a point-fifty calibre BMG. One through the engine block would do the trick.' He laughed. 'But they're not that easy to get hold of.'

'Do you know someone by the name of Kirkton Perch?' Christchurch asked.

A question I wasn't expecting. Kirkton Perch. An unusual enough name. Where did I know it from?

'I do.'

'How do you know him?'

'I think you know the answer to that,' Billy said, which didn't help me much.

'When was the last time you saw Mr Perch?' Christchurch asked.

Billy thought about that. 'Three, four months ago. August I think. Could have been later. September maybe.'

'Where did you meet him?'

'Scotstoun Stadium.'

'At a Glasgow Warriors' game, is that right?'

'That's right.'

'You're a rugby man?' It had to be a rhetorical question. Christchurch might have been a DI, but even he couldn't miss Billy's squint nose and cauliflower ear. 'Tell me what happened at Scotstoun.'

119

Billy rubbed the back of his neck. 'I don't want to bring Group Captain Perch into this.'

'Did he offer you a job?'

Billy sighed. 'We just happened to bump into each other and went for a pint after the game. I'd not seen him in years. Hardly recognised him.'

The Bulldog had sat quietly long enough. 'But you had bumped into each other before, hadn't you? Your fist had previously bumped into his nose, hadn't it?'

'Hold on,' I said. 'One minute you're asking my client about a helicopter crash, the next you're accusing him of assault.'

'If you don't mind, Detective Constable, I'll deal with this.' Christchurch said. 'Mr Paris, for the benefit of this recording, you once assaulted Mr Perch who was at that time a senior military officer. Am I correct?'

'Yeah, that's right.'

'And you spent three years in the Corrective Training Centre at Colchester before being dishonourably discharged from the Army?'

Billy nodded.

'For the record, please?' Christchurch said.

'Yeah, I spent three years in the Glasshouse, D Company, and the Army let me go at the end of my sentence.'

'What's the point of these questions?' I asked. 'None of this can be used in court. It's evidence of a prior conviction.'

The DI ignored my interruption and continued. 'In the course of your conversation with Mr Perch, after the rugby match, did he mention to you the name of Jeremy Thorn or his father, Sir Philip Thorn.'

Billy nodded.

'For the record?'

'Yes,' Billy said. 'He mentioned Sir Philip.'

'And the private airport at St Edzell Bay?'

'Yes.'

'In what context?'

'Eh?'

'Why did he mention Sir Philip and the airport?'

'He asked me if I was working and I told him I'd applied for a job at St Edzell Bay. He said if I wanted I could put him down as a referee. I did and they hired me.'

'The man whose nose you broke helped you find employment?' the Bulldog snarled.

'Thank you, Detective Wood. Again, I ask you to leave the questioning to me.' Christchurch set his elbows on the table, made a steeple of his hands and used the tips of his index fingers to play with his bottom lip, a process which threatened havoc to his perfect beard alignment. 'Mr Paris, do you know if the helicopter that crashed on thirtieth November, killing Jeremy Thorn and his fiancée, Madeleine Moreau, was sabotaged?'

'No comment.'

No comment? What did he mean, 'no comment'? Say nothing was always the way to go during a police interview. Unlike under English law, in Scotland no adverse inference could be drawn from silence, which was why the recording of a one hundred per cent no comment interview was never played in court. If a suspect was stupid enough to actually agree to answer questions, he had to keep going. It was definitely not a good idea to pick and choose. *Do you know John Smith? Yes. Were you with him on Friday night? Yes. Did you have an argument? Yes. Did you murder him? No comment.* No commenting the difficult questions sounded about as fishy as the Group Captain's name. This had to stop now.

On the basis that a solicitor was not supposed to answer questions or make statements on behalf of his client, there was not a lot I could do other than suggest that my client might wish to stop the interview momentarily in order to take some legal advice. That way, I could take Billy into a private interview room, ask him what he thought he was playing at and rehearse his lines. From now on there would be two of them: no and comment.

'I'm fine. Carry on,' was Billy's response to my offer of a time-out.

Christchurch continued. 'Mr Paris, did Mr Perch ask you to sabotage the helicopter that crashed on thirtieth November—'

'I told you. I don't want Group Captain Perch brought into this.'

'Then I'll ask you my original question again. Did you bring down the helicopter that crashed on thirtieth November killing Jeremy Thorn and his fiancée?'

'And I'll give you the same answer. No.'

'Do you know who did?'

Billy smiled. 'No comment.'

'Did you telephone the headquarters of Police Scotland on the morning of second December to ask if there was a reward for the identity of the man who'd sabotaged the helicopter?'

'No comment.'

I could see Christchurch was stuck. The art of questioning a suspect in a police station was not dissimilar to cross-examining a witness in court. It was like boxing. The tough belligerent ones you had to crowd, keep off-balance throwing rights and lefts. The clever ones you just eased off, stepped back and threw jabs, knowing that eventually they'd beat themselves. The Detective Inspector was busy weighing up my client, who I felt had hung his jaw out quite far enough already. If I had any chance of my five grand, I needed Billy out and about. If he sat there and incriminated himself he'd be going nowhere but prison, awaiting trial for double murder.

'That's enough,' I said. 'I want to speak with my client in private.'

Christchurch raised his eyebrows enquiringly at Billy. 'Would you like a word with your lawyer?'

'No,' said Billy. 'I'd like to know what makes you think I brought down that chopper.'

20

'They're just fishing,' Billy said. 'They've not got a clue.'

My client was in an excellent mood after we left Stewart Street. No wonder. After all the fuss there had been to find him, the obtaining of a warrant to search his cardboard box, all the talk about national security, and then, after a few questions, the Ministry of Defence Police had let him go.

We were walking the half mile to Queen Street Station, Billy destined for Falkirk and the bosom of his estranged family, me undecided as to whether I should go home to my daughter's sickbed or to the High Court and the rape case that was causing Joanna so much concern. By now the trial would be nearing its conclusion.

While we'd been wrapped in the warm embrace of the police station's noisy central heating system, outside it had been snowing. Now everything was covered in a thin, grey film of slush that the cars hissing by sprayed at us.

'Back staying with your missus? Your son will be pleased,' I said.

'Not as pleased as you'd think.' Billy hawked up a fruity one and spat into the gutter. 'He's had it too good too long. Just him and his mother. He thinks he's king of the castle. Things are going to change.'

'Sounds like they already have. I thought you and...'

'Maureen.'

'I got the impression you weren't on speaking terms.'

'We're not. Haven't been for years. I knocked her up when I was on leave from the Army. After that I was stationed all over and then I got the jail. I've never been around for Maureen or my laddie, but things are going to be different.'

'And she'll take you back just like that?'

'Let's just say when money talks, women listen.'

As far as I was aware, Billy subsisted on benefits.

'That's something that's about to change an' all. I'm coming into some real dosh and Maureen will be happy to share it with me.'

I was hoping to come into some dosh myself and pretty soon at that. With Billy no longer making himself scarce I was ready to collect on Philip Thorn's finder's fee.

'Has this sudden good fortune got anything to do with what you were discussing just now with the police?' I found it hard to believe how casually he'd taken the whole affair, how certain he'd been of his release.

'You see that?' he jerked his head back the way we'd come. 'That wasn't the polis interviewing me. That was me interviewing the polis.'

'Really? What about?'

'About whether they can blame the helicopter crash on me. I didn't see how they could before I went in there, and now I know they've got nothing.'

'They've got something,' I said. 'Before the interview they had you working at the airport and leaving the scene suddenly after the crash. That's suspicious. Now they've got you on record reciting your Bringing Down Helicopters Guide and, with seventeen years in the REME, you clearly have the necessary skills. I'd say the only thing between you and a police cell right now is that there's no proof the helicopter was sabotaged, although they seemed pretty certain it was.'

Billy smiled. He did a lot of that these days. Unusual for him. Even more unusual for a murder suspect.

'So who's this Perch guy?' I asked.

'Welshman. Former Fly-boy. He was also a not bad fly-half. There's an annual REME v RAF rugby game. I played in a few. In my last game he gave me this with his knee.' Billy pointed to his deviated nose. 'I waited for him outside the locker rooms afterwards.' I could guess the rest. Summary justice having been dispensed, Billy was convicted of assault and spent the next three years scrubbing toilets with a toothbrush. 'To be fair, Perch didn't want to press charges, played it all down when he gave his statement, but it wasn't up to him. There were too many folk saw me do it. I pled guilty. It was that or five years after trial.'

As we neared West Nile Street a passing lorry trundled by through a roadside puddle sending a tsunami of slush slopping across my shoes.

'So why are the cops trying to link him to you?' I asked, shaking the water off.

Billy waved one of his giant hands at me, like I shouldn't be bothering my pretty little head about such things. 'It's all politics.'

'If they find that chopper and there are copper fragments in the air-filter or compressed air in the fuel tank, they're taking you in again, and you might not be coming out,' I said.

Billy was unperturbed. 'They'll never pin it on me.'

'And why would that be?' I'd seen plenty of prosecutions built on less evidence, and if the Crown was really keen on a conviction they could always rely on some equally enthusiastic cop to fabricate more material. It wouldn't take much. Just Christchurch or the Bulldog testifying that, before I'd arrived, Billy had blurted out a confession. In my experience suspects in police stations did a lot of blurting.

'Because I know who did do it.'

I stopped, he walked on and I pulled him back by a shoulder. 'You know or you *think* you know?'

Billy's big face melted into a leer of a grin.

'Can you prove it?' I said, not wanting to mention the cardboard box straight out. Billy had given me two hundred pounds to keep it safe and now it was safe all right. Safe in the hands of the police. I was surprised he hadn't asked about it. 'Want to let me in on the secret? I'm your lawyer after all. Anything you tell me is completely confidential.'

'Not a chance.' Billy jumped a puddle and landed with the grace of a grand piano. 'The only man I'll tell is Philip Thorn and he's going to have to pay for the privilege.'

Suddenly I didn't feel so bad about selling my client's whereabouts. Not if the desire to meet was mutual.

'I can make that happen,' I said. 'For a small fee.'

21

'I can't go through all that again.' Mrs Howie blew her nose into a tissue, shaking off her husband's attempts to put an arm around her. Anyone would have thought it was her staring down the barrel at six years in the beast enclosure of H.M. Prison Shotts.

Joanna explained to me what had happened as we wandered back to the car park. The proceedings against her rape-accused had been aborted. Of the remaining thirteen jurors only ten had turned up for day four of the trial and some of those were decidedly under the weather. The case had been deserted *pro loco et tempore*, allowing the Crown the chance to re-raise in front of some fresh jurors with more robust immune systems.

'Probably best it didn't go ahead today,' I said, trying to lighten the mood. 'I couldn't help notice the client wasn't wearing—'

'Don't start on about the blue tie of truth.'

'Every little helps. You're only looking for an eight/ seven verdict, so one person can swing it.' I'd read somewhere that colours had a psychological impact and surveys showed that those witnesses wearing blue were subconsciously viewed as more honest than others.

Joanna pointed her key fob at the Merc and zapped it

from a distance. 'In that case maybe I should buy Howie a Smurf suit.'

I could tell how uptight she was. It wasn't like her. 'Don't get so worked up,' I said. 'All you can do is your best. Look on the bright side. This break in proceedings will give you the chance to ditch Brian what's-his-name.'

'Hazelwood, and there's nothing wrong with Brian for counsel. He was a depute when I was in the Fiscal Service. He knows his stuff.'

'He knows how to get people convicted, you mean. You need to bring in someone who can cross-examine a witness without sending the jury to sleep.' I'd only heard some of junior counsel's cross-examination of the complainer, but found it way too nicey-nicey, almost apologetic.

'Lady Bothkennar commended Brian on his cross-examination of the complainer.'

'Exactly. This is your chance to instruct someone to do it properly.'

Recently there had been statements made from on high, criticising counsel who attempted to destabilise complainers in rape cases through what certain members of the judiciary described as 'unfeeling questioning'. Too many were taking the criticism to heart. For me the day a judge commended counsel for the considerate questioning of an alleged rape victim would be the last day that counsel received instructions from Munro & Co. Why should rape trials be different? In any trial, someone, somewhere, for some reason, wasn't telling the truth. It didn't seem a fair distinction for the alleged victim to be treated with more compassion than the man in the dock. After all, it was the accused who was presumed innocent. There was no presumption in law that if someone complained of rape they therefore must be telling the truth; even if sometimes it seemed that way. And yet I'd wait a long time before a High Court judge waded in on behalf of one of my clients and told Crown counsel to go easy on the poor man and stop trying to destabilise him with suggestions that he was a liar and a sexual predator.

'So what you're saying is you don't think I'm doing things properly?' Somehow Joanna had managed to take that interpretation from my words. She jammed her handbag and satchel into the sports car's tiny boot, muttering that she should be trading it in for something more practical. What was eating her? She knew the car was stupidly impractical. That was why she'd thought it so great. 'Maybe you should take the case over, Robbie. Seeing how I'm making such a mess of things.'

I was about to protest, and most likely make things worse, when my phone buzzed. It was a text from my dad to say that the doctor had been round. Tina would be fine with some bed-rest. I was going to pass on the news to Joanna with a view to changing the subject, but in her current mood it would only have led to a line of questioning on the subject of me having abandoned my daughter.

Joanna started the engine. It roared into life. Five and a half litres, nought to sixty in four point five seconds, it was stupidly powerful. I'd have loved one.

'What do you think the chances are of your client getting his hands on a Pyxie Girl doll?' I asked, as we commenced our journey back to the Royal Burgh. 'He's got a toy shop, hasn't he? I've sort of gone and promised Tina one for Christmas. Well, my dad has.'

All that suggestion produced was a curt, 'I can ask

him.' I could tell the inward journey was going to be as stimulating conversation-wise as the outward. Still, a sudden change of tack often helped elicit a response during cross-examination. It was worth a try. 'Have you ever heard of someone called Kirkton Perch?'

Joanna took her eyes off the road for a second to look at me. 'Why? Haven't you?'

'In what context?'

'In the context that he's never off the telly.'

I took it she meant adult television. The stuff that came on after the kids' programmes. The stuff I never had the time to watch these days. 'Let's pretend I've not got a clue what you're talking about.'

'I'll do my best,' Joanna said, as she swung the car onto Argyle Street, heading east. 'Kirkton Perch is the Tory's only Scottish MP. He won the recent by-election in Ayrshire or somewhere.'

I must have missed that on Cartoon Network. 'What else do you know about him?'

Not much, it transpired, other than, as the only Conservative Westminster Member of Parliament for a Scottish constituency, Perch's reward had been promotion to Secretary of State for Scotland. His position had raised his media profile considerably. Whenever a Scottish current affairs programme wanted to present a balanced political view and needed a senior Westminster Tory politician to even the scales, the choice was limited to one.

Soon we were speeding down the M8 and then onto the M80-bound slip-road. I could sense Joanna wanted to ask me more about my interest in Kirkton Perch, that is, the Right Honourable Kirkton Perch, but whatever was bugging her prevented her from doing so. Two could play

131

at that game. And we did, until Joanna parked her car on the pavement outside Sandy's.

'I think I'll just nip in for some lunch,' I said. 'Then I'm going to work from home this afternoon. Tina's got a wee bit of a sniffle and I think it's best if I'm there for her. I'll come in early tomorrow. Maybe we can have a chat about dividing up the caseload in view of the legal aid problems.'

In response, all I received from my assistant was the slightest of shrugs. What was bothering her? 'Joanna—'

'She'll be a journalist, you know.'

'Who?'

'Your blind date.'

That was tonight? What with my mind full of sick children, fat cheques, rape-accused and murder suspects, I'd almost forgotten.

'I suppose if she's one of Kaye's friends it's only to be expected,' I said.

'Don't go saying anything stupid and get your name in the papers. You've already been struck off by SLAB. Try not to get struck off by the Law Society too.'

'Okay, okay.'

'I mean it. No trying to impress her with dodges you've pulled in court, and, remember, not everyone holds the same views as you do on rape trials or... well... on just about anything else to do with the law.'

'Relax,' I said, 'I'm wearing blue tonight.' I held up my right hand. 'She'll get nothing but the truth, the whole truth—'

'Yeah,' Joanna said. 'And nothing like the truth.'

22

Blue was most certainly the colour. Dark blue, almost navy, my linen suit was the perfect item of clothing for most occasions. Perhaps it was pushing it, wearing a summer suit in the depths of a Scottish winter, but I really did wonder how I had managed so long without one. Any shirt went with it and if it came across a bit crumpled-looking, hey, it was a linen suit, it was supposed to be crumpled.

'You look like you've had a shower in that thing and dried yourself in a wind tunnel,' was Malky's wardrobe critique. My brother had been called upon to babysit. Tuesday night was domino night down at the Red Corner Bar, and with prizes that included steak pies and cans of McEwan's Export there was no way anyone was keeping my dad's hands off the ebony and ivories, even if his grandchild was in her sickbed. Not that there was any scope for me to criticise. Not when I was ditching my daughter for a date with a total stranger. Why had I agreed? Joanna was right. It did all seem extremely hasty after my very recent break-up with Vikki. Was this some kind of subconscious attempt by me to get back at her?

'Keep your fashion tips to yourself and make sure that your niece is kept tucked up in bed. Give her a drink of water or milk now and again and try and have her eat something. There's bread and I've sliced some cheese so you could make her roasted cheese. She likes that. I'll not be late. Any problems, give me a call and I'll jump on a train.'

My date was called Cherry and I was meeting her in Edinburgh at the Aspen Lounge on Princes Street. She worked nearby, usually didn't finish work until late and popped in there for a drink most evenings.

'Do you want me to phone anyway? Even if there isn't a problem?' Malky asked, after I'd gone to check on Tina. He was stretching out on the couch, preparing himself for an evening of telly-watching.

'Why would I want you to do that?'

'Think about it. What if this Cherry isn't everything you've dreamed she'd be and you want to bail out? You'll need an escape plan. Say the word and I'll phone you half an hour in. If you want to pull the rip-cord, all you do is tell her something incredibly urgent has cropped up and—'

'Thank you but that won't be necessary.' Malky was plumbing new depths of shallowness even for him. 'Kaye has assured me that there's absolutely nothing to worry about. This girl's got it all, apparently.'

'Suit yourself.' Malky put an arm down the side of a cushion and salvaged the remote. 'Maybe it's her I should be giving an escape-call.'

But I was only half listening. I had it all planned out. It would be perfect. Christmas in Edinburgh. We'd have a beer or two at the Aspen, a stroll through the Christmas Market, a mug of mulled wine, a bratwurst burger, heavy on the mustard, and, to top it all, a go on the Big Wheel. How could I fail to show a girl a good time?

23

'You'd never catch me up in that thing.' Cherry sipped a cocktail through a straw and stared over the heads of the crowded room to the window. Princes Street was an illuminated wonderland. The Ferris wheel, our topic of conversation, revolved next to the Scott Monument like a slow-motion Catherine wheel. Across the rooftops of the Christmas market, the buildings on the mound, bathed in a rainbow of colours, were a cheerful backdrop for the funfair that buzzed in the gardens below, and, above it all, the Castle, shining like a diamond set on a mountain of gold. 'And never mind that death trap, how about the market? Tacky or what? All those naff wooden huts selling German sausages and novelty knitwear.'

We were sitting on stools at the bar of the Aspen Lounge, Cherry casually attired in a pair of tight-fitting faded blue jeans, and a pink cashmere sweater.

'How's your drink?' I asked. I'd never heard of a Barbotage before. I had now and so had my wallet. Cognac, Triple Sec, Brut Champagne and a twist of lemon, served in a flute glass with a straw. Cherry liked to drink them at New Year and, well, it was only a couple of weeks away, wasn't it?

She took another sip and screwed up her nose. 'I don't know what kind of champagne they're using tonight, but it's way too sweet. Did you ask for brut?'

Cherry was blonde, beautiful and expensively dressed. Her accent was a cultured mid-Atlantic, but the only bubbly thing about her was the champagne cocktail. Her gaze transferred from window to me. Then again, she was positively stunning. So what, she had a negative personality?

A man with a starched white napkin folded over his forearm materialised at my side to advise that our table was ready. Prior to that moment I hadn't realised we'd had a table, not even one that previously had been in a state of unreadiness.

Cherry placed a hand on my arm. 'I thought we'd have a bite to eat. I'm absolutely famished.'

I was pretty peckish myself, although I'd budgeted more for sausages than a sit-down meal, just as I'd come funded for beers rather than Barbotages. The restaurant was situated a few yards from where we were seated, a raised area teeming with business suits, long dresses and supercilious expressions.

'Kaye tells me you're a lawyer?' my date said, after we'd been shown to a table by the window. Her smile was as pretty as a picture and just as painted on.

'That's right.'

'What field?'

'Criminal law.'

'You're not one of those nasty legal aid lawyers are you?'

'Legal aid? Never touch the stuff. I take it, if you're a friend of Kaye's, you're a journalist. Which newspaper?'

Cherry's smile switched off. 'Seriously?'

Had I been misinformed? 'Er... yes... seriously.' I lifted my glass to find the measure of Ardbeg had already evaporated.

'Kaye told me you were a fan,' she said.

And Kaye had told me Cherry knew I was a lawyer, had heard about some of my famous victories and was dying to meet me. I rolled my eyes as though I'd been kidding, studying the inside of my tumbler, making sure it was empty. It was. Very.

'Really? You don't know who I am?'

'Is that my phone buzzing?' I put a hand in my jacket pocket and fumbled around.

'I'm Cherry Lovell from Night News.'

'I think I'll have another one of these,' I said, holding up my whisky tumbler, trying to catch the waiter's attention. Something I was never very good at.

'Night News. It's on Thursdays at ten thirty. We dig down to the dirty roots of politics.'

Ah, politics. That explained why I'd never heard of her. If there were two categories of person I really disliked, politicians were definitely in Category A. Category B was pretty much reserved for any politicians I'd forgotten to include in Category A, along with most Sheriffs.

'Half ten?' I took a sharp intake of breath. 'That's a little past my bedtime these days. Still, sounds interesting.'

The waiter at last wafted our way to drop off menus and I ordered another round of drinks.

'What do you know about Kirkton Perch?' Cherry asked, after the man in the dinner suit had drifted off.

That name again. 'Kirkton Perch?' I asked, casually, studying a menu high on price, low on portion size. 'You mean the politician? Let me see.' I put on my knowledge-able face. 'Former Group Captain in the RAF. Winner of a recent by-election for one of the Ayrshire constituencies, and, as the Tories' only MP in Scotland, now appointed

Secretary of State.' About then the information provided by Billy Paris and Joanna began to peter out. 'Oh, and he used to play rugby.'

'What do you know about spaceports?' Cherry asked.

That they wouldn't be my specialist subject on Mastermind was the easy answer, but I went instead for, 'There aren't any. Not in the U.K.'

'Got it in one.' Cherry raised her flute glass to toast my astuteness. 'What do you think Perch promised the good folk of Ayr if he got elected?'

I needed a bigger clue than that.

Cherry helped out. 'Go on. What do you think he promised the voters of the constituency which just happens to have Prestwick Airport in it?'

Taking everything in context, I suggested that Perch might have promised the honest folk of Ayrshire that he'd put in a good word for Prestwick as just the very site to host Britain's first spaceport.

'Exactly. And not just Britain's, it would be Europe's first spaceport.' Cherry took a quick suck on her straw and then with both hands made an imaginary banner in the air between us. 'Prestwick: the Place for Space. And what about Neil Armstrong?'

'The astronaut?' The Robbie Munro edition of the first man on the moon's biography would have been a short one. Possibly running to a longish sentence.

'Would you believe Perch is laying claim to him on Prestwick's behalf because the Armstrong Clan hailed from Langholm, even though Prestwick's in Ayrshire and Langholm is in Dumfries and Galloway. How pathetic is that?'

'Perch is Welsh, isn't he? You're Scottish, how much do

you know about the geography of Wales? Pathetic or not, it's a policy that got him elected.'

'And now that he is?' Cherry finished her drink, removed the straw from her glass and jabbed the wet end at me. 'What do you think is going to happen? What's *got* to happen?'

I thought about that, partially distracted by the colourful scene outside the window. My dad and Tina had been on the Big Wheel a week or so back. I'd really fancied a go. Further down the street the fairy lights on the little peaked roofs of the market stalls twinkled merrily in the cold night air. I could almost smell the sizzling German sausages.

'Well?'

'I suppose he'll have to make good on his promise – although he is a politician and so the promise-keeping thing doesn't necessarily follow.'

Cherry placed her elbows on the table and leaned forward. 'I'd like you to tell me everything you know about Kirkton Perch and his relationship to your client, Billy Paris.'

The waiter arrived with fresh drinks and to take our food order. I staved off my hunger pangs with a quick swallow of ten-year-old Islay malt, set my tumbler down again on the table and looked into Cherry's big blue contact lenses. 'This isn't a date, is it?'

She answered me with a so-sue-me raising of a sculpted eyebrow and sipped from a champagne cocktail that should have come with a mortgage.

'Then you're here on business,' I said. 'In which case I'm prepared to waive my usual consultancy fee, and seeing how Night News is paying, I think I'll have the filet mignon.' I handed the menu to the waiter. 'With chips.'

24

Wednesday morning I was at my desk, sifting through the mail and planning for a future with no legal aid. The short-term strategy involved me contriving a meeting between Billy Paris and Philip Thorn, shortly followed by a meeting between me and a fat cheque. I picked up a letter from the wire basket to which Grace-Mary had attached the printed label, 'Now', saw it was a demand for money and dropped it into the basket labelled, 'Later.' Joanna had written in pen above it, 'Much.'

Grace-Mary's stare burned into the back of my neck. Before I could reach for the next piece of correspondence, a framed photograph was pushed under my nose. A girl in a white summer frock - a white summer frock that had remained white for another forty-five seconds after the photograph was taken - smiled out at me. Tina. She had parachuted into The Life of Robbie Munro Ltd less than six months previously, ripped up the Articles of Association and installed herself as CEO.

'How is she?' Grace-Mary placed the photo back on the corner of my desk and, having divested herself of enough outer layers to insulate the loft-space, began to drape them over various radiators throughout the office to dry off.

I confirmed that Tina was doing a lot better. She'd been up in the middle of the night with a sore throat and hadn't gone back to sleep until about five, but the good news was that her temperature was normal and she was eating again. I'd come into work early so I could take time off to be with her in the afternoon.

'That's good. Will I look out the files for court?'

'Yes, give them to Joanna when she comes in. Her rape's been deserted pro loco, so she can cover the Sheriff Court this morning while I clear up some paperwork here.'

'She's not going to like that.' Grace-Mary laid a tartan scarf along the radiator under my window. 'She's been out of the office a lot recently and has her own paperwork to sort.'

'Not a problem. I can do it for her.'

'It's mostly legal aid stuff.'

'It's okay. I know her password. It's all done online. SLAB'll never know who's doing it.'

'It's not just paperwork. The High Court unit phoned to say that they want to empanel a new jury for her rape case. I'll let you break the news. It might even start on Monday if there's no objection from the client.'

I doubted there would be. Joanna's client, and especially his wife, wanted the matter dealt with as soon as possible.

'You do know that Joanna has put in for holidays starting Monday?' Grace-Mary said.

I didn't.

'Well, you should do. You signed off on them ages ago. She's got a skiing holiday arranged with her family and some friends. Flies out to Serre Chevalier on Wednesday and comes back the day after Boxing Day.'

'Christmas in the French Alps? How much am I paying her?'

'Not enough. It's a present from her mum and dad.' Grace-Mary sniffed. 'You know you're putting that girl under far too much pressure.'

'You know what they say about diamonds.'

Joanna came in and dumped her satchel on my desk. 'That they're a girl's best friend?'

'That they're lumps of coal that did well under pressure,' I said, trying not to dig a pit for myself.

Grace-Mary came to my rescue. Sort of. 'I forgot to ask, Robbie. How did it go last night? The big blind date?'

'Let's just say: as blind dates go, Cherry opened my eyes to a few things,' I said.

Grace-Mary groaned, and, there being no drying space available for her gloves, left the room.

Joanna went over to one of the filing cabinets. 'What was she like?' she asked over her shoulder.

'Blonde, pretty. Not as pretty as...'

'As?'

You, was the answer, but I wasn't saying it out loud. I didn't have to be an employment lawyer to know the meaning of sexual harassment and constructive dismissal. *My boss was hitting on me with inappropriate compliments, making me feel uncomfortable. I couldn't work under those conditions. Men don't have to put up with that sort of thing. It was sex discrimination. Thank you, Miss Jordan. How much compensation would you like?*

I coughed to cover my pause. 'Not as pretty as she looks on telly.'

'She's on TV?'

'Yes, Cherry's on some news programme.' I'd forgotten the name already.

'Night News? You were out with Cherry Lovell? That's who blind-date-Cherry was?'

'You know her?'

She did. Joanna knew all about her, as she did about

a lot of minor celebs. How could some people be so interested in other people's lives? I hardly knew what was going on in my life far less what Night News's anchorwoman got up to in her spare time. Or her working time for that matter.

'It wasn't really a date, was it?' It had taken Joanna approximately thirty seconds to discern what had taken me a trip to Edinburgh and a couple of single malts to work out. 'If you'd told me that's who you were going out with, I would have known...' Joanna's turn to clear her throat.

'You'd have known what?'

'I would have known you weren't her type.'

'Oh, you would have, would you? And what's her type, then?'

Joanna rubbed a hand down the side of my face. 'You haven't shaved.'

'I've not slept either, but that's not the point. Out with it. What's Cherry Lovell's type and why am I not it?'

Joanna wrinkled her nose sympathetically. 'I'd say she was more into the fiendishly-handsome, absolutely-loaded, daredevil-pilot type.'

I had to concede that I couldn't fly nor was my bank account in credit. 'No, it wasn't a date. It was more of a honey trap. She wanted to grill me about Billy Paris. Cherry didn't think I'd speak to her about a client in a professional setting, so she gave Kaye the job of introducing us. She said Kaye owed her one.'

'Did you tell her anything?'

What could I say? I'd gone on a social basis. Cherry was there on business. She'd brought her expenses account with her and the Aspen Lounge's list of single malts was as long as Santa's naughty list.

'Billy Paris?' Joanna pressed further. 'You mentioned him to me before, but didn't say why he was so important.'

'Old client of mine. Ex-Army. The cops think he had something to do with sabotaging the helicopter that crashed and killed Philip Thorn's son.'

'Why would he want to do that?'

'Cherry Lovell thinks Kirkton Perch was behind it.'

'Kirkton Perch ordered an assassination?' Joanna's reaction was even more extreme than mine had been when Cherry had presented that particular theory, though by that time my incredulity had been eroded significantly by several single malts. 'And why would he want to do that?'

'Because Jeremy Thorn made a late bid for his airport at St Edzell Bay to become the basis for the U.K.'s first spaceport. Until then Prestwick was more or less in a one horse race.'

'Why would he need to kill someone for that? Where's the competition? Prestwick already has a major airport and the infrastructure that goes with it. What has Saint..., whatever it is, got, other than sheep on the runway?'

I knew the answer to that. 'An eastern seaboard, easy access to the E.U., a fraction of the annual rainfall of the west coast, no major population centres nearby to endanger, yet close to areas of high expertise in IT and engineering, like Aberdeen and Dundee. Militarily it's handy for the RAF bases at Lossiemouth and Leuchars and also Kinloss Barracks, not forgetting the local MP and MSP are both Nationalists and so it will have the backing of the Scottish Government and also be able to press its case in London.'

'You sound like a lobbyist.'

'I'm a good listener.'

144

'Sounds like quite a date.' Joanna's bad mood from the day before seemed to have lifted. 'Of course, there could be another reason for the death of the handsome, millionaire pilot.'

I'd thought that too. Why did it have to be sabotage? It was more likely to have been pilot error, mechanical failure or freak weather conditions. Joanna had another theory. 'Did you know Cherry and Jerry Thorn were engaged to be married?'

'Who says?'

Apparently all the gossip websites said. Jerry Thorn's love life had been common knowledge to anyone who could be bothered to care. His romantic encounters were splashed across the internet, a lot like his helicopter and the North Sea. All I knew was that I'd read nothing about it on the BBC Sports pages; however, more conclusively, I also knew that Billy Paris had been cautioned in relation to the death of Jerry Thorn *and* his fiancée. How could that be if she had been very much alive and plying me with alcohol less than twenty-four hours before.

'I said Cherry and Jerry *were* engaged,' Joanna said. 'Then along came Madeleine Moreau and your blind date got traded in.'

'And what should I take from that? That Cherry killed her ex-boyfriend because he dumped her?' I wasn't buying what Joanna had for sale. If history had taught us anything it was that the Robbie Munro road to romance was a rocky one. I'd been given the heave-ho more often than a rope on a boat and yet had thus far refrained from any homicidal tendencies.

'You have a very twisted and suspicious mind,' I said.

'She's a woman. We need twisted and suspicious minds

to keep a step ahead of you men,' was Grace-Mary's take on things as she returned to give Joanna her marching orders along with a bundle of files. 'Robbie wants you to do the Sheriff Court today. He's going to stay here and catch up with some extremely important paperwork.'

'Robbie, I've been at the High Court for the last week. I've got my own stuff to catch up on,' Joanna said, not unreasonably.

'After that he's going home to see Tina. She's got the flu,' Grace-Mary said unhelpfully, and withdrew from the room.

'Tina's got the flu?'

'It's more of a bad cold,' I said.

'Yesterday you said she had a sniffle.'

'These things can escalate quickly with kids.'

It didn't take Joanna long to come up with her own diagnosis. 'She wasn't well last night and you were out on a blind date?'

'You know what would really make Tina feel better?' I said. 'If your client could see his way clear to finding her one of those Pyxie Girl dolls for Christmas. Have you asked him?'

'Not yet.'

'Could you?'

'Before or after I secure your lying tongue to the desk with this stapler?' Joanna asked, wielding said item of stationery.

The phone on my desk rang. I didn't care who it was, I was taking the call.

It was Maggie Sinclair. 'Robbie? We have a big problem.'

Actually, it was worse than that. We had a massive problem.

25

The massive problem had been fished out of the Forth & Clyde canal not far from Lock 16 at Camelon on the outskirts of Falkirk and was now taking up drawer space in an NHS mortuary.

The news had been imparted to Maggie Sinclair by Sir Philip Thorn. The fact that he knew Billy Paris was horizontal with a tag on his toe before I did, meant any chance of my receiving a finder's fee was as well and truly deceased as my former client.

It was nice of Maggie to pass on the news, which was why I thought it strange. Maggie being nice? To me? She'd only have bothered to phone if in some way I could be of benefit to her. Other than resurrecting Billy Paris, I was bereft of ideas.

'You met with him recently, didn't you?' she said. 'I remember the last time you were at my office you said you were going to see him that morning.'

I confirmed her understanding was correct without going into detail.

'Philip would like to know what you talked about. He's hoping to meet up with you.'

Afar off in the distance my finder's fee prospects slammed on the brakes and began reversing in my direction. 'I think I could manage that. Needless to say, I'd have certain—'

'Expenses? Naturally.' I formed the distinct impression that Maggie had already organized everything including her own arrangement fee. 'How are you placed tomorrow morning?'

'Tomorrow? Yeah, that should—'

I looked up to see Joanna shaking her head and mouthing something.

'Hold on, Maggie, I'll just check my diary.' I put my hand over the mouthpiece. 'What is it?'

'Tina. Disneyland.'

I'd totally forgotten. 'Yes, thank you, Joanna, I'd not forgotten.'

'Maggie, tomorrow morning's out, I'm afraid.'

'Out? How can it be out? This is Sir Philip Thorn. He's not one of your heroin-infused clients. He won't hang around waiting for an appointment.'

'Well, he's going to have to, if he wants to see me. Go back to him. Any other time would be okay, but not tomorrow.'

'What's so important?' Joanna asked when I'd hung up.

'Billy Paris is dead. They dredged him out of the canal earlier this morning.'

'Oh, I see,' Joanna said. 'So, while I'm running around like a blue-arsed fly, up at the High Court one minute, down at the Sheriff the next, you're faffing about with some conspiracy theory about a helicopter crash? Did you know I spent three hours at the police station on Sunday afternoon waiting to see a prisoner just because you can't take on any new legal aid cases?'

'First of all,' I said, 'I'm not faffing about. I am trying to earn a substantial private fee from Sir Philip Thorn who

148

wants advice from me on how his son came to meet his death and, secondly, don't blame me for your inexperience when it comes to dealing with police officers.'

Joanna squinted dangerously. 'Inexperience? I was in the Fiscal Service for five years. I think I know how to deal with cops, thank you.'

'No, you know how to order cops about. You can do that when you're a fiscal. When you're on the other side of the fence you have to use a bit of initiative.'

'You think I lack initiative?'

'I'm not being critical.' I noticed Joanna's grip on the stapler seemed to be tightening. 'It's just that there are certain protocols when dealing with cops that one learns through years of experience.'

'Listen, Old Father Time, you're thirty-seven, I'm coming on thirty—'

'I'm just saying, you need to employ your best asset.'

Joanna slammed the stapler down on the desk. 'Am I actually hearing this correctly? You want me to flirt with policemen? Throw myself at them in the hope I'll get to see custody clients a bit quicker?'

I didn't say it. It was corny to even think it, but Joanna was gorgeous when she was angry. 'There's absolutely nothing wrong with your more obvious, physical assets,' I said, 'but, when you're dealing with cops...' I tapped my head. 'This is the best. I didn't invent the weekend-police-station-visit kit for nothing.'

'The what kit?'

'Grace-Mary!'

My secretary sauntered through. 'You yelled?'

'Please tell Joanna what's in the weekend-police-station visit kit.'

Grace-Mary rhymed them off. 'Newspaper, family-size bag of crisps, bottle of fizzy juice. Robbie likes Irn Bru, but I don't think it matters all that much.'

I could see by the look on Joanna's face that she wasn't getting it. I thought I'd better explain. 'What happens when you go to the cop shop at the weekend? You're told to have a seat and that someone will be right with you. But they aren't right with you, are they? You have to keep going back and forward to remind them you're still there, don't you?' Joanna could only agree. 'And when they eventually show you through to an interview room, you have to wait for ages for the prisoner to be brought, correct?' Again no objection from Joanna.

'Don't tell me, the newspaper is to stop me getting bored and the juice and crisps are to stave off hunger and dehydration,' she said, wearily.

'Rewind,' I said. 'I'll be you, you be a cop. Good morning, officer, I'd like to see my client, Mr McBloggs.'

I wasn't sure if it was my high-pitched impersonation of her voice or just a general reluctance to engage in role play, whichever, it took some persuasion before Joanna would step up to the mark and take her cue. 'Hello, Miss Jordan,' she said in a monotone voice. 'Have a seat. Your client will be right with you.'

I took my tone down a pitch. 'Thank you, officer.' I pretended to flick open an imaginary newspaper. 'And feel free to take your time. I'm getting paid two hundred an hour for being here.' I don't know why but I folded the imaginary newspaper again before tossing it aside. 'Expect the arrival of your client inside five minutes. The cops hate the idea of you sitting there raking in that kind of money for reading the Sundays and eating snacks.'

Joanna saw a problem with that. 'But we don't get paid two hundred an hour, or anything like it.'

I was only too well aware of that. 'You exaggerate.'

'He means lie,' Grace-Mary translated.

'The cops don't know what you're earning. They think we're all fat-cat lawyers.'

'Not the ones who know I work for you,' Joanna muttered. She packed up her satchel with the day's files.

'Joanna,' I said. 'It's difficult just now. If it's any consolation I really don't know what I'd do without you.'

She allowed herself a faint smile and shrugged. 'I suppose I shouldn't complain. Better to be busy than not.'

I was glad she saw things that way. 'Good, because they're hoping to kick-off Keith Howie's rape trial next Monday.'

Grace-Mary gave a warning growl.

'But,' I added hurriedly, 'you're not doing it. I am.'

'You don't know anything about the case,' Joanna said.

'When's that ever stopped him?' Grace-Mary asked.

I ignored my secretary's latest interjection. 'True, but I don't know how to ski either and because it'll be a lot quicker for me to read the brief than take lessons on how to slide down a hill on slats of wood, I think it's best if you're the one who goes to Serre Chevalier.' Joanna hesitated. I ploughed on. 'I know I said it was a stinker of a case, but sometimes a pair of fresh eyes can make all the difference. Maybe I can find a new angle. An alternative line of defence.'

'He means: make something up.' Grace-Mary's translation services were beginning to get on my nerves.

'Ever the optimist, eh, Robbie?' Joanna patted my cheek. 'No thanks. It's my case and I'm going to see it through to the finish.'

'Don't be such a martyr,' I said. 'Let me do it. I've got an incentive to have Howie acquitted. He's my only hope of getting Tina what she wants for Christmas.'

'Pyxie Girl?' Joanna laughed. 'If you can find a way to have Keith Howie acquitted I'll personally find you a Pyxie Girl for Christmas. No, I'm going to stay and do the trial.' She turned to leave the room and then turned back. 'But that doesn't mean you should waste your time chasing conspiracy theories. If Tina's poorly, go home. I know what you're like when you get an idea in your head. Billy Paris is dead. Jeremy Thorn is dead. Let them go.'

But I couldn't. Not yet.

26

'I don't conduct every autopsy in Scotland, Robbie.' Professor Edward Bradley sounded breathless over the phone. 'Can we make this quick? I'm in a hurry.' For a doctor whose patients were all dead he did a lot of rushing about.

'Do you know if it's been done yet?'

'No idea.'

'Can you even tell me where the body is? The details must be on a computer somewhere. He was dragged out of a canal in Falkirk yesterday.'

'Then he'll either be at the Forth Valley Hospital or on his way to the city morgue in Edinburgh. Most of the sudden deaths end up at the Cowgate. Look, Robbie, I really have to go.'

'Then leave a note for whoever's doing the job to give me a call, will you?'

'About what? Man falls in canal and drowns. Was he a drinker?' I confirmed he was, very much so. 'Then make that: Drunk man falls in canal and drowns. Hold the front page.'

'All the same I'd like to know if there is anything unexpected or out of the ordinary found.'

'Like what?'

I resisted the obvious reply that if I knew what to

expect it wouldn't meet the strict dictionary definition of unexpected. 'I don't know. Just anything not quite right.'

'Steady, lad, don't go getting all technical on me. Just let me make a note of that for my colleague. Please check cadaver for anything... what was it you said? Oh yes. Not quite right.' With that and an exasperated, 'I'll see what I can do,' Prof. Bradley was gone. If I wanted more information, I'd have to try another source.

27

The football authorities could plough as much money as they wanted into centres of excellence and football academies. The fact was they could never repeat the success of the unfunded Boys Club system. Run by unpaid, dedicated volunteers, it had nurtured all Scotland's past generations of football talent: greats such as Denis Law, Kenny Dalglish, Graeme Souness, even Malky Munro; and it was from these same grassroots that many expected the next batch of top players would also emerge. Every boys' club coach had an ambition, and that was for one of his players to make the big-time. Which was why, at the mention of Malky being interested in young Darren, such legislative niceties as the Data Protection Act were ignored. With one phone call I had the address I was looking for.

I hadn't quite figured out the association between Billy Paris and Maureen, the wee woman in the furry hood. I knew they'd met long enough for her to conceive a reasonably competent central defender, but as for how long their actual affair had lasted I had no idea. I guessed it must have been for some length of time because Billy still kept in touch with his son through football matches, and when I'd spoken to him, just the day before, he'd been confident of a reconciliation founded upon his belief in an imminent cash windfall.

'It was on and off.' Maureen was on the back green of her terraced house, taking advantage of a rare dry spell to hang out some washing. 'When he was on the drink, I was right off him.'

I'd already offered her my condolences and they'd been received with a fairly dead-pan expression, like she'd always regarded Billy floating face-down in the canal as one in a range of possible outcomes for their relationship, such that it was.

'How's Darren taking things?' I asked.

'He's thirteen. He'll get over it. You don't miss what you never had.' She picked some pegs from the small plastic tub clipped onto the wash-line, put a few between her teeth and reached up to hang out a series of football tops.

'I just came by to say how sorry I was, and—'

'I know,' she pulled the pegs out of her mouth. 'Jimmy from Darren's team called. Said your brother was interested. Jimmy said you weren't lying. Your brother did play for the Rangers.' She was a trusting soul. Or maybe she just had the same faith in the word of a lawyer as I did in that of a politician.

'And Scotland,' I said. It was all right to speak proudly of my brother's achievements, so long as he wasn't around to hear me. 'Malky thinks your son is worth another look and maybe a referral onto a senior club for a trial.'

After the string of tops came a couple of towels, some shorts and a row of socks. Once Maureen had finished hanging them out and returned the peg-tub to her now empty wash basket, she said, 'But that's not why you're here, is it?' She picked up the basket. 'My washing's drier than Billy is and already I've had the law, twice, and now

156

you at my door. I know why the polis were here, but there's no way a lawyer is dropping by at eleven o'clock on a Thursday morning to tell me my son's quite good at football.'

'You've had the police here twice?'

Maureen stared into a sky that couldn't make up its mind. Happy that she could leave her washing out for the time being, she turned to me again. 'The first lot came yesterday to tell me about Billy. Some guy walking his dog found him. The second lot came today. They're not long away.'

'The second lot. Plain clothes? A tall Englishman with a beard and a wee angry guy?'

She nodded. 'They were here before, about a week ago, asking if I knew where Billy was.'

'What did you tell them?'

'I told them I didn't know.'

'What did they ask about today?'

'They wanted to know if Billy had said anything about a helicopter crash.'

'What did you tell them?'

'I told them what I knew.' She began to walk down the path to the back door, wash-basket on her hip. 'He's dead, isn't he? What difference does it make now?' I followed her into the house and a small kitchen. The remains of breakfast were either on the table or on the floor. She kicked a crust of toast in the general direction of an overflowing plastic bin and set the clothes-basket on the kitchen table. 'Your brother really going to get Darren a trial with the Rangers?'

'There's nothing definite,' I said, and received a grunt of derision in response. 'But I promise I'll do what I can.'

She pulled out a chair from the table and sat down. 'Billy told me the police would come looking for him. He said he needed time to sort something out. He said he'd been to see you and that everything would be all right this time.'

'When I saw Billy on Tuesday he told me he'd had a bit of good luck and that he was going to be coming into money. Do you know anything about that?'

'Aye, he said the same thing to me. I thought he was just trying to sweet-talk me into letting him move back in here.'

'What did he say?'

'That he had information. It was valuable, he said, and he was making a few final checks and then cashing it in. He said we'd be set for life. I'd heard all his crap before. The man was all arse and parsley.'

'Was it information about the helicopter accident?'

She nodded.

'When did he tell you this?'

'The day before yesterday. He breenged in here about teatime. He'd been drinking. Said he'd been at the police station with you and that he was in the clear and that everything was sorted. He wanted me to go down to the Concord Bar with him for more drink. I told him no chance. He'd had enough and, anyways, I can't stand that place. Nothing but whores and comic singers in there. He left and that was the last time I saw him.' A sudden smatter of rain hit the kitchen window. Maureen got up from her chair to look out. Satisfied that it was a false alarm, she went over to the cooker. Beside it there was a wooden chopping board covered by a red-checked tea towel. She whipped it off to reveal diced potatoes and

158

onions, and tipped the lot into a big pot. Over at the sink she filled the basin with water and emptied in a bag of carrots, letting them float there like a snowman cemetery while she raked about in a drawer. 'Darren's away to the school the day. He's in a Christmas play or something and I didn't want him to miss out just because of that big eejit.'

She sniffed and wiped an eye with the back of her hand. It was probably the onions. Eventually she found what she'd been hunting for in the drawer and brought out a rusty blade, orange string coiled around its black wooden handle. She used it to set about the carrots.

'I'll make Darren a nice big plate of soup, she said. 'That and a half loaf and he'll be happy.'

'Did Billy say what the valuable information was?' I asked.

Maureen stopped scraping. 'Oh, aye. According to him he knew who'd sabotaged that helicopter killing those folk.'

I wasn't any further forward. Billy had told me much the same thing. I also knew he'd intended to sell the information he had to Philip Thorn. Thorn would be willing to pay for the name of the person who'd killed his child. What father wouldn't? I tried to imagine how I'd feel if someone murdered Tina. No wonder Thorn had wanted to find Billy.

'I don't suppose Billy told you who did it?' I asked.

Wee Maureen shook her head. 'He just kept saying he knew who it was and could prove it and that he would sell the information to the highest bidder.'

'He said that? He actually said that he had the evidence?'

'No.' Wee Maureen took her vegetable-peeler and set about the tub of carrots again. 'He said he had left it with you.'

28

It had to be in the cardboard box. Where else could it be? Billy Paris had been in my office three times in the past two years and the only things he'd given me during that period were a couple of prosecutions to defend and most recently a cardboard box that he'd been willing to pay hard cash for me to keep safe for him. The proof of who'd sabotaged Jeremy Thorn's helicopter had to be in there.

'But it's not,' Joanna reminded me. Thursday night she'd come to say 'bon voyage' to Tina who was all set to fly out to Paris the next day. We were sitting on the living room couch in front of the TV with Tina between us wrapped in a large pink fleecy dressing gown, so that, according to her grandfather, she wouldn't catch a chill. She was more likely to suffer heatstroke.

Joanna pressed home her argument. 'We were both there when the police emptied the box. There was nothing but socks, a book, some tools...'

The tools. That had to be it. 'Socket sets usually have a moulded plastic tray that lifts out. Whatever it is could be underneath. Plenty of room to hide something there,' I said.

'Like what?' Joanna asked, highlighting the second most obvious problem. 'At least if you were searching for a needle in a haystack you'd know what to look for.'

She was right. I had no idea what Billy Paris was supposed to have left me that would prove the sabotage of the helicopter.

'We're both lawyers. Let's look at this logically,' I said.

My dad gave a short derisory snort. I was aware he'd been eavesdropping, but up until then he'd maintained a most welcome, if abnormal, silence, sitting in his armchair by the fire, either concentrating on his crossword or more likely still in the huff that I'd declared Tina fit to travel.

I ignored him and continued. 'For Billy to be so sure of himself, the evidence would have to be conclusive. Video or photos would be my guess.'

'Might not be,' Joanna said. 'We're lawyers, but he wasn't. His idea of evidence could be way out, the name of a witness or something someone told him. Who knows?'

Tina, bored with our conversation, had started to squirm.

'If there was something in the box, no matter how small and well hidden, the cops would have found it,' my dad said.

'He could have hidden a note in the box or scratched it into the metal lid of the socket set.'

'And you don't think highly trained officers of the law would have found that?'

My dad was right. And yet why would Christchurch have wanted to interview Billy Paris if he already had the proof? He hadn't so much as mentioned the box during the interview.

Joanna began tickling Tina who rolled around, giggling helplessly. Then suddenly the tickles and giggles stopped. Tina pointed at the TV. 'Look, Dad. It's you.'

I didn't immediately grasp what she was saying, and

when I did, my eyes had only a moment to focus before the image on the screen had disappeared. What I did catch a glimpse of was some stock footage of myself walking into the Sheriff Court. I recognised it from a year or so back when I'd been acting for a bogus workman in a trial that had received some brief media attention. Hard to believe it was before I discovered I had a daughter. How quickly things changed. Apart from my suit. That was still in regular service.

We were all sitting up straight now. Even my dad had cast his crossword aside.

A familiar face appeared in close-up. Cherry Lovell. *'Tonight on Night News, at ten thirty, we ask - who killed Jeremy Thorn?'*

The picture faded to a supermarket Christmas ad that had been playing regularly since bonfire night.

'Rewind, dad,' I said. He was already on the job, thumb on the remote, shunting back to the start of the clip that opened with Cherry Lovell standing on the same rocky outcrop where I'd presented Homer with my fishing seminar.

'Somewhere out there lie the bodies of Jeremy Thorn and his fiancée, Madeleine Moreau.'

Cut to a mugshot of Billy Paris, Army uniform, shaved head, looking like he was about to start three fun-filled years in the Glasshouse.

'What is the link between their deaths, the death of this man and...'

Smash cut to Kirkton Perch on a runway beside one hundred and twenty-five million pounds' worth of Eurofighter Typhoon, and from there to election night and Ayr Town Hall, where, with a blue rosette in his lapel

162

and waving to his supporters, Perch stood bookend-ed by men and women with dejected expressions and rosettes of different hues.

'*The Secretary of State for Scotland? Night News believes this man holds the answer...*'

Cue the clip of me walking into court.

And back to Cherry again. '*Tonight on Night News, at ten thirty, we ask — who killed Jeremy Thorn?*'

'Why are you on telly, Dad?' Tina asked. 'Did you see Pyxie Girl?'

The subject of Pyxie Girl was one never brought up by any adult of the Munro household in the hope that the youngest member might forget all about her. Fat chance. The super-heroine was my daughter's main topic of TV conversation.

'No, I think Pyxie Girl has gone away on her holidays,' I said, and there then followed a brief discussion as to where PG might holiday, during which I cunningly slipped in the fact that I didn't expect her to be back for Christmas, but maybe sometime early in the New Year.

Tina was impervious to such tactics. 'I can't wait for Christmas,' she told Joanna. 'I asked Santa for a Pyxie Girl and Gramps says he knows Santa and Santa always gets wee girls the toys they want if they've been good and I've been good, haven't I Gramps?' Tina climbed onto Joanna's lap. 'I wish the real Pyxie Girl could come and live with us.'

As she blabbered on about Pyxie Girl, I zoned out. How could Cherry Lovell do such a thing? I knew that discussions with the press were never off the record, despite what journalists might say. I also knew that single malt whisky was a long recognised tongue lubricant. Surely I hadn't suggested I knew who'd brought down the helicopter? I didn't even know if it *had* been brought down. So far as I was aware, helicopters were quite capable of crashing themselves without any help from outside agencies. I'd met with Cherry before my meeting with Billy's ex-partner. It was wee Maureen who'd told me that Billy had left me the evidence for safe-keeping. The most I could possibly have told Cherry was that Billy knew who was responsible. From that she must have extrapolated, with journalistic licence at full stretch, that, since I was his lawyer, he would have confided in me. Now I was going to feature on TV as the man withholding information on a double murder.

'You know, the cardboard box could be a decoy,' my dad said, looking up from the folded newspaper on his lap, tapping his teeth with a pen. 'I mean, if you think about it *properly,* logically. If this man Paris did leave the stuff with you, and the only time he was in your office was the day he brought you the box, and if what you're looking for is not in the box, then it must still be somewhere in your office.'

The way my dad talked you would have thought he'd been an ace detective and not uniformed sergeant Alex Munro, whose idea of policing had depended less on finding evidence and more on not leaving bruises.

'Seems obvious to me,' he said, returning to his crossword puzzle. 'But what do I know about solving crime? I only served thirty years on the Force, nicking criminals. I wasn't a lawyer trying to get them off.'

I hated it when he was right. Billy must have hidden whatever it was somewhere in my office. I racked my brain. What had taken place that Friday afternoon? Billy had brought the box. I remembered that much. He'd also given me two hundred pounds. I definitely remembered that, even if the taxman was unaware. What else had happened? It was all a blur now. Think. It had been less than two weeks since his Friday afternoon appointment.

'Time for me to go,' Joanna said, lifting Tina off her lap and rising to her feet.

'I'm going on a hairy-plane tomorrow,' Tina said. Arms out wide, she swooped around the room, bumping into my dad's old brass floor lamp by the light of which he was studying his next clue.

'Watch it!' He stretched one hand out to steady the lamp, another to try and collar his granddaughter.

Tina danced away, shrieking with laughter. Joanna captured her as she flitted by. 'I think it's time your dad brushed your teeth and hair and tucked you into bed. Isn't that right, Robbie?'

I didn't answer, too busy watching the floor lamp, its glass shade wobbling and casting crazy shadows on the wall above the fireplace.

'I said: isn't that right, Robbie?'

Now I remembered. I lifted Tina up, gave her a peck on the cheek. 'See you in the morning, Sweetheart. Gramps is going to brush your teeth and read you a story.' I plumped my daughter on top of the old man's newspaper, grabbed Joanna's hand and pulled her towards the door.

29

'This place looks a lot better in the dark,' Joanna said.

'Do you mind? I'm trying not to electrocute myself. Point the lamp at the ceiling so I can see what I'm doing.' I climbed onto the wooden chair and from there onto my desk, shoving files aside with my feet to clear a space where I could stand.

'This could probably have waited until the morning,' Joanna said, angling my rickety angle-poise upwards.

I disagreed. At half past ten there was to be a documentary in which, if the trailer had been anything to go by, I would be shown as the man who knew who killed Jeremy Thorn and his girlfriend. If Billy Paris had left the evidence where I thought he had, by then it might actually be true.

Joanna switched on the angle-poise lamp that sat on the corner of my table, swung it around and tilted it up at the fluorescent light strip above my desk. 'And this is definitely more than just one of your hunches?'

'No,' I said. 'It's a hunch all right, but an educated one.' The Friday Billy had come to my office with the cardboard box was the same afternoon that Grace-Mary had told me about the problem with the SLAB compliance officer. I'd spoken to her in the hall. When I'd gone back to my room, Billy had been standing on my desk sorting the fluorescent light above it. He'd said something about fixing the starter with a piece of silver paper from a chewing gum wrapper. I was no electrician, but even I knew there was a hole in the light fixture where the starter went. He could easily have stuffed something small in there. The cardboard box was a red herring. Something to divert the attention of the cops if they came looking. He'd never asked me about the box because he didn't care. He'd always assumed I'd either hand it over or have it taken from me. He had only ever intended for the box to be one thing: a stalling tactic.

'Hold it steady,' I said, reaching up and twisting the little white cylinder a quarter-turn to the left and gently easing it out. I pushed my index finger into the hole. It only went in as far as the second joint. I would have tried my pinky if I'd been a contortionist. 'You'll have to give it a try, Joanna, my fingers are too thick.' I stepped down from desk to chair to floor.

'I'm not sticking my finger in there,' Joanna said. 'What if there's a live wire? Are you sure this has been properly risk-assessed?'

'It's switched off at the wall.'

That wasn't good enough. It was okay for me to go wiggling my finger around in the circuitry, but not Joanna. She wanted precautions taken. I was too keen to find out if my guess was right to waste time arguing. Two minutes later I had switched the power off at the mains and Joanna was standing on tiptoe on my desk, me shining the torch app on my mobile phone up at the ceiling to guide her slim fingers in the direction of the hole in the side of the light fitting. No sooner had one gone in than she pulled it out again, quickly. 'I felt something there.'

'Good.'

'No, not good. It felt like a spider.'

A spider. I hadn't thought of that. Thank goodness for fat fingers. 'Don't be daft. Spiders wouldn't live in there. They'd be fried by the heat of the light-strip.'

It took a bit of persuasion for Joanna to insert her finger in the hole again. After some tentative groping around she announced there was nothing there.

'Are you sure?' I asked.

'I'm sure. There is definitely nothing in there except a wire running the length of the fitting and some frazzled arachnids.' Joanna stepped daintily down from desk to chair. On the way to the floor she snagged her heel on a wooden spar and stumbled. I leapt forward, caught her and lowered her to the ground. Our faces were close. Her hair fell across me. Realising that I was holding on rather longer than was strictly necessary purely for steadying purposes, I let her go, stepped back quickly, turned and left the room in the direction of the fuse box, hoping she hadn't noticed.

'Have you thought of looking in your desk drawers?' Joanna called through to me while I was turning the electricity on again. 'Who knows what's in there?'

For the next ten minutes we pulled everything out of my desk and found nothing remotely pertaining to a helicopter crash.

After that we had a cursory glance around my office.

'Sorry for wasting your time,' I said, as we were preparing for departure. 'I was so sure.'

Joanna smiled. 'Quite all right. It's a mistake any idiot could have made.'

My mobile phone buzzed as we were leaving the door

onto the street. I didn't recognise the number on the screen, though I knew the voice when I heard it.

'Robbie, is that you? Don't say anything. To anyone. Meet me tomorrow morning, ten o'clock—'

'I can't.'

'When then?'

'It'll need to be afternoon.'

'Okay, three o'clock. The Commonwealth Pool. Bring your trunks.'

'Why?'

'Because they won't let you in the pool with your clothes on.'

'Who was that?' Joanna asked.

'That,' I said, 'I'm not at liberty to divulge.'

30

Normally I spent Friday afternoons in the office. Court usually finished early as Sheriffs found ever new and innovative ways to be unable to sit on past three o'clock. Procurators Fiscal weren't averse to an early bath either, clocking out at four thirty. Accordingly, I found the optimum time for phoning the Crown with a view to agreeing soft pleas was sometime around the back of four on a Friday afternoon. It was amazing how those deputes, so surly and unyielding of a Monday morning, could be so cheerfully flexible when the untrammelled vista of the weekend stretched before them.

On this particular Friday, I had to leave such pre-weekend negotiations to Joanna. Having waved Tina, her Gran, aunt and three cousins off on the two o'clock Paris-bound hairy-plane from Edinburgh, I had to drive across town to the Commonwealth Pool, where at three o'clock on the dot I was wading through the shallow end in a pair of swim-shorts. Next to me was the portly figure of Edward Bradley, Regius Professor of Forensic Medicine at the University of Edinburgh, sporting an ancient pair of Speedos that may once have fitted, but were now probably a contravention of the Sexual Offences Act.

'Saw you on television last night,' he said after, in the interests of decency, I'd persuaded him to wade out a little deeper so that the water came up over his waist. 'Nice bit of publicity. If that's the sort of publicity you want.'

I usually held to the view that there was no such thing as bad publicity, but, while I'd secretly enjoyed seeing myself on screen, I hadn't liked the idea that I was being used as Cherry Lovell's political pawn. She was clearly gunning for Kirkton Perch. Some of her comments about him must have given the TV station's legal adviser a sleepless night as they verged on the defamatory.

Not that the Secretary of State's reputation suggested he was someone who'd go crying to his mum because of some bad press. An ace pilot of fixed and rotary wing aircraft, Kirkton Perch had flown combat missions in Iraq and Afghanistan. He'd trained members of the Royal Family during stints in the RAF, before they retired to a life touring factories and cutting ribbons at equestrian centres. Following a distinguished service to the country he'd entered politics and been re-routed to Scotland, where there were no safe seats for Tories, only ejector seats.

Given the daunting task of capturing Ayrshire, Perch had needed something special to put to the electorate, a vote winner, and so had centred his campaign on bringing a spaceport to Prestwick. On that platform he'd won the by-election and been all set to deliver on his promise, until Jeremy Thorn came along with a proposal that more than fitted the criteria set down by the Civil Aviation Authority, all as spelled out to me during my non-date with Cherry Lovell.

'So, tell me, Robbie. Is it true? Do you know who killed Philip Thorn's boy?'

'Haven't a clue,' I said, falling back and circling him in a clumsy backstroke.

'Well, it seems to me that some people think you do. And I'm not just talking about TV people. I mean some real, very serious people.'

That brought my backstroke to a halt. 'How serious?'

'We found something on the body of your client. Well, not actually on his body.'

'In it?'

'No, not in it either.'

Now I was confused. The man was a pathologist, if he hadn't found something in or on my client, where had he found whatever it was?

'It was on his clothing. One of my assistants was cutting the shirt from the body when she heard something fall onto the post-mortem table. It was only because the table is made of steel that it made any noise at all, the thing was so tiny.'

Tina loved to swim. I'd taken her to various leisure pools since her arrival. On those occasions, in the company of my daughter, I'd never felt at all uneasy amongst all the other mums and dads and their aquatic children. Today I was decidedly uncomfortable being one of only two men standing in the centre of the pool while shoals of non-school-age kids squealed and splashed all around us.

Thinking it best to continue our conversation in the safety of the deep end, I broke into a gentle breaststroke, thinking the Professor would do likewise. He didn't. I duck-dived and swam back. 'I think it might look... less odd, if we did some actual swimming while we are in the swimming pool.' I made to push off again, but the Professor showed no sign of drawing alongside. 'What's wrong?'

'What's wrong is that I can't swim,' he said.

'What do you mean, you can't swim? You've got a yacht moored at Port Edgar. What if you're out sailing and it capsizes? How can you be a sailor and not swim?'

'How many pilots do you know who can fly?' To placate me the Professor made some circular motions with his arms, almost whacking a kid floating nearby in orange armbands.

'Okay,' I said, 'so this thing that fell out onto the table, what was it?'

'Following your call, I had mentioned that whoever did the autopsy should keep an eye out for—'

'Anything not quite right?'

'Precisely. That's why it was brought to my attention. I hadn't the foggiest what it was until I'd had a good look at the thing under a magnifying glass.'

'And?'

'It was a bug.'

'As in a listening device?'

The Professor looked around before he nodded. 'That was my first impression, though I couldn't believe it because it was so tiny. Anyway, I took it to Joe Butler, head of Informatics up at the University. He used to work for… well never mind, that's probably classified. Suffice to say, he told me it was definitely a bug and state of the art. So state of the art he was sure it had to be Government hardware.'

'And we needed to come here for you to tell me that?'

'If your client is bugged…'

'You think I may be too?'

'I don't know. I do know that, whereas I previously said that a drunk falling in the canal and drowning wasn't headline news, it isn't really all that common either. I'm guessing it's even less common that when they do fall in they're wearing space-age audio surveillance equipment.' The Professor waited until the kid in the armbands had thrashed his way past us again, not so much swimming as beating the water into submission. 'Listen, Robbie, I want nothing to do with this, okay? If there is some defence of the realm, official secrets stuff going on, I want no part of it. I just thought you should know and wanted to tell you somewhere I didn't think anyone could listen in.'

'Do you have it with you?' I asked.

'In my locker.'

'Good,' I said. 'There's someone I'd like to show it to.'

31

'Some bosses let their staff leave work early on a Friday.' Joanna picked up one of the shirts that was strewn across my bed and held it up to the light. 'It's the week before Christmas. I've better things to do than...' She held the shirt to her nose and gave it a sniff. 'What kind of soap powder do you use?'

'None. Not yet,' I said. 'These shirts are out of the wash basket. I can't remember which one I was wearing last Tuesday.'

'You got me here to sift through your dirty laundry?' Joanna threw the shirt onto the bed again.

'The washing machine's been busy with Tina's clothes. I've not got around to my stuff yet.'

I'd made the mistake of packing my daughter's suitcase too early. All that happened was that she'd got everything else dirty, which meant I had to take all the stuff out of the suitcase so she had something to wear and then wash it all again so that it was fresh for Mickey Mouse.

Joanna picked up the shirt, more carefully this time. 'Is this really how it is for you? Every day must be a nightmare, having to decide which white shirt to wear. At least if you mixed up your colours a little you might remember the one you had on when you were at Stewart Street.'

My dad came in. 'What are we looking for?' I went

to the cupboard under the stairs and returned with a rolled-up towel. I spread it out on the bed to reveal a matchbox given to me by Professor Bradley. Inside, on a bed of cotton wool, lay the tiny listening device found on Billy Paris.

'Small, isn't it?' he said. 'What is it?'

I placed it back inside the matchbox. 'A bug,' I said, after I'd rolled it up in the towel again. 'This one was found on Billy Paris's shirt collar. Call me paranoid, but I think one of these might have been planted on me too.'

'Who by?'

'The cops.'

'Whoah.' My dad was not having any of that.

'Not your mob. Ministry of Defence cops.'

That clarified, he shrugged. 'They're sneaky enough, I suppose.'

'Let's think this through,' Joanna said. 'They've been to the office twice and you've been to the police station once. Billy Paris must have got his at Stewart Street because that's the only time the cops knew where he was. Did you see them do anything funny to him when you were there?'

I hadn't. Billy was already in the interview room when I arrived. Anything could have happened before then. Nor could I think of any contact between myself and the cops. I'd gone into the room, I'd sat down and... 'I took off my jacket. I hung it over the back of the chair, but Christchurch... That's the D.I,' I said for my dad's benefit, 'he took my jacket and put it on a chair at the other side of the room.'

'That'll have been your grey suit,' Joanna said. 'How many of those have you got?'

'Currently, I have a suit for every day of the week,' I

176

said, taking off the jacket I was wearing. 'And this is it.' I laid it on the bed. The three of us pored over it, feeling every inch of the cloth.

'Found it!' From the collar of my suit, Joanna gently removed a bug identical to that in the matchbox. She placed it on the palm of her hand. It was black, slightly bulbous at one end and with a thin tail that came to a sharp point. The whole thing couldn't have been more than five millimetres long and when the tail was embedded in the fabric of my suit, just at the collar, it was practically invisible. 'It looks a bit like a…'

'Like a what?' my dad asked.

Joanna hesitated.

'Like what?' my dad repeated.

'Like a spermatozoa… Obviously a lot larger…' Joanna had spent too much time studying forensic reports in rape trials. 'Or a comma… Or—'

'Or a tadpole that's been on a diet,' I said, trying to help, while at the same time thinking back to my walk through the streets of Glasgow with Billy Paris and what had been said. Anyone able to listen in would have picked up the fact that Billy knew who had killed Jeremy Thorn. They would have also heard him refuse to reveal that information to me. And then I remembered yesterday morning. I'd visited Billy's ex-partner. Her words came back to me. Billy had also told her he knew the identity of the saboteur. But more than that, he'd told her he'd given the evidence to me.

A knock at the front door. My mind still racing, I answered it to a smartly dressed young man who I felt sure had more than one charcoal grey suit and half a dozen white shirts in his wardrobe. His smile was well rehearsed. 'Robbie Munro?' he said confidently.

'Who wants to know?'

The young man held out a hand. 'Alfie Platt. PA to Messrs Greg and Tony Glass.'

I recognised those names from somewhere. But where? 'Who?'

The young man's smile vanished. 'Greg and Tony Glass,' he said, as though his repeating the names would be enough for me. It wasn't. 'They'd like to meet you.'

'Why?' It was all becoming a little surreal.

I became aware of Joanna standing behind me. 'It doesn't matter why,' she said. 'We're going to meet Glazed Over!'

32

I was a music lover and therefore not a fan of boy bands. Not that I was culturally illiterate. I had heard of Glazed Over. I knew the titles of their most famous albums and could hum the tunes of a lot of the tracks on them. I could also recite most of their lyrics given that they didn't seem to use that many and those they did took a bit of a pounding. What I hadn't bothered to learn was their actual names, favourite colours or star signs. Joanna had. Saturday morning we were taking her car, so as not to be shown up by the state of mine, and heading for St Andrews. The Glazed Over boys were playing in one of their regular pro-celebrity golf matches and had asked to meet me at the nineteenth. They'd teed off at ten o'clock to get the best of the light and so I'd arranged to be at the Old Course Hotel by three. Joanna was tagging along because I had no wild horses available to stop her.

'Can you believe it? Glazed Over. Tony's nice, but Greg...' she sighed. 'He's just dreamy.'

'Is he really?'

'I know what you're thinking. He's not the best singer, and it's Tony who writes most of the songs, the good ones anyway, but all the same, ding-dong.' She licked the tip of a finger and flicked at an eyelash, checking it in the rear-view mirror.

'Keep your eyes on where you're going,' I said, only too well aware of the occasional tatty bunch of roadside flowers, memorial to an inadvisable overtaking manoeuvre on the twists and turns between Kinross and Auchtermuchty.

'You're very grumpy. What's wrong? Missing your wee girl?'

That must have been it. Tina had phoned to say she'd arrived safely, but I'd hardly got a word in before my dad took over.

'I'll bet Greg is never grumpy,' I said, feeling slightly queasy and putting it down to Joanna's cornering.

'Neither would I be. Not if I had his money.'

'Money's not everything,' I thought I heard someone say in a voice very similar to my own.

'I can't wait to meet him. Do you think I'm looking okay?' Joanna said, as though she'd ever not looked so much better than okay. 'I thought at first I was maybe too informal, given that this is really a business meeting, and then I saw your linen suit and now I'm wondering if I'm too straight-laced? I don't want Greg to think I'm the local librarian.'

Greg bleeding Glass. Oh, he's so handsome, such a good singer and stinking rich too. I hoped he drove his golf ball into the Swilken Burn at the last, duffed a chip into the Valley of Sin and finished off with three puts.

Upon our arrival we came across quite a crowd hanging around the entrance to the Old Course Hotel. Inside wasn't any quieter. We hacked our way through the swathes of autograph hunters to the reception desk, and when a few minutes later word of our arrival had filtered through, an immaculately attired Alfie Platt came to meet us in the company of a very large, black man wearing slacks and a houndstooth sports jacket that looked like it had been assembled by a group of tailors working from scaffolding. The Glass brothers' gofer leading the way, their bodyguard bringing up the rear, we were escorted to a private elevator and from there to the Royal & Ancient suite on the top floor. Alfie swung the door open and with a sweep of his arm gestured for us to enter. 'Mr Robert Munro and...'

'Joanna Jordan.'

'Mrs?'

'Miss.'

Alfie started again. 'Mr Robert Munro and Miss Joanna Jordan to see you, Sir,' he said, like he was announcing our arrival at the court of the Sun King and not the hotel room of a couple of clapped-out popstars. At first I had no idea exactly who his grand introduction was aimed at, until I made out a pair of Pringle-patterned socks poking from one end of a period couch that was upholstered in a luxuriously thick, fern-patterned, two-tone fabric.

'Thanks, Alfie.' The socks disappeared and in a moment a tousled-headed man of about my own age stood, smiling across the room at us. Beyond him a floor-to-ceiling window looked out on to the seventeenth green. The Road Hole was said to be the most difficult hole of golf in the world. I was yet to find an easy one.

'Thanks, boys, I'll give you a bell if I need anything,' Mr Socks told our escorts, and with that Alfie and man-mountain in a sports coat backed out of the room.

While he'd been addressing the staff, I'd taken the opportunity of clarifying with Joanna just which of the Glass brothers this was. I knew there were two, them being twins, and that one was thin and camp with black hair. This had to be him. The other was blonde, taller, more athletic. It was their names I couldn't attribute.

'Tony,' Joanna told me out of the side of her mouth. He seemed pleasant enough. He was wearing a pair of vibrant pink trousers and a darker pink jersey over a white polo shirt.

'Robbie, Joanna, come away in,' Tony said. 'We just finished our round ten minutes ago. The rain kept off for sixteen holes, lashed down for the last two, but, hey, that's the danger of playing in December and you can't play the Children's Hospice Christmas celebrity match-play in the summer can you?'

He invited us to sit, which we did on a couple of Edwardian armchairs either side of a low Italian marble table that was scattered with golf tees, markers and sweet wrappers.

'Greg's in the shower,' he said, 'and the wives...' Did a guy who wore pink trousers have a wife? 'They'll have gone for lunch and then hit the spa. Watching me and Greg play golf, even at the home of golf, is just another day at the office for them. They show face at the first tee for the cameras and then disappear.'

'How'd your round go?' I asked, after he'd offered and we'd accepted a glass of sparkling mineral water.

'Pretty terrible, as usual,' he said, twisting the cap off a bottle of spring water. 'One day I'll break ninety, but not today. What did you make of Alfie?'

'Alfie? You mean your... what is he? A butler?'

Tony laughed. 'He's our new PA. Slightly over-the-top, don't you think?' Over-the-top? The guy was moustache-twirling, leaping out of a trench blowing a whistle with a

182

service revolver in his hand, over-the-top. 'Don't worry, we'll tone him down. He's really extremely efficient. He found you quickly enough for us.'

'Hi.' A man I took to be Greg Glass entered the room and stood under the crystal chandelier, one hand leaning on the dining table, the other holding a bottle of German lager. I say I took him to be the other half of the singing, now golfing, duo, but only because the other was sitting a couple of metres away. I certainly wouldn't have recognised him. What I vaguely remembered from years gone by was a head of wavy blonde hair, tight-fitting clothes and an athletic physique. Not a shaved scalp, white-towelling dressing gown and a torso that looked to be expecting twins of its own.

'Greg, this is Robbie and his colleague Joanna,' Tony said.

Greg gave us a friendly salute, took a long swig from his bottle of beer and dropped onto the couch next to his brother. 'Never,' he paused to burp, 'play golf with a hangover. You a golfer, Robbie?'

I admitted that I had been known to swing a golf stick on occasion.

'Any good?' Tony asked, to which question I could only shrug modestly. When it came to golf I had plenty to be modest about.

Greg rolled the cold bottle along his brow and groaned. 'Ever play the Old Course?' I had, once, many years before. 'How'd you do?'

Terrible, would have been the historically accurate answer. It had been blowing a gale off the Eden estuary that day, but you didn't turn down the chance of a round at St Andrews.

'I almost got blown away, but I did narrowly miss out on a spectacular hole-in-one at the eighth by only a couple of shots,' I said.

Greg grunted a laugh. 'The East Neuk of Fife. Best golf in the world and some of the weirdest weather, eh?'

Tony took up the chat as his brother restored his electrolyte balance with another couple of slugs of beer. 'We didn't really want to play. It's the first time we've had the clubs out since.... Look, it's good of you to come all this way, and so I'll get straight to the point. We saw you on TV, Thursday night. Cherry Lovell's investigation into the death of Madeleine and Jerry.'

That was the first time I'd heard anyone say the names of the crash victims that way around. Sometimes it would be Jerry and Madeleine. Mostly it was Jeremy Thorn and his fiancée.

'And if there is a fee for this afternoon, I quite understand,' Tony continued. 'Just give the details to Alfie and he'll sort everything out for you.'

'Why do you want to know?' Joanna asked the question I'd have asked myself if I hadn't been wondering what kind of fee I might be able to wring out of a situation such as this.

Greg shoved the debris on the marble table to one side and put his feet up, hairy legs crossed at the ankles. 'We want to find out if Robbie really knows who killed Madeleine and Jerry.'

The Glass brothers' eyes were fixed firmly on me and there was silence in the room for several seconds, until Joanna asked, 'You knew them well? Madeleine and Jerry?'

'Maddy was our PA,' Tony said. 'Before Alfie.'

'Long before that clown,' Greg confirmed.

'How much do you know about us and Philip Thorn?' Tony asked. 'Other than that Phil was the man who made us.'

'We'd have made it without him,' Greg interjected.

It was like watching a tennis match, the two of them sitting at opposite ends of the couch taking turns to talk.

'I know, I know,' Tony said. 'But we can't not recognise how much he did for us in the early days, even if it doesn't mean that he owns us.'

'If he had any decency he'd cut us loose,' Greg said.

'That doesn't look like it's going to happen any time soon,' I said. 'You and Thorn are on opposing sides of a civil court action, aren't you?'

Back to Tony. 'Yes, we're making some rich lawyers even richer.'

'But one thing's for sure,' Greg said, punctuating his words with another belt of beer. 'I'm not letting Philip Thorn get his hands on Cut Crystal if it's the last thing I do.'

I felt I shouldn't have to ask, but I did. 'Cut Crystal ?'

'Greg and Tony's musical,' Joanna said, patiently, as though I was her senile uncle or a 1960s High Court judge being advised that The Beatles were a popular beat combo.

Tony's turn to serve. 'But that's not why we've asked you here. Madeleine and Jerry were our friends. Maddy was with us for six years. It might not seem that long a time, but she became like a sister to us. I don't know anyone who ever met Maddy and didn't just love her. Jerry, we've known forever. When we were first signed we were eighteen, Jerry was twenty.' He allowed himself another sip of fizzy water, and in unison Joanna and I did the same. 'In the early days, Jerry went everywhere with us, or maybe that should be we went everywhere with him. There were fast cars, nightclubs, drugs, women...'

'Lots of women,' Greg confirmed, with a final pull from the beer bottle and an accompanying release of gas. 'I never thought Jerry would settle down, but when he met Maddy a few years ago it really looked like he would.'

'Then along came Cherry Lovell.' Tony placed his glass on the coffee table. 'She'd been following the court action and wanted to interview Jerry who was pig-in-the-middle.'

I could pick up the story from there on. 'Jeremy and Cherry became an item, got engaged and then—'

'And then Jerry came to his senses.' Greg climbed out of the couch and disappeared into the kitchen area, returning with another bottle already cracked open and emptying fast.

'Greg's right,' Tony said. 'He broke things off with Cherry and he and Maddy got engaged.'

Greg took his seat on the couch again, legs akimbo, the halves of his dressing gown threatening to part. He leaned forward, one hand on top of the other, both resting on the beer bottle. 'If Maddy and Jerry were murdered, we'd like you to tell us who did it.' To my relief he leaned back and closed his legs.

'Join the queue,' I said.

'I don't suppose that sort of information comes cheap,' Tony said. 'What'll it take?'

Here was a man I could get to like very quickly. The trouble was, he was willing to buy and I had nothing to sell. I could tell them what I knew, which wouldn't take long, charge a smallish fee for my troubles, and go home – or make something up. If it was good enough for Night News…

'Robbie doesn't know,' Joanna said, before my creative juices were fully flowing. 'Cherry Lovell stupidly assumed that because Billy was his client he'd have told Robbie everything.' She laughed. 'Clients seldom tell their lawyer everything, which is usually just as well.'

Tony and Greg were clearly disappointed at the news. They glanced awkwardly at each other, not sure what to say.

I looked around my luxurious surroundings and knew exactly my next move. It was the week before Christmas and twelve days since my main revenue stream had been cut off. My daughter was seven hundred miles away and I was in a five-star hotel in the company of the lovely Joanna and two has-been, but very wealthy, popstars.

'Joanna's quite correct,' I said. 'I don't have a definitive answer for you. What I do have is one extremely plausible theory. If you're interested, that is.' They were. 'Then make yourself comfortable. This is a story that will take me some time to tell.'

33

'It was completely shameless.' Joanna pressed her foot on the accelerator and the Mercedes sped along the eastbound carriageway of the M90 motorway. Monday morning and the re-trial of HMA -v- Keith Howie had been transferred to Edinburgh in the hope there'd be fewer flu-infested jurors there.

It hadn't been easy, but on pain of death-by-secretary, I had persuaded Joanna to fly out for the Alps on Wednesday with her family and friends. That morning she was dropping me off at the High Court before heading for Livingston where she'd deal with any new legally-aided custody clients the cells might have received over the weekend. First of all, Joanna wanted to meet with the client and advise him of the change-over.

'I didn't hear you complaining when you were being wrapped in seaweed and force-fed canapés and chilled glasses of Veuve Clicquot,' I said.

'That's because you wouldn't have heard anything over the sound of your own voice spouting a lot of nonsense about a helicopter crash you know practically sod all about.'

That was unfair. I'd known enough for an excellent dinner and overnight stay at a top-class hotel. It had been great to live the life of a superstar, even that of a couple of burnt-out ones, if only for the night. Greg and Tony were good company and no expense, nor geriatric single-malt, had been spared.

Sunday morning I awoke to find fresh underwear, shaving kit and toiletries, all provided by the hotel, as well as my linen suit, dry-cleaned, lightly pressed and smelling wonderful.

'Greg and Tony seemed quite interested in what I had to tell them,' I said.

My client being dead, I'd felt unfettered by confidentiality issues and, although I'd been unable to say categorically how their friends had met their end, what I could tell them was that I had it on good authority, if Billy Paris could be described as such, that the helicopter had indeed been sabotaged. I had also been able to reveal that prior to his untimely death my client had proclaimed he'd had proof of the saboteur's identity, missing out the part about him supposedly having given that evidence to me. From there on I'd explained Cherry Lovell's view of things, and then speculated on a few more ideas that sprang to mind. Assisted as they had been by a bottle of red wine and several whiskies, it was true to say that my theories had grown wilder as the night wore on; however, while they may have not been wholly, or even nearly, accurate, the Glass brothers had found them entertaining enough to pick up the tab.

'How much whisky did you have to drink, by the way?' Joanna eased us off the M90, through a long uphill bend and onto the City Bypass.

'A good meal like that deserves a few digestifs,' I said, 'and however much I had to drink, your hero Greg had a lot more.'

My words caused the needle on the speedometer to continue north. It was a shame. Joanna had been so excited about meeting her girlhood crush, only to discover that he was now a bald porker with a drink problem and an unnatural amount of excess body-gas. I was really pleased.

'Go on, admit it. You had a good time. And that seaweed's worked wonders.'

Joanna couldn't keep a straight face any longer.

'By the way, good job in talking the legal aid board into granting sanction for senior counsel,' I said, changing subject to the matter at hand, namely, Keith Howie's rape trial. Junior counsel Brian Hazelwood had sadly, if very fortunately, fallen victim of the lurgy and somehow Joanna had persuaded the bean-counters at SLAB that the procedural problems occasioned by the collapse of the first trial, and the lack of counsel due to the flu epidemic, meant that only a QC could adequately step into the breach and defend the accused at such short notice.

'I have my uses,' she said. 'But do you really think Fiona is the best choice for a case like this?'

The best choice? Of course Fiona Faye was the best choice. She was always the best choice. 'Trust me,' I said, 'we're in for some proper cross-examination now. If there's anyone who can tear a hole in the Crown case and pull your client out, it's the Princess Fi-Fi.'

'The case is hopeless, Robbie.' Fiona Faye was the best advert for feminism I could think of. She was intelligent, witty, superb at her job, and prepared to allow men like me to carry her bag if they were daft enough to offer.

Counsel's library was up three extremely long flights of stairs. We had stopped halfway so I could catch my breath.

'I'll grant you, it's challenging,' I said, 'but hopeless?'

'Robbie. Me scaling Everest in my bra and knickers – that's challenging. Your client's defence is flying to the moon in a paper aeroplane.'

My own much lighter briefcase in one hand, I heaved Fiona's semi-suitcase, stuffed full of goodness knows what, onto my shoulder to save my aching arm.

'I take it you weren't one of the feminists who complained about Pyxie Girl and ruined my daughter's Christmas,' I said, hoping she'd take the hint and perhaps offer to carry my briefcase the rest of the way. She didn't.

On the subject of Pyxie Girl, Fiona had heard me before. Many times before. 'Don't start blaming women for that,' she said, leading the way. 'If you ask me, it was a load of confused, right-on men who did all the complaining, trying to impress a bunch of women who couldn't give a toss. Now, is there any chance you could shut up about dolls and talk to me about this case you've landed me with? It's not that I'm not hugely grateful for instructions in yet another rape, but I'm not.'

One of the problems with being both counsel and a female was that you tended to receive instructions in a lot of sex cases. This was partly due to a school of thought that believed if a jury saw a woman acting for a male accused, they would think he must be innocent because surely a woman would never represent a man she thought guilty of such a heinous crime? I didn't think jurors were so stupid. I instructed Fiona because I thought she was the best.

'What I'd give for a murder or even a robbery,' she said. 'Anything that doesn't involve me asking questions about people's genitalia for once.'

191

'I'll see what I can drum up,' I managed to gasp. 'However, coming back to this case, there really isn't that much to it.'

'Least said soonest mended, eh?'

'Yes... Apart from when you tear strips off the complainer.'

Fiona grimaced. 'I'm not sure strip-tearing is all that wise in the present climate, Robbie. Could impact on sentence.'

I thought it appropriate to mention that I'd been thinking along the lines that, with some robust questioning and a dash of luck, there might be an acquittal and no sentence that need be impacted upon.

'Have you read the brief?' Fiona asked, when we'd reached the top of the stairs and I'd put down our respective baggage in order to open the door for her.

I confirmed I had.

'And you're still optimistic? What do you know that I don't? And please don't tell me you've come up with one of your surprisingly clever lines of defence.'

There was only one defence I could think of. 'If our client didn't rape the girl, then she must have had sex with someone else.'

Fiona stopped in the doorway to the library and clapped her hands. 'Brilliant, Robbie. Honestly, I don't know why you haven't taken silk.'

'Let me finish,' I said. 'She'd been out at a party before she came to our client's home.'

'Yes, and according to your client, in his very helpful interview with the police, she seemed fine. By the way, how come you let the accused shoot his mouth off to the cops? I've never seen such a long statement.' I knew what she meant. I couldn't shut the guy up. When they transcribed Howie's statement they'd probably had to skip some of the punctuation in order to save a few trees. 'Whatever happened to the Munro & Co. sacred oath of omertà?'

Inside the library a few fellow advocates were dotted around an enormous dining table upon which were scattered the daily newspapers. They looked up from what they were reading, briefs or the sports pages, to acknowledge Fiona's arrival.

'Some of the witnesses say that they think she'd been drinking,' I said.

'So what? Her mum and dad are away, she's a young girl who went to a party.'

'She's sixteen.'

'Is that the best you can come up with? Underage drinking? That's going to rock the world of an Edinburgh jury. A sixteen-year-old girl has a couple of alco-pops of a Saturday night? The little minx.'

'She's a Mormon. She's not supposed to drink.'

'So she has to repent. It doesn't give anyone the right to rape her.'

'What I'm suggesting is that she's been drinking, and, because she's not used to it, she's got drunk, had her way with someone at the party, regretted it in the morning—'

'And pinned the blame on dear old Uncle Keith?' Fiona sat down at the table and flicked open a Daily Mail. 'Did that come straight out of this year's Robbie Munro's Dodgy Defences Christmas Annual? Can you not give me something I can actually use? Tell you what. Why don't you go back to your man and see if he can come up with something slightly more credible — like an alien abduction. If I have to pull the trigger, I'm going to need some ammunition. Don't have me standing there firing blanks.' She pulled out a chair and sat down. 'Well, at least you and him have got another day to think about it.'

'What do you mean?'

'Sorry, I meant to tell you before you came all the way up here. The clerk called first thing. Lady Bothkennar's not well, poor soul. The case isn't calling today. Mind you, were your client to change his plea, I could have him called this morning in front of Lord Tait. You know his views on rape: woman with skirt up, run faster than man with trousers down. Your client wouldn't be looking at any more than a quick six, out in four. Maybe a five if the judge's team won at the weekend.' She looked across at an older advocate in a nicotine-stained wig. 'Did it, Fraser?' The older counsel shook his yellow wig. 'Still, we could *try* for a five. The girl wasn't injured, was she?'

'He's not pleading,' I said.

'You sure? You know who is prosecuting, don't you?' Fiona bit her top lip to show her front teeth.

'Not Cameron Crowe?'

'Just our luck, eh?'

Nosferatu in pinstripes. I should have known the undead wouldn't come down with the flu like the rest of the population.

Fiona groaned. 'I wish people would stop calling it flu. Anyone who's able to say "I've got the flu," hasn't got the flu. The flu's like the Glasgow Bar Association's annual dinner. If you can remember it, you weren't there. I should know. I had the real thing last year. Went to bed and never saw daylight for a week.'

'Are we talking about the flu or the GBA dinner?'

'Funny, Robbie. All I'm saying is that what's doing the rounds at the moment is just a nasty cold-bug, a forty-eight-hour thing, maybe seventy-two if you're a child,' she turned the page of her newspaper, 'or a man.'

With the trial not proceeding, I could have phoned Joanna and Grace-Mary to let them know I'd become unexpectedly free, but they'd only have found work for me to do.

'What's your sudden interest in this rape anyway?' Fiona asked, putting the Daily Mail down and moving to her left physically and politically to pick up the Guardian. 'I thought this was Joanna's case?'

'It's complicated,' I said.

'It's not that complicated, Robbie. I mean we're not talking Father's Day in Falkirk. If you ask me, he did it and now it's all about damage limitation.'

'I'm not talking about the case being complicated. I'm talking about Joanna and me.'

Fiona lowered the newspaper and raised an eyebrow. 'Complicated? In what way? Have you and Miss Jordan finally...'

'Fiona, is there something wrong with your eye?'

'I'm winking,' she said, 'I'm just not very good at it. These eyelashes don't help.'

'Why?'

'It's the stuff you have to glue them on with, it's—'

'No, why are you winking?'

'Come off it, Robbie. You and Joanna? Everyone can tell...' She looked around the table, on the circumference of which sat four highly disinterested advocates. 'Well, I can tell.'

I sat down next to her. 'Tell what? There's nothing to

tell. We're work colleagues. She's my employee.'

'Come off it.' She gave me a nudge. 'I've seen how you look at her.'

'I'm a man. We all look at Joanna that way. It's hard not to.'

'And I've seen how she looks at you.'

Yeah, askance, most of the time.'

'Don't do yourself down, Robbie. You've got a lot to offer a woman.'

'Yeah? Like what?'

Fiona skimmed through the newspaper until she came to the law pages. 'Well, right now I'd happily accept a coffee. And see if you can't rustle me up a choccy biscuit.'

34

'You set me up.'

Kaye was sitting on the floor of her office, surrounded by rolls of brightly-coloured paper, swathes of ribbons, gift tags and glue. Monday was always a slow news day at the Linlithgowshire Journal & Gazette. It was a weekly paper and the deadline wasn't until Thursday. Plenty of time for the editor to wrap a few Christmas presents. She didn't bother to look up. 'It's always got to be either tears or tiaras with you, hasn't it, Robbie? Where was the harm in it?'

'You told me it was a blind date.'

'I know. I lied. You're a lawyer. You should be used to people lying to you.'

'I am, but not my friends, strangely enough.'

'Well maybe it could have turned into a date if you'd tried a wee bit harder.'

'Tried harder? I was wearing my best suit.'

'Good. Glad to hear you've got rid of that blue linen thing at last,' Kaye ripped sticky-tape from a dispenser and stuck the ends of a parcel down, finishing it off with a ready-made gold bow.

'And I took her to an expensive cocktail bar in Edinburgh.'

'Robbie, sometimes us women don't want best suits

197

and stuffy old cocktail bars. We want spontaneity, candy-floss, a go on the big wheel, something fun. Edinburgh at Christmas. What could be more romantic?'

'She thinks Ferris Wheels are death traps and that the Princes Street Christmas Market is tacky.'

Kaye tossed the present onto the completed heap and pulled over a candle in a jar that was next to be smothered in cheery Yuletide paper. 'Yeah, I can imagine Cherry might be a tough shift. You probably dodged a bullet there, actually.'

'I want to meet her again.'

Kaye pulled out a length of paper and neatly ran the scissors along it. 'Not happening.'

'You can make it happen.'

'Nope.'

'You made it happen before.'

'That was different. I only had to fool you. This time I would have to fool Cherry and that wouldn't be so easy.'

'How do you know? Maybe she liked me and is too shy to call.'

Kaye reached for the glue-stick and studied it carefully. 'Sorry, I thought I must have left the cap off this and you'd been inhaling the vapours.'

'You owe me,' I said.

'No, Robbie. I don't think I do. On the other hand I did owe Cherry, which is why I lied to you. Now I don't owe her anymore and you had a nice night out with a pretty girl who got your face on TV. If anything, I'd say you owe me.'

'Did you watch that nonsense the other night?' I asked.

'No, but I heard about it. One of your clients is in the frame for downing the helicopter that's gone missing with

Philip Thorn's boy on board. Though, when I say missing, I understand it's been found again.'

The phone on Kaye's desk rang: her husband wondering what was for tea. She told him he'd have to phone for a pizza because she still had a few loose ends to tie up at the office.

'Did you say that they'd found Jerry Thorn's helicopter?' I asked, after she'd replaced the handset and was busy wrapping again.

'Oh, *Jerry* is it? You two on first name terms? Yeah, came through on the news feed. They found it early this morning. A fishing boat snagged something off Montrose. It was the helicopter.'

'Bodies?'

'No sign of any. Only to be expected after three weeks at the bottom of the North Sea.'

'Look, Kaye. I really need to speak to Cherry Lovell and you're the only point of contact I have. Do this and I'll definitely owe you.'

'And what have you got to repay me with? Don't think you can buy me off with chocolate. Not this time. Well, not just chocolate.'

'You know how I was the lawyer of the man they think downed that helicopter?' I bent over to put my finger on a knot. 'What if I told you I was also the lawyer with the evidence to prove who *actually* did it.'

Kaye let go the ends of the ribbon. Now she was paying attention.

'You set me up a meeting with Cherry and when I reveal who sabotaged that helicopter, you'll—'

'Be the first to know?'

'No... but possibly second or third.'

35

'So what did you think of young Darren?'

Malky was driving me back from Grangemouth. I'd talked him into going down to watch Billy Paris's son play in the team's last match before the winter break. In the space of just over a week the Sunnyside pitch had gone from water-logged to frozen solid, and so Saturday's postponed game had been shifted to under the floodlights of Planet Soccer's 4G astro-turf pitch at Little Kerse, near Grangemouth.

This time there had been no team talks by Malky. We hadn't even spoken to the coaches, but I'd made sure Maureen saw me making good on my promise.

'He's a good big lad. Not the quickest, but reads the game well, which makes up for it,' was Malky's take on young Darren. 'With the right partner, someone quicker across the ground than he is and him marshalling things at the back, you could have the makings of a decent central defender.'

'At what sort of level?'

'Too early to say at this stage. He's a stick-out now because he's big for his age. If he stops growing and everyone else catches up, things could be a lot different. If he keeps growing, eats a few less burgers, who knows.'

'But you will recommend someone comes and takes a look?'

'I'll speak to some people.'

'Thanks.' Happy that I had kept my word, I reclined in the comfort of the BMW's heated leather seat and relaxed as much as I could relax when my brother was driving. 'Malky... you know Joanna?'

'Remind me.'

'Joanna who works with me?'

'Oh, Joanna as in...' Malky's took his hands off the wheel and made a parallel wavy gesture which I took to be his contour estimation of my assistant's torso. 'What about her?'

'I was speaking to someone the other day who thought that maybe she... I don't know... liked me.'

Malky pinched my cheek. 'Of course she likes you. You're her boss. She's paid to like you. You pay her to like you.'

'I was thinking, after what that person was saying, I mean, that there might be more to it than that.'

'You mean that she might fancy you?' I supposed that's what I would have meant — if I'd still been at school. Malky squinted sideways at me. 'Have you been eating those mushrooms that grow up by the third tee? Joanna's way out of your league. I mean *way* out. She could even be out of my league,' he said, laughing at the ridiculousness of that last remark.

'It doesn't matter who I go out with, you always say they're out of my league.'

Malky shrugged. 'What can I say? There are a lot of leagues above you.'

'You said it about Vikki too.'

'And look what happened. Red-carded.'

Even those conversations with my brother that weren't

201

about football were usually littered with football analogies. I let it go. This was no time to fall out with him. He'd already done me one favour. Now I needed another.

'You know Cherry Lovell?'

'The girl from that news programme you were on? The wee blonde thing? Don't tell me she's got the hots for you too. You really are smoking. I don't know why I bothered to turn on the heated seats.'

Before we'd left for the game, Kaye had tried calling Cherry, who wasn't picking up. After several attempts she'd managed to get through. The news presenter wasn't keen to meet me again and neither was her expense account. So far as she was concerned she'd spread enough muck about Kirkton Perch as she could legally do at that moment and, until someone came up with hard evidence on him, she had moved onto her next exposé.

'She's working on a Night News special on sectarianism inside football,' I told Malky. 'It's to coincide with the first Old Firm New Year game since 2012.'

The 'inside' football wasn't completely true. Actually, it was completely untrue, but then the truth wouldn't have lured my brother into the trap I was trying to set for that evening.

Everyone knew how fond the supporters of Rangers and Celtic football clubs were of gathering at stadiums, singing folk songs before later meeting at pubs around Scotland and welcoming each other with open razors, but my brother had always maintained that the players remained apart from all the hate. Some of Malky's best pals were his former hooped rivals and had the bruises to prove it. It annoyed him to think people thought otherwise, and his keenness to set the record straight, as well as the chance to try it on with Cherry, would be the perfect bait.

Malky turned off the Cadgers Brae roundabout and onto the M9 motorway. I had to talk him round before we hit the Linlithgow turn-off. I had approximately two miles.

'It was her I was out with on that blind date the other night,' I said. 'We had dinner at the Aspen Lounge on Princes Street.'

'Two reasons why I know you're lying, Robbie. One—'

'Has the first reason got anything to do with league divisions?'

'And two, the Aspen Lounge is way outside your income bracket.'

And, three, your lips were moving when you said it.'

Two miles with Malky driving was a distance measured in seconds, not minutes. He flicked on the nearside indicator.

'Well, you're right about one thing,' I said. 'She wasn't keen on me. You, on the other hand, up there in the premier league…'

'Go on.'

'Cherry's a big fan. Loves your show. Thinks you're wasted on the radio and should be on telly.'

Malky began to slow. 'Really?'

'I bet I could set you up. After all, I owe you one for coming to watch Billy Paris's boy.'

'Do it.'

'It would have to be tonight, now, in fact, because I'm dead busy the rest of the week.'

'Now? Where?' He turned the wheel to take the off-ramp.

I gently tugged the steering wheel in the opposite direction keeping him going straight ahead. 'Edinburgh.'

36

The Monday before Christmas, the Aspen Lounge was heaving with office staff from the various financial institutions on St Andrews Square and along George Street.

From what I could see Cherry and my brother had got along famously. I wasn't all that surprised. They had a lot in common. Narcissism being the most obvious.

In gratitude for serving up my brother, I'd been granted an audience. 'I'll give you five minutes,' Cherry said, when she'd eventually finished with Malky and I'd gone over to sit opposite her. She was occupying a corner table on which some papers with scribbled notes were scattered. 'Malky was great, except I'm not sure how much of his material I can use. I'm more trying to focus in on the hatred between both sides of the Old Firm, than the camaraderie amongst players from yesteryears.'

Yesteryears? Please tell me she'd said that to Malky.

'Yeah, sorry, about that,' I said. 'Malky was always very ecumenical during his football career. He didn't mind who he clattered. Still, not to worry, I'm sure you'll manage to invent something and do a programme on it anyway.'

I took a sip of ginger beer and looked over to the bar where my brother had already gathered a few well-wishers, whose eagerness to offer the former Scotland centre-back a refreshment was matched only by his willingness to accept. Halfway between Linlithgow and Edinburgh we'd agreed that I'd drive back so he could have a drink. Now that he'd apparently conceded defeat with Cherry he was going to crash at my dad's house, since Tina was away and there was a bed free.

'I don't invent things. I report. Anyway...' Cherry put a hand to her mouth, yawned and started gathering her notes. 'I don't care what you think. We're quits now.'

'Quits? You hung me out to dry last Thursday night and despite that I bring my brother to you for your next piece of sensational TV drivel, and you call us *quits*?'

'Drivel?'

'I have not the faintest idea who killed Jeremy Thorn or Madeleine Moreau, I've already got the cops planting bugs on me because they think I'm withholding information on a murder, and you go throwing petrol on the flames of their suspicion. By the way, you can use that last line when you record your apology,' I said.

'Drivel?'

'What gives you the right, without my permission—'

Cherry reached over and placed a hand across my mouth. 'Enough. That *drivel* happened to be the culmination of weeks of intensive journalistic research. Tell me one thing that wasn't factually correct.'

'How about two for starters? First of all, at the time the programme went out the helicopter hadn't been found and so no one could truthfully say it had crashed, far less been sabotaged.'

Cherry clicked her pen and dropped it into an expensively vulgar, lime-green handbag that had gold fitments hanging from it and the designer's name in bold metal letters. 'Okay, so I was ahead of the curve on that one.'

'Secondly, there is no actual evidence to say that the helicopter was sabotaged.'

Cherry rolled her eyes. 'That's practically the same as the first, and, anyway, you told me your client had said it had been sabotaged.'

'Then, thirdly—'

'It's still only secondly.'

'Even *if* the helicopter was sabotaged, I never so much as suggested to you that I had any idea who was responsible.'

'But you do have an idea, don't you?'

'That's not the point. You had no right to broadcast a load of speculation as though it was the truth. *Night News believes this man holds the answer*. What did you think you were doing?'

'What I thought I was doing was saving your life,' Cherry said, folding her notes in two and stuffing them in her handbag.

It was a defence to my accusation I hadn't anticipated. 'Oh really? Saving my life? How's that, then?'

'Your client. What happened to him? Just strolled into a canal one evening, did he?' She snapped her handbag shut. 'You may think I'm some blonde bimbo who spouts drivel on the telly, but when it comes to politics I know a damn sight more than you ever will.'

Guilty as charged.

'For instance,' Cherry said, 'do you know that the Business Secretary estimates that space innovation, launching satellites, space tourism, all that sort of stuff, will be worth four hundred billion a year to the global economy by two thousand and thirty? Well, it will, and both the Scottish and UK Government want a slice of it.'

206

I could only sit back and listen as she continued at full volume in order to be heard above the general hubbub.

'It's just a matter of time before there are calls for another referendum on Scottish independence. All the Unionist parties are desperate to do something for Scotland that'll help keep Britain together. Out of the seven sites identified by the UK Space Agency as suitable for a spaceport, somehow five were in Scotland. Then, when Kirkton Perch was elected, the shortlist swiftly came down to one: Prestwick. That is until the late arrival of St Edzell Bay.'

What had this got to do with Billy Paris being found in a canal or Cherry saving my life?

'If Prestwick wins, it's a triumph for Kirkton Perch and the UK Government. Strange, don't you think, that when St Edzell Bay appears on the scene and starts ticking all the right boxes, the owner dies in a helicopter crash and the person most likely to have caused the crash ends up in a canal? Remember what happened to Dr David Kelly when he criticized Tony Blair's WMD dodgy dossier?'

I did. If the dossier on Sadaam Hussein's alleged weapons of mass destruction had been dodgy, Dr Kelly's suicide verdict was even dodgier. Why else would the subsequent Government inquiry have resulted in an order that all evidence relating to Kelly's death, including photographs and post-mortem examination reports, must remain classified for seventy years?

'If the Government is prepared to kill its own weapons expert, half a million Iraqis and spend four and a half billion pounds to get its hands on a share of some oilfields, what do you think it will do for a chunk of four hundred billion from space?'

Although I was on the receiving end of a ticking off, I

207

thought I might actually be starting to admire Cherry. On the face of it she seemed like just another TV mannequin; however, scratch the surface and here was a woman passionate about her job. There was only one thing I didn't understand. 'So why does you announcing to the world that I hold the very same information that got Billy Paris assassinated protect me from the sharp end of a poisoned umbrella?'

'Thanks to last Thursday night, the Government knows I'm onto them. So do one point four million Night News viewers. And word is spreading. Kirkton Perch is slipping down the greasy pole. Questions are being asked at both Westminster and Holyrood. There are conspiracy theorists all over the country, all over the world, watching to see how this plays out. If anything happens to you, if you get struck by lightning or are hit by a runaway iceberg, the Government is getting the blame. They wouldn't dare risk it; however, you never know, they might come up with some other way of keeping you quiet.' She rubbed a thumb and forefinger together. 'If they do, it'll be your turn to buy me dinner. Happy now?'

'I know someone who has a different take on things. A conspiracy theory that doesn't involve Her Majesty's Government,' I said.

Cherry got to her feet and looked down at me, which was figuratively what she did most of the time anyway. 'Is that so?'

'While everyone is concentrating on Jerry Thorn's death, they keep forgetting there was someone else in that chopper.'

Cherry's expression changed swiftly from cocksure to what would be best described as dangerous. I battered on, fearlessly. 'People don't kill only for money and power. They kill for jealousy too. How about that for a documentary?'

As I did my best to wipe ginger beer from my face, I watched Cherry weave her way through the Christmas party crowd to the exit. It was hard not to admire her style and enthusiasm. Or her bottom...

'Not a bad rear view, eh?' Malky said. 'Had her eating out of my hand with all my football chat. Women love that sort of stuff. He slurped the head off a pint of lager. 'She wasn't really my type though.'

'Yeah, I know how much you hate the beautiful, blonde ones,' I said, wringing out my hanky into the now empty tumbler. 'Still, she liked you. Said your chat reminded her of an evening with her dad, talking about what football was like in the good old days. Yesteryears, I think she called it.'

'Really? She said that?' Malky smiled thinly, took another long pull of ice-cold lager, held the pint tumbler up to the light in order to admire it all the better and smacked his lips loudly. 'I like it here. Maybe we'll stay a wee while longer. Let me buy you another ginger beer.'

37

'I take it that when the mouse is away, the cat goes down the pub?' Joanna said.

Tuesday morning and we were bound for the High Court. Driving to the city that hates motorists was sheer madness at any time of the year, far less the week before Christmas, and so we'd taken the train. The Glasgow to Edinburgh rail line was Scotland's busiest. Finding a seat was like finding a politician without a dubious expenses claim. Joanna had managed to squeeze in beside a fat bloke who thought he was two people. I'd had to stand all the way. I wasn't too disappointed. Five minutes on the platform, being asked my opinion on ski-wear, as my assistant skimmed through an online catalogue on her iPhone, had been enough for me. I didn't need more of the same on the twenty-minute train journey to the capital.

'Why? Am I looking a bit rough?' I asked, as we walked up the ramp from Waverley Station and veered left. It was a cold and frosty morning and our white breath billowed, merging into one cloud as we spoke.

'Just a tad. I mean, I'm not your mum or anything, but drinking on a school night? Tut-tut.'

'Trust me, it's definitely not drink,' I said. 'I had a late night. It's lack of sleep.'

'How come, when Tina's not here?'

'I went through to Edinburgh to see Cherry Lovell, and—'

'You did what! I mean, you did what?'

'I wasn't happy about being thrown to the wolves in that documentary last week.'

'And so you went through to give her a piece of your mind?' Joanna sounded less than convinced.

We'd reached the foot of the News Steps. One hundred or so of Edinburgh's steepest steps leading from Market Street at the foot of the mound to the rear of the High Court of Justiciary on the Royal Mile. I offered to take Joanna's satchel. The one containing the case file for Keith Howie's rape trial.

'Why?'

'Because, like I say, I was pretty angry with her.'

'No, why do you want to carry my satchel for me?'

'Will saying because it's heavy and you're a woman get me a slap?'

Joanna's smile was as tight as her grip on the satchel. 'Try and find out.'

I didn't want to know that much, and, anyway, I already had my own case to carry. By the time we'd reached the top I was breathing like a dirty phone call.

'Oh, by the way,' I said, pretending my news was so important I had to stop to impart it, rather than admit it was so I could catch my breath. 'I mentioned to Cherry your theory that she might have sabotaged the helicopter to get back at her ex-fiancé. It got me a ginger beer shampoo.'

Joanna seemed unduly pleased about that. 'I thought it was looking particularly lustrous this morning,' she said, giving the top of my head a rub.

Our rape-accused client was waiting for us at the front door of the court, stamping his feet against the cold, his perpetually distraught wife by his side looking pale, drawn and thoroughly miserable.

'You've met Mr Munro before,' Joanna said, as I shook hands with the Howies in turn. 'As I mentioned yesterday, he's going to sit in and instruct counsel at the trial today. I'll be here for a while this morning, just to bring him up to speed and make sure we're all set to go.'

The client seemed less than thrilled at this. He wandered off to stand beneath the statue of David Hume, nowadays better known for his lucky golden toe than his thoughts on radical philosophical empiricism. Joanna followed. They spoke for a few minutes and then my assistant returned alone.

'If Howie thinks buffing up Hume's shiny big toe is going to bring him luck, he might have to think about using power tools,' I said to her.

'Robbie, we need to talk. Let's go upstairs to the agents' room.'

I was happy to talk, though I had a better location in mind than the stinky wee hole of a room the High Court provided for the use of solicitors.

'Does everything with you have to revolve around food?' Joanna asked, looking at her watch. Food-wise, the café beside the court had not scaled the dizzying heights of Bistro Alessandro, but it could put together a bacon roll that was almost at the same culinary altitude as one of Sandy's. Unfortunately, they were out of bacon and I had to make do with a toasted cheese croissant.

'Not just food,' I said, lifting the lid and squirting in a sachet of brown sauce, 'coffee's very important too.'

It didn't take Joanna long to apprise me of the situation. Our client had been doing some thinking. Generally it was better if clients didn't, but he had and come to the conclusion that he didn't want me. He wanted Joanna. Who could blame him?

'Too bad. He'll just have to make do,' I said. 'You can't not go on holiday because of that sex-beast.'

'*Alleged* sex-beast. Remember?' Joanna said.

'What's wrong with me anyway?' I wanted to know.

'Do you want details, or will bullet points do?'

'Funny.'

Joanna screwed up her face sympathetically as though I might be suffering a crisis of confidence. 'It's nothing personal, Robbie. Well, actually it is. Why did you have to go and call him a numpty?'

'I didn't. Not exactly.' When I'd first met Howie in the police station all those months ago — before the interview in which he'd found it necessary to try and be helpful — I'd told him only a numpty would answer any questions the cops asked.

'That's sort of the same thing. Isn't it?' Joanna said.

'It was a turn of phrase. A joke.'

'Hugely amusing, Robbie, and look where your sense of humour has got us.' Joanna, who'd turned down the offer of food, tore a hunk from my croissant and popped it into her mouth. There were no calories that way. 'It makes sense me staying, whichever way you cut it. Even if you could do Howie's case, who'd deal with the Sheriff Court business?'

'It's easy.' I pulled my plate a little closer. 'You go skiing, I'll contact Paul Sharp and ask him to cover all our cases for the rest of the week. He can just adjourn

213

everything. Everyone is winding down for Christmas. No Sheriff is going to get worked up at the thought of having to go home early by putting a few cases off until next year.'

'And new work? Who does that? Robbie, this is the busiest time of the year.' Joanna had made up her mind. She would not be found clad in a shocking pink glacier ski-suit gracing the snowy slopes of les Hautes-Alpes this winter season. 'Even if I stay, we're going to need Paul to help out anyway. This case is going to take two of us. I want you here to keep an eye on Howie's wife. She's liable to become hysterical and I don't want it rubbing off on him. I want her nowhere near the courtroom when he's giving his evidence.'

Babysitter for a client's wife? Was this what I'd come to?

'I think you're mistaking me for some kind of manservant. The Howies aren't the Glass brothers and I'm not wee Alfie. This is legal aid.'

'Don't start, Robbie.' Joanna snatched another piece of croissant before I could fend her off. 'If you didn't go around calling the clients names, it could be you in court and me keeping Mrs Howie under control. As it is, you might as well be doing something useful, seeing how you can't get paid to do anything else. Have you thought about what's happening next week? It's Christmas and the week after that is Hogmanay. There'll be tons of new custody cases.'

Joanna's timetabling of statutory holidays was impeccable. She was equally correct to be worried about the next few days and the potential loss of business for the firm. Christmas was the season of goodwill and blazing

214

family rows. The Lord Advocate's zero-tolerance policy on domestic-related incidents was the Crown's gift to defence lawyers. Every sherry-fuelled Christmas quarrel between spouses or partners was now considered a crime. Hordes of accused, many who'd never dreamt they'd ever fall foul of the law, were crammed into police cells like toys into a defence lawyer's stocking. They all needed legal representation, and we at Munro & Co. were happy to provide it.

I tried to console myself with a bite of what little croissant was left. It didn't work. Not even one of Sandy's bacon rolls would have.

There was no time for further discussion. It was knocking on for ten o'clock and court would be starting soon. Joanna departed, leaving me to finish my breakfast. I was reading a newspaper a previous customer had left behind, when the light from the window was eclipsed and I felt the urge to look up. 'You've got to be kidding.'

DI Christchurch gave me a polite nod. Thankfully he'd left his bulldog outside. 'Morning, Mr Munro, I'd like you to accompany me, if you don't mind, there's—'

'I do mind.' I tossed the newspaper aside, aware that those at nearby tables were becoming interested at what was going on at mine.

'If you'd keep your voice down and let me finish, Sir.' Christchurch pulled up the chair recently vacated by Joanna and sat down. 'There's someone who'd like very much to meet you.'

'And who would that be?'

The DI leaned across the table. 'The Secretary of State.'

I hadn't totally forgiven Cherry Lovell for pouring a drink over my head, even though I'd probably deserved it.

Still, I had to hand it to her, she did know a lot more about politics than I ever would. I could visualise those fingers from the night before, rubbing together, and remembered her words, *they might come up with some other way of keeping you quiet.*

I was a solicitor and an officer of court. It would be an insult for the Government to think it could offer to buy my silence. But seeing how I didn't know anything, I was happy to let it try.

38

Edinburgh likes a statue and that of Robert Dundas, 2nd Viscount Melville, Member of Parliament, First Lord of the Admiralty and Governor of the Bank of Scotland, has pride of place in the middle of the street named after him.

Prior to that Tuesday afternoon I'd given no thought to the address of the Secretary of State's Scottish head-quarters. I knew his office in London was based at Dover House in Whitehall and had mistakenly assumed that when north of the border, Kirkton Perch would have a berth down at the row of upturned boats at the foot of the Royal Mile. Not so, instead he was to be found in the West End on one of Edinburgh's grander thoroughfares.

Number One Melville Street was in the New Town, situ-ated on a corner of crossroads next door to the Japanese Consulate and consisting of five floors, including attic rooms and a basement. If it hadn't been for the Union Flag and Saltire flying either side of the royal blue front door, it would have gone unnoticed as just more office space in the New Town.

Since Christchurch had been sent on the errand to find me, it was even clearer now that the Secretary of State was using the Ministry of Defence Police as his own small army. Despite the spotlight shining on me and my now deceased client, I'd not felt so much as a tug from an officer of Police Scotland, and from that fact it was safe to assume the regular Force had been told to back off while the MDP took care of things. Kirkton Perch thought he had me on a string. Well, if he wanted a puppet show, he was going to have to pay or I was bringing out the scissors.

Flanked by the two MDP officers, the security checks on arrival were dispensed with, and upon our entry I was asked to wait in the lobby. Two minutes later a compact man in brown suit, checked shirt and no tie bounded down the stairs. 'Mr Munro? Kirkton Perch.' He strode across the hall and shook me firmly by the hand. If he'd once had a Welsh accent it was now AWOL. 'I'm stepping out,' he called to anyone listening who might be interested, and, placing a hand on the small of my back, gently ushered me out of the front door again and down five or six well-worn sandstone steps to the pavement.

Once on the street I had a better chance to take him in. Oozing energy, he was lean and athletic with an excellent head of sandy hair and a smile that wouldn't have hindered his career as a baby-kisser.

'Come on,' he said, marching ahead of me. What position had he played in his rugby days? Scrum-half? Or was it fly-half? He certainly wasn't big or ugly enough for a forward, but as someone who'd traded broken noses with big Billy Paris he must have had a lot of nerve and, I noticed, access to a better plastic surgeon.

Trotting to catch up, I pulled level with him as he crossed the road and took to the cobbles, up Walker Street and then left along William Street. With any number of licensed premises to choose from, Group Captain Perch selected the nearest. The two MDP officers had tagged along and took up position outside.

'A swift medicinal or two is just the thing for this damn flu that's going about,' he said, once we'd found a table. 'I've too much to do to let it take a grip.' Judging by the broken blood vessels on his cheeks and invisibly-mended nose, keeping a step ahead of ill health was a constant chore. 'What are you having?'

It was eleven o'clock and, strictly speaking, too early for me; however, to refuse would have seemed churlish and, since the Secretary of State was paying, I graciously accepted a pint of lager-tops. Perch had the same, minus the dash of lemonade and with a very large brandy to keep it company.

'Thanks for coming to see me,' he said. 'You'll know why I wanted to speak with you.'

'Night News?'

He nodded. 'Cherry what's-her-name didn't do either of us any favours, did she?'

I wasn't so sure now. It depended on what Perch thought I knew and how much money he was prepared to throw at me to find out.

'If you know who caused that helicopter crash, you also know it wasn't me. Am I correct?'

I stalled by taking a drink of beer.

'So, I need your help,' Perch continued, fighting off the germs with a nip of brandy. 'I need you to hand over to me all the evidence you have relating to Jeremy Thorn's helicopter crash.'

I thought it about time I said something and so played along. 'Let's say, for argument's sake, that I do have the proof. If I were to give it to you, thus allowing you to vindicate yourself...' I paused to let him take up where I'd left off. He didn't. There was no subtle way to say it.

219

It was all I could do to refrain from rubbing my fingers together. 'What would be in it for me?'

'In it?'

I nodded encouragingly.

'For you?' Puzzled, the Secretary of State thought another sip of brandy would assist his deliberations, before eventually coming up with, 'Why, the truth would be in it for you,' he said, washing the distilled grape juice down with a swig of lager.

The truth. Why did it insist on rearing its ugly head every time I was homing in on a few quid?

Perch killed any remaining bugs with one final gulp of brandy. 'Are you saying that you'd be happy to conceal the evidence that would clear my name? That you'll let that reporter ruin my political career unless you are paid?'

At last he was getting there. Or, actually, no he wasn't. 'I don't think so, Mr Munro.'

'Then maybe I should give the information to Cherry Lovell,' I said.

He shrugged his ministerial shoulders. 'Perhaps you should. At least then Ms Lovell wouldn't be able to accuse me of falsifying the evidence.'

Was he telling the truth, or was this a test to see how much I knew? He seemed genuine enough. But then again, he was a politician. Which was it? Refuse to assist and I could be doing him a grave injustice. Help him out and, if Cherry was right about things, I'd be signing my own death warrant. According to her, whatever it was I had was the only thing keeping me alive.

With another short draught of lager, Perch rose to his feet. 'I'm leaving now,' he said, in case I hadn't got the message. The smile was gone, together with any traces of flu. He couldn't resist a parting shot. 'You know the problem with people like you? There's always got to be something in it for them. No sense of duty, no sense of standing up for what is right.'

I got to my feet a lot quicker than he had. Any more from him and he'd be hoping he'd kept the phone number of his nose surgeon handy. 'You're getting all teary-eyed because you're being wrongly accused by Cherry Lovell? Well, I stand up in court every day defending the rights of people who say they have been wrongly accused by the State, Mr Perch. That's what I stand for. You've bombed some foreigners, I'll give you that, but what have you actually ever stood for – except Parliament? You're Welsh. Had you ever been to Ayrshire before being parachuted in from Tory HQ? What was in that for you – Mister Secretary of State? I'm a lawyer. My business is funded in the main by legal aid. It's not much, but it's a living. At the moment I am struck off the Criminal Legal Aid register which means that—'

'Times are hard. I understand perfectly.' Perch was cool under fire.

'No, I don't think you do, sitting up here on Melville Street or down in London with your ministerial salary, copper-bottomed pensions from the RAF and now Westminster, I don't think you do know what it means to me, my employees or my family.'

'I'm sorry, Mr Munro. I'd hoped you'd see reason, in which case I might have been able to bring to bear what influence I have to help you out of the difficulties you find yourself in professionally, but I will not use the public purse to bung you for information that on any view of decency and natural justice should already be in the public domain.'

He turned on a heel and strode to the door where Christchurch and the Bulldog were waiting for him, leaving me standing at the table with most of a pint to drink.

'Would it help if we didn't say bung and called it a consultancy fee?' I shouted after him.

He didn't reply. Probably just as well, for whatever evidence I had, there was still the small matter of finding it.

39

There are many analogies used to describe the criminal justice system. It is often likened to a game, a sport, two sides pitched against each other, attack and defence. In actual fact there is very little sporting about a competition between the State with its unlimited funds, ranks of police officers, procurators fiscal, advocate deputes, precognition officers and clerical staff on one side and on the other a legal aid lawyer who hasn't seen a pay rise since dinosaurs ruled the earth.

To stick with the theme, the best comparison I could think of was poker, and a professional, high-stakes gambler, surrounded by stacks of chips, facing off across the green felt at a schoolboy clutching his pocket money. The prosecution could afford to bet high and only when it held all the aces. No bluffing required. Not so for the defence. The defence had to play the cards it was dealt, albeit after some expert shuffling.

Which was why I was used to making the most out of what little I had. Bricks without straw. Sometimes bricks without bricks. It was a skill I hoped to put into good use when negotiating with Philip Thorn. I badly needed to cut a deal to pilot Munro & Co. through the financial turbulence thrown up partly by my bureaucratic failings and partly by the Scottish Legal Aid Board's unwillingness to see that the ends justified the means – even if the means were not time-recorded in triplicate.

To go back to the card-playing analogy, what I really needed was an ace up my sleeve. I thought I had one. Billy Paris had told me he had the evidence to prove who'd killed Jeremy Thorn, and he'd told wee Maureen that he'd given it to me. The problem was that, after a great deal of searching, I'd been unable to bring the card up my sleeve down into the game. I didn't even know for certain it was there. Which was why I needed help.

'Oh, no, it's you,' were Wahid Sattar's warm words of welcome as he threw the front door open and a blast of central heating hit me full on. He looked me up and down. 'Robbie Munro. If you're here, either I'm in big trouble or you are, and, having seen you on TV the other night, I'm going to guess it's you.'

I invited myself in, pushing past Wahid and letting him close the door before we lost any more of the polar ice-caps. He followed me through to the sitting room which smelt less of nappy than I recalled it had on my last visit.

'How's Deeba?' I asked.

'She left me.'

Wahid's high-flying, corporate-lawyer wife had flown off. There'd been a custody battle, he'd got the kids, and, to be fair, a nice little piece of real estate in the New Town, only a short walk from Kirkton Perch's residence.

I flopped into an armchair. Wahid seemed happy standing. 'And how are the kids? Fara and...'

'Latif. They're both fine. I have to collect them from nursery in...' He glanced at his watch. 'Goodness, is that the time?'

I could take a hint, but only if I wanted to. 'I'm looking for some advice, Wahid.'

'How long is this going to take?'

'Probably safer to stick the kettle on, but if you're in a rush to pick up the kids, I can—'

'Go away?'

'Wait here until you come back.'

The thought of leaving and returning home to have to deal with me and a couple of sprogs was too much. 'I can give you fifteen minutes without coffee, or ten with,' he said.

I had a compromise solution. 'I'll talk while you make.'

'So let me get this straight,' Wahid said, when, twenty minutes later, I'd finished my coffee and filled him in on my predicament. Prior to that it had only taken a brief spell of cross-examination to ascertain that he didn't have to collect the kids for another two hours. 'You want to fool Philip Thorn into thinking that you know the identity of his son's killer in order to fleece—'

'Fleece?'

'Would you rather I said extort?'

'Fleece it is.'

'In order to fleece him out of a lot of money?'

'You were always quick on the uptake,' I said.

He laughed. 'But I couldn't possibly advise you on something like that. It's unethical.'

I laughed too, until I realized that Wahid's had been a serious laugh. 'Sorry, I can see how it could be viewed that way,' I said.

'Is there any other way to view it?'

'Surely it comes down to a question of *mens rea*? If there's no evil intent on my part to obtain money on false

225

pretences how can it be unethical? I truly believe I have the proof. I just don't know where it is.'

Wahid held that argument under reservation for the moment. 'So, what do you want from me?'

'Even though I don't have the information Thorn wants, I'm sure I'll unearth it eventually.' I would unearth it even if I had to level my offices in the process. 'I was wondering about drawing up a written contract, something he can't wriggle out of.'

'It's possible, I suppose. You'd need to move quickly though. He's bound to want to put a backstop on it time-wise.'

'How come?'

'They've found the helicopter. Given the publicity and the slur against Kirkton Perch's good name, there will almost certainly be a fatal accident inquiry. He'll be desperate to have himself vindicated.'

'So?'

'So, who do you think is going to be witness number one? You'll be cited to the FAI and have to answer any questions put to you. Solicitor/client confidentiality privileges will mean nothing. Refusal to testify will be contempt of court.'

He was right, and, whether I agreed to testify or not, my offices would be thoroughly searched by people who knew how to find things. They might even bring in a team of mothers. *Found it. Right here in his desk, second drawer down on the left.* If that happened, I'd have no leverage to extract a payment from Philip Thorn. I had to find the evidence, and quickly.

'Of course if there isn't an FAI then maybe the conspiracy stories will have been right all along,' Wahid said.

226

I didn't want to think about that. 'How rich is this guy Thorn? I've Googled him and most of the stuff on the internet is about his civil action with Glazed Over.'

Wahid knew all about the court proceedings. 'That case has been trundling through the Court of Session for years. It's a dispute over the performing rights to Glazed Over's back catalogue.'

'What happens if Thorn loses?'

'He won't.'

'What happens if he wins?'

'Nothing. He's the one being sued. Glazed Over say they signed unfair contracts back when they were young and without proper advice. The court is never going to buy that. They had a manager and if he didn't adequately protect their interests any claim is against him.'

'Who was their manager? Whoever it is, I hope he's insured.'

Apparently, he wasn't insured. He was their dad and he was dead. They'd never told me that part.

'I met them,' I said. 'Tony and Greg. They bought me dinner at St Andrews last weekend.'

'You met Glazed Over?'

'Everyone thinks I know who killed Jeremy Thorn and they're as keen as his father to know who that was.'

Wahid finished his coffee, placed his mug on the arm of the couch. 'I don't know how you do it, Robbie. Dinner with Glazed Over, rendezvous with Phil Thorn. You get everywhere. Like sand.'

'How's business with you?' I asked.

'So-so. My clerk still tries to send me instructions, but with the kids to look after I'm hardly ever up at Parliament House and, I'm afraid, out of sight is very much out of mind. I scrape by doing the occasional opinion, drafting pleadings, revising agreements. Anything that'll put food in our mouths.'

'Then draw me up a contract so tight Houdini couldn't escape from it and I'll weigh you in for five per cent of whatever I can fleece Philip Thorn for.'

But Wahid's ethical principles weren't for sale. Not for a measly five per cent. He got up from the couch, walked to a sideboard and removed a sheaf of A4 paper from a drawer. 'Let's call it ten.'

40

I called Paul Sharp on the walk to Haymarket Station. He was happy enough to cover any new legal aid cases for me so they could later be transferred into Joanna's name.

That gave me the rest of the afternoon to search my office for Billy Paris's missing evidence. With the help of Grace-Mary I emptied every filing cabinet, every desk drawer, hunted in every nook and cranny of my room where something, no matter how tiny, could be stored. And found absolutely nothing.

At five o'clock my secretary left for the day, and I nipped down to Sandy's for a coffee. While I was there I had an idea.

'My client's next-of-kin wants his belongings back.'

The crisp, eloquent tones of DI Christchurch floated back down the airwaves to me. 'Mr Paris wasn't married and had no partner, only an ex-partner. Despite my best endeavours, and believe me I've looked, I can trace no next-of-kin other than his illegitimate thirteen-year-old son, who I doubt very much will be a big Alistair MacLean fan, nor take size twelve in a boot. Are you quite sure you have instructions?'

'Where's the box?'

'Safe.'

'I want to see it.'

'Why?'

'Sentimental reasons. Billy was a valued client of mine for years.'

'Is it the socks, the boots, the socket set or the paperback edition of the Guns of Navarone that holds particular emotional worth?'

I was getting fed up with the whole thing. I had a business collapsing about my ears, no love life, a daughter with no Christmas present, and a father who'd never let me forget any of it. 'How about you just tell me if you found something?' Surely the MDP would have had a team of experts x-raying the box, dismantling it and sifting through everything piece by piece.

There was a pause on the other end of the line. Maybe Christchurch heard the desperation in my voice. 'You don't know anything, do you, Mr Munro? You never have.'

'Waste of time you pinning those bugs on me and my client then, wasn't it?' I said. He didn't answer. 'If you want them back, by the way, I can do you a good price.'

'Good-bye, Mr Munro.'

I threw my phone onto the table, striking my cup of coffee. Some slopped out. Sandy came over with a cloth. 'Temper!' He lifted my cup and wiped underneath. 'What's the matter — there's no Joanna tonight? '

'Joanna's busy doing legal work and making money,' I said. 'Like I should be.'

Sandy made a face. 'Someone's not very full of Yuletide cheer.'

'I don't have a lot to be cheery about,' I said.

'Away. I know what's wrong with you. You're missing your bambino.' Sandy's grip on the Italian language was as about as secure as my financial future.

230

'Tina's a girl,' I said. 'She's a bambina not a bambino and she's part of the problem. You know that Pyxie Girl doll that everyone wants?'

'You didn't promise her one for Christmas?'

'My dad did, but it'll be me getting the blame if Santa doesn't get his hands on one.'

'On the news it says that there will be plenty in the New Year.'

'I know. *Lady* Pyxie. But that's not good enough. I need the girl version and I need it for Sunday morning.'

'You should have had a little Italian bambina. In parts of my home country they don't open presents until epiphany. That would give you another twelve days.'

Overlooking the fact that Sandy's home country, despite his attempts at an Italian accent, was the same as mine, I thought putting Christmas on hold while I changed my child's nationality was too big a step to take for the sake of a stupid doll.

Sandy was drying my phone with a tea towel when it buzzed. It was Joanna checking in to say that Keith Howie's trial had started and without any trace of a sick juror they were rattling through the evidence. It seemed certain to finish by Friday.

'The Crown case will finish Thursday morning at the latest,' Joanna said. 'Mrs Howie is next up for the Crown and not looking forward to it. She's the classic two-edged sword. Heard nothing unusual at the time the rape is supposed to have taken place, which is good for us, but the Crown want her to confirm that her husband was the only male person in the house and, just as importantly, she speaks to the girl's distressed state.'

It sounded to me that one edge of the blade was a lot

keener than the other, and it wouldn't take long for an expert cross-examiner like Cameron Crowe to blunt the defence edge even further, by pointing out that the reason Mrs Howie had heard nothing unusual was because she'd been sound asleep.

'I'm just checking that you're going to be free to come to the High Court on Thursday,' Joanna continued.

'Why, what's the problem?'

'Mrs Howie. Just like I thought, she's going off the deep end. Every time I even mention about her husband giving evidence, or what will happen if he's convicted, she goes hysterical on me. I was hoping you could come through and, you know...'

'Hold her hand? The hand of the woman whose husband I called a numpty?'

'Please?'

I relented. 'I'll do it, but only if you remember to ask him what the chances are of a Pyxie Girl at trade price.'

'I think he has other more important matters on his mind at the moment, Robbie.'

'Then we'll have to hope the jurors are in Christmas spirit and come back with a not proven,' I said.

'That's right. Always look on the bright side,' she said.

Was there a bright side? For me or my rape-accused client? I had Sandy pour the rest of my coffee into a cardboard cup and took it and the telephone call onto the High Street. 'Joanna, we need to talk about the business. I don't know how things are going to be in the New Year. I just don't think there is going to be the turnover for two lawyers at Munro & Co.'

'But—'

'I can maybe scrape by on my own. Who knows? I might have to fold the whole thing.'

'What about your partnership offer?'

'It was unfair of me to even suggest it and expect you to take on the lion's share of the work. Maybe it would be better if you did get back your old job at the PF's.'

'Stop this right now, Robbie. I'm supposed to be the pessimistic one, remember? What happened to Mr Rainbows and Unicorns? In January you can hit the Legal Aid Board with a New Year's resolution that you'll promise to try harder. In fact, who needs it? We can take on more private work. Move up the social strata of criminal clients. In the meantime, we can ride the storm out. Me and you.'

'And until then?'

'You'll think of something.' Joanna laughed. There was nothing remotely funny about my situation; nonetheless, hearing her smile down the phone at me somehow helped. 'You always do.'

41

It was a bad day for fishing. The tide was out, the rocky outcrop was surrounded by sand and five hundred miles of mountainous waves lay between us and the Norwegian coastline.

Homer was at his usual place in the security hut on the access road into the airport. The haar was rolling in off the North Sea, visibility was registering poor to pea-soup and St Edzell Bay airport was closed for take-off or landing.

I'd left home early that Wednesday morning and arrived shortly after ten. According to Maggie Sinclair, when I'd called her at home the previous evening, Philip Thorn was in Scotland, settling his son's affairs. He'd decided not to pursue Jeremy's spaceport tender and was listening to offers from prospective purchasers. Some said that the tragic death of his son had knocked the fight out of the usually rambunctious music mogul, others that he simply didn't have the funding to continue his son's grand scheme. The fortunes of his own business, Blunt Instrument, were on the slide. They had been since its top two assets had opted for early retirement. That was all I could get out of Maggie during our thirty-second telephone call. She'd been hosting a sherry party and not amused at the interruption.

Homer came down to the barrier to greet me.

234

'How's the fishing?' I asked.

'Caught a few flatties on lugworm,' he said. 'A good size, but murder to fillet. And it's getting too cold. I think I might put the rods away until the spring. What brings you back?'

'I'm here to see Mr Thorn.' En route I'd asked Grace-Mary to phone and make sure that he was at the airport.

'Oh, yeah. Was that your office who called?' Homer scratched the back of his head, pushing the peak of his baseball cap down to meet the rim of his mirrored shades. He puffed his cheeks and blew. 'I'm sorry, you've just missed him. He was here first thing with some folk wanting to see round the place, in fact he's not long away.'

'Do you know where he's gone?'

'No, but I could try and find out,' he said, ducking back into his hut. Two minutes later he was out again. 'I've phoned the rest of the boys. No one knows where the boss is or when he's coming back. If it's okay, you've to wait here because Oleg's coming over to see you.'

My first impression of the man who, seconds later, pulled up at the security gate in a little golf-type buggy, was of someone you seriously did not want to piss off. There was nothing soft about him. Not a smooth edge anywhere. Not from the buzz-cut of grey hair above a large-featured, craggy face, to the gnarled knuckles of the hands that gripped the steering wheel. He looked like head of security all right: security for the President, not a remote airport clinging for dear life to the Scottish coastline. He alighted and shook my hand. Unlike his colleagues he did not favour blue overalls with a hi-vis tabard, but a dark suit over a white shirt and a black tie knotted tightly around his broad neck.

'You are looking for Mr Thorn,' he said, in an accent that was a cross between St Petersburg and Peterhead. 'He have to leave on urgent business. I am to let him know when you get here.'

I really hoped I hadn't had a three-hour drive for nothing. The Russian seemed suitably apologetic and although I thought he might tell me to wait in my car, or join Homer in the glass hut, instead I was invited into the buggy, scooted over to the main terminal building and from there led up a flight of stairs to a small office. Other than the dark green, metal locker parked against a far wall, the rest of the fixtures and fittings consisted of a stainless steel desk and chair, both situated in front of a bank of video screens. Judging by the rundown state of the building, I'd have expected a few fuzzy CRT monitors, not plasmas showing high definition images from around the airport. It all looked very new.

'Impressive,' I said.

'Civil Aviation Authority make us upgrade. And also we get many VIP. So surveillance very important.' VIPs? Oleg must have picked up on my unspoken incredulity. 'Many of Jerry's friends visit. This is like playground to them. They race their sports cars along the runway. Fly in the helicopters. You need top-notch security. There are many nutters who want to see them. One day we have a nutter parachute in. Another time a speed boat full of them arrive. Many nutters come along the beach also. It's not easy to keep them out. We are not allowed to make the security fence go past the high tide mark. Her Majesty, she owns the rest down to the sea. But you are a lawyer. You know this.'

I did recall once having to skim through something

about the Crown's ownership of the foreshore during my University studies. After the exam I'd felt I had better use for the brain space than cluttering it up with riparian law and water rights.

'Oh, yeah, the Queen likes to hit the beach,' I said. 'What about Glazed Over? Ever see them here?'

'Yes, Tony and Greg very big pals of Jerry. He try to teach them to fly. Flying a chopper it is like patting your head and rubbing your belly at the same time while tapping your foot. Not easy. Greg could never get the hang of it. Tony very good pilot.'

'Can't be much fun sitting here watching nothing happen all day.' I said.

Oleg agreed it wasn't. Which was why the security team took turns, rotating in two-hour stints. 'It is worse since we go digital. Nothing but trouble. The old system was not good, but it worked all the time.'

'Were you here the night Jerry's helicopter went missing,' I asked.

'Nyet.'

'But you were here the day before.'

Oleg's face hardened as though I'd accused him of a dereliction of duty. 'I supposed to work 'til five o'clock. That day it's very busy. Mr Thorn visit Jerry and Jerry getting ready for many friends to come here. I have to work late, six, seven maybe.'

'That's why I'm here. I want to talk to Mr Thorn about his son's death. Find out some more information. Maybe help him discover the truth.'

Oleg stuck out his bottom lip and shrugged. 'You want to know the truth?' I took that to be rhetorical. 'Jerry did something stupid.'

237

I asked the Russian what had made him come to that conclusion and discovered that for Jerry Thorn doing something stupid in a chopper was a regular occurrence. He'd previously been disqualified from flying for three months for carrying excess passengers. In the latest stunt he'd flown extremely low over Loch Tay with a couple of mates in wetsuits on either skid. He'd dropped them in the water then gone back later to pick them up, carrying out the same dangerous manoeuvre and narrowly missing a speedboat in the process. This time they'd taken his licence away for a much longer period.

Oleg frowned. 'Three years. It is very bad. A lot of people come here to see Jerry and have lessons with him. When they ban him, he has an idea to make this place better. Make it into a spaceport.'

Oleg picked up what looked like a large cellphone with a stubby black aerial protruding from the top. 'Satellite phone. The signal is rubbish out here. Hold on.' He punched a few numbers and was connected remarkably quickly. 'Oleg from St Edzell, Mr Thorn. Mr Munro is here to see you now.' There was a longish pause before, 'Yes, Mr Thorn. I will tell him.' Oleg pressed a button and set the phone back in a charging cradle on the desk. 'Mr Thorn is very sorry, but he has business in Aberdeen. He will come back here to see you if you don't mind waiting. We could send you in helicopter, but we have no pilots today because the weather is very bad.'

'How long will he be?'

'Two, maybe three hours. Mr Thorn says that you make yourself comfortable until he gets back.' I looked at the single metal chair. Comfortable wasn't going to be easy. Thankfully, the head of security had other ideas.

238

'It is a wee bitty breezy today,' he said, as I followed him out of the main building and down a side path towards a large, prefabricated structure set well back from the runway in an area of garden ground that had a rectangular lawn to the front, marked out as a five-a-side football pitch and bordered by a white picket fence.

At the front door Oleg unclipped a bunch of keys from his belt, selected one and let me out of the 'breeze' that had threatened to blow my head off. Inside it was dark. Oleg squeezed by me, opened a small metal cabinet on the wall by the door and flicked a series of switches. Immediately row upon row of ceiling-mounted LED lights illuminated to reveal the finest airport lounge I'd ever seen, if that's what it was. It seemed more like a man-cave. Jukebox, retro video game machines, pool table, dartboard, and a well stocked bar. The walls were lined with photographs of cars, sportsmen, aircraft, attractive females in various stages of undress, and television monitors. Around the room soft furnishings were scattered, beanbags, sofas and lazy-boy chairs, even a four-poster bed in one of the corners. Hot air blowers hummed in the background.

'Please make yourself at home,' Oleg said. 'You will find everything you want here.'

I believed him. The lounge/man-cave would be a fine place to spend a few hours waiting for my host to arrive, even if it meant playing pool and darts with the dour Ruski, but if I was going to bluff my way to a few quid with his boss it would help if I could speak with some knowledge. I only wanted to sound out Thorn. I didn't have the information he wanted. Not yet, though, with time, I was certain I'd find it.

'Oleg, would it be okay if you gave me a tour of the

239

airport? You know: the hangars, helipad...' my aviation terminology was drying up fast. 'Stuff like that?'

Oleg shrugged again. 'Sure. Where you want to see first?'

The place I wanted to see first and last was the hangar where the crashed helicopter had been stored the night before its final journey. Oleg took me in the buggy to the largest of the three main hangars where two choppers were parked. He pointed to the nearest. 'Euroeagle BC one-fifty. Five hundred shaft horsepower gas turbine engine. We have three of these before the crash. Can take four passengers, has maximum range of three hundred and fifty nautical miles.'

I could see it was definitely a helicopter. A yellow one. The one next to it was red. I liked the yellow one.

'Jerry was ace pilot. He gave me lessons too. Said if I passed the test he would get me a pilot job here, flying the famous people about. I liked Jerry. He helped my mother when she was ill back home in Volgograd. He gave me money to send to her. I am sorry he is dead.'

After admiring the choppers for a while, I looked around and noticed a CCTV camera in a corner of the enormous structure. 'Does the CCTV system record?'

Judging by the length and volume of his sigh, Oleg had been asked this question before. 'Yes, but not the night Jerry goes missing, if that's what you ask. That night the camera is broken again. Homer tells me before I go home. I log the breakdown and tell Homer to call the maintenance people. He says they will come out next day to fix it.'

'So the person on monitoring duty would not have seen if anything strange happened?'

Oleg shuffled his feet and stared down at the concrete floor. 'That is true.'

The head of security had already told me he hadn't been on duty that night and, although I only knew one other member of the security team, I had a funny feeling I also knew who'd been roped in that fateful St Andrew's Day nightshift. I didn't even have to ask. 'Billy was on duty. One of the boys phone in not well and I ask Billy to cover for him. He did that sometimes. It was no big deal.'

'And the next day Billy left and never came back. Does that not seem strange to you? The CCTV camera in the hangar where Jerry's helicopter was probably sabotaged is out of order when Billy is on duty and then he disappears the next day?'

'It was not the first time the CCTV camera is broken. I am fed up with it. The system cost fifty thousand pounds. It was my idea to upgrade. Mr Thorn wasn't happy to pay for it. When it broke again I phone him and tell him to ask for his money back. He come here very angry.'

'What about these two helicopters? Was there any problem with them?'

There hadn't been because they had both been hired out. Only one had been left in the hangar overnight; the one Jerry had used to take his fiancée on a late night/early morning flight. It had been green.

We returned to the warmth of the man-cave where Oleg, acting like my very own butler, put some coffee on to brew.

'What is it you have to tell Mr Thorn?' he asked.

It was a fair enough question. What *did* I have to tell him? Not very much. More and more it was distilling down to a choice between two scenarios. Either Jeremy

241

had pulled one crazy stunt too many or the helicopter had been sabotaged. The latter would leave Billy Paris in the frame, Cherry's conspiracy theory intact and the Secretary of State's political career on a shoogly peg. The pending report from the Air Accident Investigation Branch would decide the issue. My sole reason for being there that blustery morning was to put a finder's fee agreement in place, one that Thorn couldn't back out of. I might not have anything to tell him, not yet, but I would, and since I was doing all the work I didn't see why we need involve Maggie Sinclair.

What I had to tell Mr Thorn was private, I told the security man, and was halfway through a mug of coffee and biting into my second caramel log when from somewhere a phone began to warble. Oleg went behind the bar and came out with another satellite phone. He held it out to me. 'Mr Thorn for you.'

I chewed rapidly on my mouthful of biscuit to clear my mouth, in the process inhaling some desiccated coconut and collapsing into a coughing fit. Strange that even while trying to catch my breath I remembered Billy Paris's preferred way of bringing down a helicopter: impregnating the air filter with copper fragments. A handful of them would destroy the turbine engine much in the same way as the pieces of toasted coconut were threatening to do to my lungs.

'Hello?' I managed to croak.

'Mr Munro? Philip Thorn. Sorry, I can't see you today after all. I'm bogged down in business talks up here in the Granite City. I'd have let you know earlier and saved you a trip if I hadn't been so wrapped up in everything that's going on. Are you free later in the week? How does Friday suit?'

Friday didn't suit. I was picking Tina up from the airport. 'I can do tomorrow. No, wait...' I'd promised Joanna I'd do some hand-holding with her client's wife. 'It would need to be first thing in the morning.'

'No problem. I'm an early riser. And this time I'll come to you.'

We left things on the basis that he'd call me later to make the necessary arrangements.

Oleg took the phone from me. 'You are meeting Mr Thorn. Are you going to tell him who killed his son?'

'If I did, what do you think he would do with that information?' I asked.

'Do?'

'Would he... you know. Do something about it?'

'What do you mean – do something about it? Do you mean kill somebody about it?' He was a plain talker. I liked that about the Russian. He came closer, the expression on his face looked as if it had been carved using hammer and chisel. 'You tell me who killed Jerry,' he said, 'and I kill them myself.'

42

That night it was just me and my dad, sitting in his living room, a small glass of whisky in hand, and a coal fire seething away nicely in the hearth. Thankfully there was mid-week football on TV and little need to converse, other than when criticizing players who missed scoring chances we agreed we each would have tucked away with some aplomb.

'I wonder how the bairn is,' my dad said, after the first forty-five minutes, raising himself from his armchair to give the coals a poke. His granddaughter's letter to the fat man in the red suit, all three pages of it, plus a subsequent appendix, had gone up the chimney weeks ago. 'There's a lot of crazies over there in France. The rag-heads are running wild. Remember that Charlie Hedgehog magazine thing? And then there was the bombs at the football and the hostages and everything.'

I assured him Tina would be having the time of her life. 'If you're so worried, you could have gone with her if you'd wanted. Mrs Reynolds wouldn't have minded.'

'Who? Me? Go to France so I can stand in a queue all day just to go on a roundabout and be bothered by a load of folk in fancy dress?' was my dad's take on the wonderful world of Disney experience. 'No thanks. There's enough clowns in this town without having to cross the Channel to see them, and, anyway, how could I afford a trip like that?'

His words hung like a juicy lugworm wriggling beneath the waters of St Edzell Bay. I let the bait hang. I was too comfortable, and relations between myself and the old man were sufficiently delicate that I decided not to rile him further with mention of his generous police pension or of his historical whisky collection, the latter something of a sore point. He'd started the collection several years before he was set to retire, buying collectable bottles to sell later at inflated prices in order to supplement his pension. Then when he did retire he'd thought, what was the point? He'd only spend the proceeds on more whisky, and as he had the whisky already... Suffice to say the collection was no more and, with whisky prices rocketing and his consumption plummeting since the arrival of his granddaughter, it irked him to think about it. No, I'd save that juicy morsel for later. I had something else to wind him up with.

'Imagine,' I said. 'Paris, the sun setting over the Magic Kingdom. Just you and the rich widow Reynolds... ooh, la la.' I think it was my wink, and click of the tongue that especially annoyed him.

Without a word he stomped off through to the kitchen. I waited until he returned to give us each a half-time refill. 'Come on, Dad. It's thirty-six years since Mum died. You're not too old to get married again. Don't you want a wife?'

'No thanks. I'm just fine wanting what I don't have. It's a lot better than having what I don't want. It's you who should be finding a mum for Tina.'

'Me and Malky managed without one,' I said.

'Aye, but you were boys. Boys just need someone to keep them on the straight and narrow.'

'And to give them a skelp when they stray off it,' I said.

'Ach, a clip round the ear never did you any harm. Girls are different, though. You can't hit a girl. A girl needs a mum, someone to learn womanly things from. A female role model.'

'The helpers at the nursery are female and when Tina starts school so will most, if not all, of the teachers be.'

'That's not what I'm talking about. I'm talking about someone to look up to, to go shopping with, that sort of thing. What are you going to do in a few years' time when Tina starts talking about bras and... well, you know, that other stuff that comes by every month.'

'I've got female friends. There's Grace-Mary, and Kaye helped out the other night, remember? And then there's Joanna—'

'Now you're talking. Joanna. She'd do fine. She's never away from here as it is. Always dropping in to see you about something.'

I had to admit that over recent weeks I had seen a lot of Joanna, and not just at work. Some evenings she'd pop by to discuss a case or say hello to Tina. Perhaps Vikki had also noticed, put two and two together and come up with a pretty solid five.

'Never mind Pyxie Girl. Tina thinks Joanna is a super-hero. That lassie can do nothing wrong in Tina's eyes.'

I didn't want to engage in this topic of conversation, but I could see no other way of avoiding us getting onto the subject of Tina's missing Christmas present now that it had been raised. 'Dad, Joanna's not interested in me. She's my employee for one thing, and for another she's about seven years younger than me.'

There was a break for more TV ads before the players came out for the start of the second half. I didn't have long to stall, normal father/son non-communications would resume shortly.

'Nonsense, don't let a little thing like age difference get in the way,' he said, pausing to strain whisky through his moustache. 'What about me and your mum?'

'What about you? You were both the same age.'

'Aye, but she died when she was younger than you. Anything could happen to you or Joanna. Remember what happened to Tina's real mum. One minute she was alive, the next...'

Joanna had said I was an optimist. Now I knew where I didn't get it from. The referee blew his whistle and the second half kicked off. So far, according to the commentator, it had been a case of no goals but plenty of action. In the first minute of the restart the home team was awarded a free-kick in a dangerous position. As the defensive wall was setting itself up to block a shot at goal, a blue graphics banner appeared and a message began to scroll along the bottom of the screen. *AAIB findings indicate Jeremy Thorn's helicopter sabotaged.*

I waited for the striker to balloon the ball over the bar and then switched to a news channel where the helicopter crash and its repercussions were making all the headlines. Cherry Lovell's Night News documentary had not gone unnoticed at Westminster. Now, after this initial report from the Air Accident Investigation Branch, not only was the Secretary of State for Scotland implicated, but the Minister for Aviation and the Business Secretary were also in the firing line. A lot of disgruntled opposition MPs who had backed an English-based spaceport, claimed it had gone to Scotland only to defuse calls for another independence referendum. Like Cherry they pointed to a Secretary of State forced to deliver the goods whatever the cost, and highlighted his connection with the man most likely to have brought down the helicopter. People wanted answers. There was talk about recalling Parliament early after the festive break and a vote of no confidence against a Prime Minister who could condone an act of terrorism if he thought it would save the Union.

Lights shone through the curtains. Outside I heard a car door slam.

'Santa's either come early or it's for you,' my dad said.

I answered a knock at the door. It was DI Christchurch and his ugly little helper. 'Evening, Mr Munro. Please listen carefully. There is a posse of journalists and TV news crews headed this way. Unless you want to end up a prisoner in your own home, pack a change of clothes and whatever else you need and come with us.'

43

Milton Street, Edinburgh was a road lined either side with towering, sandstone tenement buildings, every other window the frame for a Christmas tree. It began at Abbeyhill, at the foot of the Royal Mile and ended at the boundary wall of Holyrood Park.

The first floor flat at number thirty-one was a safe house, used by the Ministry of Defence Police to hide people they didn't want other people to find. With a curt, 'Goodnight,' Christchurch opened the front door, the Bulldog tossed my holdall through it and then the two of them left. There was no need for further discussion. Things had been made abundantly clear to me on the drive through to Edinburgh. I had a choice to make, the easy way or the hard way. Voluntarily hand over the evidence given to me by Billy Paris or have my office pulled apart by an MDP search squad, who, if they found nothing there, would move onto my dad's cottage, then onto Malky's place, then Joanna's and so on down the list of people I was related to, worked with, or with whom I was otherwise acquainted. I didn't want to meet Grace-Mary after they'd kicked her door in.

Christchurch, as usual, was the epitome of reasonableness. The platitudes spilled from his lips. I should do myself a favour. Do the right thing. We were all on the same side. For Queen and country. Seekers after the truth.

Having patiently, but firmly explained that whether I cooperated or not, the outcome would be the same, the Ministry of Defence officer said he'd let me sleep on it. I couldn't. At four thirty next morning I climbed out of a rickety single bed, walked through to the front room and looked down on a road that was sparkling with frost.

I paced the room. What should I do? I wasn't under arrest. There were no bars on the windows, no guards at the door, just a posse of newsmen hot on my trail.

Christchurch wanted me to do myself a favour by doing what he said was the right thing. The trouble was the two were mutually exclusive, and it didn't matter if I slept on it all night or all the next day for that matter. It wouldn't alter the fact that there was nothing in it for me if I cooperated with his government, that is the Westminster Government. Of course, if I chose not to cooperate with that lot in London it would please those sitting in power at Holyrood. But what did I owe a Scottish Government that banged on about access to justice, and yet hadn't increased the funds available to prepare a criminal defence in a quarter of a century? A government whose quango had recently taken away my livelihood because I hadn't filled in a few forms correctly. Kirkton Perch said the evidence would vindicate him. Well he would, wouldn't he? If, or rather when, I found the proof, and if I did hand it over to him, what guarantee was there it would ever see the light of day? And where would we be then? The Secretary of State happily climbing the greasy pole, and me still skint. If Philip Thorn wanted justice and was ready to pay, who said he had any less of a claim to the evidence than the politicians? It was his son who'd

250

died, and while Thorn's idea of justice might differ from theirs, it was more likely to coincide with mine had it been my only child who'd been murdered.

Somehow, while wrestling with my thoughts, I managed to fall asleep, awaking in the early hours scrunched up on a two-seater sofa feeling exactly like someone who'd fallen asleep scrunched up on a two-seater sofa. After a shower and change of clothes I felt better. Not coffee-and-a-bacon-roll better, but fresher and clearer of mind.

Inside a kitchen cupboard I found and dismissed a jar of supermarket own-brand instant coffee. The only food item was a pack of high-fibre cereal guaranteed to clear out a digestive system faster than a pull-through with a Christmas tree. I was checking the fridge for anything remotely edible when my phone buzzed. It was Philip Thorn. He hadn't lied. He was an early riser and was already on the road south to my office. I told him to steer a course for Edinburgh. He reckoned he'd be there inside a couple of hours. Plenty of time for me to go off in search of a decent cup of coffee and bacon roll and, before that, to make one very important phone call.

'Robbie!' Cherry Lovell greeted me as though I were her long-lost brother. 'You won't believe this, but I'm outside your house right now. Where are you? Can you spare me some time for a quick chat over the recent developments? How about lunch? I'm paying.' She knew me so well.

'I was thinking more along the lines of breakfast,' I said. I didn't have to say it twice. By seven o'clock I was crunching on finest crispy Ayrshire bacon. By eight o'clock Cherry was sitting beside me on the sofa in the safe house, a cameraman tinkering with the lighting and a sound technician twiddling knobs.

Christchurch arrived as final arrangements to the furniture were being carried out. 'What's the meaning of this?'

'This,' I said, 'is an interview with Night News. Have you met Cherry Lovell? Stick around and you can watch yourself on TV tonight. Ten thirty.'

For the first time the DI looked flustered and annoyed. Maybe he wasn't a morning person. 'Get out, this minute. All of you.'

The Bulldog moved closer, keen to get in on the action. The camera turned on him, the light shining in his face.

Cherry produced a microphone and stepped in between camera and Detective Constable. 'The investigation into the deaths of Jeremy Thorn and Madeleine Moreau moved a step forward last night with an AAIB report stating that their helicopter had indeed been sabotaged. We're here at a secret location to interview Mr Robbie Munro, solicitor, who is currently being held by Ministry of Defence Police. Mr Munro, I understand the police are keen on you assisting them with their enquiries...' The Bulldog stepped forward menacingly. Christchurch reached out and placed a hand on his colleague's shoulder, reining him in.

'Can you fill us in on what's been happening?' Cherry asked me.

I could and I did. The more I'd thought about it, the more I'd come to believe Christchurch was bluffing. Obtaining a warrant to search a solicitor's office was not an easy thing to do, even if the office was mine and the Sheriff being asked to sign off on it was my old adversary, Albert Brechin. For one thing, the cops would have to have a reasonable suspicion that I possessed evidence that might secure the conviction of the person responsible for murdering Jeremy Thorn. That in itself raised certain tricky issues of client/solicitor privilege, and the only way Christchurch could explain his suspicion was by reference to his clandestine eavesdropping. To prove the point, I produced a matchbox with the two tiny bugs resting comfortably on a wad of cotton wool. In case I was wrong, and Christchurch had obtained the necessary authority to plant a bug on me, I explained to camera – for the benefit of those members of the Scottish Parliament who might later watch — how police officers, not from Police Scotland, but acting on behalf of the Westminster Government, were attempting to run roughshod over due process and a Scots citizen's right to privacy.

In truth, much of what I had to say would not have borne any degree of jurisprudential scrutiny, nothing too unusual there, but what my speech to camera would do, once broadcast, was buy me time. Cherry would take what I gave her, tuck it under her arm and charge head-down towards the goalposts of a government conspiracy. What would happen to the evidence if I had it and it was taken from me? Would it ever see the light of day? Would the public ever know the truth about Kirkton Perch's role in the death of Jeremy Thorn? The involvement of MDP officers, instead of good old Scottish bobbies, only went to show it was all part of a Westminster cover-up.

As I reached the pinnacle of my high-dudgeon, Christchurch and his companion drifted away. Cherry wasn't finished. 'Mr Munro, what do you know about the death of Jeremy Thorn and his fiancée?'

'No more than you,' I said.

'Your own client Mr William Paris was considered a suspect and it has been alleged that you hold evidence vital to finding the murderer. What have you to say on that?'

In law, possession was defined as having the knowledge and control of an item. If the evidence was in my office it was arguably under my control; however, if I had no idea where it was, how could I have actual knowledge of its presence? 'I'm sorry, Cherry, but for legal reasons I am unable to confirm or deny if I possess the evidence to prove the identity of the person responsible for killing Jeremy Thorn or Madeleine Moreau.'

It wasn't the answer she'd hoped for, but it was sufficiently ambiguous for her to put on it whatever slant she wanted. More importantly it gave me time to strike a deal with Philip Thorn without Christchurch and the Bulldog breathing down my neck.

'So, is it the case that you are unwilling to assist with any enquiries to establish the truth?'

'No,' I said, 'I am simply stating that for certain reasons I can't help anyone at the moment.'

And I couldn't. Not yet. But when I could, the person I'd be looking to help most was myself.

44

Christchurch and his colleague were long gone, and the
Night News crew all packed up and away, when, holdall
slung over a shoulder, I walked to the end of the street
and exited via a door cut into an ancient sandstone wall,
leading to Holyrood Park. By nine thirty I was sitting on
a frosty bench on the east edge of St Margaret's Loch,
watching a pale disc of sun struggle to climb the ruins of
St Andrew's Chapel.

A couple of joggers ran by, breathing hard and startling
the flotilla of swans that was heading my way in a futile
search for bread. Behind me I heard the throaty growl of a
high-powered engine and turned to see a bright red E-type
Roadster pulling up by the side of Queen's Drive. Two
men alighted. One I recognised immediately as Oleg, head
of security at St Edzell Bay, the other, dressed in a long
camel coat with a felt collar and tobacco Trilby, could
only be Philip Thorn. I stood and the latter marched over
to me, leaving the Russian standing by the car holding
a metal briefcase that was handcuffed to his wrist, no
doubt in anticipation of the evidence his boss thought I
was about to deliver.

Thorn tugged off a brown leather driving glove and
shook my hand. 'Mr Munro?'

I confirmed my identity and would have complimented

him on his choice of motor car had he not come straight out and asked, 'How much?'

Here was a man with whom I could do business. 'Forty thousand,' I said, preparing to haggle.

Thorn looked as though I'd picked up a swan and slapped him across the face with it.

'Cash,' I said.

Thorn snapped the fingers of his ungloved hand. Oleg marched across and set the briefcase down on the arm of the park bench. Thorn turned the combination dials, clicked the lid open, reached inside and removed four bundles of notes. He didn't open the lid far, just far enough for me to catch a glimpse of many more similar bundles inside. Was I selling myself short? Was his surprise not at how much I was asking, but at how little? He closed the briefcase again. Without a word Oleg withdrew to the roadside.

I'd not expected this. I'd thought there'd be a lot more negotiation, more questions, that I'd have time to stall him while he got the money together so that I'd have time to find the very thing he'd come for. Faced with the cash, I wasn't sure what to say.

'I've not got it,' I blurted.

Thorn looked more confused than angry.

'When I say I've not got it, I mean not with me. It's at my office.'

'I don't understand,' he said. 'We arranged to meet today. You must have known why.' He looked about anxiously. 'Is this some kind of set-up?' He tucked the wads of cash into the inside of his coat and summoned Oleg again. The Russian was by his side in an instant. 'Search him.'

Searching me wasn't easy with a cash-stuffed metal briefcase hanging from one wrist, and I lost a button from the front of my shirt before Oleg returned his verdict. 'Nada.'

'I don't like this, Mr Munro,' Thorn said. 'I was led to believe that you were in possession of the evidence proving who killed my son.'

I felt uncomfortable with Oleg this close. The man who'd been so amenable a host during yesterday's visit to St Edzell Bay, today had a face on him like the Crags beneath Arthur's Seat.

'Let's walk,' I said, taking to the path, followed by Philip Thorn and the gaggle of overly optimistic waterfowl.

'I want to know what's going on,' Thorn said, when he caught up with me.

So I told him. I told him I had the evidence, I just didn't know where it was. I realised how weak that sounded and so qualified the statement. 'I'm ninety-nine per cent certain I will find it.'

'How long until you do?'

'Not long,' I said. 'In fact, very soon.'

'And you haven't seen it? You don't know what it consists of or who is responsible for Jeremy's death?'

I had to agree I knew none of these things.

'So whatever you have, if indeed you have anything at all, could prove to be nothing? I could be wasting my time and money?'

'Let's not be too hasty,' I said, remembering Billy Paris's high hopes. 'No, it's definitely something. But I won't know what exactly until I find it. That's going to take a lot of searching, and I'm going to have to drop everything to do it. Christmas is coming up, I've got a family and the police are extremely interested. Right now they're trying to obtain a warrant to ransack my office.'

Thorn stopped walking. He was smiling now. 'All right. Forty thousand. You have two days.' He spun on a heel, took a couple of paces.

I called him back. 'I'd like you to sign this agreement.' I pulled the document Wahid had drafted for me from my pocket and held it out to him. He took it from me, crumpled it in a leather glove and tossed it back. He thrust a hand inside his coat, pulled out the bundles of notes and pushed two of them into my chest. 'That's half. If you want the rest, you bring me the evidence before Christmas.' He stepped closer, frosty breath hitting me in the face. 'If you don't, it'll not be Santa coming down your chimney Christmas Eve. It will be Oleg.'

45

It may have been winter on Arthur's Seat, but in my heart it was spring. Twenty grand tax-free was one of the best remedies I knew for driving out the iciest of cold blasts, and the thought that the same again awaited me only helped stoke the warm feeling that perhaps it wasn't going to be such a bad New Year after all. Set against that, of course, was the thought that I might not be able to make good on my promise to Philip Thorn. That did send a slight chill down the back of my neck. I didn't fancy the idea of an irate Russian security guard abseiling into my fireplace on Christmas morning, but I still had time on my side. It was Thursday. Christmas wasn't until Sunday. Kirkton Perch and his Westminster lackeys would stay away from Munro & Co. for the time being, especially after Cherry Lovell's show was broadcast that evening. All I need do was rally the troops and give my office the fine-toothed-comb treatment.

I was reaching for my phone to call Grace-Mary and place her on stand-by when it began to buzz: Joanna.

'Robbie, where are you?'

'Edinburgh.'

'Good. I'd thought you'd forgotten.'

'Forgotten?' I laughed. 'Me?'

'You have forgotten, haven't you?'

A moment's hesitation on my part was enough for Joanna to accurately assess the situation. 'Wherever you are, whatever you're doing, get your butt up here to the Lawnmarket. Keith Howie is giving evidence today and his wife is practically suicidal.'

When had it become part of my duties to molly-coddle a rapist's wife? No, I had to correct myself, not rapist, alleged rapist — until the jury came back with its verdict, at any rate. Perhaps it was because of Howie's dislike for me, or maybe it was because I had a daughter of my own and thought that jail was too good for the type of men who took advantage of young women; whichever, I really had very little concern as to the outcome of HMA -v- Howie. If he was guilty, and it had been my daughter, he'd have found jail the safest place to be.

Sadly, there was no way I could back out. Not having told Joanna I'd help. How churlish would it be if I wasn't willing to take an hour or so out of my day when she had foregone a ski-holiday? So, resigned to the task ahead and with more urgent and important things to be doing, I set off from the bottom of the Royal Mile to my destination at the top, all set for a morning spent patting Mrs Howie's hand and telling her everything would be all right, which of course it would be — right up until the verdict was returned.

It was one brisk fifteen-minute walk later when I poked my head in the door of Courtroom 4 to find a forensic scientist busy explaining to the jury, with the aid of Cameron Crowe, the advocate depute, all about semen, sperm heads, swabs, stained underwear, and the significance of these findings apropos a charge of rape. Unfortunately, the jury seemed to be listening intently.

Courtroom 4 was situated on the first floor of the High Court. The accused sat in the dock with his back to me, Lady Bothkennar straight ahead, elevated high on the bench with the jury to her right. In the well of the court, opposite the lawyers for the Crown, and to the judge's left, Joanna sat beside the voluminous presence that was Fiona Faye QC. Joanna looked up from her note-taking and gave me a tight smile. This case meant a lot to her. Every case meant a lot to her. She was a winner. She was just what Munro & Co. needed, now more than ever.

As I stood in the doorway, a court officer approached. 'Are you coming in or not?' she whispered.

I backed out, beckoning the court officer to follow. 'Is this the last witness?'

She nodded. 'Lady Bothkennar's been keeping things moving along. She was panicking in case we weren't finished this week because she wants away early tomorrow and then that'll be her until the sixth of January. Okay for some, isn't it? There's no chance she's going to let this case spill over into next week.'

The court officer returned to her duties and I paced up and down the carpeted hallway, waiting for the expert witness to finish. There was no need for me to listen in. The forensic evidence was only being led as a formality to establish the fact that sex had actually occurred. Whether it had been consensual wasn't an issue. Howie had denied any sexual contact. Even if he hadn't, and had lodged a defence of consent, it would have made little difference so far as I could see. Once intercourse was proved, the jury would take into account the complainer's evidence, her distress, as witnessed by the accused's own wife, the age difference, and the big question: if it was consensual why would she say otherwise? And that was before anyone applied Malky's football league analogy and the yawning chasm between the accused's and complainer's respective divisions. In my book it all pointed to a unanimous guilty verdict.

After the expert witness had testified, Cameron Crowe formally closed the Crown's case and there followed the customary break in proceedings to allow the defence a chance to get itself organised. This usually involved some last-minute words of encouragement for the accused and a few tips on how to testify effectively. Every lawyer had their own theory on that.

'Stand up straight, look whoever is asking you questions straight in the eye and speak loudly and clearly,' Fiona told Howie once the four of us had gathered in the corridor. 'If you don't understand a question, say so and ask for it to be repeated. Whatever you do, keep your hands away from your face. Everyone assumes that's a sign of someone lying.'

That last piece of advice was commonplace and one I felt sure more likely to make a witness face-fondle than if nothing had been said on the subject.

Howie blinked a few times and nodded. His complexion matched his tie. His green tie.

I took the end of it and held it up. 'Why aren't you wearing a blue one?' I asked.

Joanna and Fiona did some synchronised eye-rolling.

Howie reclaimed the tie and patted it flat onto his white shirt. 'I like this one. It's my favourite.'

'Yes, but it isn't blue. You need a blue tie when you're giving evidence. Joanna must have told you. A blue tie signifies truth, it's a psychological thing. Green doesn't signify truth it says…' Red was arrogant and aggressive, I knew that. Pink said you were either gay or making a statement that you were so secure in your heterosexuality that you could get away with it. Yellow was just stupid, brown was yuck, navy was not blue enough, black was for mourners and waiters. What was green again? 'A green tie is something else. What it's definitely not is a blue tie of truth.'

Howie was unrepentant. 'I don't care. It's the tie I wore when I proposed to my wife. It's lucky.' With a face like his he must have had something going for him.

'Maybe after the trial we can ask Mrs Howie if she agrees,' I said.

Joanna butted in. 'That's enough, Robbie. You're not helping.' Mrs Howie, who had been standing sobbing a distance away, heard her name mentioned and made her way over to us, dabbing each eye in turn with the corner of a handkerchief. Joanna shoved me in her direction. 'Stop her.'

I did as I was told. If the accused wasn't prepared to take my advice, then he and his emerald neck-wear would have to take their chances.

'Have you had any breakfast?' I asked, intercepting Mrs Howie and steering her away from her husband. 'They do a lovely bacon roll next door and the coffee is—'

'No,' Mrs Howie shook her head, 'I couldn't possibly eat at a time like this.'

I could. Very easily. Breakfast was but a fond memory. Taking her by the arm, I manoeuvred her towards the swing doors at the end of the hall. 'Then let's go for a walk. If you stay in the courtroom you'll only upset your-self and the last thing you want to do is sit worrying in a

263

witness room for the next hour or so. There'll be plenty of time for that when the jury is out.' Mrs Howie stifled a short howl with her hanky. 'Come on. Let's get some fresh air inside you. You'll feel better.'

Somehow, I managed to propel her against her will through the doors. Halfway down the stairs to the main lobby she asked, 'Will he really be in there an hour or more? How will he stand it? I was only in for twenty minutes when I gave my evidence and it seemed like days.'

'He's going to be a while, but if they go full steam ahead he should be finished by lunch.' Outside the big bronze front doors, the weather had taken a turn for the worse. On the High Street the rain was stotting off the cobbles and gurgling down the gutters. I tried again. 'Are you sure you won't have a coffee?' She was sure. 'Then how about you watch me drink one?'

46

Keith and Elizabeth Howie had been an item since their school days. They'd married young and had children late. He owned a small toyshop on Linlithgow High Street. She was a freelance writer, penning poems and sentimental slush for greetings cards and the In Memoriam sections of newspapers.

'His name was Fred and now he's dead. That sort of thing?' I asked, but Mrs Howie didn't see the funny side of that, if there was one.

During the time it had taken us to scurry the fifty yards or so to the café, find a table and place an order, I'd introduced any number of topics of conversation in an effort to take the woman's mind off what was happening next door in Court 4. None of them worked.

'He'll die in there, you know,' she said, matter-of-factly. Mrs Howie alternated between states of extreme calm and hysterical weeping. I liked the extreme calm moments the best. 'If they send him to jail, he'll not last a day.'

There was little doubt that the scent of fresh meat like Howie would have the wolves circling, but I could hardly tell her that. 'Prison's not so bad,' I said. 'It's the thought of going that's the deterrent. A lot of people who do go are surprised at how normal it is. It's just a matter of getting into the routine and treating it like a job. Except with fewer holidays.'

Mrs Howie's face twitched, a sign I'd come to recognise as the precursor to tears. I really couldn't be doing with any more crying. 'I'm sure everything will be fine,' I said.

'Do you really think so?'

Of course I didn't. 'Of course I do. The case has been prepared meticulously by Miss Jordan, and Fiona Faye is one of Scotland's top criminal QCs. In fact, she is the top. Once she gets her go at the jury they'll be putty in her hands.'

'I can't help thinking that if Keith is found guilty, I'll somehow be to blame.' I wasn't sure what to say. Perhaps in a way she was to blame. If she hadn't been such a sound sleeper she might have heard her husband getting out of bed and tiptoeing through to the next room in the middle of the night. Then she could have gone after him and asked what the hell he thought he was doing. 'They made me tell the jury that I saw Ruby upset and crying and screaming to be let out of the house.'

Until recently a spouse could not be compelled to give evidence for the prosecution unless the case concerned violence between husband and wife. The Scottish Government had changed that age-old rule, though a lot of people had argued that forcing one spouse to testify against another was a breach of the marriage vow.

In the present case, Ruby Maguire's evidence had been that she'd been raped by Keith Howie. Her word alone on the matter was insufficient, another long-established rule of evidence the Scottish Government was keen to erase, even though corroboration was one of the few things that God and Scotland's most famous philosopher and atheist, David Hume, saw eye to eye on.

For a conviction in any rape case three crucial facts

had to be proved. Firstly, that there had been intercourse; secondly, that it had been non-consensual and, thirdly, the identity of the rapist. The forensic finding of sperm had taken care of any doubts as regards intercourse. That it had been non-consensual was spoken to by Ruby Maguire and supported by the evidence of Mrs Howie and her description of the young woman's distress. The only thing left was identification of the rapist, and by a process of elimination, who else could it have been other than the only male inside a locked house?

'You had no choice but to give evidence and tell the truth,' I assured her. 'Anyway, hearing you speak so fondly about your husband, and the jury seeing the kind of woman you are and that you are standing by him, can only have helped to give a good impression.'

'Do you think so?' Mrs Howie sniffed and fumbled in her handbag for her hanky.

Though I was doing my best, I could tell we were in danger of tipping from calm to hysterical, and so to change the discussion I brought up the one subject no mother could help herself talking about: her children.

Our drinks arrived. Coffee for me and tea for Mrs Howie who had eventually succumbed to my suggestion of a hot drink. She steadied herself, blew her nose into the sodden hanky and sat up straight. 'You're right. I have to be brave for the children,' she said, visibly steeling herself and sounding like the heroine from a Sunday night TV costume drama.

'I take it your kids don't know what's happening?' I asked, checking the coffee for temperature and scalding my tongue.

'We've said nothing to them.' Mrs Howie poured milk

from a little jug and sighed. 'Fortunately the twins are too young to ask questions. The oldest suspects something's going on. I've told her it's all to do with a Christmas surprise.'

That certainly would be a surprise on Christmas morning. *Surprise! Your dad's doing six years for rape!*

'It's three girls you've got, isn't it?' I said, seeing an opportunity. 'What are they getting for Christmas? Your husband owning a toyshop, I bet he's not had any trouble getting his hands on a few Pyxie Girls.' Looking back, perhaps that wasn't the best way of putting it. I manufactured a casual little laugh.

'Don't get me started on Pyxie Girl,' Mrs Howie said, peering at me over the top of her teacup.

'No, please,' I said. 'Get started.'

She wet her lips. 'Back in August, Keith ordered in two dozen of the things. They were flying off the shelves and I told him to keep three back for our girls. No need, says he, I'm going to order in a lot more for Christmas. Then the big carry-on started about the doll's name and since then no one in the trade, far less any customers, has been able to lay hands on one. You wouldn't believe the sums of money Keith's been offered by some parents.' I could. 'Do you have children, Mr Munro?'

'A daughter,' I said. 'One's enough for me. Three must be difficult.'

Mrs Howie couldn't deny it. 'My sister has two sons and a daughter and says that the girl is more bother than both her brothers. She says with boys you only have to feed them, put them out to play and make sure they wash behind their ears occasionally. With girls everything is a negotiation.'

It wasn't just Tina then. My cup was cooling. I attempted another sip of coffee across my furry tongue. 'Did you ever think fourth time lucky for a boy?'

At that moment Mrs Howie came as close to what I could reasonably describe as a smile as she had on the few occasions I'd met her. 'No, that wasn't a risk I was prepared to take. Twins run in my family, and I wasn't falling into that trap again.'

I could imagine. Twin girls. Much as I loved my daughter, the thought of Tina in duplicate made me shudder.

'As soon as I saw the first scan and knew I was having twins I had Keith booked in,' she said.

Having established my coffee was drinkable, and there being some time to go before lunch, I was toying with the idea of a bacon roll. I glanced around for the waitress, stopped and then turned to Mrs Howie again. 'Booked in?'

'Yes.' She winced slightly. 'You know?' She set her teacup back down on its saucer, released her grip on the handle and made scissors with the index and middle finger of her right.

'Your husband's had the snip?'

Her previously pale cheeks took on a faint sign of colour. 'Keith said it was quite painless.'

I took that as hearsay and as such quite possibly unreliable evidence.

Mrs Howie must have noticed the expression on my face. 'Trust me, he'd have found it a lot more painful to have another mouth, or, perhaps, another two mouths, to feed.'

But my expression had nothing to do with excess children or even the thought of someone closing in on my gentleman's parts with a blade in their hand.

'Mr Munro, are you all right?'

I jumped to my feet with a loud squeal of wooden chair legs on ceramic floor tiles. 'Mrs Howie, I'm going to nip over to the court for a moment. Could you wait here? And if the bill comes, maybe you could take care of it.'

47

There were easier courts to slip into unnoticed than Courtroom 4 at the Lawnmarket, especially if you were in a rush.

From the doorway, I could see Fiona Faye had completed her examination-in-chief of Keith Howie and Cameron Crowe was on his feet cross-examining.

The demeanour of the two, advocate depute and accused, could not have been more different. Crowe, cool and collected, leaning a languid arm against the jury box, shot a taught line of questions across the well of the court at the accused who, sweating like a cheese, did his best to walk that tightrope in the knowledge that one slip and it was all over.

The design of the room meant I had to sidle past the jury box and at least make a pretence at being inconspicuous, ducking my head slightly as I passed between Cameron Crowe and his prey. When I reached the defence side of the table, I sat down on the nearest vacant chair and gently pushed myself along the floor until I could waggle my way in between Joanna and senior counsel.

The questioning of witnesses under Scots procedure was straightforward enough. The side calling the witness, be it prosecution or defence, went first. There then followed cross-examination to test the reliability and credibility of the evidence that had been led in chief.

271

The third stage was re-examination. This was an opportunity for the side that had originally called the witness to clarify any matters raised during cross-examination. Like me, I knew Fiona Faye preferred not to re-examine. It was a sign of weakness. It sent a message to the jury that the prosecution's questioning had been effective, and that you were trying in vain to rivet on some iron plates to stop the holes in a defence battleship that had been torpedoed by the Crown.

'Fiona,' I whispered.

'Go away, Robbie.' The QC didn't look up from the notepad she was doodling on.

'I need you to ask a question.'

'No.'

'It's very important.'

Joanna tapped my shoulder. 'What's the matter?'

'I want Fiona to re-examine.'

'Howie's not doing so bad,' Joanna said. 'Crowe's chucking everything at him, but he's sticking to his story.'

'I put it to you, Mr Howie that you are nothing but a bare-faced liar...' Cameron Crowe was winding up his cross in what was a trailer for his speech to the jury rather than any actual examination. 'That you crept into that young woman's bed after she had entrusted herself to your care, and in the middle of the night, while your own wife and three daughters slept soundly next door, you raped her.'

Howie stood in the witness box visibly shaking. The accusation hanging in the air, Crowe strode back to his seat. As with a dramatic flap of his gown he sat down, Fiona rose to her feet.

'M'Lady, if that last tirade was supposed to be a

question, perhaps Mr Crowe would at least allow my client the opportunity of answering it.'

Lady Bothkennar stared down to her right at the advocate depute. 'Mr Crowe?'

With a great deal of unnecessary effort, Cameron Crowe climbed to his feet. Hands planted on the table in front of him, he fixed his serpent-like gaze on the witness and sneered. 'Well?'

Howie gripped the sides of the witness box, partly in anger, partly I was sure, to stop himself from collapsing. 'No, Sir, I am not a liar and I did not rape Miss Ruby Maguire.'

Crowe took his seat again, behind him row upon row of grim-faced jurors. No matter how brilliant Fiona's closing remarks, there was no way she was going to wring an acquittal out of that lot. Not unless she listened to me.

Lady Bothkennar looked down at the defence huddle. 'Is there to be any re-examination?'

I tugged at Fiona's gown. 'You must re-examine Howie.'

'No, Robbie. It's as good as it's going to get,' she said, rising to her feet to address the judge.

I stood too.

'Just leave it,' Joanna whispered up at me.

How could I just leave it? Before the trial Fiona had asked me to come up with some ammunition. *Don't have me standing there firing blanks.* Ironic, because the only person firing blanks was Keith Howie.

'Is there a problem, Miss Faye?' the judge enquired, as I leaned in closer to the QC.

Fiona favoured the bench with one of her smiles. 'I'm just taking some instructions, M'Lady.' She turned to me and hissed. 'What is it?'

273

'Ask Howie if he's had a vasectomy.'

'What?'

'Ask—'

'I heard you. Why didn't you tell me this before?'

Now Joanna was on her feet. 'Vasectomy?'

'Didn't you ask him if he'd had the snip?' Fiona asked me.

I turned to Joanna. 'Did you?'

The judge wasn't happy at the delay. 'Miss Faye, really...'

Fiona hesitated. There was a general stirring amongst the jury who no doubt just wanted to convict the rapist in the witness box and get on with some last-minute Christmas shopping.

I tugged again at the QC's gown. 'His wife says he was cut three years ago. You've got to ask the question.'

Fiona knew that too. The problem was how to get the question in. The purpose of re-examination was to deal only with any matters raised during cross-examination. If a subject had not been mentioned by the cross-examiner, you couldn't go there. Crowe would be on his feet objecting the moment Fiona strayed off the path and tried to lead new evidence. If the judge ruled the vasectomy question invalid, as the rules of procedure said she must, then it would go unanswered and as such form no part of the evidence the jury would subsequently have to consider before returning a verdict.

Joanna and I sat down. There was nothing we could do but leave things in defence counsel's hands.

'If your Ladyship pleases.' Fiona turned to the witness. 'Mr Howie, the advocate depute mentioned that you have three daughters. Is that correct?'

Howie looked puzzled. 'Yes.'

'How did you come by those three children?'

Cameron Crowe got to his feet. 'Is my learned friend asking if the witness's children are adopted? If so, what possible relevance has that to these proceedings?'

Lady Bothkennar tended to agree. 'Is that what you're asking, Miss Faye?'

'No, M'Lady, it's not.'

'Then,' said the judge, 'I expect Mr Howie came by his children in the same biological fashion men and women normally come by their children. Is that correct, Mr Howie?' The witness, hugely embarrassed, could only agree. A few of the jurors laughed politely at the judge's comments, and Lady Bothkennar couldn't resist a glance at the jury box to accept their acclaim.

'Thank you for raising that point, M'Lady,' Fiona said graciously, squeezing herself through a procedural eye of a needle. 'If I might ask just a few questions to clarify further on that?'

Lady Bothkennar looked down at the Crown's side of the table. She having asked a question of the witness on the subject of human reproduction, the judge could hardly sustain an objection to a follow-up question.

'So,' Fiona continued seamlessly, 'we can take it that nine years ago one of your intrepid sperm entered an egg belonging to Mrs Howie, resulting nine months later in the delivery of a baby girl?'

The witness looked decidedly wobbly. He was handed a glass of water by the macer and moistened his mouth before answering. 'I suppose that's what must have happened.'

'And three years ago by the same process you became the proud father of twin girls?'

Across the table from me, Cameron Crowe huffed and puffed at a line of questioning he regarded as inane, no doubt thinking it to be some feeble attempt by the defence to remind the jury of the accused's darling daughters in the hope of securing a sympathy vote.

'And can we expect any more little Howie girls?' Fiona asked. She was in full flight mode, her presence filling the small courtroom, the eyes of every juror upon her. Crowe twitched slightly as though he might object then thought better of it. He knew how strong the Crown case was. Why not let the defence flap about like a fish on a beach for a few minutes longer? He had no idea that the prosecution case he'd so skilfully brought to life and paraded before the jury was about to breathe its last.

'No,' Howie said.

'And why is that?' Fiona asked.

On the prosecution side of the battlefield, Crowe's radar sprang to life, picking up danger signals to which he was swift to react. But not swift enough. Before he could rise to his feet, the answer to defence counsel's question was already out and in front of the jury.

'I had a vasectomy after the twins were born.'

Fiona Faye pivoted on a stiletto and addressed the judge while Cameron Crowe sank slowly back into his chair, looking like the drink-driver who goes to bed happy, believing he's got away with it, only to wake in the morning and find a dead pensioner on the bonnet of his car.

'I think my learned friend might appreciate a short adjournment,' she said.

48

Dead horses and the flogging of them was something of a specialité de la maison for Cameron Crowe, and yet even he couldn't raise a whip to the deceased nag of a Crown case that had collapsed at his feet.

How could he possibly go to the jury with the unchallenged evidence that the sperm found on the swabs taken from young Miss Ruby Maguire, the Mormon virgin bride-to-be, could not possibly have belonged to the blank-firing accused?

The Crown's motion for an interlude was granted. Howie was taken to a cell in the basement and his wife sent home to find her husband's vasectomy certificate. Meantime prosecution and defence had a joint telephone conference with Professor Edward Bradley. The forensic pathologist confirmed that the purpose of a vasectomy was to avoid the release of sperm, yes, even one or two because that's all it took. If the accused's vasectomy had been certified successful, the Crown would have to look elsewhere for the person who'd deposited the sperm.

I thought that was that, until one of the prosecution team mentioned something about naturally reversing vasectomies. This developed into a further discussion and a longish delay while a small glass jar was sent down to the cells and we waited for a man with a white coat and a large microscope to arrive.

It was well after lunch before the first concrete signs of capitulation. I noticed the Crown team was no longer referring to young Ruby as the victim, but, rather, the complainer, and a short time later she was taken along with her parents and boyfriend, all of whom had been sitting in court watching proceedings, to a witness room for a chat with the advocate depute and a female PF.

The defence team was standing in the corridor at the end furthest from the witness room when Crowe emerged minus the complainer or his female colleague, but accompanied by the sound of wailing from within.

'We're no longer seeking a conviction,' he said, calmly, as though he'd decided against a bottle of Sangiovese with his veal cutlets that evening and was going to opt for plain old Chianti instead.

'That's it?' Joanna asked.

'We'll ask the judge to have the jury formally return a verdict of not guilty,' he said, and turned to leave.

Joanna wasn't finished. She strode down the corridor towards him. 'What did she say to you in there?'

'That's confidential.' Crowe closed the door to the witness room to dampen the sound of tears.

'She nearly had that man sent down for six years!' I'd never seen Joanna this angry before, not even when she'd belted the Bulldog.

'She's a child,' Crowe said. 'That makes it complicated.'

What constituted a child in Scotland was certainly complicated. A sixteen-year-old like Ruby Maguire could join the Army, but not drive, was old enough to vote for Guy Fawkes if he stood as her local MSP, but not to buy fireworks. She could have sex so long as she didn't smoke

278

a cigarette afterwards, and if she sent her boyfriend a naked-selfie, they'd both end up on the sex register, she for distributing child-porn and he for possessing it. Yes, complicated summed up a criminal justice system that prosecuted you as an adult, but treated your photograph as a child.

'What's complicated about perjury?' Joanna asked.

'Look,' Crowe said, 'we've spoken to her, asked her to be honest with us and she's admitted having made a terrible mistake.'

'Mistake?' Joanna almost choked on the word.

Crowe's mockery of a smile revealed no teeth. 'When we spoke to her just now, she wasn't under caution so we can't possibly prosecute.' He could be magnanimous when it coincided with Crown Office policy. 'Your client should be happy he's getting off.'

'How can he get *off* with a crime he didn't commit?'

'Let it go, Jo.' Fiona put an arm around Joanna's shoulders. Having once served as one of his deputes, the QC was only too familiar with the surreal world inhabited by the Lord Advocate. If it was Scottish Government policy to convict more rapists, even if it meant diluting the law and rules of evidence that had stood for centuries, it wouldn't do to advertise that sometimes women made false allegations.

Joanna shrugged her off. 'No, I'm not letting it go. I think my client and his wife deserve to hear the girl's story, given that it will never be heard in court.'

Fiona looked at Crowe. 'Actually, Cameron, I think we'd all be interested in knowing what happened.'

Personally, in my book, a not guilty was a not guilty whichever way you cut it. I was keener on heading back to Linlithgow to start turning my office upside down in the search for Billy Paris's missing evidence.

The prosecutor sighed. 'Very well, but this better go no further.' He cleared his throat. 'It seems that, while the boyfriend was working offshore, Miss Maguire was at a party and had a little too much to drink. She met some boy and they well... I don't have to paint you a picture. When she woke in the early hours and realised what had happened she thought she might be pregnant or that in some other way her boyfriend would find out she was no longer...' He gave a little cough, cleared his throat. 'She's actually not all that bright—'

'Bright enough to pin the blame on my client,' Joanna said.

Crowe bared his teeth at Joanna. 'Quite.' He turned to Fiona. 'We'll bring the judge on in five minutes and put this whole sorry mess to bed.'

'So to speak,' Fiona said, but her adversary was already floating off down the corridor in the direction of Courtroom 4.

'It's a disgrace,' Joanna said, watching him go.

'Never mind that wee trollop,' Fiona said. 'You should be thanking your lucky stars that we found out about the vasectomy before our man was convicted. Imagine if it had been discovered a few years into his sentence. Talk about inadequate legal representation? Did you never think of asking him?'

If Joanna looked pretty when she was angry, she looked absolutely stunning now. 'The man's been in my office half a dozen times! I've gone over the forensic reports with him... I don't know how often. We've talked about practically nothing other than sperm and sperm heads.

How was I supposed to know his dad never told him about the birds and the bees? Forgive me if I credited the client with an ounce of intelligence.'

'Best not too,' Fiona said. 'Not clients, and especially not men. But you're young. You'll learn.'

I wasn't quite sure how Joanna would take the QC's patronising tone, only that it was my painfully gained experience that quarrels between women never ended well for any man who sought to intervene. The two of them could hammer it out like schoolgirls in a playground if they wanted. Me? My sensible and mature decision was to make a tactical withdrawal, return to the courtroom and, while awaiting the formal verdict from the jury, gloat like a schoolboy across the table at Cameron Crowe.

49

There are a great number of shocking things one learns during a career as a defence lawyer. The one that comes as the biggest surprise is the ingratitude of clients.

Take Keith Howie. Here was a man charged with one of the most repulsive crimes known to the law of Scotland. A man who, thanks to a good accountant, and the need to support a wife and three children, had had his legal expenses paid by the State. A man whose lawyer had set aside a trip to one of Europe's most beautiful ski resorts just so she could see his trial through to conclusion. Whose lawyer had persuaded her boss to babysit his emotionally shaken spouse. A lawyer who had secured an acquittal that had sent him home for a Christmas in the bosom of his family, while she'd probably spend the big day eating a microwaved vegetarian meal off her knee in front of the telly. And what did this man give his lawyer to express his indebtedness? A limp handshake and a *thanks very much for all your help, Miss Jordan*, as though she'd given him a hand to hang up a few decorations in the front room.

'You don't have to be quite so melodramatic about it, Robbie,' Joanna said, as we rumbled our way back to Linlithgow on the four o'clock train. Neither of us had managed to find a seat and we were crammed into the compartment by the doors.

'I'm being perfectly rational,' I said. 'You can't buy a cup of coffee without being expected to leave a tip. Get someone off a rape charge and—'

'When did you last leave Sandy a tip?' Joanna asked, laughing. 'In fact when did you last pay for a coffee?'

'That's different. Sandy treats me like a savings scheme. He knows I'll square him up some time.'

'Or your dad will.'

'Either way he knows the money will come in. That client of ours…' I said, aware that other passengers might be listening. 'You save him from six years in the nick and what do you get? A handshake and a less than hearty thanks very much. That won't buy you much Christmas cheer.'

'The look of relief on his wife's face was all the thanks I needed,' Joanna said. 'And also, you have to see it from Mr How… from the client's point of view. He's been to hell and back. Through his eyes, me, you, Fiona, Cameron Crowe, we're all just part of the system. Why should he be grateful for being acquitted of a crime he didn't commit?'

Sometimes I worried about Joanna's objectivity. The knack of seeing things from both sides of an argument, was… well, there was something unlawyerly about it.

We were swept off the train at Linlithgow in an avalanche of returning shoppers and folk who'd knocked off early from work. It was a five-minute walk from there to the office. Joanna's car was parked en route, outside Sandy's. In the near distance I could see Grace-Mary bustling down the road towards us. Another worker who thought the Christmas holidays had come early.

'Can't stop,' she said, 'I've got to catch the butcher. Turkey emergency.' She showed me the palm of a furry

mitt. No, really, you don't want to know.' She was right
— I didn't. 'I've left you some phone messages. Your dad
called to say he's away late-night shopping in Glasgow
and then going to Malky's radio station for their drinks
party. He's staying overnight at your brother's and will be
back about lunchtime. I've to remind you about collecting
Tina tomorrow. Oh, and I confirmed our booking for the
Star & Garter. I've told them we'll be there at one thirty.
It's a bit later than planned, but that way you'll be able
to pick up Tina and bring her with you.'

I'd almost forgotten about the Munro & Co. Christmas
lunch, and almost, but not quite, about the twenty thousand pounds nestling in the inside breast pocket of my suit
jacket. I'd spent all day at the High Court. If I had Tina to
collect from the airport tomorrow, followed by the office
Christmas lunch, it wasn't leaving me much time to carry
out the root-and-branch search that I'd planned. I'd have
to start now. I wanted that second twenty-grand instalment almost as much as I didn't want a visit from Oleg.

News imparted, Grace-Mary hurtled off to save her
Christmas dinner.

'Is it too late for you to catch a flight out to the Alps?'
I asked Joanna as she searched in her handbag for her car
keys. 'The court diary's empty and I should be all right
dining with Grace-Mary alone. I've done it before and this
time I can ask Tina to chaperone if need be.'

'Are you kidding? Me miss the Munro & Co. Christmas
lunch just so I can slide down a hill on my backside?'

'What about Christmas Day? If your family's away, I
take it you'll be going to your boyfriend's?'

'Only if I can find one by then.'

Joanna didn't have a boyfriend? What kind of crazy

world was I living in? 'You're welcome to come to my dad's. I know Tina would love it. But I have to warn you, we will be eating dead things.'

Joanna laughed. 'No, I'll be fine.' She opened the car door and threw her handbag and satchel onto the passenger seat.

'What are you doing tonight?' I asked.

She looked at me. 'Tonight? Nothing. Why?'

'Care to work some unpaid overtime?'

Joanna retrieved her baggage and slammed the car door. 'Sure. Why not?'

50

By midnight we had emptied every single filing cabinet and searched every single case file. We had pulled the cabinets out from walls, looked down the back of them and combed through a disgusting mixture of dust, ooze, deceased insects and paperclips. After that had come the window blinds, then the pot of my desiccated umbrella plant in case something had been buried in the rock-hard soil. We had looked under the rug and behind the picture of Linlithgow Palace at sunset, painted for me by famous local artist Effie McIntyre and which hung on the wall behind my desk. Nothing.

The sleeves of her blouse rolled up, Joanna turned to the last remaining item of furniture: my desk.

'I've already searched it,' I said.

'And now we're going to search it again. Properly, this time.'

We started off with the desktop and everything lying on it: case files, mail trays, the angle-poise lamp, the box of tissues reserved for tearful clients; and from there moved onto the drawers. There were six of them, three down either side. They took us the best part of an hour to go through, taking them out, emptying the contents on the floor and sifting through them like a couple of Klondikers panning for gold. We found things I'd thought were lost, things I didn't know I'd lost and things that I didn't know I even owned. What we didn't find was any sign of Billy Paris's missing evidence.

Joanna closed the final drawer and dropped into my chair. 'Did he go to the toilet when he was here?'

Not that I could remember; nonetheless, I searched in there as well, inside the wee white medicine cabinet, under the basin, down the back of the loo and inside the cistern. I met Joanna as I came out drying my hands on some paper towels. 'Zilch.'

'Same here,' she said. 'I've just had a good look through the waiting room.'

That only left reception, where Billy might have passed through fleetingly when he called at the office to see me that Friday afternoon at the beginning of December.

'And there's Grace-Mary's room,' Joanna said.

I doubted it. Grace-Mary's inner sanctum where she did the cashroom work was always kept locked unless she was in it.

'It's too late now,' I said. 'I'll come in first thing before I go for Tina and do both rooms.'

It was after one when I locked up and walked with Joanna down the stairs and though the close, lit only by the orange glow of the sodium security light.

'It's really bugging you, isn't it?' she said at the door to the High Street.

'You wouldn't believe how much.'

'Let it go. Your daughter's coming home tomorrow. Christmas is around the corner. Have some fun.'

I smiled and nodded in fake agreement. How could I possibly let all that money go when come the New Year I'd be struggling to keep my business afloat? What if I

287

didn't find the evidence? What if Thorn's second payment slipped through my fingers and Oleg the Russian returned to remove the first instalment and my kneecaps with it?

Joanna read my mind. 'The New Year will take care of itself. We'll get by.'

We? Would there be a 'we'? With no legal aid money, I'd have to seriously cut my overheads for a start. Take on fewer cases. Be more selective in whom I acted for, namely, only those who could afford to pay. If the poor wanted access to justice they'd have to go somewhere else, to someone whose paper-pushing skills were better honed than my own. Yes, I probably could get by, but there'd be no room for Joanna.

We stepped out onto the pavement. It had been raining and the frost had turned the walkway into an ice-rink. Joanna slipped. I grabbed her and as she steadied herself I gazed into those beautiful dark eyes. Was this what was really worrying me? That I would lose Joanna?

'Watch your step.' My attempt at a light-hearted laugh was more of a croak.

'I don't think I really gave you the credit for today's result,' she said, as still with a grip on my arm she let me guide her down the High Street towards Sandy's café and our cars. 'When you came charging into court at the end of the Crown's cross-examination, I thought "here we go", and could have strangled you. Then when I heard you tell Fiona about Keith Howie's vasectomy, I could have kissed you.'

I stopped, took Joanna's other arm and gently turned her to face me. 'Really? Then why don't you?'

She smiled. 'Strangle you?'

'No,' I said. 'Kiss me.'

51

'That was highly unprofessional of us,' I said, waking up in the darkness of Christmas Eve's eve, an arm around Joanna to stop her falling out of my single bed.

'I wouldn't say that,' she said sleepily. 'It was definitely better than amateur.'

I switched on the bedside lamp and sat up, looking around at a floor covered in scattered clothes. 'We're work colleagues. This isn't how we're supposed to behave.' I was hearing myself talk and at the same time wishing I'd shut up about it. 'In fact, it's worse. I'm your employer. I should never have allowed that to happen.'

'Allowed?' Joanna budged me over with a shove of the shoulder so that she could sit up too and share some of the pillow. 'Would you feel better if I lodged a formal grievance?'

'You know what I mean,' I said. 'How are we supposed to work together if—'

'Oh, stop worrying.' She kissed me on the cheek. 'These things happen. It couldn't be helped.' She made it sound like it had all been a minor mishap. Like we'd bumped into each other, our clothes had dropped off and we'd accidentally fallen between the sheets.

Joanna jumped out of bed and disappeared through to the bathroom. When she returned a few minutes later she had on my dad's enormous Paisley-pattern dressing gown that could have contained her and a family of asylum seekers. She walked to the window and threw the curtains open. No effect. Scotland in winter, the sun only made guest appearances during the day and certainly not at seven in the morning. She switched on the big light. The glare was painful and I had to shield my eyes and squint to see her.

'Right,' she said. 'I'm hitting the shower. That'll give you time to decide which white shirt you're wearing today.' She picked up my suit trousers from the floor, gave them a shake in the hope it might smooth out some of the creases, and then draped them over the back of a chair.

'Joanna, I'm sorry about what happened.'

'Sorry?'

'I'm not sorry it happened.'

'I thought you just said you were.'

'I'm not. I just think it was a bad idea.'

'Do you?'

I didn't. As ideas went, sleeping with Joanna was probably the best idea I'd ever come up with. 'What I'm trying to say is that this could make things awkward at work.'

Joanna came to the side of the bed and frowned down at me. 'So, this was a one-off?'

'I never said that.'

'Good.'

'But it has to be.'

She sat on the edge of the bed. 'And why's that?'

'Because… well there's our ages for one thing. I'm eight—'

'Seven and a half—'

290

'Years older than you. My business is going down the tubes. I'm a single parent. I don't even have a house of my own. I live with my dad.'

'There you are, then. At least you know I don't want you for your money.' She picked my jacket from the floor and gave it a similar crease-loosening shake. Two wads of cash fell out and onto the floor by her bare feet. She picked them up. 'Scratch that last remark. How much is here?'

'I can explain.'

Joanna tossed the bundles of notes onto the bed. 'I think you'd better.'

52

'What were you two up to last night?' were Grace-Mary's first words as Joanna and I arrived at the office to resume the great search.

If guilty looks were evidence, Grace-Mary could have hanged me on the spot. Fortunately, she was too busy staring at the mess created the evening before.

'You should have known if Robbie was putting that much effort into finding something, it would have had less to do with solving a crime and more to do with money,' Grace-Mary said, once Joanna had provided a summary of events so far in the who-killed-Jeremy-Thorn saga.

'I'm trying to run a business here,' I said. 'Santa Claus doesn't pay the salaries.'

'I notice he doesn't pay a Christmas bonus either,' Grace-Mary said.

'Find this thing and there might be a New Year bonus.'

'In which case,' with a bang of her hip, Grace-Mary straightened up her desk, 'I'll start looking for whatever it is, after the holidays. There's no time today. You've got your daughter to pick up and then there's lunch.' She pointed a finger at me. 'And we *are* having lunch together this year. No skipping off to court like last Christmas because one of your clients was caught shoplifting.'

'It was armed robbery of a Post Office.'

'Leaving me sitting there on my own like—'

'The last turkey in Tesco's?'

Grace-Mary narrowed her eyes at me. 'Like a bride at the altar.'

Joanna put an arm around Grace-Mary, and, with me following, led her through to reception. 'Don't worry. We're all going for lunch.'

'But before we do,' I said, 'we're going to turn reception upside down and if we don't find what we're looking for there, your room will be next, Grace-Mary. So the sooner we get started, the sooner we'll be wearing party hats and pulling crackers.'

Two hours later and the only thing I'd pulled was a muscle in my shoulder, trying to shift a filing cabinet. At noon I gave up. Whatever it was, it wasn't on the premises. It couldn't be. There was nowhere left to look. The thing we were trying to find probably wasn't that big, but then neither were the offices of R.A. Munro & Co. and I'd been all over them. Twice. I'd even checked inside the swear-box. I didn't understand. My mind kept going back to the cardboard box Billy had left with me that Friday afternoon.

'You'd better get going,' Grace-Mary said. 'Tina's plane lands in half an hour.'

I grabbed my keys. 'Keep looking and phone me if you find anything.'

I jogged down the stairs, thinking about that cardboard box. Had it been a red herring designed to put the cops off the trail? Why else pay me two hundred pounds to keep a box with contents that were worth a fraction of that?

Once in my car I phoned DI Christchurch. He answered almost immediately. 'Mr Munro? Do you have something for me?'

293

I started the engine. 'I'm phoning to ask you the same question.'

'Are you driving while using a phone? I hope you're hands-free.'

'Yeah, I am,' I said, 'I'm steering with my knees. Now listen. The cardboard box. Did you find anything?'

'That's classified.'

I pulled out into traffic, phone clamped between ear and shoulder. 'You must have found something, then?'

'What makes you say that?'

'Because how can nothing be classified? I can understand how *something* can be classified, but—'

'All right, I get it. No, we found nothing of interest in the box.'

'Are you sure you've looked properly?'

'I'm entirely sure. It's been at the forensic labs for the last ten days.'

'Well, if it's not there, it's gone,' I said. 'Either that or it never existed, because I've just spent the last two days blitzing my office and there is no way there can be anything of interest to you there.'

'Really? Then what would you say if I sent a team round just to make sure?'

'I've just told you, I've already turned my office inside out.'

'With respect, Mr Munro, I'm talking about people who really know how to search.'

He made it sound as though I'd have trouble finding my backside with both hands and a mirror on a stick. 'How many are there on your search team?'

'Six, maybe eight, highly trained operatives.'

'Are they tidy or do they have the same furniture-hurling technique as DC Wood?'

'You'll never know they've been.'

'Then it could happen,' I said, hurtling down the Blackness Road towards the motorway. 'On one condition.'

'And that would be?'

'Whatever you find, you give to me.'

'That's one hell of a condition.'

'Whatever it is, you can take a copy but it's my client's property, remember?'

'Yes, it's your deceased client's property. Your deceased client with no next-of-kin.'

'And...'

'There's a second condition?'

'It's an addendum to the first. I want six hours' complete radio silence on what is found.' That would be long enough for me to fulfil my contract with Philip Thorn.

There was a lengthy pause on the line while Christchurch thought that over. I switched the phone to my other shoulder.

'You're going to sell it, aren't you?' He was good. 'You're going to sell it to that woman from Night News.' He wasn't that good.

'If you agree to my terms, I promise I will not release the information to any media outlet or otherwise cause it to be published.'

There followed another long silence while the Detective Inspector considered his options. 'Tomorrow morning,' he said at last. 'Ten o'clock, sharp.'

The phone slipped from my shoulder and down the side of the seat. By the time I'd retrieved it, Christchurch was gone.

53

She'd only been away a week and yet I'd missed my daughter so much. The girl herself was fairly blasé about the reconciliation with her old man, though she did have a lot to tell me and used the journey back to Linlithgow to relay her entire trip, paying great attention to detail.

Tina's one regret was the absence of Pyxie Girl at Disneyland, and, rather than try and explain the intricacies of TV franchising and intellectual property rights, I explained that PG was on holiday until the New Year.

My dad phoned as we were eastbound on the M9. I wasn't taking any calls while transporting so precious a cargo and so Tina extracted the phone from my coat pocket and the two of them kept blethering until I pulled onto the pavement and into my usual parking space outside Sandy's.

'The bairn sounds in fine fettle,' my dad said, once I'd wrestled the phone from Tina's grip.

'Yeah, she's had a good time. I'm taking her to the Munro & Co. Christmas lunch. Have a good night at Malky's Christmas do, did you?'

He took a moment before replying. 'Free bar.' Two words that for most Scotsmen translated, twelve hours later, into one: hangover. I arranged to meet him later back at the cottage, and, since we'd made good time, Tina and I walked along to the office where Grace-Mary was making some last minute adjustments to her hair in the toilet mirror.

'I don't know who you think is going to type that,' she shouted through to Joanna, whose voice I could hear dictating an urgent letter. 'This is me 'til the third of January.'

There then followed heated talks between the two which I neatly avoided by way of a detour into my room. I plonked my wee girl down onto the clients' wooden chair, legs swinging, while I reclined in my big black leather one. Joanna walked in. She'd changed into a clingy black dress and her hair was different somehow. More *up* than it had been before.

'Is Tina not back from Disneyland, yet?' she asked, looking around everywhere except on the very chair on which my daughter was seated.

'I'm here!' Tina yelled, jumping off the chair and giving Joanna a hug.

Joanna held her at arm's length. 'Is that you? Look how much you've grown in a week! I thought you were one of your dad's clients, sitting up there on the big chair. Are you ready? Grace-Mary's just finishing off a letter for me and then we're off for lunch.'

Joanna perched on the edge of my desk while Tina climbed back onto the wooden chair, kneeling, facing the wrong way and rocking backwards and forwards.

'Tina?' I said, calmly. She didn't reply. I tried again, this time with an edge to my voice as the rocking became more extreme. 'Tina?' She must have heard me. Was this some kind of test? 'Tina, would you please stop swinging on the chair?'

She looked at me over her shoulder. 'No,' she said, her wee face fixed in a scowl. There was no denying whose granddaughter she was. 'I like swinging.'

I got up from my seat as Joanna came to my assistance. 'Tina, do as your Dad says. You might fall off and hurt yourself.'

'I'm not going to fall off.'

The chair pivoted backwards. For a second it stayed perfectly balanced and then with a creak and a loud crack it began to topple. I reached out, grabbed my daughter's arm and pulled her away as the chair crashed to the floor.

Tina found the whole thing hugely amusing, as apparently did Joanna although she was doing her best not to show it, covering her mouth with a hand.

I had no idea what to do now. I couldn't smack my own wee girl, neither did I want to shout and make her cry again, but I was her dad, and she'd disobeyed me. What was I supposed to do? I glanced at Joanna. She shrugged helplessly. I stalled, directing my attention to the chair that was now lying with its back and arms resting on the floor, four legs pointing upwards, one of them at a strange angle.

'Yuk!' said Tina. 'What's that?'

I looked closer. There was something in a corner of the underside of the seat. What was it? I prodded the blob with the AIDS pen Grace-Mary kept handy for junkies to sign their legal aid forms. The pen sank deep into the grey mass.

'It's chewing gum,' Joanna said. 'A great big blob of chewing gum.'

I tugged a bunch of tissues from the box, took a grip of

298

the blob and pulled. Strings of grey bridged between my hand and the base of the chair.

'Yuk, it's all germy,' Tina said, face screwed up.

I wrapped the gum in the tissue and shoved the lot in my jacket pocket.

'What are you doing with it, Dad?'

'I'm going to sell it,' I said. 'But first we're all going for lunch.'

54

The Munro & Co. Christmas lunch turned out to be a fairly lavish affair. It helped when the boss had twenty thousand pounds in cash stuffed in a shoebox under his bed and the means to acquire twenty thousand more wrapped in a bunch of Kleenex nestling in his suit pocket.

Around about four o'clock I dropped a slightly tiddly secretary off at her home and took Tina to the cottage where my dad was waiting for her.

Back at the office Joanna was waiting for me. I retrieved the sticky wad of gum and, using the tissues, carefully peeled it back to reveal a small, black rectangular object. It was plastic, no more than two centimetres long, one centimetre wide, and a couple of millimetres thick. A neat piece of IT equipment and IT was something I left to others when at all possible.

Joanna took it from me gingerly, using the fingernails of thumb and middle finger. She studied it carefully, cleaning it with the tissue. 'Sixteen gig nano-USB memory card,' she said. 'You can buy these anywhere for a few pounds.' She examined it some more and, when satisfied the terminals were sufficiently gum-free, slotted it into a port and switched on my PC.

The computer took an age to boot up. Eventually it was up and running and Joanna went to work while I paced my room like an expectant father, every now and again asking her for an update. Whether it was excitement or three ginger beers and a coffee, I had to go to the toilet. On my return, Joanna was staring at the computer screen, an annoyed look on her face. She lifted the mouse an inch or two off the desk and slammed it down on the mat. 'It's no good. It won't work.'

I came around the back of the chair and leaned over her shoulder. 'What do you mean, won't work?' I could sense she was counting to ten before answering. 'Okay, I know what "won't work" means. Have you any idea why not?'

She leaned down and ejected the USB. 'All I know is that it's got some kind of video file on it, about eleven gigs' worth. Unfortunately, it won't run on this PC. I've searched the internet and can't find the right codec to download. It must be some kind of proprietary brand.'

I pursed my lips and nodded. 'I see. Just one question... Do you think we could go back to where I asked why it won't work?'

Joanna stood up and handed me the piece of black plastic. 'It's not broken. It's just that the video won't play without the correct software.'

'Maybe it's for the best,' I said. 'This has to be what Philip Thorn wants. I'll take it to him, get paid and he can do what he wants with it.'

'And it won't matter if it doesn't work?'

'Thorn's got enough money to pay people to make it work.'

'Don't you think maybe you should...?'

'Give it to the police? What if it contains evidence that implicates Billy Paris?'

'There's no conflict of interest. He's dead.'

301

'But what if—'

'Stop trying to think up excuses, Robbie. Decide what it is you want the most, the gratitude of the government or hard cash.'

I knew where Joanna was placing her bet. That's when I remembered my agreement with DI Christchurch who, accompanied by a team of expert searchers, was due to invade my office on Christmas Eve morning. I tossed the USB stick in the air and caught it again. 'Why can't I have both?'

55

'Because we have an arrangement. That's why not.' Philip Thorn wasn't keen on my have-cake, eat-cake suggestion. 'The deal was you give me the evidence and I give you the rest of the money. Remember?' he said, speaking slowly and clearly as though my IQ was a minus figure.

'What's so bad about the police having it six hours after you?'

'Speak up, the line is terrible.'

I wandered to the other side of my room. It was dark outside, had been for hours. Gusts of wind shook the window frames, rain spattered against the glass. All I could see in the glow of the fluorescent strip light was my own streaky reflection and Joanna, a shadow in the background, her black dress merging with the leather chair. 'I said, why can't I give it to the police a few hours after I've given it to you? I could leave it a couple of days if you like. That would give you time to...' What was he going to do with it anyway? 'I don't even need to tell the cops you have it. That information could be kept in strictest confidence.'

'Mr Munro, you either give the video file to me exclusively or we no longer have a deal, in which case I'd expect my money back.'

I'd been afraid he might say something like that.

'I don't really understand your difficulty,' he continued. 'You tell me it's a video file, but you say you haven't been able to view it. Therefore, you don't know what evidence it contains. Correct?'

'Billy Paris left it with me, so I'm pretty sure—'

'But you don't know for certain, do you? For all you know it might show nothing at all.'

It was certainly possible, and, yet, Billy had been sure enough that what he'd stuck to the bottom of my chair was worth a great deal of money to somebody. If it wasn't proof of the identity of the person who'd sabotaged the helicopter, what else could it be?

'There is no reason why you need to help the police at all.' Thorn was unrelenting in his speech to the hard-of-thinking. 'If you don't know what you have, how can you possibly be under any moral or legal obligation to hand it over to the authorities? After all, the Government could very well be implicated. A lot of people seem to think it is.' If he pushed any harder on the swing door that was the Robbie Munro conscience, he'd fall flat on his face. 'In any event, I happen to believe that what you have in your possession is my property, so if you don't hand it over to me it would be tantamount to theft.'

It was certainly a persuasive argument, then again, persuading me not to hand over something to the police, in exchange for a tax-free lump sum, had to be one of life's easier arguments to make. 'Okay,' I said, 'where are you?'

He was in Aberdeen trying to sell St Edzell Bay Airport to a company providing offshore helicopter transportation services to the oil industry. It wouldn't go for Spaceport prices, but at least it would net Philip Thorn a few quid. It seemed the race for space had been won by Kirkton Perch and his Ayrshire constituents.

'It's nearly six o'clock now,' he said. 'Let me see... I've still one or two things to clear up here. I can meet you at St Edzell, say, the back of nine tonight. How would that suit?'

It suited fine. If I put the boot down I could do the round trip and be home by midnight.

'You could do it even quicker if you took my car,' Joanna said. She dangled the key to her car at me. 'That vehicle of yours is just a series of rust spots flying in close formation. It'll probably break down halfway.' Another person who had no trouble persuading me to do something. 'And when I see you next, I want you to have made your mind up about us and where we go from here.'

Why put the onus on me? I thought I'd left the ball firmly in Joanna's court. Hadn't she been listening to my single-parent, failing-business, living-with-my-dad speech that morning? We swapped car keys. Unsure how exactly I should go about leaving, I gave her a peck on the cheek. As I began to walk away, she grabbed me by the lapels, pulled me to her. 'For luck,' she said and kissed me hard on the lips. 'See you later. Unless you damage my car, that is. In which case, don't bother coming back,' she laughed and then stopped. 'I mean it, Robbie, when you get back we've got a lot of things to talk about. Or, if you prefer, we can talk now.'

Meaningful relationship talks with women seldom went well for me. Past performance was not necessarily indicative of future results, but like the weather I couldn't see how the forecast was going to improve any time soon. I suggested it would be better if we held discussions at

305

a time when I wasn't working to such a tight schedule. Joanna agreed it was best. Another thing I was right about was the weather. When I crossed the Forth into Fife, the snow was starting to fall. At Perth the snowploughs were cutting about on the M90 and by Dundee, with a good forty miles still to go, I could hardly see the road ahead. The rapid deterioration in conditions meant that I didn't reach St Edzell Bay Airport until around ten o'clock, where by some means or other they'd managed to clear the final stretch of service road leading to the security barrier. This time the small glass hut was occupied by a youth reading the Press & Journal. He was swathed in layer upon layer of winter clothing, a woolly hat pulled down, almost meeting the Burberry scarf that was wrapped around his neck and across his nose and mouth. He didn't bother coming out to see who I was, forcing me to leave the warmth of the car and go up to the window. When I knocked he opened it an inch or two and gave me a muffled greeting.

'Robbie Munro. I've got an appointment to see Philip Thorn,' I said, shouting to be heard, the wind slapping my cheeks.

He pulled the scarf away from his face just enough to make his mouth work. 'He's not here.'

'Where is he?' I hadn't bothered with a coat and the tail of my suit jacket was flapping like a seagull in a hurricane. 'He told me he was on his way down from Aberdeen to meet me. He was supposed to be here at nine o'clock.'

His scarf back in place, the youth found it easier to raise his hands in a what-can-I-do? gesture than speak.

From the direction of the control tower and main building, a pair of headlights shone through the curtain of white. A golf buggy with a four-inch cushion of snow on its roof sailed across a sea of snow towards me and pulled up at the barrier. Oleg jumped out, marched over to the door to the glass hut and yanked it open. Like me he had no coat on. Unlike me he seemed impervious to the freezing conditions. 'Frankie! Have cleared this area of snow immediately!' he bellowed, and the young man leapt from his seat. Oleg turned to me, shook my hand and gestured to the buggy. 'Please. Come.'

I climbed in beside him and together we trundled off through the snow, down to the main building. After kicking the slush from our shoes, we ascended to the same small room I had visited previously, the gloom illuminated by banks of CCTV monitors and the single bar of a portable electric fire glowing orange in one of the corners.

'Mr Thorn is not here,' Oleg said. He let me have the only seat and leaned himself against the metal desk where a mug of coffee steamed gently. 'You want coffee?' He picked up the mug and drank from it.

I declined. 'When is he going to be back?'

Oleg shrugged. 'In the morning. Maybe. The A90 north is closed at Stonehaven. No traffic moving on it for nearly two hours now. I am stranded too. I cannot go home.'

'Can you phone him?'

'There is no need. Give what it is you have to me and I will make certain he gets it.'

I wasn't sure about this change of plan. 'I'd need to speak to Mr Thorn first. He's got some money for me.'

The door was slightly ajar. Making an unconvincing show of hugging himself and slapping his body, Oleg walked over and closed it firmly. 'Very cold tonight.' He came over to where I was sitting and held out the flat of a hand the size of a snow shovel. 'Give it to me and you can have money later.'

I stood up. Our faces were only inches apart. 'Get Mr Thorn on the satellite phone or I'm leaving.'

Oleg held my stare and then abruptly turned away. With a screech of metal he yanked open the desk drawer and removed the phone.

'You know who killed Jerry?' he asked, punching buttons.

'Haven't a clue.'

'You are Billy's lawyer?'

'I *was* Billy's lawyer. Billy's dead.'

'But he tell you who killed Jerry and his girl, yes?'

'No,' I said. 'He didn't.'

He handed me the phone. I put it to my ear, eyes fixed on the Russian.

'Oleg?'

'No, Mr Thorn, it's me, Robbie Munro. I'm here at St Edzell Bay. I gather you've had some travel problems.'

'I'm not far away, stuck in a snowdrift. I'm waiting for a recovery vehicle. But never mind that. Have you got it with you? Good,' he said, after I'd replied in the affirmative. 'I do not want you to give what you have to Oleg, understand? Take an envelope. If you are in the main building, there should be plenty lying around. Place what you have inside and seal it. Then I want you to go to the VIP guest lounge. Oleg will take you there. Behind the bar is a hidden safe. The combination is forty-three, twenty-two, thirty-six. You will find your money inside. Leave the envelope, close the safe and go.'

'That's very trusting of you,' I said.

'There is no reason why I shouldn't trust you. We are

308

both businessmen and this is a business deal. You have what I want, and I have what you want. It's a fair swap.'

A business deal. That sounded so much better than concealing evidence from the authorities.

'Oh,' Thorn added. 'But if I have misplaced my trust, Oleg is ex-KGB. I will have him find you. Find you and do cruel and horrible things to you.'

56

The man I was confident would not require to do anything cruel or horrible to me, led me out of the main building and down a small path to the prefabricated structure where I'd been a few days before. The heating was on just enough to avoid frozen pipes, but it was a lot warmer than outside where the snowfall had become a skin-tearing icy sleet. He flicked the electricity switch, the lights came on and the hot air system began to hum.

'What is it that Mr Thorn say?' he asked.

'I've to open the safe, put what I've brought with me inside and take my money,' I said. 'After that I've got a long drive home.'

I raised the flap in the counter and slipped behind the small bar. It took me some time to find the safe, concealed as it was behind a false front of shallow shelves on which sat miniatures of vodka, gin and malt whisky. I pulled it open to reveal a squat dark-grey safe, bolted to the concrete floor.

'You want vodka make you warm?' Oleg asked. I thought what I had to do was best done with a clear head and so rejected the offer of alcohol and hunkered down in front of the safe. The dial was black with white numbers from zero to ninety marked out in fives. In between the numbers were white lines. I turned the dial left to forty-five and clicked it once more. Forty-six.

310

Oleg came around the counter and stared down at me. 'What is it you have?'

I really wished he'd stop asking questions. 'I've got what Billy Paris gave to me. Mr Thorn says it belongs to him and so I am giving it back.'

'You are giving it back for money?'

'It wasn't easy to find.' I had no more to say. If Philip Thorn didn't trust the airport's own head of security, he had to have a reason. I wasn't about to risk twenty thousand pounds finding out what that was.

I pushed his leg, forcing him to step back and let some light in so that I could see the notches on the dial more clearly, cupping my hand around it so that he couldn't.

Right, twenty-two. Left thirty-six. The combination worked. I hauled the door open. Inside was a canvas bag, some papers and several blocks of money similar to those I'd been given in Holyrood Park. First things first, I slipped a chunk of cash into each of my jacket's two outside pockets. Then I reached into an inside pocket and removed the white A5 envelope stamped with a TAS logo into which I'd already placed the USB stick. I laid the envelope on top of the remaining stacks of notes and was swinging the door closed when Oleg lifted a foot and shoved me with the sole of it sending me sprawling.

I jumped to my feet. Oleg took a step forward. So did I. He pushed me aside, knelt and removed the envelope.

'Put it back,' I said.

He didn't. He ripped the corner off the envelope and emptied the tiny black memory card into the palm of his hand.

'I go look at this,' was all he said, before turning and walking through the gap in the counter.

311

'You're wasting your time. You won't get the file to open. I've tried. It's encrypted or something,' I called after him.

'It will work here,' he replied, not looking back, striding for the door.

It was amazing how a surge of adrenalin helped concentrate the mind. If the USB stick did indeed contain the evidence of who killed Jeremy Thorn, I realised that up until that moment I had not included Oleg in my otherwise limited list of possible suspects. How could I have overlooked him? As head of security, the Russian could access all areas of the airport at all times and raise no suspicions. Why was he even here tonight? I thought he didn't work nights? And who'd ever heard of a Russian getting stuck in the snow?

If the evidence did implicate Oleg, all he had to do was destroy it and say I'd never brought it with me. Thorn would be none the wiser and simply assume I'd tried to rip him off. I had to think. What were my options? Leave the money and go? The go part of that was an attractive proposition, not so much the part where I left the money behind. No, I had to persuade the Russian to return the USB to the safe and lock it up just as his boss had ordered. I darted after Oleg, overtaking him as he reached the door. 'Look, be reasonable about this and put the envelope back,' I said as calmly as possible.

Oleg wasn't to be so easily persuaded. I discovered that a split-second after he'd propelled the heel of one of his iron hands into my solar plexus. I staggered, thumping my back off the door. He grabbed me and threw me aside. I bounced off the pool table and landed on the floor, chest heaving, sucking in great sobs of air. The Russian had gone, slamming the door behind him, before I could drag myself to my feet. I looked around and found a rack of pool cues on the wall. I grabbed one and broke it across my knee. Holding the heavy half by the jaggy end, I opened the door and stared out at the snow-covered path leading down to the picket fence. Beyond it Oleg marched purposefully onwards, his feet leaving deep gouges behind as he went. I hefted the broken half of the pool cue, slapped it into the palm of my hand, took a few deep breaths and followed in his snowy footsteps.

I hadn't taken more than a few paces when I heard a bleeping. The phone behind the bar. It might have been that noise in the silence that brought me to my senses. Why did I care who killed Jeremy Thorn? I'd never known him. He'd lived, loved, crashed and died before I even knew he existed. Did Billy Paris sabotage his helicopter? Did he do it on the instructions of Kirkton Perch as part of some political conspiracy to land a spaceport at Prestwick? Or was it Oleg? And, if it was, what could I realistically do about it? Fight the Russian, wrest the evidence from him? Me against the ex-KGB man? He'd probably take the thick end of the pool cue, shove it somewhere it fitted snuggly, roll me in the snow and make the world's biggest ice-lolly.

What was I thinking? I had a daughter waiting at home for me, a beautiful woman who for some reason seemed to think I was playing hard to get and twenty grand in readies on my hip with the same again stashed under my bed. Why should I care if multi-millionaire Philip Thorn did think I'd ripped him off? Let him send Oleg to find me if he liked. I knew people who for a lot less than forty grand would find the Russian for me long before he found

West Lothian, far less Linlithgow, far less my chimney.

I threw the broken pool cue away. With the adrenalin draining from my system like anti-freeze from a leaky radiator, I started to feel the cold again as I set off for the shelter of Joanna's car and a treacherous drive home.

As I approached the security barrier, the miniature full moon of a torch shone my way, the beam swinging from side to side. The young security guard shone the light in my face, hooking a finger over the edge of his scarf and pulling it down to his chin. 'You leaving? Where's Oleg? I'm just after trying to get him on the phone.' The young man tapped the satellite phone tucked inside a leather holster that was strapped to his belt. 'Mr Thorn called to say he'll be here in a couple of minutes. He got his roadster stuck. Rear-wheel drive. Murder in this weather. Council had to pull him out. Come on, I'll take you back to the VIP lounge. You'll freeze to death out here.'

'No thanks,' I said. If I was going to meet with Thorn after all, I wanted to catch him as soon as he arrived. 'I'll wait in my car.' I'd hardly finished my sentence when a red, snow-topped, E-Type came skidding to a halt alongside Joanna's Merc, and Philip Thorn alighted wearing a heavy coat, a white scarf and a furry hat with ear flaps that would have brought back memories of home to Oleg. I met him at the barrier as he walked through with a regal salute to the young security guard who had now been joined by a familiarly bulky shape in a hi-vis vest. Homer's face was bright red and his hands shook as they clasped a mug of something hot. I took it he'd been out on patrol. He gave me a stiff little wave when he saw me.

'Everything sorted?' Thorn asked. 'Good,' he said, not waiting for me to answer.

314

'Mr Thorn—'

'It's Philip. Come on, I'm frozen. You must be too. Let's go have something to heat us up.' His hand in the small of my back, he guided me down the central avenue. 'Envelope in the safe all right? I take it you've got your money?' He smiled. I wasn't sure why, but I didn't like that smile.

I stopped. 'You know, I've a long drive ahead of me and with this weather...'

'Nonsense.' Thorn slapped my back. 'Have something to warm you up before you go.' He pushed me forward with more hollow words of encouragement. A few yards away the stocky figure of Oleg materialised through the falling snow, silhouetted by the arc lights on the front of the main building.

'Mr Munro's going to have one for the road,' Thorn told him when we met outside the main building, and the three of us returned to the VIP lounge where Thorn squeezed behind the bar while Oleg and I drew up high stools on the other side of the counter. 'And you have still not managed to view the video file yet?' he said.

I hadn't, but I was fairly certain Oleg had, though, if I said as much I was sure the Russian would deny it. What should I say? It had been made very clear that the security guard was not to be given the video evidence.

Thorn set up two shot glasses and filled them to the brim with vodka. He pushed one towards me.

'I tried to play it,' I said, 'but couldn't get it to work. It seems it needs specific software to run.'

Thorn liked my reply. Lips pursed he nodded gently. 'Good. In that case...' He withdrew the shot of vodka he'd offered me. 'I think I'll have my money back. You can keep the first instalment.'

315

A few days ago during my discussions with Maggie Sinclair, five thousand, even three thousand pounds for delivering up Billy Paris and his evidence, had seemed like a good deal. Now I was feeling short-changed at the suggestion I take twenty thousand.

'The deal was forty,' I said.

'Well it's twenty now. Think yourself lucky.'

'What about the trust between two businessmen?'

In answer Thorn raised his hands to show me the shiny palms of his brown leather driving gloves. 'I'm afraid in business there is no such thing as trust, Mr Munro, only winners and losers. Now hand the money over.' He cocked his head at Oleg.

There was no need to involve the Russian. I pulled the two wads from my pockets and laid them on the counter. Thorn shoved the shot glass towards me again, lifted his own and drank. If drinking that Russian paint-stripper would end this sorry deal and see me back on the road to civilisation I was all for it. I picked up the shot glass, careful not to spill any, and tossed it down my throat.

Thorn stacked the two bundles of notes, one on top of the other, and squared them up. He stared at them hard for a moment and then, smiling, looked me straight in the eye. 'Oleg, I think we can say goodbye to Mr Munro now.' I felt the Russian's heavy hand on my shoulder. Thorn edged further along the bar, dipped down and swung open the safe door. 'Why isn't this locked?' He stood again, not smiling anymore, the canvas bag from the safe in his hand. 'Where is the envelope?'

What had Oleg done with the memory card? Was it him on that video file? Had he killed Thorn's son? Was that why he'd wanted it so much? If so, at that moment our interests might coincide. He wouldn't want to admit to having taken the USB. I could use that to my advantage.

'I didn't bring it,' I said. 'I didn't trust you and it looks like I was right. Give me my money as agreed and then I'll send the USB on.'

Thorn reached across the counter and grabbed me by the throat. 'Where is it?' he snarled.

I seized hold of his wrist and wrenched his hand away. I stepped back, bumping into Oleg.

From the canvas bag Thorn produced a compact semi-automatic pistol. Was it real or a replica? If in doubt always assume the former. 'Search him.'

Oleg didn't move.

'I said search him!'

Oleg stood rock-still for a second or two before very slowly reaching with two fingers into the breast pocket of his suit jacket and pulling out the tiny USB card. He placed it in the palm of his other hand and slapped it down onto the bar top.

Thorn lowered his gaze, placed a finger on the small plastic rectangle and then looked up at his head of security, the confused expression on the music mogul's face gradually morphing into one of tired resignation. Oleg's granite left hand clamped down on the hand holding the gun, pinning it to the countertop while with his right he straight-armed Thorn, sending him crashing into the rows of bottles and glasses on the shelves behind. I knew how it felt to be hit like that. It hurt. A lot. Thorn's legs folded. He hadn't hit the floor before I was on the move, my only thought to put as much distance as possible between myself and the Russian.

'Mr Munro!'

I turned. Oleg took a stride towards me. I backed away with a quick glance at the row of pool cues. It would be like stopping a charging reindeer stag with a sprig of holly.

'You are lucky man,' he said, 'but you are right. A deal is a deal.' One after another he tossed the two wads of notes at me. 'Better you take this too.' He flicked the tiny USB card. It arced through the air. I reached out to catch it with a stack of fifties in either hand and fumbled. It fell. I stooped to pick them up from the floor.

When I looked up again Oleg had about-turned and was walking back towards the bar from where came the sound of groaning and soft whimpers of pain. 'Yes, you are lucky,' he said. 'Not like Jerry.'

I saw no one on my trudge back to the barrier. It was even colder now. The wind had dropped and the snow had stopped falling. Homer was clearing the path to the gatehouse. Best to look busy when the boss was on site. I presumed his young colleague was having the pleasure of perimeter patrol.

I climbed into the Merc and commenced a three-point turn, thinking about Oleg's bizarre and violent behaviour. I couldn't fathom why the Russian had acted like that, or his parting words to me. Yes, I was lucky. I was another twenty thousand pounds lucky. And Jeremy Thorn? Of course he was unlucky. He'd been murdered.

Why had Oleg turned on his employer? Was it so that he wouldn't find out the truth that it was Oleg who had killed his son? It didn't make sense. The Russian had taken the video file and presumably viewed it. If it incriminated him, why not scrub the USB or destroy it? Why give it back to me? I'd given him the perfect opportunity. All he had to do was let Thorn think I'd reneged on our deal. That way he wouldn't have had to terminate his employment in such a dramatic fashion.

I stopped the car, got out and walked back to the barrier.

'Stuck?' Homer asked, shovelling snow and tossing it onto a mound against the wall of the glass hut. 'I can give you a push.'

'The car's fine,' I said. 'I was just wondering, Homer. Were you actually on site when Jeremy Thorn's helicopter went down?'

He stared into a sky that was fast clearing of clouds to reveal bright stars pinned to a black velvet cushion. 'Not this again.'

'Remember before, when I said I was Billy's lawyer and you wondered if people were trying to blame him for the crash?'

Homer stuck his spade into the mound of snow, rested a boot on it and pointed the finger of a black, fleecy-glove at me. 'That was you on telly. I told the wife it was you. They said on that programme the chopper was sabotaged and that you knew who done it. That's right, isn't it?'

I shook my head. 'Don't believe everything you see on TV.'

'Come on, you can tell me. Who was it?'

Why would no one believe me?

'I'm betting it wasn't Billy,' Homer said. 'Him and Jerry got on great. Everyone here got on fine with Jerry. Best boss I ever had, that's for sure. Best job too, meeting all the famous folk. My daughter's got a book full of autographs

319

thanks to me.' He winked. 'I used to make them all sign in twice. Once for the timesheet, once for my wee girl. 'Won't be like that again. Don't know if us lot will even be kept on if the place gets sold.'

'I was speaking to Oleg,' I said.

'Ivan the Terrible? I know, young Frankie told me he was on the prowl.'

'Oleg told me that Jerry was banned from flying for doing crazy stunts, like skimming across Loch Tay for instance.'

The red face creased along well used laughter lines. 'Aye, that was Jerry all right. Did he tell you about the time he tried to fly under the Glenfinnan viaduct? You know, the Harry Potter one?'

I joined in with his laughter before breaking off. 'The night he died, why was he flying if he was disqualified?'

Suddenly, Homer wasn't finding things quite so amusing. 'I dunno. Just taking his girl for a spin, I suppose. Showing off to her when there was no one around. So what?'

'You were on duty the night he disappeared, weren't you?'

'No, I was back-shift. I finished at ten.'

'But before you went off duty, did you know that Jerry was going flying later that night?' Homer's already flushed face reddened further. I took his complexion as answer enough. 'Then why didn't you do something about it? You're supposed to be a security guard.'

'Aye, and Jerry paid my wages.'

'That the best you can come up with? What was wrong with the CCTV in the hangar? Oleg says you reported it wasn't working the evening before the helicopter disappeared. That just a coincidence? Have the police asked you about that yet?'

The security guard rubbed a ruby jowl, a fleecy glove catching the stubble on his chin. 'You're a lawyer, right? What I tell you is off the record?'

'Try me.'

'All right. Jerry went up in the whirligig back and forward. He was a pilot. He liked flying. Usually he just went up himself, late on or early in the morning. He was the boss. What was I supposed to do?'

'And the CCTV system? Was there really something wrong with it?' The look on Homer's face confirmed my suspicion. 'What did you do? Disconnect it so there'd be no record of the flights? Do it just before Oleg finished work, tell him you'd call out maintenance and then sort it yourself the next day after Jerry was back, with no one any the wiser?'

'What harm was there in it?' Homer kicked some snow off the top of the mound with a steel-toecapped boot. 'I got a wee bit extra in my pay packet, Jerry buzzed about for a couple of hours. Big deal.'

'Why would Oleg think that Jerry was unlucky?'

'He crashed, didn't he?'

True, but if Jerry had been unlucky, someone had been very fortunate indeed. I thought back to Stewart Howie's rape case. He'd seemed so obviously guilty. That was because one vital factor had been overlooked. When the lawyers had read the forensic report, they'd concentrated on the evidence that was there. No one had realised that what was there shouldn't have been. Was Jeremy Thorn unlucky to have had his helicopter sabotaged? Yes, but he was all the more unlucky if he

321

should never have been in that helicopter in the first place.

'How many chopper pilots work here?' I asked.

'Three, if you include Jerry.'

'I'm not including him.'

'Just Pete and big Davie, then.'

'Which one was supposed to be flying the chopper that crashed?'

The eyes set deep in the ruddy face narrowed to gaze past me into the mid-distance.

I turned to follow his line of vision and saw Oleg lumbering through the snow towards us. There was no sign of Philip Thorn. 'So, Davie and Pete, they were just lucky it was Jerry's chopper that was sabotaged and not theirs?' I said.

Homer pulled the spade from the snow pile and began to set about the path with renewed vigour. He dug deep. The blade of the shovel scraping along the tarmac beneath. 'Aye, I suppose they were lucky. But not,' he hurled a wedge of snow over his shoulder, 'as lucky as some other folk.'

57

I'd been a parent for less than six months. Tina was nearly five years old. I'd missed her birth. I'd missed her first words and her first steps. Of course, I'd also missed her first nappy and the last nappy and all the many nappies in between, so there had been an upside to arriving late on the scene. One day I'd read her a last bedtime story and we'd play our last game of dominoes. One day, many, many, many years from now, I'd meet her first boyfriend. This Christmas it was Pyxie Girl, soon it would be designer clothes, expensive perfume, luxury handbags. It was life. Things moved on, children grew up. Six months. I'd learned so much about child-rearing in such a short space of time.

Tina had learned a lot too. She'd learned very quickly that in order to have her own way she needed to play her Dad and Grandpa off against each other, that telling Malky he was the best uncle in the world was the quickest route to a pocketful of sweets, and that if she remained very quiet around about bedtime there was a chance I'd forget she was there and so she could stay up a few precious moments longer than normal. One thing she hadn't yet learned was to distinguish between my stomach and a trampoline. To her my body wasn't so much a temple as a bouncy castle.

'It's Christmas Eve!' she yelled, landing a child's size five right where my six-pack would have been if I'd had one.

It was Saturday. I'd not made it back from St Edzell Bay until after three that morning. Four and a half hours of painfully slow driving, peering through the frequent snow flurries and trying to stay on the road, had left me with a splitting sore-head. The red digits of the radio alarm said eighty twenty. Late, by Tina's standards. My normal routine when receiving an early morning visit was to send my daughter through to see her gramps on some fictitious errand. That was usually good for securing a few extra minutes' shut-eye, but not that morning. That morning the old man was in my room too, standing at the bottom of the bed wrapped in his Paisley-pattern dressing gown looking nothing like Joanna and a lot like the Ghost of Christmas Past His Sell-By Date.

'You'll need to get up,' he said. 'There's a TV crew outside and some lassie called Cherry who's very keen to see you. She says she's a pal of yours.'

I sprang out of bed on the legs of a newborn gazelle, tottered to the window and pulled back the curtains. Through the misty murk of a mid-winter morning I could see human shapes, bundled against the cold. They were standing around holding big square silver cases, poles and tripods, blowing white as they spoke to each other, stamping their feet to keep warm.

Two minutes later, face washed, teeth brushed and outside of a couple of paracetamol, I was at the kitchen table, a cup of coffee in my hand, Tina on my knee and Cherry Lovell sitting across from me.

'I couldn't very well let the lassie stand out there in

324

the cold while you took an age getting ready,' was my dad's reasoning for allowing this intrusion, although he'd thought standing about in the cold to be good enough for the male contingent of the Night News team.

'Thanks very much for this, Robbie. All I want is your response to the news. We can set up in your front room. Ten minutes and we'll be out of your hair.' Cherry reached across and tweaked Tina's nose. 'I'm sure you'll have lots of last-minute Christmas shopping to do for this little lady.'

'What news?' was the most I could manage even after a reviving sip of coffee.

'You must have heard on TV or the radio?'

I hadn't.

'Where have you been?'

I'd been in bed. Before that I'd been driving down the A90 at twenty-five miles an hour trying not to run Joanna's Merc off the road and into a field. I'd listened to the radio all the way down. There had been no sensational news, just lots of crap Christmas music.

'Philip Thorn's dead. He was found washed up on the beach at St Edzell Bay earlier this morning.'

'Dead?'

'They're calling it suicide. There's some chat that he shot himself, but there's no official word on the cause of death yet. I'm betting he…' Cherry made bunny ears with her fingers, '*drowned*. Just like your client.' The news of Thorn's fatal soaking didn't seem to have dampened her Christmas spirit any. 'And, guess what? Kirkton Perch is not available for comment. There's a shocker.'

Philip Thorn was dead? I sucked in more caffeine. It was awfully early in the morning and my head was too sore to take in the news properly, or to focus on Cherry's conspiracy theory. Not that my fragility was going to stop her rehearsing it anyway.

'Kirkton Perch wanted Prestwick for a spaceport. Only Jeremy Thorn stood in his way, and...' Cherry looked at Tina who was listening intently in the manner children only do when they shouldn't be. 'Well, we know what happened to him, according to the Air Accident Investigation report.'

'I was in a hairy-plane yesterday,' Tina said. How much of this was she taking in? I tried to lift her down from my knee, but she wasn't for budging. She leaned across the table at the reporter and sniffed. 'You smell nice. You smell like Vikki. Joanna smells better though. Dad, does Joanna smell better than this lady? I think she does.'

As a general rule, I didn't comment on the fragrance of those women I came across in my day-to-day life. There may have been a proper time and place for passing such a compliment. If there was, I was sure my dad's kitchen at half-eight on a Saturday morning wasn't one of them, and, anyway, telling a woman how good she smelt? It sounded to me like the sort of creepy chat-up line someone might make before inviting the female in question back to his place and making a lampshade out of her skin.

Cherry, a little put out by my daughter's opinion on matters aromatic, continued anyway. 'Your client William Paris told you he knew who'd carried out that sabotage, didn't he?'

Tina wanted to know what a sabotage was. I looked to my dad who was also listening in keenly to the conversation. Reluctantly, he removed Tina from my knee and carried her kicking and wriggling through to the living room.

'Not in so many words,' I said, 'but don't let the facts get in the way.'

'The facts?' Cherry said, now free to speak. 'Let me present you with the facts. I'll try and make them very simple for you.'

'That would probably help,' my dad said, reappearing, having plonked Tina down in front of some Saturday morning TV. I really hoped it wasn't a Pyxie Girl re-run.

Cherry gave us her painting-by-numbers version. 'William Paris knew who killed Jeremy Thorn. Paris is dead. Your client *must* have told you who was responsible—'

'How do you come to that conclusion?' I asked.

'Because he was your client and because you had an arrangement with Philip Thorn to sell the information to him.'

How could she possibly have known that?

'Oh, don't look so shocked. I'm an investigative journalist. I investigate. Do you think I just let you wander off after our interview on Thursday morning? We filmed your meeting with Thorn. Unfortunately, telescopic lenses don't carry telescopic microphones, but why else would you meet with him? What would he want more than to know who had murdered his son?'

'All the same, I think I'll pass on the interview,' I said.

'Talk sense to him, please,' Cherry appealed to my dad. 'Now that Thorn's also sleeping with the fishes, that leaves one person who knows the truth and we all know what that means.'

My dad looked confused enough for both of us. 'No, what does it mean?'

'It means,' Cherry said, rising from her chair, 'that it

would be inadvisable for your son to go anywhere near Linlithgow Loch unless he wants to end up in it.' She placed both hands on the table and leaned forward at me. 'Do this interview. Blow the story wide open before some government spook pushes your head under the water too.'

'That's not going to happen,' I said.

'How can you possibly say that? When you met Thorn at Holyrood Park the other day, do you know who that was with him? Oleg Pasportnikov, ex-KGB or FSB as they call it now. There are scores of them over here. After nine/eleven the West turned all its attention to Islamist extremists. It's been open season for Russian spies ever since.'

'Cherry, the man is head of security at a nothing airport in the middle of nowhere. They have three helicopters, a couple of light aircraft, a few microlights and a handful of staff. Until the crash, the most exciting thing that ever happened was when celebrities were helicoptered back and forward to play golf and Oleg had to hold back the autograph-hunters.'

'And if it became a spaceport? Nice for the Russians to have someone undercover right from the start.'

'Then why would he kill the very person whose idea it was to create a spaceport at St Edzell Bay?'

'He wouldn't. Aren't you listening? Ex-army Billy Paris, working for the Government, killed Jeremy Thorn. It's obvious. The Government then had him killed and now they've killed Philip Thorn too. They can't kill Pasportnikov because the Russians will know they're onto him. They'll track him instead. See what they can learn. It's all wheels within wheels.'

But it wasn't. Not even Russian dolls within Russian dolls. 'Listen to me, Cherry. You think you know what's going on, and I can understand why. If you look at things in a blinkered way, make certain presumptions—'

'What other way is there to look at them? This is the British Government sanctioning the execution of UK citizens to further political aims. The pieces all fit, you've got to agree.'

That the pieces now all fitted together, I did agree, except in doing so they'd formed a completely different picture to Cherry's image. I stood up when we were joined by Tina who was wondering what had happened to breakfast. She opened the fridge door and on tiptoe lifted out a box of eggs.

'Come on,' Cherry said. 'One quick interview. We'll have it all wrapped up in no time at all. Just look shocked and surprised. You can do that, can't you?'

'Okay,' I said, 'I will.' I took the box of eggs from Tina before she scrambled the contents on the kitchen floor. 'But not here and it's going to take a lot longer than ten minutes.'

'I don't understand.'

'I know. If you did…' I held up the box of eggs. 'You'd realise that what you have is an unfertilised hen's ovum and from it you're trying to hatch a chick. Trust me. There's no government conspiracy going on here.'

'Yeah? What then?'

'Just one very serious cock-up.'

58

There would have been quite a crowd trying to cram itself into my office that Christmas Eve morning if I hadn't phoned ahead to tell DI Christchurch that his team of expert searchers needn't come. What he was looking for, my daughter had already found and was safe in the back pocket of my jeans. I was ready to let the Ministry of Defence policeman have it, subject to certain conditions. First of which was:

'You want me to bring the Secretary of State to your office? This morning? What happened to your other condition that, if we found the evidence, I had to guarantee you six hours' radio silence?'

'It no longer applies. Tell him not to worry, though, I've thought of some other conditions especially for him,' I said, hanging up.

Later, a bacon roll to the better, Cherry and I left Sandy's for my office and waited in reception while a camera crew set up in my room pending the imminent arrival of Kirkton Perch.

'I must say, this is really good of you, Robbie,' Cherry said, sitting on the reception desk, legs crossed. It was a short skirt to be wearing in such cold weather.

'Not at all. You being here helps me as much as it helps you.'

She lowered herself to the floor and came over to where I was standing, leaned close and picked a speck of fluff from my shirt. Tina was right. Cherry did smell nice, although, I had to agree, not as nice as Joanna.

'Can't you tell me what's happening now?' she asked. 'Or are you really going to make me wait until—'

'Until when?' Joanna didn't only smell nice, she sounded great. If a little angry.

'Hi Joanna. How did you know I was here?' I asked.

'Your dad.' She threw my car keys on the desk and held out her hand. 'Key, please.'

Make that very angry.

I walked over to her. 'What's the matter?'

'Nothing.'

'It's just that you seem a little upset,' I said.

'She's not upset, she's jealous,' Cherry said.

'Of what?'

'Not of what. Of who.'

'What are you on about? Who's Joanna jealous of?'

'Me,' Cherry said.

'Why? What have you got that Joanna hasn't?' Both myself and my daughter would testify as to who smelt better.

'You,' Cherry said. 'She thinks I'm making a move.'

Why would Joanna think that? She knew I wasn't Cherry's type. She'd told me that herself. I thought it best to clarify just in case. 'You're not, are you? Making a move?'

Cherry let rip a loud snort.

I turned to Joanna. 'See?' She still didn't look happy. I'd no time to wonder why. Kaye Mitchell burst into reception. A deal was a deal.

331

'The Secretary of State's on his way,' she said, leading the way to my room where a row of lights blazed bright atop a tall tripod and a man in a Christmas jumper balanced a TV camera on one shoulder.

The Bulldog was the first of the government personnel to arrive. Without acknowledging any of those present, he scouted round all the rooms before going to the top of the stairs and shouting an all clear.

From my window I looked down to where a black limousine and a black van were parked on the double yellows directly outside the office. A couple of uniformed officers with firearms stood on the pavement, one looking east along the High Street, the other west.

The Bulldog entered again and took up position by the door. Next was Kirkton Perch looking a tad bleary-eyed and behind him Detective Inspector Christchurch.

Christmas Jumper swung his camera at them.

'Not yet,' I told him.

'What is this?' Raising a hand to shield his eyes from the light, Perch turned to Christchurch. 'Nothing was said about television.'

The DI glowered, beard pointing at me accusingly.

'Don't worry,' I said, 'there will be no filming until I've shown everyone what DI Christchurch has been trying to have me disclose to him for the last month. Mr Perch, I know the pressure you've been under recently due to certain...' I glanced over my shoulder at Cherry who was busy being wired for sound, 'unfounded allegations. And I also know that you are completely innocent of them. Who better to interview you and let you clear your name than the reporter who made those accusations in the first place?'

Cherry, who was clipping a battery-pack to the waist of her skirt, stopped and stared across at me like a vampire who'd just been told blood was off the menu. 'Innocent?'

I took the USB card from my back pocket, went over to my desk and swivelled the computer monitor around to face outwards. Christmas Jumper came forward to sit in my chair. He'd assured me that if there was a video file on the USB and an internet connection available, he'd find a way of getting it to play. I bent down, pushed it into a slot in the PC case and turned to Perch. 'I'm about to save you and your government's reputation. You've already said you won't pay for my service to Queen and country; nonetheless, while we're waiting for the show, there are a couple of matters I'd like to draw to your attention, and as regards which I am sure you will be able to bring your influence to bear.'

59

Christmas Eve.

Tina hung her stocking out after tea, ate the last advent calendar chocolate and placed a carrot for Rudolph alongside a glass of whisky on the hearth. Though Scotland's strict drink-driving laws probably meant the real Santa should have been left a glass of milk, and not a single-malt, there was another man with a set of white whiskers who'd argued otherwise.

If on any other night I'd wanted to send my daughter to bed early and without supper, I'd have had to have trumped up some pretty serious charges. Not tonight. Tonight, of her own volition, Tina had gone to bed earlier than she ever had before. The logic gene she'd inherited from her dad had told her the sooner she fell asleep, the sooner Christmas Day would arrive. If only life did operate logically. Unfortunately, like a lot of plans based on logical thinking it was good in theory, not so effective in practice. Unable to sleep, she'd come tottering through to the living room on several occasions, her wee face pinched white with the terrible excitement of it all. This in turn had led to a few hurried replenishments of the whisky glass, lest Tina notice and think Santa had been, knocked back a quick straightener and shot off on his sleigh again, forgetting to leave any presents behind.

334

At least that was my dad's very own application of logic.

When I'd poked my head into Tina's room at ten o'clock I'd found her sound asleep. At last I could settle down, watch TV and wait. Some people were waiting for Mr Claus, I was waiting on a phone call.

My dad, dozing in his armchair by the coal fire, fired off a volley of snores. I poured myself a dram, sprawled out on the couch and trawled through the various revolving twenty-four-hour news channels.

The story surrounding the death of Philip Thorn had gone out early evening. It had been a nice Christmas present from me to Cherry Lovell. Her production company had sold the news item around the world. It hadn't been too bad a gift for Kirkton Perch either. The pressure the Night News' documentary had placed him under had been growing by the day. Now the same investigative journalist who'd led the campaign of persecution was vindicating him and his government completely.

It didn't take many flicks of the remote to find a station where Thorn's story had come around again on the news carousel.

'...*it all started here on St Andrews Day and finished on Christmas Eve when the body of Sir Philip Thorn, one of Britain's best known music executives and entertainment managers, was washed ashore.*'

Cut to Cherry Lovell wrapped in a big white coat, scarf and furry hat, standing, microphone in hand, on the runway at St Edzell Bay Airport to where, ironically, she'd been helicoptered earlier that day.

'*According to police sources there are no suspicious circumstances.*'

According to the police. But not according to me.

335

No, for me the jury was very much still out.

His body was found by this man, Oleg Pasportnikov, head of security at Thorn Aviation Services.

Three seconds of footage showed a man in a dark suit walking along a deserted shoreline. Not long, but long enough for me to remember his words: '*Tell me who killed Jerry and I kill them myself.*'

There then followed a brief montage of Thorn and the various artists he'd brought to fame. The sound of music woke my dad. With a loud splutter and a noisy clearing of his throat he sat up from his slouch. He looked across at me and then at the TV. The camera panned the offices of R.A. Munro & Co., where a bunch of tinsel brought some festive cheer to my umbrella plant, and I sat in my chair looking pretty pleased with myself as I held up a small, thin rectangle of black plastic.

'Do you never weary of watching yourself?' my dad asked.

It was true. I had watched the clip a fair few times, but I had to make the most of it. There wouldn't be too many more opportunities. I'd already noticed that my cameo was being edited shorter with every broadcast. One or two stations now omitted my moment of fame altogether, as other breaking news stories vied for screen time.

'Quiet, we're getting to the good part,' I said, as Cherry's voice cut in again.

'*Why would someone who had it all, take their own life? One man held the answer.*'

That one man was me.

He might have been a violent, binge-drinker, but Billy Paris had not served seventeen years in the Royal Electrical and

Mechanical Engineers without learning how to fix a loose wire, especially a simple sleeve connector.

Oleg had been right, Jeremy Thorn was unlucky, but the head of security had also been wrong. There had been nothing the matter with the new CCTV system. The only time it malfunctioned was when Jerry wanted to go for a late night or early morning spin and didn't want the fact recorded. On those occasions Homer would unclip the connection, cut the signal, and away Jerry would go. Next day Homer would reconnect the cable and normal service would resume. Only he and Jerry knew about the arrangement. When Homer had reported the 'fault' to Oleg, the Russian had passed on to Philip Thorn the news that the expensive new surveillance system had packed in yet again. The lack of CCTV cover provided someone with an opportunity. That someone hadn't taken into account the technical skills of recently hired handyman, Billy Paris, who'd been pressed into security duty when a colleague called in sick.

The picture on the TV screen went blank and there followed a period of static, clearing to reveal the face of Billy Paris, even more misshapen than normal by the wide-angled lens, staring right out at me. His hands came into view, made a few adjustments to the camera and then, satisfied, he moved out of shot.

Some later editing deleted the ensuing two hours or so that had then elapsed between Billy's minor repair job and the time, shortly before midnight, according to the digits in the top right corner, when a dark figure entered the helicopter hangar. It was difficult to see who it was at first under the dim illumination of the security lighting. Then the camera zoomed in and there was no mistaking

Philip Thorn. He had some kind of canister in his hand.

Had Billy known what was happening? Had he known who Philip Thorn was? Or, so far as he was concerned, was the person on screen just one of the maintenance crew carrying out routine servicing to a helicopter? A helicopter that next morning, piloted by Tony Glass, would fly the Glazed Over boys further down the coast to a St Andrew's Day celebrity golf tournament. Whatever, Billy had certainly realised the relevance of that late-night visit when the chopper never returned, and he'd intended to cash in, just as soon as he could work out who'd pay the most for the information and how best to put on the squeeze. Billy had known he'd come under scrutiny. Being of no fixed abode he had to leave the evidence somewhere safe. The cardboard box he'd left with me was an excellent decoy.

I hadn't given my old client the credit he'd deserved when he'd attended the interview at Stewart Street police station. He'd mentioned a number of ways to bring down a helicopter, but not the one that was actually used: expanding foam in the fuel tank. When Jerry had taken his fiancée for an early morning flight, the fuel gauge had registered full. In reality there'd been scarcely a litre or two in the system. Just enough to take the pair of them far out into the North Sea.

Earlier reports had questioned why a father would want to kill his son. Those had now disappeared. Everyone knew the real targets. CNN played a 2013 interview with John Branca, co-executor of the Michael Jackson estate, when he'd admitted to journalist Robin Leach that the entertainer had made more money in the four years since his death than he'd made during his lifetime. The week after David Bowie's death in January 2016, his albums accounted for a quarter of the Top 40.

To the man who held the biggest share of the rights to Glazed Over's portfolio, the Glass brothers were an asset worth a lot more dead than alive.

I'd severed the piece of string tying my dad's cordless phone to the table in the hall. The handset rested on the arm of my dad's chair so that when it rang he could grab it before it woke Tina, which he did, impressively so. 'Hullo?'

I could have answered it myself, but it wouldn't have been the same.

'Who shall I say is calling?' My dad put his hand over the phone. 'She says you bloody well know who is calling.'

'Tell her I won't be a moment.'

I took a small sip of whisky, held the glass up to the flames in the fireplace, and tilted the tumbler so that it caught the soft flickering light from the fire, bringing to life the amber tones of a fine Islay malt.

'Yes?' I enquired, having gracefully accepted the receiver that my dad had chucked across the room at me. 'Is that Miss—'

'Yes, it's me. You know it's me. I'm at a carol service and I've been dragged away by a policeman—'

'Short, squat, would look at home in a kennel?'

'To tell you,' she of the red-lacquered fingernails continued, 'that you are no longer suspended and may resume the provision of criminal legal assistance under the legal aid scheme.'

'I see. Anything else?'

There was a clearing of the throat followed by a quiet,

'We don't feel there is going to be any need to compliance-review your case files in the near future.'

'Thank you. Anything else?' There wasn't. She hung up.

I waited. It wouldn't take the Bulldog long to remind her. The phone rang again less than a minute later. 'Merry Christmas,' she said.

'And a Happy New Year to you and the Karate Kid when it comes,' I replied too late. She was gone, replaced by the Bulldog with some less happy news. There were certain things Her Britannic Majesty's Government could not achieve with less than twenty-four hours' notice, not even with a Ministry of Defence police officer delegated to the task. Finding a Pyxie Girl action figure was one of them.

'You're a bigger wean than Tina,' my dad said, when, having reattached the handset to the leg of the telephone table, I was back in the living room, lying along the couch and waiting for my cameo to come around again.

He was right and I didn't care. Christmas brought out the child in us all and if, having saved its reputation, the best the United Kingdom Government could do for me, was give me back my livelihood, I might as well get some fun out of it.

'When are you getting the doll?' he asked.

The old man had done nothing but harp on about that doll for weeks and how I was spoiling Christmas for everyone. Now, on Christmas Eve, despite the fact that his son was a media sensation, he still couldn't come to terms with the fact that I'd failed as a father.

'The doll's not happening, Dad.'

'You know the wean will be devastated.'

'She's getting plenty of other toys.'

'Not the one she wants.'

'Tina's tough.'

'What Tina is, is a wee girl who lost her mum less than a year ago and now this.'

There was no point arguing with him, but I did. 'And if she can come to terms with her mum dying of cancer, she'll get over not having a doll that will be old-hat come the next TV fad.'

The phone saved me from any comeback. I went through to the hall to answer it, speaking softly so as not to waken Tina. Surprisingly, it was the Bulldog again. 'Mr Munro... I just wanted to say that when your girlfriend slapped me—'

'My colleague.'

'Whatever, when she hit me, the DI was right, I did deserve it.' It seemed the Yuletide spirit had fallen upon everyone. 'I don't like double-dealing shysters — no offence — but I shouldn't have brought up the safety of your daughter. I've got a daughter. For what it's worth, she wanted a Pyxie Girl too and I couldn't get her one either.'

'Then you're in for as hard a time as I am tomorrow.'

'Maybe not,' he said. 'You see, I have a plan B.'

I couldn't bring myself to admit it to the Bulldog, but Plan B was brilliant. Not that Keith Howie quite shared my enthusiasm for it when I phoned his house around half past ten. He was even less enthusiastic when asked to go down and open his shop. I was waiting for him.

'This really isn't good enough.' Howie selected one from a bunch of keys and unlocked the front door. The only reason he'd come out was because his wife had answered the phone and I'd told her how important it was to my daughter. Joanna was right, Mrs Howie was lovely. I could understand why she'd been more concerned for the accused's wife than the accused himself during the recent High Court trial. 'My children are in bed, and if I hadn't been helping Liz prepare the vegetables for tomorrow, I would be too. I can't abide being taken advantage of.'

I could have reminded him that, but for yours truly, he'd be having plum-duff courtesy of the Queen the next day, but instead made no comment. Unlike Howie I was good at that. I didn't want an argument. I just wanted what I'd come for. A Pyxie Girl outfit. Why bother with the action figure when you could dress up and look just like your hero? Zooming about in a mask and cape would appeal to Tina's imagination; much better than a stupid doll, and it was all thanks to Joanna. That slap across the Bulldog's chops had brought him to his senses and his belated apology had saved Christmas Day.

Once inside, Howie disappeared through the back of the shop, returning shortly with some large square plastic packages, each with a picture of a happy child dressed as Pyxie Girl on the front. He threw them down on the counter between us. 'That'll be twenty-nine ninety-nine,' he said, holding out a hand. 'Let's call it thirty. I'm not opening the till, and after all us numpties have to make a living too.'

I'd wondered when he'd bring that up.

'I thought you might see this as, if not a Christmas present, as a sort of thank you,' I said.

Howie took a step back in fake astonishment. 'I've to be thankful have I? For being found innocent of a crime

342

I didn't commit? I'm afraid being thankful didn't stop somebody putting my kitchen window in with a half-brick last night. You know, I've been thinking. If you or Miss Jordan had asked me about my vasectomy at the start, I needn't have been put through the hell of a High Court trial —- twice!'

'And I've been thinking too,' I said, digging into my jeans pocket, bringing out some cash and floating three tenners down on to the counter, 'that if you don't know why your tubes were cut, that's nobody's fault but your own. Maybe you should have listened more carefully to your biology teacher.'

'Or maybe I should have got myself a better lawyer.'

Fists clenched, I planted my knuckles and leaned across the counter. 'Have you a complaint to make about the way Miss Jordan managed your case? Because if you have, I'm sure I could deal with it now.'

Howie snatched the money and backed away. 'Just get out.'

I picked up one of the packages and clamped it to my chest. With my daughter's present problem sorted, it was hard not to feel good, even if Howie was doing his Scrooge-like best to put a damper on things. I walked to the door. Sometimes I wondered why I bothered. Clients, mad, bad or sad, it was the ungrateful ones that annoyed me most. Still, who cared? I reached for the handle, pulled open the door and looked out at a chilly night, thinking of a warm Christmas morning to come.

60

Here it was at last. Christmas morning. Peace on Earth and good will toward men.

'You complete idiot!'

Perhaps not all men.

'Age ten to twelve?' My Dad hurled the plastic package at me. 'Some great idea. You can't give Tina that, it will drown the lassie.'

How was I to know Pyxie Girl suits came in small, medium and large sizes? I'd just picked up the nearest. It hadn't been until I was back home and doing a spot of late-night present wrapping that I'd made the discovery. There'd been no point trying to contact Howie for an exchange. On the burnt-boats scale we were talking Pearl Harbour.

Tina trotted through to my bedroom while my dad was holding forth on my intellectual shortcomings, something of a specialist topic for him, and I hurriedly threw the Pyxie Girl costume under the bed.

'When's Uncle Malky coming, Dad?' she asked. Christmas morning, half-eleven. Tina had been up for hours. She'd opened her presents, played with her toys, tried on her new clothes and eaten her body weight in chocolate. Now she was wondering when her guest would be arriving. Thankfully, in all the excitement, the absence of Pyxie Girl the action figure had seemingly gone

344

unnoticed. Until now. 'Do you think Santa will have given Uncle Malky my Pyxie Girl doll to bring with him?'

Glowering, my dad bumped me out of the way as he left the room. I picked Tina up and took her to the window. 'I don't think so, pet.' Life sucked. If anyone should know that it was Tina, with no mum and only a dad who couldn't even get her what she wanted for Christmas. At least I had someone to blame. 'I think Santa's made a mistake. He's like Gramps. He's getting on a bit and his memory is not that good. But he's brought you lots of other nice things, hasn't he? When he gets back to work in the New Year I'll have Gramps phone and ask him to bring you a brand new Lady Pyxie doll. How's that?'

Not good enough by the look on her wee face. The heat was taken off momentarily when Malky arrived bearing gifts. My daughter ripped through them like a tornado in a Tennessee trailer camp, and only I heard the knock at the door. It was Joanna, bottle of champagne in one hand, carrier bag in the other.

'Well, you did offer,' she said.

I didn't know what to say.

'Don't look so worried. I've brought my own lunch.' She held up the plastic bag. 'Chestnut, spinach and blue cheese *en croute*. Just slam it in the oven for twenty minutes and you carnivores can get stuck into the dead bird. Maybe after lunch you and I can talk a few things over.'

By *a few things* I took it she meant either business or what had happened on Thursday night. I'd been doing a lot of thinking. More about Thursday night than business.

'I've got some good news on the business front,' I said, 'but it will keep until the New Year.'

345

Joanna smiled. 'Great. Then there'll be more time to talk about us.'

Us. Why was she so keen to talk about us? Was there an *us*? Did she want there to be an *us*? Why would she? The woman needed to speak with my brother and learn all about League Divisions and our relative standings.

I helped Joanna off with her coat. She was wearing the same little black number she'd had on at the Munro & Co. Christmas lunch. Talk about an action figure! She walked past me down the hall. As she reached for the handle on the living room door I had an idea. I caught her arm and ushered her further down to my bedroom. 'Would you mind waiting in here for a couple minutes?' I said.

'In your bedroom?'

'It's... a surprise. I'll explain in a moment.' I pushed her in and closed the door.

'You've already ruined the wean's Christmas, don't make it any worse by falling out with Joanna,' my dad said, after I'd taken the Munro boys through to the kitchen for a conference.

I wasn't to be put off. 'No, it's perfect. Tina wants Pyxie Girl—'

'It's the doll she wants,' my dad said.

I clenched my teeth. 'I know. But we haven't managed to get her one.'

'*You* haven't,' he growled back at me.

'And why's that? It's because *nobody* can get one, and the only reason Tina is having difficulty understanding that is because someone...' I hoped my stare left my dad in no doubt who that someone was, 'said that he had Santa on speed-dial.'

346

My dad rejected any criticism with a snort that parted his moustache.

'As I was saying, Tina wants Pixie Girl, Joanna would do anything for Tina and—'

'Even if that was true, do you think that by getting her to squeeze into a child's play costume—'

'Yes,' I said. 'It's the ideal combination. Tina loves Joanna even more than Pyxie Girl, and she's got a vivid imagination.'

'You'll not *need* an imagination if you have a full-grown woman squeeze into that thing!'

'But—'

'But nothing. It'll be far too tight.'

'Hold on, hold on,' Malky said, intervening, an oasis of calm in the storm of words between his father and brother. 'Let the man speak, Dad.' He turned to me. 'Robbie, this costume, just how tight are we talking?'

'It will be pretty tight,' I admitted, 'but it's Lycra, it's stretchy.'

'There you are then,' Malky said, with an air of finality, surprisingly on board with the whole suggestion.

So, motion carried by a majority, I left them to keep Tina amused while I had the somewhat daunting task of trying to persuade Joanna into saving Christmas. She was waiting patiently in my room, sitting on the edge of the bed, looking through the presents I'd opened earlier. Socks and toiletries featured prominently. She held up one of a number of deodorant sets.

'Do you ever think people are trying to tell you something?' she asked.

'That I smell and have holes in my socks? Yes, sometimes.'

I sat down beside her.

'Okay, so what's the big surprise?'

'Joanna, there's something I have to ask you.'

She smiled and gave me a shove. 'Robbie, I know I said I wanted to talk about us and the future, but don't you think we should get Christmas dinner out of the way first?'

'I'm not talking about the future. I'm talking about this time, this place, *pro loco et tempore.*' I wasn't sure if Latin would assist. It often did when speaking with fellow lawyers. 'Joanna, when I ask you this I don't want you to answer, not straight away. At least hear me out and think it over carefully before you say no.'

She seemed interested and why shouldn't she? Though Sheriff Albert Brechin had once described me as a man whose legal submissions were unrestrained by relevancy, this request was well reasoned, logical and directed at someone who was actually prepared to listen. Joanna was a good sport, but if things did become tricky, and my hand forced, there was an ace up my sleeve. If it came down to it, I'd remind her of her words to me shortly before the retrial of HMA –v- Howie, '*If you can find a way to have Keith Howie acquitted, I'll find you a Pyxie Girl for Christmas.*' Well, I had found a way. Now it was time for her to keep her end of the bargain.

'You like Tina, don't you?' I said.

Joanna frowned, puzzled. 'Yes…'

I laughed lightly. 'In fact, you, me and Tina, we're a bit of a team.' I gave her a friendly tap on the shoulder with my fist.

She gave me a less friendly tap on my shoulder with hers.

348

'Then I want to ask if you'd do something to keep that team bond strong.'

'Would you hurry up and ask?'

'It's Christmas—'

'I'd noticed.'

'And at Christmas it's easy to become overly sentimental, too full of Christmas spirit, I know that, we all know that, but it's also the time to think of others, good will toward men, and all women and especially children, and I was wondering—'

'Robbie, really, what are you going on about?'

'Okay, okay. Here's the thing.' I took her hands in mine. 'This will seem slightly crazy to you, embarrassing even, but—'

'Robbie...' Joanna warned.

I thought it was best just to show her. I slid off the bed and dropped onto one knee, reaching a hand under the bed to retrieve the Pyxie Girl costume.

In hindsight it was the dropping to one knee that probably caused the confusion.

Head bowed, I fumbled around for a second or two until I found the package. I looked up. Why were there tears in her eyes? 'Joanna, would you...' The words *put on this costume and pretend to be Pyxie Girl?* never made it out of my lips. It was difficult to talk when someone was kissing you. I found it even more difficult when that person was Joanna because I couldn't help kissing her back.

We stood up together. 'Yes,' she said. 'It is crazy, but I *will* marry you.' Tears streamed down her face. She wiped at them with the back of a hand, smudging mascara. She was searching for a tissue when she noticed the package at my side. 'What's that?'

I looked down at the package and swallowed hard. 'This? This is... a present for you to give to Tina.'

'Robbie, I put my gift for Tina under your Christmas tree last week.' She took the package from me. 'Age ten to twelve? It's going to be way too big for her.'

They say that at the time of death a person's past life flashes before their eyes. I hesitated for a moment, only for a moment, and in that moment I saw, not the past, but a life still to come. 'Maybe we can have it taken in. Can you sew?'

'Not even slightly.'

'Then she'll just have to grow into it,' I said, and, putting an arm around my fiancée, led her out of the door, from the present tense towards a bright, if uncertain, future.

Author's Note

As readers of the earlier stories in the Best Defence Series will have heard me mention before, many of the characters, cases and incidents are based, often very loosely, on my time as a criminal defence lawyer.

While I have been involved in a number of alleged conspiracy theories over the years, generally the workings of certain clients' feverish imaginations, I have to admit none has involved a helicopter, nor indeed a potential spaceport. On the other hand, the trial of Keith Howie is almost identical to a case in which I was involved back in the late Eighties, when I was a good bit younger than Robbie Munro.

My client, a middle-aged man, was charged with the rape of his teenage neighbour, whom he had known since birth and who referred to him as 'uncle'. When the girl's parents were away one weekend, she asked to stay with my client and his wife rather than alone in her own home. My client's only child, a son, was grown up and away so there was a spare bedroom. On the Saturday night, the girl went out for the evening and arrived at my client's house around midnight, slightly the worse for wear. She thereafter went to bed, and about six the next the morning, woke screaming and highly distressed claiming to have been raped in the night. She tried to leave the house only to find the door locked. The key to the door was hidden on a window ledge under a vase and my client had to let her out.

In due course, my client was interviewed by the police and, despite my best efforts to have him make no comment, insisted on providing a lengthy statement to the police in which he denied having gone near the girl, thus ruling out any possible defence of consent.

Although I never called this particular client 'a numpty', there have been times when I have been less than diplomatic towards clients who feel they have to tell the police their side of things. It's not that I don't understand the urge to do so, but in all my years of sitting in on police interviews I have never heard one end up with a policeman telling a suspect, 'Well, thank you for clearing that up. You are free to go.'

Unlike in the 'Howie' case, the evidence of distress, which corroborated the girl's own allegation of having been attacked, was not provided by my client's wife, but spoken to by someone who met the girl shortly after she had left the house that morning; however, as with the 'Howie' case, corroboration of penetration hinged on the forensic report, and it was anxiously awaited, my client being certain it would vindicate him.

Back in 1988 or 1989, DNA was forensically in its infancy, and, although it had been used in some extremely high profile and serious cases in England, was not widely available, as I recall, in Scotland. Instead, the Crown forensic experts relied on blood grouping, not the standard A, B, O system, but a much more precise version, which in my client's case disclosed, firstly the presence of sperm (thus corroborating sexual intercourse) and, secondly, that blood-group-wise the sperm matched my client's, a group that was shared by only 9% of the population. It wasn't the billion-to-one odds that regularly feature in DNA reports today, but a nice adminicle of evidence nonetheless. Not that DNA is the be all and end all. Even today, there are many cases where the presence of sperm can be identified, but DNA cannot be extracted, often due to the passage of time.

As defences go, my client's *it wasn't me, honest,* line wasn't the best, but it was all we had. The Crown was in a much stronger position. There was a clear sufficiency of evidence enhanced by that one major factor upon which many a Crown case hangs: why would the young woman lie about such a thing?

I needed counsel to conduct the trial at the High Court. I asked my brother, James, also a criminal lawyer, for his thoughts and he recommended a junior counsel by the name of Paul McBride, newly called to the Bar and whom he described as 'a fighter'. Paul turned out to be more than merely a fighter, he was a brilliant lawyer who had graduated in law age nineteen and went on to be Scotland's youngest ever QC at age thirty-six. Young Paul had one look at the stinker of a brief and thought it might be in order for me to seek sanction from the Legal Aid Board to instruct senior counsel. That request was refused. Some things never change.

So, on the first day of the trial, we were walking towards Court 9 in Parliament House, Paul on one side of the client, myself on the other, like two corner men leading their out-of-shape amateur boxer towards a confrontation with the defending World Champion. On the journey, I happened to mention to the client that it was good to see his wife was standing by him, as it had been a constant feature during my preparations how adamant she was that her husband was innocent. Paul then asked how sexual relations between the client and his wife were, possibly in case it was suggested that there had been some sort of sexual frustration behind the alleged attack. Unlike today, back in the Eighties, there were no holds barred when it came to asking witnesses questions to do with their sex life.

'Great,' was my client's response. 'If anything they've improved since my vasectomy.'

At this point you have to imagine solicitor and counsel screeching to a halt, while the accused marches on down the corridor, oblivious to the import of his remarks.

Needless to say, the trial did not proceed. I was dispatched to the University of Edinburgh's Medical School to return with Professor Anthony Busuttil, Emeritus Professor in Forensic Medicine, while the accused's wife was sent home to bring back her husband's vasectomy certificate from the hospital. There then followed a great deal of discussion, a deposit was made into a small jar for a man with a large microscope and, after a very long day, the case was deserted.

No action was ever taken against the complainer. She'd been at a party. Her boyfriend was working away from home at the time and she'd had too much to drink to the extent that she'd been sick into a carrier bag. Whoever's sperm had been donated it wasn't my client's. Why she'd picked on my client, I never found out. Maybe she'd been drunk and confused. Perhaps she'd had some kind of drunken nightmare. Those would be the charitable views to take. A less charitable view would be that in the days before the 'morning-after' pill she'd had unprotected sex at the party, thought she might be pregnant and rather than tell her boyfriend that she'd had sex with one of his pals, decided to accuse my client of rape. Who knows? Only one person.

Just as in Present Tense, my client's subsequent acquittal did not prevent a mysterious person(s) putting his windows in with a selection of half-bricks later that night, and, no, I never got a thank you. However, neither did my client criticise me for not establishing the fact of his vasectomy at an earlier stage. I think I would have felt aggrieved if he had, for he was not a stupid man. He held an important job in the local community and we had gone over the forensic report and talked about the presence of sperm and associated blood groups on numerous occasions in the lead-up to the trial. Perhaps sex education back in the day wasn't what it is now, but if nothing else, one would have thought if he was going to let a doctor come near his delicate areas with a scalpel in hand, he might have wanted to know the reason why.

One man, though, never let me forget. Over the years, until his untimely death in 2012, I would often come across Paul McBride at the High Court and whenever he saw me, whether I was instructing him or not, and whether the case I was involved in was rape, murder, robbery, whatever, he could never resist a dig and would shout across the room at me, 'Have you checked to see if your client has had the snip?'

Ever since it has been the first question I ask of any rape-accused.

WHS McIntyre.